# PLAIN FEAR

# FORGIVEN

A NOVEL

# LEANNA ELLIS

sourcebooks
landmark

Published by Sourcebooks Landmark, an imprint of Sourcebooks, Inc.
P.O. Box 4410, Naperville, Illinois 60567-4410
(630) 961-3900
Fax: (630) 961-2168
www.sourcebooks.com

Library of Congress Cataloging-in-Publication Data

Ellis, Leanna.
  Plain fear : forgiven : a novel / Leanna Ellis.
      pages cm
  (paperback : alk. paper) 1. Amish—Fiction. 2. Life change events—Fiction. 3. Vampires—Fiction. 4. Good and evil—Fiction. 5. Pennsylvania—Fiction. I. Title.
  PS3605.L4677P567 2013
  813'.6—dc23

                            2013010792

         Printed and bound in the United States of America.
               VP 10 9 8 7 6 5 4 3 2 1

## ALSO BY LEANNA ELLIS

*Plain Fear: Forbidden*
*Plain Fear: Forsaken*

To those who daily put on the "full armor of God"
and "fight the good fight."

*He uncovereth deep things out of darkness,*
*And bringeth out to light the shadow of death.*

JOB 12:22

# PROLOGUE

DARKNESS CLAWED AT HIM, its talons sinking deep, hooking into his heart. Jacob Fisher tried to clear away whatever obstruction prevented his eyes from seeing, but there was nothing. Nothing but darkness, thick as molasses and cold as the heart of the universe. It shrouded him, pressing in on him, and he felt the weight of it against his chest. He could not move or struggle or fight or even scream.

And he wanted to scream. Scream for someone. Someone to come to his rescue.

Worse than the darkness though was the silence. The quiet pulsed and throbbed, around him and through him. Nothing—if there was anything around him—moved. Only in the tiny recesses of his mind could he hear anything, his thoughts writhing and struggling as a creature pushes out from the womb. Fears tormented him. Bits of verses and poetry knotted and tangled as he reached for them—as if by grasping them, they could take him away from here, lead him somewhere else, or at least anchor him and keep him from going mad.

*Abandon all hope, ye who enter here.*

For hope was absent from this place—if it was a place... or a time...or somewhere between times and places. The emptiness felt like an enclosed tomb and yet also seemed to stretch on forever.

*Only a look and a voice, then darkness again, and a silence.*

A silence that seemed never to end. If he could scream, he doubted he would be heard. For he was alone.

*He will keep the feet of his saints, and the wicked shall be silent in darkness; for by strength shall no man prevail.*

He was no saint. So was this his punishment? *Where was he? What was this?* Fear seized him. He struggled, against nothing and everything, but it was useless. He could not move. *Was he still alive? Trapped in a wooden box and buried six feet underground? With no way to escape, no way to breathe, no way to scratch or claw at the sides, lid, or seams?*

From somewhere deep inside him came a continuous scream. But it had no outlet, just ricocheted around inside his head and heart, proving his own impotence.

Then out of nothing and yet from somewhere beyond came a shriek that pierced his eardrums. With it came pain. Intense pain, sharp and searing, sliced through him. As the first shriek died away, another chased after it. Each time, as the pain dulled, more replaced it and pounded relentlessly against him. Wave after wave of shrieking and throbbing crashed over him.

In that splinter of a moment, Jacob realized something cold shackled his ankle. He aimed to kick out but couldn't as another band slithered around his other ankle, the long, fingerlike strictures icy and rigid.

A sensation of forward movement carried him and the rush of wind against his face surprised him. Yet he could see nothing. There was nothing to hold on to and fight this force. He had to let go.

# CHAPTER ONE

THE FIRE BLAZED, ROARING upward into the bleached sky, and its reflection burned in Samuel Fisher's soul. Guilt and anger combined into a powerful explosion of emotions. Smoke shifted with the wind and coughed into his face, making his eyes water. Sweat poured off him, soaking his cotton shirt and trailing down his back. He mopped his forehead with his arm, clearing his eyes of the stinging saltiness.

"You okay?" Roc Girouard paused his footsteps. He'd been living with Samuel's family for a few weeks, yet only today's events had revealed his reasons for being here. An ex-police officer, an *Englisher*, Roc had come to protect Rachel, who wasn't really his wife, as they'd proclaimed. It was a lie, as so many things Samuel had learned were. "Samuel?"

At Samuel's nod, they shuffled closer to the fire, the heavy load dangling between them. He tried to blanket the questions in his mind and the reality of what they were doing. Tried but failed.

When they were but three feet from the fire, the heat pulsing against one side of Samuel's face, Roc set the body on the ground, releasing the wrists slowly and respectfully so the arms crossed the blood-soaked chest. Samuel couldn't take his gaze off of the pale, deathly still features of his brother, Jacob.

"This is wrong," Samuel said, his throat charred by the smoke and tight with constricting emotions. "We should bury him. Not...this."

"It's the only way," Roberto Hellman intervened. The priest had a soft-spoken but steely tone. A man of conviction. A man who knew God's word.

"You ready?" Roc prodded.

They'd fought a battle together. But was this what it felt like to win? To save loved ones? To defy evil? Samuel wasn't sure of anything anymore, especially the truth.

"Let go now, son. We can take a moment." The priest's hands settled on his and helped him relinquish his brother's ankles, where he'd held him as they carried him from the house to the open field. "Would you like me to say a prayer?"

"Roberto," Roc's tone turned brusque, "don't—"

"It's his own brother, Roc."

"No, it isn't. Samuel, that wasn't your brother you shot. That creature was—" Roc made an exasperated sound at the priest's glare and fell silent.

The priest took it as agreement and made the sign of the cross. They'd ridden together on Samuel's motorcycle from the bus station in Louisville, but even in that short amount of time, Samuel recognized the priest's kind soul. When the prayer ended, he realized the words had been another language. Latin, he suspected, even though most of the Bible he had heard growing up was read in German. Still, the Word of God carried the same weight in any language. Raw emotions shook Samuel. He shuddered with effort as he resisted shouting at the world and God.

All three stared into the fire, knowing what must be done and yet allowing Samuel one last moment. *But for what? To say good-bye to his brother?* He'd already done so three years ago when he believed his brother had died. *Had his father been wrong then? Or had Pop lied?*

Because Jacob had appeared again today.

Jacob had come to harm Rachel. But why? Rachel and Jacob had grown up together. They even went off during their *rumschpringe* years. But Rachel had returned first, and alone. It was after that when Jacob returned and died suddenly in an accident at their father's woodworking shop. Or so Samuel had been told. Rachel had married Josef Nussbaum, who had died in some kind of an accident, leaving Rachel a pregnant widow. Then she'd showed up here with Roc, saying she was married to this *Englisher*. But Samuel now understood Roc had been waiting, anticipating Jacob's arrival, ready to do battle.

Samuel had only known of an intruder. And he'd shot. But he'd shot his brother. How could he have known? He'd stopped Jacob from hurting Rachel or Roc or anyone else. But he'd killed his brother.

What was there to say to Jacob now? I'm sorry? Was he? Oh yes. But how did one ask for forgiveness from a corpse? He'd done what his family and faith believed was the worst sin imaginable. He'd stolen a life. And somehow he would have to live with that.

He had no prayer to offer. Praying was too audacious an act after what he'd done. The body at his feet was proof of his unforgivable sin. And he would pay for that.

Choking on smoke and tears, he bent once more and grabbed Jacob's ankles. When he straightened, he sensed the other two men watching him. But he couldn't look at them. He couldn't look at Jacob's face. He stared into the flames, felt the searing heat, and gave a sharp nod.

Roc cleared his throat and took hold of Jacob's wrists.

"On three." Samuel swung his brother's body away from the flames as Roc said, "One."

Two.

Three.

And Samuel released his brother into the carnivorous flames. But he held on to the guilt and anger. That fire could never be quenched.

# CHAPTER TWO

A SHARP LIGHT SLASHED THROUGH the darkness. Jacob's descent came to a sudden, jarring halt. Shrieks exploded around him, like an angry chorus, each attempting loftier notes. The cacophony of sounds stabbed him.

Then just as abruptly, blessed silence. This silence, rather than suffocating as it did before, comforted. A sudden, blinding light transfixed him. It came from a long, thick blade—a sword—and the brightness radiated outward, forming a circle of hope in the darkness of despair. But as his eyes adjusted, Jacob realized the light came from a man.

Tall and muscular, the man—or being—was unlike anything Jacob had ever seen. Beautiful beyond words. Majestic. Powerful. His skin glowed like melted silver and rippled over thickly corded muscles along his chest and arms. Every sinew and bone was finely crafted, each muscle honed and well defined, coiled with readiness. Fierce blue eyes glared at the dark creatures now cowering at Jacob's feet.

He saw them now, what had wrapped around his ankles and dragged him deeper into desolation. These creatures were dark and distorted, like shadows with substance and form and spindly arms. They held on to Jacob's ankles, and he kicked to break their hold. One edged away, its body moving like liquid. But the other leered toward Jacob, hissing and snarling, its features grotesque and misshapen.

Fear gripped Jacob, and he trembled all over, tried to draw back, but he could not move. He could do nothing to defend himself. The creature's foul breath wafted over him, a lethal concoction of decaying fumes.

"Enough!" the being with the sword spoke. Although not shouted, his voice resonated through every fiber of Jacob. The dark creatures at Jacob's feet recoiled, their shapeless bodies quivering in response to the being's commanding tone.

A fluttering behind the being alerted Jacob as a wing arced behind his head. No, two wings stretched high above the being and trailed down below his feet, unfurling a strength that matched the thickly muscled torso and limbs.

*Was this an angel or some demon?*

Gripping the sword's hilt, the being pointed the blade downward in an imposing, authoritative stance. "This one," he spoke to the cowering creatures, "is not yours."

"But he is!" one of the creatures responded in a shrill voice. "We were told."

Another form stepped out of the darkness and into the dim outreaches of the light still emanating from the angel. This being—or was it a beast?—also held a weapon, which caught the light and, instead of reflecting, absorbed it. He, like the angel, had a mighty build with carefully defined muscles, but the likeness ended there. The face, rather than open and commanding, was pinched and distorted, heavily lined with fury. This creature could frighten even the likes of Stephen King. "He is ours to take." The beast spoke with a crusty voice that set Jacob's heart pounding. Black, lifeless eyes turned toward Jacob. The beast gave a slight bow. "Akiva. You are known—"

"His name," the being Jacob interpreted to be an angel spoke, "is Jacob Fisher." In spite of the powerful tone, he moved not one muscle. "His name is written in The Book."

The two dark creatures cowered and repeated, "The book. Oh, the book!" They edged toward the dark beast, which demanded, "Do not release him."

The angel never flinched. Was he weighing Jacob's worthiness? Did he even merit the effort of a fight? Why would this angel fight for someone such as Jacob anyway? What had he ever done to garner help on this side of life?

If Jacob could have spoken, he would have pleaded for help from this powerful angel, who looked as if he could land a deadly blow with that mighty sword. But Jacob was rendered speechless. Fearing he would have no choice but to go with the creatures and beast, Jacob ached with every ounce of will to go into the light. Yet hope for such as that seemed pointless after all the sins he had committed.

When he thought the moment had stretched beyond its breaking point, the bright sword flashed, slashing ever so close to Jacob's feet, and sparks burst from the bonds that held him as they shattered. Shrieks and howls erupted from the creatures, and they swirled upward in a dizzying flutter and vanished into darkness. Then the angel whirled around with lethal grace, wielding his sword overhead in a swirl of steel and light, and halted before the beast, pointing the tip of the blade at the dark monster's throat.

As he held the beast at bay, the angel reached toward Jacob with an open hand. His eyes, a steel-blue force, met Jacob's for one second, yet the unrelenting gaze seemed to last a lifetime. "Take my hand."

Jacob could move then, and he clasped hands with the angel. Whisked behind the powerful wings, Jacob saw only the great expanse of white feathers, which were like no feathers he'd ever seen, shimmering with an indescribable iridescence.

The clash of steel startled him. His view blocked by the

immense wings, he heard the grunts and parrying of battle.
Dodging away, he sensed more of those frightening yet timid
creatures in the darkness beyond, so he kept beneath the shadow
of the wings. Sword clanked against sword, the sound echoing
in the stillness beyond. The black, encrusted sword thrust forward and barely skimmed the angel's wing. Jacob fell backward
as the dark blade came too close. Then the swords banged and
clanged. A ringing filled the gaps between the heavy blows.

"This battle is already over," the angel said. "Why waste
effort on this one?"

"Why indeed?" With a huff, the beast yanked his sword
away, slapping aside what looked like a cape or covering, and
stalked into the shadows and darkness, but his voice carried
through the stillness. "You will regret this. You'll change
your mind. You'll beg me to take him."

The angel did not move until the beast disappeared, then
his wings carefully folded and came to rest, secured between
his shoulder blades. Turning, sword still at the ready, he said,
"Come, Jacob."

"You know me? But—"

"Completely."

"And w-who are you? An angel?"

He inclined his head, indicating yes.

"Do you have a name?"

"Remiel."

Jacob whispered the name, and his pulse leapt. "Where
are we going?"

"Come now." The angel began moving away from him,
taking his circle of light.

Sensing others in the dark watching and waiting, Jacob
scrambled to his feet and hurried to keep up. "What is happening? Where am I?"

Without slowing, the angel said, "You are dead. Do you remember?"

The memory shot through him, just as the shotgun blast had hit him in the chest. It struck him as odd that he should view his own death so dispassionately. It brought no resurgence of pain or grief. It was as if he no longer cared about the life he had known, as if the shackles and burdens had fallen away, and he now felt lighter and safer than he'd been moments before. "So this is it? This is death and dying? Heaven and hell?"

The angel again said nothing. A head taller than Jacob, he had long strides, which made it difficult for Jacob to keep up. Out of breath, Jacob rushed after him, his thoughts trailing way behind, lingering in the earthly realm. "But what about—?"

The angel kept moving.

"Wait!" Jacob stopped. "I can't go anywhere. I can't leave. Not yet. Not until… What about my brother?"

Remiel's gaze, hard and stony, leveled on Jacob, yet the depths of his eyes flickered. "Do you mean, Samuel?"

Awestruck at the angel's knowledge, Jacob nodded. "Yes, Samuel. There's danger. We have to go back. I—" He hesitated, not wanting to admit he was the danger. "Akiva wasn't the only vampire there. Samuel is in trouble. You've got a sword. You can help him. But we have to hurry."

The corner of the angel's mouth curled. "It's too late. The moment has passed. Samuel does not want help."

"What do you mean?"

"You cannot force help on those who resist. That is true in life and beyond."

Desperation reared up inside Jacob like a startled horse. "But he's my brother!"

"Yes, and stubborn, like you. He must learn. If he chooses to learn at all."

"But that's dangerous."

The hint of a smile disappeared, and only Remiel's strong, fierce features remained, his eyes those of a warrior who had seen into eternity. "Yes, it is."

Slowly, the angel assessed Jacob, then continued in the direction he'd been heading. A halo of light encircled him, the light emanating from his ivory skin.

Jacob jogged a couple of steps. "I have to help Samuel. I have to—"

"Are you willing to sacrifice your eternity for his?"

The question caught Jacob off guard. He'd seen what darkness awaited, the painful torture. Pain had throbbed through his very bones and shaken him to the core. He'd heard the infinite, excruciating silence of an eternal darkness yawning before him. And he'd met frightening creatures. Creatures that had cowered before Remiel. Without Remiel, Jacob would have been at their mercy. And they offered no mercy.

Yet, Remiel suggested all that Jacob had experienced might be waiting for Samuel. *Would Jacob take his brother's place? Was his love strong enough to give his brother such a gift?*

Samuel was young, two years younger than Jacob, and infinitely unschooled in the ways of the world, especially the unseen, unknown world. Jacob had done many things in his life to deserve eternity in fiery hell. So without much hesitation, he responded, "Y-yes." He rushed ahead before cowardice made him recant his words. "Yes," he repeated more firmly, "I will trade."

Remiel stared off into the vast darkness as if judging distance or time or something Jacob could not begin to comprehend. "You think you can redeem yourself by helping Samuel?"

"I don't know. I don't know anything about this place. I don't know the rules."

"You know more than you think."

Jacob didn't understand. "You tell me the answer."

The angel's gaze never wavered, and no answer was forthcoming.

Jacob knew, if he could, if there was a way, he would help Samuel and keep him from falling into the same pit. "Can I at least try?"

# CHAPTER THREE

"SAMUEL, WON'T YOU EAT some more?" Mamm called from the kitchen. She'd fixed his favorites: fried chicken, mashed potatoes and gravy, along with buttermilk biscuits. He'd retreated to his room and lay on his bed, hands folded over his empty stomach, legs outstretched, and eyes closed.

"Samuel?" Her voice came closer, and he heard her footsteps. "Are you ill?"

But he didn't respond, and her footsteps receded into the other room. She spoke softly to Pop, but Samuel rolled onto his side and faced the wall.

Three months had passed since Jacob's death. The real one. The one Samuel couldn't ignore, forget, or deny. Each day since, Samuel had risen early, completed his chores, worn himself out doing more than was expected. But his appetite had waned, and sleep evaded him. When he found refuge in short, sporadic dreams, Jacob appeared. And Samuel woke in a sweat with a cry on his lips and chest heaving.

Winter had taken hold of the land, and snow blanketed the ground. Samuel labored on his chores until his muscles quivered with fatigue. Only then did he seek the shelter of the house. His parents were already eating supper at the kitchen table when he walked in the back door, doffed his hat and coat, and headed toward his room.

"Aren't you hungry?" his mother asked.

His father harrumphed. "Your mother worked long and hard on this fine meal."

But he didn't respond. He flopped onto his bed. For a long while he stared at the ceiling until his eyes closed.

A knock on the door jarred him. The doorknob twisted, and his father entered.

"Samuel," his voice boomed, "this has to stop."

Samuel blinked but did not answer. *What was there to say?*

"Now, I want you to get up and go in there and eat. Do you understand me?"

He couldn't move. He felt nothing, as if he too were as dead as Jacob.

"Samuel, are you listening to me?" His father strode farther into the room and leaned over Samuel. "Is it that *English* girl you've been seeing?" This time his voice was quieter, as if he didn't want Samuel's mother to overhear. "Is it?"

He hadn't gone to see Andi in a week. Only because he had not yet joined the church and was still in his "running around" years had his father kept quiet this long. Still, surprise that his father knew he'd been seeing an *English* girl made him sit upright. When he'd drunk too much, smoked some weed, and showed up at Andi's door, she'd taken him in, taken him to bed, and he'd tried to forget. But he'd ended up weeping like a baby, his head cradled on her shoulder.

"Is this woman turning you against us?" Pop demanded.

Samuel met his father's gaze with a challenge. "You didn't tell me the truth about Jacob, did you?"

His father's eyes narrowed and he straightened. "And you're turning into him."

Those words were meant to wound, and yet Samuel held on to them. At least Jacob hadn't lied to him the way his father had.

"You heard me right, Samuel. Your brother believed we were hiding some big truth from him. And look where it got him! Is that what you want to happen to you?"

Words piled up in Samuel but could find no release. His hands shook as rage boiled inside him. The one thing his father had tried to teach him about God and faith Jonas Fisher had obviously known nothing about. Maybe Jacob had been right. Maybe there was more out there than the way they'd been raised.

His father stared down at him, waiting for an answer, an acceptable answer that Samuel couldn't give. Finally, he left.

Later, as the room darkened with shadows, Mamm brought him a tray with buttered toast and strips of beef swimming in buttery noodles. "I thought you might be hungry."

He forced himself to sit up on the edge of the bed.

She set the tray beside him and handed him an envelope. "This came for you."

Samuel recognized the careful penmanship of his older brother, Levi. His mother's fingers lingered on the envelope a second longer than necessary. *Had Levi ever written to her?* But she finally released the envelope into her youngest son's hands and left him alone. Pennsylvania seemed so far away. So very far away.

All three of the Fisher boys had been born in Lancaster County and raised there in the district of Promise. When Samuel was fifteen, Pop told them of Jacob's death. They'd all gone to the grave site and prayed together. Yet each of them had held on to grief. Their family might have survived Jacob's death…or first death, except Pop decided he couldn't live in Promise any longer. That decision had severed their family in ways Jacob's death hadn't. With his parents, Samuel had moved to Ohio, Levi had stayed behind, and Samuel had felt as if he'd lost both brothers. If he'd been older, then maybe he would have done the same as Levi. Or if he'd been sweet on a girl the way Levi had been on Hannah Schmidt. But Samuel hadn't been given a choice.

Now, almost four years later, Samuel hadn't seen his older brother since then. Levi had married Hannah, Rachel's younger sister, and they were expecting a baby soon. Life in Pennsylvania had continued on.

But here in Ohio, it seemed to have stopped. Longing welled up inside Samuel. His fingers sought the sealed flap and tore it open.

*Dear Samuel,*

*Roc brought news of your safety. I was relieved to hear that you are well and that no harm came to you. You must not feel guilty for what happened. We choose our own path, and Jacob chose his. I will never understand why, but maybe it is not for me to understand. Or maybe I only understand what I wish to.*

*Hannah shared with me a book of poetry Jacob loved. This passage has brought me comfort.*

> *When some Beloveds, 'neath whose eyelids lay*
> *The sweet lights of my childhood, one by one*
> *Did leave me dark before the natural sun,*
> *And I astonished fell, and could not pray,*
> *A thought within me to myself did say,*
> *"Is God less God that <u>thou</u> art left undone?*
> *Rise, worship, bless Him, in this sackcloth spun,*
> *As in that purple!"—But I answered Nay!*
> *What child his filial heart in words can loose,*

*If he behold his tender father raise*
*The hand that chastens sorely? Can he choose*
*But sob in silence with an upward gaze?—*
*And my great Father, thinking fit to bruise,*
*Discerns in speechless tears, both prayer and praise.*

Samuel stretched back out on the bed and reread the poem, his lips moving slightly as he read the words that had meant so much to Levi. Maybe his older brother could offer prayers and praise to the good Lord, but Samuel could not. Levi didn't know the sin Samuel had committed. He was alone in this dark grief and stifling anger.

Clenching his hand, he wadded up the letter but stopped himself from throwing it away. A part of him wanted to hear his brother's voice, to feel as if their family was once again whole, to know that all was not lost. And he opened the crinkled paper once more and read the rest of Levi's letter.

*For I know at the end, Jacob chose love, a sacrificial love.*
*Love carries beyond the grave, as we know of our dear Lord's*
*great sacrifice and love for us.*

*Choose wisely, Samuel, how you will live. You are in my*
*daily prayers.*

*Always your brother, Levi*

Samuel's thoughts lingered on the last. *Sacrificial love.* Jacob may have sacrificed his life in the end to save Rachel, but it was Samuel who had killed him. The choice he had made could never be undone.

*The hand that chastens sorely?* Samuel reread bits and pieces of the poem. Had it meant something to Jacob too? Jacob had revered words and stories, poems and books. What had spurred him beyond the confines of his Amish upbringing? What had pushed him to do so? His father's lies? Had Jacob seen through the façade? Or was it simple truth in poetry? Words strung together on a page? How could words have lured him away from home, family, and faith? Could the words he'd read, the rhythm and cadence, have acted like a balm to his wounded soul? Had they held profound truths?

Either way, resolution and redemption seemed out of Samuel's reach.

He was being watched.

Samuel felt a suspicious shiver run down his spine as he walked along the darkened street. Living in an Amish community, wearing the plain clothes, made one stand out, and all his life he'd been aware of the *English*, who liked to observe. It could have easily been the last bite of winter, as it clawed and scratched its way into late March, but the prickly sensation at the base of his neck told him it was more than the cold.

He glanced over one shoulder, nothing grabbing his attention, and jerked his gaze in the opposite direction. Again, nothing. No tourists. No *Englishers*. No one. Dismissing the sensation, he hunched his shoulders inside his jacket, tucked his chin, and stared at the glistening sidewalk as he trudged onward.

Rain puddles speckled the sidewalk and gave a shimmer to the pavement where dirt and sludge from the last snowfall had been pushed to the side of the roadway. High above, streetlights made tiny halos at the top of the poles in the misty night air. He felt like a man with a foot in two worlds, and his path was as murky and indistinguishable as light from dark on this cold, foggy night.

The bitter wind tugged at his coat, but he fisted a hand over the opening, the same way he held on to the Eden of his childhood, now lost to sorrow and heartbreak and sin. As a child, life had been simple—not easy, but comfortable. Comforting. And he longed for it once again.

He crossed Eighth Street and angled toward the building. Through the glass door, he entered this world so unlike his own, where artificial lights replicated the sun, an automated spring breeze cooled off rooms, and sleek steel, solid brick, and shimmering chrome replaced wood. In this place, technology reigned supreme, media took the place of teachers, and books were honored.

But in the Amish world, sun and sky, wind and rain bowed only to the hand of God. Furniture and attire reflected the natural world and order. Nothing seemed complicated. Everything adhered to simplicity. And only one book, God's Word, held any value. His parents owned only two others in their home: a book of hymns and one of martyrs. But those, especially the Bible, had been displaced by others, which Samuel had delved into in an effort to understand what had happened to his brother.

For the past six months, he'd thought of nothing but Jacob, and each time, he felt the jarring shock and guilt jabbing into his heart. *Oh, Jacob. What happened? How did we come to this? How should you be remembered? As a victim? A villain? Or simply a martyr?*

Levi had said Jacob gave his life. Gave it? No, Samuel had taken it, like a thief. Their father wouldn't discuss Jacob or his death, wouldn't acknowledge that something disturbing and beyond the natural world had happened, wouldn't admit he'd lied about Jacob's first death. Or fake death. But as much as Samuel wanted to unload his own guilt, he couldn't.

He'd attempted to banish the questions, shun the memories, but they hounded him like coyotes after a stray cat. The questions gnawed at his bones and flesh. He'd finally taken refuge in a place he hoped held the answers.

The library had become his church, where he bowed his head over pages and words, searching for truth. Now, passing an elderly woman and bank of computers, he took the stairs to the third floor, a path well worn by his scuffed boots over the last three months. Down below, teenage laughter carried up through the atrium, bouncing around the walls and off the windows. Here above, the top floor appeared deserted. The reference desk stood empty. Samuel wandered through the maze of bookshelves, searching for the librarian who had helped him over the past few weeks.

Julie worked Sundays, Tuesdays, Wednesdays, Thursdays, and Fridays. Midweek, most patrons stayed away. He'd learned to arrive a few minutes before closing, when she didn't have anything much to do.

It had become a set time when Samuel returned books, chatted with Julie, learning she had grown up in Cincinnati and wanted to one day be a writer, and picked up more books she had ordered for him through interlibrary loan. He got the sense she anticipated his visits, as last week she'd said, "You're late." But maybe he was reading too much into her awareness.

Julie had graduated from University of Kentucky and was a couple years older, but she was always eager to help, her green eyes sparkling with enthusiasm, her smile quick and easy, if not on the edge of shy. Her long blond hair was usually pulled back at the base of her neck. She wasn't one of those *English* women who wore a lot of makeup, and he liked her wholesome plainness. She was pretty in a simple way. She'd told him once, "I love books. Love them." Her grin had been as broad as the state of Ohio. "Really, I just can't help myself."

When he'd confessed he appreciated the darker poems, she'd suggested the obvious: Poe. But Edgar Allan had nothing on Aleister Crowley and his works. One line in "A Saint's Damnation"—*My poisonous passion for your blood! Behold!*— stopped Samuel cold. Deeper and deeper he dug into occultist practices and rituals, and Julie had eagerly supplied the tools, even pointing him toward musicians who were followers of "The Great Beast": Led Zeppelin, The Doors, and Sting.

"Are you looking for something in particular?" a deep voice interrupted his thoughts. Samuel turned toward a man with dark hair, silver threaded through the thick mass. He bent his head slightly forward at an angle. His awkward stance made the man, who might have been in his midthirties, seem embarrassed by his own button-down shirt, the fabric of which was a funny pattern and too bold for Samuel's tastes.

"Yes." Samuel cleared his throat. "I'm looking for Julie Redding. She's a librarian here. She, uh, usually works on Wednesday nights."

The man nodded. "You must be Samuel."

*How would this man know his name?* Hope sparked inside him. *Had Julie spoken of him?* "I am."

"Julie said you'd be coming by." The man adjusted his thick glasses, pushing them along the bridge of his nose with his forefinger. "I've got a stack of books earmarked for you."

A pinprick of disappointment stabbed Samuel, but he was grateful she'd remembered and kept her word. "Thank you."

"Sure, come on back this way and I'll get those books for you." The man turned away and meandered through the bookshelves, leading Samuel back the way he'd come, toward the reference desk. He shifted one shoulder downward and looked back, gazing at Samuel over the dark rim of his glasses. Something in that shadowy look reminded Samuel of someone…but he couldn't place the features with a name.

"Have we met before?" Samuel asked.

The man turned away and shuffled along. "Don't think so."

"You look familiar is all."

The man walked around to the other side of the counter, keeping head and gaze downcast. "If you come to the library often, then I expect you've seen me here."

"That's probably it." Samuel watched the odd man search the shelves and carts for a stack of books with Samuel's name on them. "Could have sworn I put them here." He tilted his head as if he had a tic, then squatted down, his knees popping, and hunted below the desk and through a couple cabinets. Despite his ungainly movements, he had broad shoulders and a solid build. "They could be in the back." He took off, walking with an odd gait, gesturing with his hand. "Come on, you can help me look. If you don't mind."

Samuel figured the poor guy needed help all right.

The man opened the door, holding it with a foot. "Appreciate the help. Don't want this to take all night, now do we?" He waited for Samuel to step over the threshold before releasing the door. "Julie said nice things about you."

Heat prickled the tips of Samuel's ears as he entered the "Librarians Only" area where he glimpsed carts stuffed with books, a door marked *Restroom*, and a container of toilet paper and cleaning supplies lining one wall. How could he ask about Julie without giving away his own interest? "Have you worked with her…Julie a long time?"

"Not too long, no."

"And what's your name?" Samuel asked. "So I can tell Julie the next time I see her how helpful you were tonight."

The man grinned. Behind the dark rim of his glasses and thick lenses, his even darker gaze glittered. "I'm Brydon."

# CHAPTER FOUR

F ROM A PLACE BETWEEN places, Jacob Fisher glared at the vampire standing too close to his younger brother, Samuel. *Brydon.* Jacob should have left him for dead in New Orleans. After all he'd done to help the ungrateful vampire! The traitor. Now Brydon wanted to kill Jacob's younger brother. The blood didn't have to advertise his intentions; Jacob simply knew. What else did a vampire want? For there was no other reason a vamp would hang around a human. It was their way. Another way to pass the endless time. Another game. Another meal.

Smiling like a shark inviting a fish to dinner, Brydon forced the door to the back room of the library closed. It was a restricted room, out of sight from any patron or anyone who might intervene. Brydon was now alone with Samuel. All alone.

Except for Jacob. But neither Brydon with those black eyes or Samuel with his weak human ones could see into the other world. Would that prove to be an advantage? Or a disadvantage? The lights in this area were dimmed. Farther ahead, where the room hooked left, a fluorescent light twitched and buzzed. Samuel perused the book carts, looking for something, but behind him Brydon straightened to his full, imposing height.

Would he toy with Samuel first? Or would he attack quickly? It was only a matter of heartbeats before Brydon struck.

Anger fired inside Jacob, and he launched himself at Brydon. But instead of slamming into flesh, he fell right through Brydon's body, as if blood and flesh didn't exist, and rolled across the floor, chest skidding, arms flailing. Samuel stepped straight through Jacob's abdomen, but Jacob felt nothing—and he accomplished less.

Brydon and Samuel didn't notice Jacob lying on the ground as they continued their casual conversation.

"Have you known Julie long?" Samuel trained his gaze on the stacks of books on shelves and carts, not paying attention to Brydon, who crept closer and closer.

He had his prey so close, his body rigid with the coiled posture Jacob recognized all too well. "I've known Julie a fairly short time," Brydon answered, his tone mild. "She's nice." His voice lilted, as if dulling Samuel's senses. "And she's quite beautiful."

Scrambling to his feet, Jacob growled deep in his throat and threw himself at Brydon's back. But again, he tumbled through the vampire as if he were vapor and sprawled across the floor.

Which is when he saw it—the toe of a shoe. Where the room curved sharply to the left, a discarded shoe protruded from behind a cart. Jacob scurried around the metal shelves and came face to face with a young woman. Actually a corpse.

Her blond hair fell around her shoulders in tangled waves. Her neck gaped—a bloody, mangled mass. Her eyes remained open. This was Julie.

If Jacob didn't do something quickly, Samuel would soon be lying beside her. Equally dead.

A roar of frustration and fear reared up inside him, and he swung around.

Brydon was watching Samuel with that hungry look. Jacob's hands fisted. *What could he do? How could he stop Brydon?*

"Hey!" Jacob called.

Remiel stood in that typical stance, with his sword plant-ed. His wings were drawn back and relaxed. But even tran-quil, he had a ready-for-action posture, his features hard.

Jacob ran toward him. "Do something! He's going to kill Samuel! You have to stop him."

"He is not my responsibility."

"What do you mean by that? Aren't you supposed to help people?"

"My job is to secure you. That is all."

"Secure me? What does that mean?" Jacob shook off the question. "It doesn't matter. Just do something. Save my brother!"

"I cannot interfere."

"But I can?"

Remiel shrugged. "That is to be seen."

Jacob swung around, his body taut. Brydon chatted ami-ably with Samuel, toying with his dinner.

"How?" Jacob pleaded with Remiel. "I tried to stop him."

"Physically."

"So? What am I supposed to do? Pray?"

"You are not of the physical world anymore."

"But—"

"Talk to him."

"Him? Samuel? Isn't hearing physical?"

"There are many ways to hear."

Jacob scowled. He didn't understand, and he didn't have time to waste.

"Sounds like you might be interested in Julie," Samuel said to Brydon, bending over to read the titles of the books crammed into the shelves.

Behind him, Brydon removed his glasses, and his black

gaze glinted with anticipation. "In some ways, I suppose I am interested. Or was. She was...is," he corrected himself and licked his lips, "sweet."

Samuel checked a square piece of paper bound to a book by a rubber band. "What changed your mind?"

Jacob rushed toward his brother and squatted beside him. He cleared his throat. "Samuel!"

Samuel didn't blink, turn, or respond in any way. Instead, he listened to Brydon talk about the virtues of some girl. Some dead girl.

Desperate, Jacob snapped his fingers in Samuel's face.

No response.

"Hey, Samuel! Are you listening? Hey! Get out of here. This guy is no good. He's dangerous." Jacob planted himself in front of Samuel, trying to block Brydon, but Samuel looked right through him. "Run, Samuel! Get out of here!"

Samuel dipped his head downward and rubbed his temples. "Tell Julie I was here. I'll be back next week. I come every Wednesday. You know, to check out books."

"Hey, Remiel!" Jacob yelled across the room at the angel. "He can't hear me! Do something! You can appear in front of Brydon, can't you? I've seen that when I was...well, before. So, come on, do it."

"I have no stake in this fight. No authorization to—"

"You can't think for yourself? Come on, time is running out here."

The angel turned his head, looking not at Jacob or Samuel or Brydon, as if he didn't care what was happening in this room, as if he was looking somewhere else, and then he said, "There is someone who might help."

# CHAPTER FIVE

NAOMI WAGLER STARED OUT her bedroom window at the full moon beaming down on the Pennsylvania farmland like a proud papa smiling with pride at his youngest child. But would God be so proud of her? She doubted it.

The weak moonlight created deep shadows. She sat on top of the quilt over her single mattress with her legs tucked against her chest and her arms wrapped around her knees. In spite of the cool, spring weather, the room she had once shared with her sister felt warm and stuffy. She scrambled across the bed, unlatched the lock, and raised the window to allow in the breeze that teetered between winter and spring.

The path below led away from her parents' house, toward the road. It was only two miles to her sister Grace's new home, but it might have been two hundred for how isolated and far away her sister seemed. Earlier today, Grace had come over to help clean the house for Sunday services, which would be held at the Waglers' farmhouse. Traditionally, church services rotated every two weeks between families in the district, and tomorrow, folks would be arriving early to set up the benches. Naomi would help her mother finish preparations and prepare the noon meal. It was always enjoyable, as many women from the district came to help, making the drudgery of hard work light with their many hands and cheerful conversation.

But the day of cleaning had impacted her in an unexpected way. She pressed her cheek to the soft fabric of her nightdress stretched over her knees and felt the hot sting of tears. Breathing in the scent of sun-warmed cotton, she could hear one of her mother's typical sayings: don't put a question mark where God puts a period.

She blinked back the tears. Was she questioning God? Her emotions felt like an unformed blob, not a solid question, but maybe they were. Had God put a solid barrier in front of her dream? She wasn't sure. Not yet anyway. And yet the emotion she'd felt all day bubbled up and threatened to spill over but she squeezed her eyes closed.

*It is of the Lord's mercies that we are not consumed, because his compassions fail not. They are new every morning: great is thy faithfulness.*

*Oh come, morning! Bring the mercies of the Lord*, her heart cried. Mulling the scripture verse, she wondered if morning would ever come. Even when it did, would God's mercies cover her?

She struck a match and lit a candle on the bedside table. Warm candlelight flickered through the room, pushing the shadows of doubt and envy further away. She reached for a tiny notebook and ink pen she kept on the table. Her fingers slid into position as if the pen were an extension of her hand... or heart. The tip of the pen hovered over the paper as God's spirit once hovered over *the face of the waters*...like a shadow.

She saw her own shadow darkening the wall and straightened her back, watching her shadow shift and change. Then she relaxed her shoulders and allowed them to curl forward as pen touched paper.

*My shadow sees*
*What I cannot*

*My mirror image*
*My soul pleas.*

Mother always said faith gave courage to face today and billowing expectations for the future. So why did it feel as if hope had shriveled? She'd placed her hope in one and lost him. She wouldn't be so foolish again. But had she also lost her faith? No, of course not. Perhaps she'd dropped the harness of obedience, as her father often said when disciplining one of his children. She searched her memory and her heart for something she'd done, something she'd said, something she'd thought…some rebelliousness, disobedience, or unimaginable sin.

Her constricting thoughts bound her. Jealousy of her sister; her best friend, Rose; and even Hannah Fisher tightened its hold on her and proved she was full of sin. She should be happy for Grace, who had told Naomi and Mother she was expecting a baby, her first. Of course, Naomi hugged and congratulated Grace even as she felt her throat tighten. She should be happy for Rose too, who had whispered to Naomi that her father was planting extra celery this spring, which could only mean Rose was planning a fall wedding with Adam Borntreger. Then Hannah Fisher's mother, Marta, had chatted unceasingly about Hannah's newborn twins.

Everyone knew the heartache the Schmidts had suffered last year when Hannah's sister Rachel disappeared, then returned to marry an *Englisher* of all things. Marta had been heartbroken. But now she had such joy, and Naomi should rejoice with her. But all of the happy news had felt like broken glass inside Naomi's chest.

To make matters worse, Marta had confided to Naomi that Hannah needed a helper with her twin boys and asked if Naomi would be willing to do so. Of course, Levi would pay. It would be a worthy task, and yet the thought of it brought tears to the surface again. She sniffed back her resentment. Maybe she needed humbling. She vowed she would do her best to help Hannah. Maybe then God would open a new door for her. Maybe this was preparation for what she hoped—to be a mother one day. Or maybe it was a consolation prize and she would only be a helper, never truly worthy.

Pen touched paper once more.

*My God knows*
*What I cannot*
*My heart prays*
*My soul groans.*

# CHAPTER SIX

ANDI MITCHELL HUDDLED INSIDE her coat and stared at the downtown Cincinnati public library. *What was Samuel doing here of all places?* Since he'd broken off with her a few months back, he hadn't contacted her. Not once. But she couldn't stop thinking of her farm boy. She missed him more than she'd ever imagined. But she never would have thought he'd go to a library. *What was he looking for?* The Kama Sutra?

Smiling at the idea, she thought of what else she could teach him. Or maybe by now, he could teach her. He'd been nothing more than a boy toy when they'd first met and she'd seduced him. Seduced was probably too strong of a word, as it hadn't taken more than a few winks and flirtatious suggestions to get him into bed. He'd been young, inexperienced, right off the farm, but a quick learner. Over the months, however, her feelings for him had grown. There was something about him that she'd found missing in every man she'd ever known. At first it had been hard to identify the missing quality. Was it innocence? Naïveté? Honesty? He had strength, not just of bone and joint and muscle but character, and something she'd rarely come across in others—integrity.

He'd lost his brother early last fall and had broken up with her. She'd thought he needed time to sort things out and grieve. But he hadn't come back.

She suspected he'd found some sweet Amish girl to keep him busy. Or maybe he'd gotten baptized and married. He'd told her how kids married at a young age in his district. Worried that he'd actually jumped off that cliff, she'd gone to his house way back in Harmony Hollow, parked down the lane, and watched for him. It hadn't been easy waiting, but finally he'd come tearing down the drive on his motorcycle, making her heart flutter once again with longing, and she'd followed him. When he'd driven over the covered bridge and toward the main highway leading back to Cincinnati, she'd suspected he was banging some other English girl. Was she here at the library of all places?

Now jealousy picked up her pace along the sidewalk. Andi kicked a glob of ice and mud out of her way. Was he into some nerd? A library dork? It didn't matter, because some bookworm wouldn't be too much competition for her.

The temperature took another dip. Andi hunched her shoulders and dug her hands deep into the pockets of her wool coat. Spring felt months away when it should be around the corner. To dispel that myth, the wind howled at her. It sounded like a voice, a cry.

Samuel.

Was that his name gliding on the wind or only her mind conjuring hope? She looked around but saw nothing out of the ordinary. Downtown on a Wednesday night wasn't the most happening place.

Stamping her feet to keep warm, she looked longingly at the glowing lights in the library windows. She never had much of an interest in hanging out in such a boring place. What was there to do in there anyway?

As a kid, her mom had sometimes dropped her off at their local library while she'd gone on a date. Andi had found a self-help section, which included books on sex, where, with the help of pencil drawings, she'd learned about life. Other books had actual pictures of men and women making love. She'd moved from there to the romance section, always skipping the boring parts of sea battles or pouring tea and going right for the sex scenes. Eventually, Andi found a boy equally bored, and they'd done the deed in the backseat of his mom's car while she was reading *Redbook*. Andi had become well acquainted with the upholstery of Camrys, Chevrolets, and VW bugs, finding cookie crumbs and petrified French fries along the floorboards, and discovered which seats left rug burns on her back and legs and which didn't. Leather, she'd learned, was the best.

Back then, she and whatever boy she was with had fumbled around, experimenting and discovering, until by the time she was in eighth grade, she'd moved on to seniors in high school, then college boys, a teacher or two, and somewhere along the way, a principal. But older men weren't always the most savvy when it came to women. Finally, in her search for fulfillment, she'd met a biker who knew a thing or two. Then along came Samuel, and she'd enjoyed tutoring him in the art of screwing.

He, in turn, had shared his family and religion with her, how they lived like it was back in the olden days without electricity. She'd said, "You're nuts. Why suffer when you don't have to?"

More often than not, she'd listened as Samuel explained about his family and older brothers, especially the one who had died—who she later learned had only been declared dead by Samuel's father. *What was his name? Oh yeah, Jacob.* He'd been a bookworm, a pseudo-intellectual, and apparently bent on destruction, because since then, he really had died. Andi hadn't worried his fatal intellectualism was a family trait because Samuel rarely had the patience to read even the *TV Guide*. But now Samuel was in the intellectual center of this town.

Another blast of cold wind punctuated by damp, icy spray made her decide to brave the interior of the library. What did she have to lose? She might meet a bookworm and educate him on the Dewey decimals in the nonfiction section. At least she'd be warmer than she was now. So she jogged across the street and entered through the glass doors.

Some teenagers were giggling at the computers. Wanting to avoid them, Andi headed up the stairs, the movement kicking her heart into gear and warming her limbs..The farther she went, the more empty the building felt.

Isolated, she searched for someone...anyone. Maybe Samuel needed her now more than ever. The way some people sensed a change in the weather approaching, she felt a prodding and pushing, as if there were an urgency for her to find Samuel. Not believing in Samuel's prayers or his God, she placed more faith in gut instinct, a sixth sense, premonitions, and psychic powers. Her intuitive radar made her heart pound.

Something was wrong.

But there didn't seem to be anyone on the third floor either. Desks and chairs, cubbyholes and computer banks were empty, neatly squared with tables, nothing out of place. An eerie hum of silence vibrated through the vacant rooms. She angled across the carpeted floor, passing bookshelves. A creepy sensation crawled up her spine. It felt colder here than it had outside.

*Call him.*

The pressing need rose up inside her, but she pushed it

away. She stood in the middle of the open area, hands on hips, and turned in a circle. *Maybe Samuel was downstairs. Maybe he knew those teens. Could he be part of a library gang?*

*No! He's here.*

Was her thought strictly intuition? Was she suddenly psychic? Maybe she could tap into some major supernatural powers and have her own reality TV show.

*Call him!*

That inner voice intruded on her wayward thoughts. Even though she felt stupid and hoped no one could see her, she whispered, "Samuel?"

Of course, there was no response, because he would have had to be standing within two feet of her. So she took a deeper breath and trusted her instincts. "Samuel."

Again, nothing. This was ridiculous. Maybe the stupidest thing she'd ever done. Had she had some sort of emotional meltdown? With a huff, she turned back.

*Call him again.*

She shook her head. This was crazy. Maybe she was turning into that Jack Nicholson character in that creepy movie in the empty hotel. It had taken him months to go loony tunes and grab an ax. At least there was nothing more dangerous than a pencil in the library.

But she'd had enough. She headed back toward the stairs.

*Stop!*

She did. A tingle crept along her spine like an icicle sliding upward, defying gravity and intelligence. Maybe this was like that movie with the little boy who saw dead people. Was she seeing…or hearing dead people? Now, that really was crazy.

But she'd seen that crazy blond-haired chick on TV who saw dead people and talked to them too. Was it even possible? Maybe you had to be open to the possibility. Yeah, she was sure the woman with the Jersey accent had said something to that effect.

*Samuel.*

"All right. Fine." She spoke louder this time, "Samuel?"

No response. That's freaking it. She was going home before someone saw her.

Then a door creaked. Andi whirled around. The door behind the main desk shifted, and Samuel stuck his head through the opening. His eyes widened at the sight of her. "Andi?" He carried a stack of books under his arm. "What are you doing here?"

"I came to…I was here, ya know, and thought I saw you…or heard you…" She hesitated, unsure how he'd feel about her following him—not to mention the voices-in-her-head phenomenon. "And, well, here you are!"

She produced her best smile, held out her arms for a hug. But he stood there staring at her. Not moving. So she took an awkward few steps forward and hugged him. One of the books poked her in the stomach. Awkward didn't begin to describe the situation. He hadn't changed much, but he looked older, leaner, harder. He no longer had the baby face he used to have.

Tossing her hair over a shoulder, she attempted normal. "So, how are you?"

"Good." His voice sounded deep and rattled her. "And you?"

*Missing you*, she thought but didn't dare say something so eighth grade. Where was a glib *Gilmore Girls* line when she needed it? Then a movement behind Samuel caught her eye, and she shifted slightly to look beyond his shoulder.

The door he'd come through swung closed, and she caught a glimpse of an odd-looking man with dark hair and even darker eyes watching them. "Who's that?"

But when Samuel turned, the guy was gone. "Oh, probably the librarian." Samuel shrugged. "He was helping me find these books."

"Oh yeah?" She reached for them. "Whatcha got?"

But Samuel shifted away, pressing the books protectively against his chest. "It's almost closing time. I better get these checked out."

"Oh, sure, yeah, you're such a party animal, Samuel. Shutting down the library."

Then she caught those dark eyes watching them through that door's window. "I think that guy has a hard-on for you."

Samuel didn't look back. "What are you doing here, Andi?"

"He's a real creeper." She matched Samuel's stride and slipped her hand through his bent arm as they began the downward descent toward the lobby. "So, what have you been up to lately? Seeing any farm implements?"

He remained silent, and panic rolled through her, flattening her hopes. This was not going well.

"How are your folks?" she asked, hoping to recover.

"Okay. You?"

"Oh, you know. Same ol', same ol'. Working. You know, stuff."

Samuel felt her hand on his arm, the familiar gesture seemingly natural but not. He couldn't say he was sorry to see her. He'd experienced the telltale excitement at the sight of her. Her eyes were bright, her cheeks red from the cold. Her fair skin made her flush easily. She wore a blue scarf around her neck, trapping the ends of her flaming hair.

She stayed beside him while he checked out his books, and he wished she hadn't seen the ones on poetry.

"What are you into now?" she asked, reading the titles. "Got some girl you're trying to impress?"

"Just doing research."

Her lips tightened, and she didn't look happy about his answer. But how could he explain? Samuel slowed when they reached the sidewalk along Eighth Street.

"Where's your car?" he asked. He should at least see her to her car safely.

Those big, green eyes held his gaze. Her fingers plucked at his sleeve. Was he misinterpreting the longing? "Can we talk, Samuel?"

He shifted uncomfortably. He wasn't sure it was a good idea. And yet, what could it hurt? "I don't know."

"Did you get baptized, then?" she asked.

He nudged a chunk of ice with the toe of his boot. How could he? "Not yet."

"Then it wouldn't be against any rules, right?"

"I suppose."

"Are you"—she hesitated, something he couldn't read flickering in her eyes—"seeing anyone?"

He thought of Julie. Maybe he'd misread her signals too. "No, I'm not."

Andi's features relaxed, and she took a steadying breath. "It'd only be for a few minutes. I promise not to keep you out late."

He wavered in his resolve. Too easily, he remembered her body pressed against his, her mouth hot and sweet, her hands—

Breaking eye contact, he checked out the buildings in downtown Cincinnati. "Is there a coffee shop nearby?"

"Sure." Her smile ignited something inside him. "Absolutely." She kept smiling, bubbling. "Coffee. That would be great."

"Yes," he repeated, unable to stop himself. "Coffee."

An all-night diner around the corner provided a place to talk, and yet there didn't seem to be much to say between them. Whatever Andi wanted, she seemed to be having a hard time saying it as she stirred cream into her coffee, twirling the spoon and fiddling with her silverware.

Besides the waitress who'd served them coffee in mugs, there didn't seem to be anyone else around. The booths and tables were empty. The waitress tucked away her order pad in her apron when they told her they just wanted coffee and headed to the kitchen.

What could he say to Andi? How could he explain what he had been through—killing his brother—and the metamorphosis he'd experienced in the following months? She wouldn't understand. Or would she?

She'd never spoken much about her own folks, and he sensed there was something that had happened between them. Maybe she could relate to the simmering anger he felt each time Pop spoke to him about obeying God and getting baptized. No, that part she wouldn't understand at all.

"Work going well?" he asked, to break the tension and silence between them.

Giant tears welled in her eyes and spilled over, running down her cheeks.

"Andi?" *What had he done? What should he do?* He rubbed his palms down his thighs and cleared the uncomfortable tightness in his throat. He should be used to women crying. Mamm often turned away and dabbed at her eyes with her apron. Usually Samuel gave her an awkward pat on the shoulder or (and he was ashamed to admit this) sometimes he simply pretended he hadn't seen the pain or tears in her eyes. But Andi…he'd never seen her even sniffle.

Wiping her eyes, she waved a hand. "I'm sorry. Really. I didn't mean to do this." She dug around in her purse. "I just...I don't know." She tipped her head sideways and dragged her bottom lip between her teeth. "I just miss you is all."

Without any more thoughts or questions, he slid out of his side of the booth and eased in next to her, wrapping an arm around her. She pressed her face against his shoulder, and he breathed in the flowery scent of her hair. When she lifted her head to look at him, his gaze rested on her parted lips, and he couldn't help himself. He tasted her once more.

# CHAPTER SEVEN

OUTSIDE THE WINDOW SPORTING a sign about Cincinnati chili, dark, heavy-lidded eyes watched the couple.

Brydon liked observing people, especially before he dined on them. It somehow made the experience that much tastier. And he had been watching Samuel for a long while. Longer than usual. He'd been more patient than was his natural course, but this one he could take his time with. This one was special.

He wanted the moment to be right.

During his years as a cop back in New Orleans, he'd learned the chase gave him the most fun. Once he'd caught a criminal, he felt a letdown. The anticipation...the hunt... that was the thrill. So he would wait...and enjoy getting revenge on Akiva. He only wished Akiva could witness it.

Akiva should have let Brydon, a rogue vampire, die. He'd wanted to die. He'd allowed Roc to slit his throat. But Akiva had brought a blood sacrifice, and as weak and near death as he'd been, Brydon had drunk fully of the offering and revived. He'd then owed Akiva, which had been the purpose. He'd drawn the line though and refused to kill Roc, his ex-partner on the police force.

He hadn't exactly felt sorrow when Akiva or Giovanni had been destroyed. But at that point, he'd recognized the position in which Akiva had placed him. So, Brydon nursed the hatred and resentment growing inside him, and he'd begun following Akiva's little brother, Samuel.

Killing him would be simple, and yet he'd begun to feed a new idea: transforming Samuel. That might be the best revenge of all. Akiva had hated being a vamp—as had Brydon at first—until he gave in and learned to appreciate the benefits. It would be fitting for Akiva's younger brother to become one. Samuel clung to his Amish white-bread existence. What a shock it would be for him to learn there was a whole new world, a world he'd never imagined. Samuel would appreciate the salvation of an awakening and embrace all that this kind of life promised and provided.

And if Akiva was watching from hell, then he'd burn even hotter at the sight.

# CHAPTER EIGHT

S AMUEL AWOKE WITH A start.

He jerked upright and shook himself. A kink knotted his back and neck, and he shifted and stretched, sitting upright at Andi's kitchen table. He rubbed his jaw, and stubble scraped his palm. A dream pressed into his mind like the edge of the book imprinted on the side of his face where he'd slept. His dreams had turned dark and sinister, reflecting either his reading material or all he'd seen the night Jacob died.

No clock was needed to tell him night nuzzled morning; he knew from his years of being awakened for chores. Pushing up from the chair, his muscles stiff, he gathered the books about creatures of the night: demons, witches, legends, myths, and the fuzzy line between this world and the next. He stuffed the hardbound books back into his leather satchel, slipped on his crumpled shirt, and tied his work boots.

He'd followed Andi home and they'd gone straight to her bed. It had felt good to hold her again, to lose himself in the tastes and scents and touch of her, to forget, even for a few minutes, all the thoughts and feelings wrestling inside him.

After she'd fallen asleep, he'd slipped out of bed, tugged on his jeans, and settled at her kitchen table. There, he'd opened the library books and had begun to read until his eyes grew bleary. He'd fallen into crazy dreams of being chased and chasing something he couldn't name, couldn't see, couldn't understand.

Scribbling her a note now, he left it on her pillow, brushed the hair back from her face, and kissed her bare shoulder. She sighed and rolled over, revealing the soft curve of a breast before scrunching down further under the covers. Maybe he'd made a mistake breaking it off with her a few months ago. He'd missed her more than he had realized.

Careful not to close the door too hard and risk waking her, he then made the hour drive back to his folks, which took even longer on the slick, icy roads. Pop was just entering the barn when Samuel parked behind the structure. He left his satchel of books attached to the motorcycle, not wanting to frighten Mamm or Pop if they were to find them. He went straight into the barn and began doling out feed.

Linda stood in her stall watching for him, her breath steamy in the morning chill. She eyed him with those limpid brown eyes and nosed his arm. "You as hungry as I am this morning?" He chuckled and poured the feed into her bucket. As she snuffled around in the oats, he rubbed her neck and scratched along her mane. When he turned around, he pulled up short. "Good morning, Pop."

His father stood in the stall's opening as if he'd been watching him for a few moments. "You are a hard worker, Samuel. Never missing work. Even when you stay out awful late, as you did last night."

The usual accusation was there but it ricocheted off Samuel. "No reason anyone else should suffer on my account."

"It grieves your mother, this carrying on with an *English* girl." He raised his hand to stop Samuel's protest. "It matters not how I know. Word travels."

Old news, like a withered grape, still lingered on the grapevine. Samuel rubbed the mare's nose, readjusted its bridle, anything but look at his father.

"There are nice girls here in Harmony Hollow," Pop said. "Girls who share your faith. Girls of marrying age."

His faith. And what was that? Samuel's lips twisted with the effort to control an outburst. "Pop, I'm not interested—"

"Are you planning on marrying her then? This *English* girl? Bringing her into our family and district?" He said it as if Andi were a disease, as if bringing her to their home would expose the family to some horrible malady—the way Pop believed Jacob had.

"She has a name."

Pop said nothing.

"Andi," Samuel supplied, anger rising in him. It rankled him that all his father would ever see would be their differences. Pop saw life in black and white, never gray. But that's all Samuel could see. "Her name is Andi."

Frown lines pulled and stretched Pop's features downward. "A boy's name?" Then his eyes widened. "Is it—?"

Samuel laughed, but humor remained aloof. Pop would never accept an *Englisher* in his family any more than he'd ever accepted Jacob's questions. With Pop, you either adhered to the law—his law—or you were bound for hell. For the first time, Samuel felt a true kinship with his dead brother.

"It is not a funny matter, Jacob."

Samuel felt the air around him shatter. "I'm not Jacob, Pop. But even if I was, it would be better than being like you."

Pop blustered, cleared his throat. "I didn't..." He broke off, unable to finish. Finally, he said, "How will you explain this...this...*Englisher* to your mother?"

"There's no way Andi would ever come here. So don't

worry about that." He exited the stall, brushing past his father and scooping up the next bucket of feed.

Pop trailed him. "Are you going to turn your back on your family, your beliefs, your district then?"

With an exhausted sigh, Samuel dumped in the grains and straightened. He had wanted to avoid this discussion, especially when his stomach was growling, but it might as well be said. He faced his father, meeting his unrelenting gaze, and the banked fire in his gut ignited again. "Those are your beliefs, Pop. Not mine."

His father blanched, his skin turning as white as the hairs in his beard. Samuel might as well have slapped his father hard across the cheek. He'd gone too far. Maybe his father's beliefs weren't his *yet*. Maybe they never would be. The fact was, Samuel didn't know what he believed anymore. Nothing made sense. He couldn't explain his feelings to his father, who would never understand and would only condemn them.

Back when Jacob was alive and living under the same roof, heated words were often hurled across the kitchen table. Jacob had dared voice his questions. Slammed doors and disapproving gazes followed. Like kindling, Samuel had taken the explanations and questions and laid them on the angry fire in his heart. He didn't know if he'd ever embrace his father's beliefs; Jacob never had. Pressure to conform and rebel yanked him in two directions. A white picket fence divided his world and poked at him. At some point, he'd have to make a decision and climb over into the serene yet penned pasture of the Amish or into the wide expanse of freedom beyond, in the *English* world.

But now was not the time. Backpedaling, Samuel said, "There's more out there than what I've been taught. Jacob knew it and—"

"*Ja*, and Jacob paid the ultimate price. Have you not heard of the tree of knowledge of good and evil? There are some things not worth knowing."

Arguing was pointless. "Jacob went to learn what he'd missed, and I am trying to understand so I can make a more informed decision before I bury myself in some district—"

"Is that what you think I've done?"

Samuel could no longer meet his father's gaze. "You lied to me."

Pop stepped back as if struck.

"You lied to me about Jacob."

For a long moment, Pop remained quiet. *Was he trying to figure out an answer, an excuse?* It didn't matter. Nothing could explain it away. Samuel slammed the lid back on the feed bin. Pop would never admit he'd been wrong. That wasn't his way.

"Would you"—Pop's voice sounded brittle—"would you break your mother's heart by going down the same destructive prodigal path?"

Guilt rose inside him like steam. How easily his father could stoke that fire. Samuel wanted to ask, "What about your heart, Pop? Would you care?" but he dared not. In some ways, his question was born more of a desperate plea rather than anger, but Pop would never understand that either. "Why are you asking me this today?" he asked. "I still have chores."

The corners of Pop's firm mouth pinched tight. "Because I must take a trip."

"A trip?" Rarely did Amish leave their homes or travel. Moving the family, or part of the family, from Pennsylvania to Ohio had not been the usual actions of a man steadfast in his Amish faith. "Where?"

"Will you be here to watch over your mother and take care of the workshop?"

Amish husbands and fathers didn't just go off and leave their families and businesses. "What's happened?"

His father sighed wearily. His shoulders, narrow and thin, seemed to carry the weight of the world. "It's Levi."

Of course, they'd been sent word that Hannah, Levi's wife, had delivered twin boys. "Something wrong with the babies?"

"Nah, the boys are healthy and strong. Although Mother would like to go and see her first grandbabies, which I suppose would be good for her, it is a long journey."

And Samuel knew neither would leave him alone for fear of what he would do. The words never had to be spoken, but Samuel understood the unspoken message. Regret heaped on top of his guilt.

But something must have happened. "Then what about Levi," Samuel asked, "is causing you to go back?"

"If you'd been home last night instead of off who knows where, then you would have been here when we got word."

Samuel pressed his lips together and kept from arguing.

Pop finally said, "Levi took a fall. Broke some ribs."

Samuel's muscles tensed and he felt a deep ache for his oldest brother. Then suspicion clouded his thoughts. Was Pop telling the truth?

"He'll be all right in time." Pop waved away what he read as Samuel's fears. "But he needs his rest. Since he and Hannah bought that farm, it's a critical time for planting, *ja*? So I'll go and help out as I can. You stay with your mother while I am gone and—"

"No, Pop."

His father's eyes registered shock, bulging slightly.

The urge to leave welled up inside him. Whether Pop was telling the truth or not, Samuel had to do this. He needed to get away, to see Levi again, to think about his life on his own terms. But again, he couldn't explain that to Pop, so he simply said, "You should stay here with Mamm. Levi is my brother. I'll go. Besides, I can travel faster and easier on my motorcycle. I'll be there in half the time you would by bus or train."

Pop's eyes narrowed. "That's not a good idea. Levi expects me—"

"What are you afraid of, Pop?" Exasperation got the better of Samuel. It was one of those off-handed comments that he immediately regretted. He'd mouthed off, much the same way Jacob used to do, and now he braced himself for his father's wrath. But for the first time in Samuel's life, he didn't see his father jerk his chin defensively. Instead, the look in the older man's eyes twisted something in Samuel's gut. He read fear—fear mixed with sorrow.

Of course, Samuel understood. Pop feared losing another son the way Samuel feared losing his only other brother. Jacob's death had changed their lives forever.

"If you go," Pop said, his voice deeper than usual, "will you come back?"

Maybe Pop wanted him to go. Maybe he had planned this, knowing Samuel would volunteer. Maybe it was all a ploy to get him away from the English girlfriend and save his soul. *Would Pop lie about Levi? Yes*, Samuel decided, *he would*. His father would do anything to get his way. Samuel jammed his hands in his pants pockets. "I don't know."

# CHAPTER NINE

IN TRUTH, THE POETRY book drew him to Pennsylvania. It tugged on Samuel's soul like a magnet. He wanted to hold it in his hands, touch the pages, and read the words Jacob had once valued. Could he find something, other than aggravating Pop, in common with his lost brother?

With his clothes folded and packed into a duffel bag, he hugged Mamm, who stood on the front porch. He dodged her gaze and the tears in her eyes. Quickly, he shook hands with Pop, avoiding his gaze.

"You'll let us know when you arrive, *ja*?" Mamm said, her voice constricted.

He wanted to tell her he'd be okay, that he had to do this, but she didn't know Pop had lied to her too. To her, Jacob had died over three years ago and was buried in an Amish cemetery in Pennsylvania. So he kept his thoughts wrapped inside himself. "Of course, Mamm."

Without a backward glance, he took off on his motorcycle over the winding, curving roads leading out of Harmony Hollow. Even though the countryside still looked like the dead of winter, with gray, wilted brush and bare-limbed trees, the sun led the way, brightening his path and warming up the day like hot apple cider. Samuel skimmed over the blacktop roads, weaving around pits and broken limbs, before he hit the highway.

It was the right thing to do, he decided, as he swung by the gym where Andi worked as a personal trainer. It took him way out of his way, but he couldn't just leave without saying good-bye.

He'd been in the chrome and glass workout place a time or two in the past, and the receptionist recognized him and told him Andi's location. Music blared from hidden speakers. Beyond the bank of televisions, which chattered like magpies, stationary bikes, treadmills, and Stairmasters all whirred and created a cacophony in Samuel's ears. Andi had explained to him once about all the equipment and tried to get him interested in working out with her, but he hadn't seen the need. Working in the shop and doing chores around his folks' place was enough to keep him fit and trim.

Across the weight room, he saw her. Andi wore a tight-fitting warm-up suit that accentuated her slim curves. The jacket was only half zipped and revealed a good portion of cleavage. The man she spoke to seemed focused on her assets, not on her advice. Immediately, Samuel felt a kink in his gut.

Andi placed one foot behind her, and the man copied her movements, wobbling until she steadied him with a hand. His balance was obviously thrown off by his rounded belly and his inability to quit looking at Andi's curves. She led him to an elliptical machine, got his feet placed correctly on the pads, then his hands on the handlebars, and set a bunch of buttons. The machine started, and the man glided along, getting nowhere quickly. Smiling, she made sure his movements were correct, then patted his arm reassuringly. Samuel had a feeling the man and others like him came here for reasons beyond cardio and BMI.

When Andi noticed Samuel, her smile brightened, which eased the knot in his abdomen. She said something to the man, then walked toward Samuel. Her smile was playful, secretive, making him remember all they'd shared last night, and coiled his insides with a new, more delightful tension.

"Well, hello," she said as she approached. "Missing me already?"

Samuel became aware of others watching—a woman lifting weights nearby, a man walking on a treadmill. Samuel edged back a few steps to give space for a private conversation. Andi pressed her body against his, looping her arms around his neck and kissing him, declaring to those around: *look but don't touch*. He hoped it would say the same to the men ogling her backside, but he suspected it would only act as a challenge to overblown egos.

She'd told him how the club was a pickup hot spot, where the ladies were always scoping out the men just as much as men were the ladies, unless their pleasure leaned toward their own sex. That shocked him, and she'd laughed and called him "farm boy."

She cupped his shaved jaw. "I didn't like waking up without you."

He squeezed her waist, and he wasn't sure if he wanted to push her back a notch or pull her closer. "There were chores to be done."

"Oh, I had a chore for you. You'll have to come back and take care of it." She winked and kissed him again. Just when she had him wanting more, she eased out of his grasp. "Wanna have dinner tonight? I have to work until four, but—"

"I came to say good-bye." There. He'd said it. Better to put it out there and let her know before she muddled his mind.

Her smile congealed, then disappeared altogether. Her eyes turned hard as glass. "What are you talking about?"

"It's my brother. The one in Pennsylvania—"

"I didn't figure it was the dead one." Her tone sounded flat.

"Levi got hurt," he explained. "Fell off the roof of his new house or something and broke some ribs. He needs my help. He's just bought a farm in Promise, and it's time to prepare the fields and begin planting. If the work doesn't get done, he won't be able to make a living this year." Samuel shrugged a shoulder. "So I'm going out there to help."

Andi narrowed her eyes. "You told me neighbors help neighbors. So let 'em."

"I need to be there."

She crossed her arms over her stomach, pushing her breasts higher. "It's more than that, isn't it?"

He felt his heels sinking deeper into his decision.

She stepped back. "How long will you be gone?"

"Not long." He looked over at a barbell lying deserted on a mat, the way he'd abandoned the truth. His own reluctance to share his hopes and plans brought back a memory. He'd stood at the end of Jacob's bed as his brother had packed his own bag so many years ago.

"New Orleans isn't so far," Jacob had offered as a consolation.

At fourteen, Samuel had resented Jacob's ability to take off for parts unknown. Sounding even younger with his voice cracking, Samuel asked, "How do you know?"

"Because I've read all about it." Jacob slapped a hand against Samuel's chest, then grinned. "Don't worry. I'll come back."

He had, yet he hadn't. The Jacob who had returned to his family months later had been different. And their lives had never been the same.

He sensed similar emotions now. Whatever awaited him in Pennsylvania would change him irrevocably. From the look in Andi's eyes, she understood that too.

She drew a deep breath as if fortifying herself. She'd told

him of breakups she'd experienced in the past. She wasn't the type to give her heart easily, and she protected it with a vengeance. He could see her rebuilding the walls even now, protecting herself. "You'll forget all about me. Hey, maybe I'll forget about you too."

"Never." He reached for her, and she tried to tug loose, but he was stronger and pulled her close. Still, she remained stiff and unresponsive in his arms. He tipped her head back and stared deeply into her eyes, seeing the green spiked with bits of gold and brown all swirled together. "I love you, Andi."

It was the first time he'd used those words, and he meant them. He loved her. But words held little meaning for her. She'd told him enough about her past, her parents, and ex-lovers for him to understand actions spoke much louder than even he could shout. He regretted the words even now. Not that he didn't believe them or feel them in the very beat of his heart, but because those were the last words her father said when he left Andi and her mom—for good.

Her wounded gaze skittered away, and her mouth tensed. So he kissed her as hard and as long as he knew how, trying to express all the things he couldn't say. When she began to soften beneath him, he pulled away. "I can't promise you anything, Andi. Not now. Not yet. I don't know what my future holds. But I want...I hope—"

She touched his lips with her fingers. Tears glimmered in her eyes, but she blinked them away and backed out of his arms. "Shut up. Just go."

# CHAPTER TEN

THE SKY REMAINED A dark gray, clouds blocking out the stars and moon, and the air felt still, as if it held its breath—waiting.

Andi too was in wait mode. Waiting to hear from Samuel. Waiting to find out if he'd ever return. And she hated waiting.

As a girl, she'd watched her mother waiting on the couch, arms and legs tangled in knots of worry, as she waited for her latest boyfriend to come home. But first, she'd waited on Andi's father hand and foot, fetching a bottle of beer out of the fridge when he snapped his fat fingers, washing his stinking clothes, which he never bothered to put in the clothes bin, and playing the little wife every chance she got. Vicki Mitchell waited on her man when he went to work, on the rare occasion he did. And she waited on him when he went out with the boys for a beer and came home smelling of whiskey and cheap perfume. Then Vicki waited for him to come home one last time, after he tossed over his shoulder, "Love you, baby." But he never darkened her door again, and Andi had known he never would.

Well, Andi wasn't like her mother. She wasn't the waiting type.

She slammed the door to her apartment, not bothering to lock it, and threw her bag and keys on the coffee table. Samuel could go off to who the hell cared where, but she was not going to sit around waiting for him to come back. No, sirree.

Stalking into the bedroom, she refused to look at the bed—the mussed sheets, which hung off the mattress, and the note he'd left that morning. She stared in the bathroom mirror and stripped off her work clothes, scattering her warm-up suit, then stood under the hot shower spray. The loofah scrubbed and scratched at her skin, as she rubbed it over every inch of her, chafing away the memories of his touch, punishing herself for caring what he did or where he went. She was a fool. Just like her mother.

When she couldn't scrub deep enough to erase his memory, she shut off the water, batted away the shower curtain, and tramped into her closet, dripping water on the carpet. She chose her sexiest outfit with the skimpiest neckline and shortest skirt. First went the thick lotion, next extra sprays of Juicy Couture, then a thong, and finally the stretchy dress fabric over her bare skin. Towel-drying her hair, she shaped the curls with her fingers, leaving it in sexy disarray. She drew heavy lines around her eyes, as if the black liner could make it look like she hadn't shed one tear, then she smeared her lips with gloss.

If she had looked through the mirror to her heart, she might have seen a lost little girl, pretending not to care. "It's okay, Momma. We can help each other."

"Shut up. You don't know nothin'."

But now, Andi didn't bother with self-help talk. She slipped on five-inch heels and walked back into the den, where she came to a sudden stop.

A dish towel partially hid a book on the kitchen table. Samuel's book. Red, hot rage rumbled deep through her and then erupted in a blast of quick, jerky movements. The book hit the wall, splatting onto the carpet, splitting the spine and twisting pages. She gave it an added kick, and her shoe bolted, knocking into the television. Teetering on one heel, she gasped and sputtered and fought the tears until she wrestled them back under control and forced them into that deep, dark, secretive place.

Brushing chaotic strands of hair out of her face, she stood in the living room of her apartment. Silence beat against her ears. A new eruption followed, not as violent as the first, but an eruption nonetheless. She kicked off her other shoe, gathered up the book, and shoved it into a grocery bag. Dumping it at the door, she drew a steadying breath, readjusted her skirt, shoved her feet into her shoes again, grabbing the wall for support, and hooked a lock of hair behind her ear.

There. That was good. She'd toss the book in the Dumpster. Then she'd go have a drink. Or two. Or ten.

She breathed easier now, expanding her lungs and drawing in the promise of hope. Her life wasn't over. So what if Samuel had left? Who needed him? There were plenty more men out there, just waiting for a chance to meet a woman like her. She'd be more particular this time. She wouldn't get some stupid farm boy. No way. She'd find a man, a real man, a grown man, who wore a dignified suit. Maybe one who worked in a bank. One who made lots of money. Somebody who knew how to treat a woman.

Buying into that hope, she grabbed her keys and snatched up the book. But she bypassed the Dumpster. What would be the point? Samuel wouldn't know if she threw it away. Or care. Worse, he'd never do that to her. With a heavy sigh, she reconsidered her initial plan. What she loved...liked about Samuel was that he always did the right thing. And the right thing to do was return the book to the library. Yes, that's what she would do. Tonight. Then she'd move on.

The drop-off box at the library had cones blocking the lane, so she parked and carried the book to the return box. She held open the latch, placed the book in the opening, but couldn't release it. For one long moment, she clung to the book as if it was all she had left of Samuel. Maybe she should keep it, just for another couple of weeks, in hopes that Samuel would return.

But then she'd be waiting for him.

"How'd the book work for you?" a male voice said, startling her.

She spun around, the slot clanking at her quick release. Pressing the book against her abdomen, she stared at a guy not much taller than her. He stood near the driver's door of a Ford pickup truck. "Do I know you?"

"You're Andi, right?"

Her gaze narrowed. Her heart thudded. Had this guy followed her from the club?

He didn't advance toward her but kept several feet between them. Slowly, he flipped a set of keys around his index finger. He kept his gaze on hers, not looking down the way most men did. Maybe he was gay. He had that buffed and polished look. "Don't worry, you don't know me," he said as if he'd read her mind. "I only know about you because of Samuel."

*Samuel.* He knew Samuel? She released a pent-up breath, but her brow remained puckered. "How do you know him?"

"I was helping him do some research here at the library."

"I see." A nerd, but a nerd who knew Samuel. And a decent looking one at that. "I'm not sure if the book helped or not. Samuel had to leave town."

"Good thing about the library, he can always check 'em out again."

She didn't care. Yet she held on to the book and walked back toward her car, fingering her own set of keys. Maybe this idiot could be upbeat about the whole scenario but she couldn't. Not yet.

Then he stood beside her, not brushing against her, not touching her in any way, yet there. Only slightly taller than her, he still outweighed her by much more. Not that he was overweight. She could see the bulge of muscle through his shirtsleeves.

"I'm Brydon, by the way." Up close, he had a nice smile, straight teeth, and decent clothes. For a nerd. "Let Samuel know that if he needs anything else…"

But she blocked out the rest of what he said as an idea occurred to her. The book she carried turned out to be about laws. Written by someone named Crowley. Was this a business book? A judicial one? Why was Samuel reading this? The cover looked worn, the text and binding from another time, and yet it appeared from the plastic-coated cover as if few had checked it out. Not a bestseller. When she'd first gone out with Samuel, he hadn't been much of a reader. Why now? Did it have something to do with his dead brother? If there was a trail, then maybe she could follow…or even lead, if she could figure out what he was searching for.

The librarian took a step toward her, and she gave him a slow once-over meant to intimidate. He had a way of standing, a slouch really, dipping one shoulder as if he didn't have much confidence. She suspected he was harmless. "Maybe we could both help Samuel."

"How's that?" he asked.

"Do you know anything about this, Bryon?"

"Brydon," he corrected her, emphasizing the last syllable. "I might."

"So you wanna have a drink and discuss it?"

He gave a noncommittal shrug. "What's in it for me?"

"We'll figure something out."

Nodding, he said, "No use taking two cars."

She gave him her most beguiling smile. "I'll drive."

A few minutes later, the silence in her Toyota Yaris was unnerving as she felt Brydon's gaze stuck on her—even when she jerked the wheel and switched lanes. Nervous, she stirred her thoughts for something to say. Just above his collar peeked the jagged edge of a white, lumpy scar. "What happened to your neck?"

Only then did he look away from her. He rubbed a hand over it. "Car accident."

"Some accident."

"You should have seen the car."

Awkwardness unsettled her stomach. She punched in a CD to fill the silence and "Stairway to Heaven" blared from the speakers. She gauged his reaction. Samuel had never particularly liked her taste in music, but Brydon kept time, thumb against thigh.

"You like Led Zeppelin?" she asked.

He gave her a sly smile. "Did you know there's a connection—" he thumbed toward the backseat—"between the band and your book?"

"My book?" In the rearview mirror, she couldn't see the book on the seat. But its presence loomed, filling the spaces in the car with shadows. "It's not mine."

"There's still a connection."

# CHAPTER ELEVEN

I T WAS AFTER DARK when he arrived, late by Amish standards, as most households turned in at the close of daylight. Each farmhouse Samuel passed looked as innocent as a sleeping babe. Night snuggled in, shadows deepened, and the cool spring air burrowed into his bones. His cheeks felt numb, his ears hollow from the wind, and his backside dead from the thrum of the motorcycle.

Samuel found the Yoder's homestead, which now belonged to Levi and Hannah Fisher. He remembered his mother telling him that poor Ruby Yoder had died. Was that why her family had left Lancaster County? Had they wanted to escape the memories the way Pop had wanted to put distance between his family and Jacob's death?

His old home was not far from the Yoder's, just out Slow Gait Road, but he didn't bother going by, not at this time of night—maybe never. Someone else lived there now. He didn't even know who had bought the shop and house; he'd never asked. *Would it do any good to stir up old memories and more pain? But wasn't that what he was doing in his quest to connect with Jacob?*

Shoving aside confusing thoughts, he turned onto the gravel drive. The headlight of his motorcycle cut through the darkness and shone across the mailbox, which read *Fisher*, and the beam slanted over a wagon and push-powered lawn mower. Not much else could be seen in the dark, but a distant yellow light highlighted one window along the front of the house. From his past visits to the farm, when he was a boy, he knew the barn was off to the left, near the silo, and the washhouse to the right, near the garden. Pasture and farmland extended out behind the one-story house. He wondered if Levi had plans to expand the quaint house as his family grew.

A shagbark hickory provided shelter for his bike. The three-quarter moon slid out from behind a cloud and revealed the tree's bare branches, stretching outward in all directions. As he walked toward the house, the white-painted porch railing glowed like ghost's teeth. An odd feeling stirred the hair at the back of his neck as Samuel climbed the steps. Before he could knock, the door swung open.

"Samuel?" Hannah Schmidt Fisher greeted her brother-in-law with a warm and welcoming smile. She wore her blond hair pulled back in the traditional Amish style, beneath a prayer cap. Tiredness crinkled the corners of her eyes, but she still looked happy and content. No longer the skinny young girl he'd known a few years back before he'd moved with his folks to Ohio, her figure was now a bit plumper and her face rounder. But then again, she'd just had twins.

"Come on in," she said, her voice soft and welcoming. She gave him a hug as he came through the door. "Did you eat on the way? Or are you hungry?"

He laughed softly. "I ate, but…"

Her grin widened, highlighted by the flickering light of the kerosene lamp. "But you could probably eat again, *ja*? Come, sit at the table, and I'll fix you a plate."

She led him into the kitchen, which looked like most other Amish kitchens. A propane-powered refrigerator took up space in the corner. An eating table sat in the middle of the room. A calendar hung on one wall. It had not yet been turned to April, and the picture above the March grid was of a meadow filled with yellow buttercups. Next to the stove, two quilted potholders hung not only for decoration but purpose.

While she scooped food out of containers, she caught him up on the latest. "The babies are sleeping, but they'll be wanting a snack soon."

"Pop said they were healthy."

"Oh, *ja*. We are blessed. Levi went to bed early, plumb worn out."

"I can see them all in the morning," Samuel said, his stomach rumbling as he smelled the delicious scents coming from the stove. "I'm sorry I kept you awake."

"I was glad to stay up." Hannah pulled a plate from the cabinet. "I like the quiet when everyone has settled down for the night. It's the only chance I have now to breathe deep and reflect." She faced him, plate in hand. "Levi was so excited when he heard you were coming."

Hannah set a plate in front of him. Roasted pork, creamed sweet potatoes, green beans, and pearl onions, along with two slices of bread, filled the plate to overflowing. She added a glass of sweet tea next to the fork.

"*Danke*, Hannah. This looks awful good."

"I hope it will be enough to fill you. But if not, there's more, along with a butterscotch pie for dessert."

"If I'm not careful, I'll grow lazy and fat with all this good cooking."

She sat opposite him. "We'll see if we can't find something for you to do around here. Levi and I appreciate you coming all this way."

He offered a quiet prayer of thanks, then set about eating. "How is Levi?"

"Right as rain." Another voice supplied the answer. His big brother leaned against the doorframe, his shirt loose and unbuttoned, one sleeve empty and limp at his side. An arm crossed his bare stomach, and his other hand gripped a wooden cane. A bandage encircled his rib cage, and dark bruises emerged from beneath.

Tightness seized Samuel's chest. Pop hadn't lied. Levi was hurt. He jumped up from the table and rushed toward Levi. It had been over three years since he'd seen his oldest brother, but he stopped just shy of giving Levi a big, bone-crushing hug. Grinning at the beard Levi had grown since he'd last seen him—the sign of a married man—Samuel clapped him on the shoulder.

Levi winced yet still grinned back. "It's awful good to see you, Samuel."

"I reckon he may be taller than you now, Levi." Hannah smiled at the two brothers, who eyed each other levelly. She moved between them and slid Levi's other arm through his sleeve, then settled the shirt on his shoulders.

"And stronger," Samuel added.

"That's not too difficult, given my poor state of late." Levi peered closer at Samuel's chin. "You having to shave yet?"

"Three times a day," Samuel joked.

"Time to find this man a bride then." Levi winked.

"I'll wait for a while on that." Samuel helped his brother to the table. "Right as rain, eh?"

"Let Samuel eat while the food is hot," Hannah chided softly. "Would you like some pie now, Levi?"

"Of course. I smelled that butterscotch baking. Woke me from a sound sleep."

"Your stomach rumbling probably woke you." She tilted her head toward Samuel and lowered her voice. "He hasn't been eating well since the accident, so I've been tempting him with his favorites." She went to the counter and cut the pie, sliding big, thick pieces onto plates.

"What did happen that caused all this?" Samuel eyed his brother's weakened condition.

"You two have much to talk about." Hannah carried the plates to the table. "So I'm going off to bed if you don't mind. The boys will have me up soon enough."

"It's good to see you, Hannah." Samuel nodded toward his sister-in-law. "*Danke* for the good meal. You're an awful good cook."

"You're always welcome here, Samuel. But I can't take the credit for the meal. It was Naomi who cooked all of this for us."

"Naomi?" Samuel asked.

"Naomi Wagler," she clarified. "She's about your age, I believe. Are you eighteen now?"

"Almost twenty." His voice sounded strangled.

"You remember the Wagler family, don't you?" Levi asked. "Lizzie, Noah, Nathan, Grace, Naomi…"

Oh, he remembered her. Her family. Samuel's heart kicked up a notch, and he forced himself to add to the list of Wagler children. "And Dan, but I can't remember the little one."

"Deborah." Hannah smiled. "But they have two more now: Matthew and Mary."

"I have a lot to catch up on," he said, wondering what he would say to Naomi when…if he saw her again. Of course, he would see her. It was too small of a community not to bump into someone.

"There's plenty of time." Hannah hid a yawn behind her

hand. "Samuel, you'll be sleeping in the back bedroom. Levi can point you in the right direction. If you need anything, let me know." She placed a hand tenderly on her husband's shoulder. "Don't stay up too late, Levi. Just leave the dishes, and I'll clean up in the morning."

"I'll be along shortly," Levi reassured her. "But first I'm going to enjoy this pie."

Smiling, she left the room.

The two brothers ate in silence. For a moment, it felt like old times. Samuel remembered when Levi, Jacob, and he had gobbled up their mother's cookies, snatched muffins, and gorged on whole loaves of hot bread. Samuel had tried to keep up with his older brothers, who had been able to stuff more food in their stomachs. But if Levi could eat a whole pie, then Samuel could eat two. If Jacob ran two miles, then Samuel ran three. Looking back now, Samuel realized his older brothers had egged him on. Once Jacob bragged, "I ate thirteen apples!" So of course, Samuel had to beat that, and he had managed fourteen and a half. But he'd paid the price for that overindulgence.

Mamm had laughed at their antics. "You boys must have hollow legs."

She'd always been proud of her three and enjoyed cooking for them. Now the family was separated by too many miles and too much heartbreak.

When Samuel finished his second piece of butterscotch pie, he scraped the plates and cleaned up, so Hannah wouldn't have to in the morning. She had enough to keep her busy with two babies and an injured husband. Knowing Levi was indeed hurt changed Samuel's plan. He would have to help his brother. But for how long?

"We can discuss what needs doing tomorrow at breakfast,"

Samuel said, seeing the circles beneath his brother's eyes. No matter what Levi said, he obviously wasn't well. "I'll get up and feed the stock. That much I can figure out on my own."

Levi nodded, explained which animals needed special care or food, and then they headed off to separate beds, Samuel watching his brother's slow, careful footsteps. At the door to his bedroom, Levi turned back. "I'm glad you're here, Samuel."

"Me too."

"Even if you eat like an elephant." Levi grinned.

With a matching smile, Samuel said, "That's why I'm taller."

# CHAPTER TWELVE

WHAT POTIONS HAVE *I drunk of Siren tears...*
With realization came a sharp inhalation. No. He couldn't go there.

Jacob turned away from the Amish farm they approached. Words failed him even now. The landscape of tranquil countryside stretched outward in peaceful waves, a respite from the turmoil of this world. Home. Yet not anymore. Not for a long time. Still, awareness stirred tumultuous emotions he could not begin to decipher. He simply couldn't go into *that* home.

He wasn't sure how he knew, but he *knew*. She was there. He couldn't see *her*. Not again. Not now. Not ever.

*Hannah*. He had loved her, yearned for her, and yet he'd also hated her. She'd driven him mad with desire, and he'd come back for her, hoping to change her as he'd been changed so they could live together. Forever.

He'd never expected her to be a pushover, and so he'd set in motion a plan to cajole and lure her toward him. But she'd given her heart to Levi. His own brother. Now they were married.

So how could he look into the depths of her eyes again? How could he watch her with Levi? Know her heart had chosen another? And yet how could he not see her for what might be the last time?

"Did you not say you wanted to help Samuel?" Remiel asked, brushing past him.

Jacob watched the angel approach the lonely farmhouse as if all was safe and well, as if there were nothing to fear in such a tranquil place. Then the angel circled back and peered closely at Jacob. "What is it you fear?"

A fierce resilience reared inside him. Jacob had never feared anything. Truth sliced through him. That was not the honest answer. He'd feared losing Hannah. He'd feared living for eternity without her. But mostly, he'd feared dying—because he knew what he deserved. Now seeing Hannah again might be more torture than being doomed to hell, and so beneath the beam of Remiel's gaze, he confessed, "I fear seeing her."

"*Her*," the angel repeated, tasting the word as if it was new, then he looked past Jacob toward the farmhouse, as if he could penetrate the walls with one look. "Hannah? This woman you loved?"

Jacob's throat contracted.

"Come." Remiel placed a hand around Jacob's upper arm and drew him toward the farmhouse, not giving him a choice or chance to flee, and as they approached, their speed increased. Jacob couldn't have stopped the momentum or escaped if he'd tried. The inhuman grip was solid and stern. *Had this been the plan all along? Was this his eternal torment, the torture for all his sins?*

All of a sudden, they entered a room, a bedroom it seemed, the furniture simple and functional. The shades were pulled low, the light, provided by a gas-powered lamp, dim. Levi, his older brother, was there.

Jacob's chest swelled with an overwhelming love. He ached to rush forward and throw his arms around Levi.

But something wasn't right. Levi lay upon a bed, propped in a sitting position by thick pillows. He wore no shirt, only his regular pants, the suspenders looped over his broad shoulders, and a bandage wrapped around his ribs.

*What was wrong? What had happened?* Jacob searched for an answer through Remiel, but the angel's features were like stone. It didn't matter if he knew any answers or not, Remiel wasn't about to divulge secrets from either world.

If only Jacob could talk to Levi, to explain the mistakes he'd made, and yet he could not get through this filmy barrier that seemed to come between the world of reality his brother knew and the world of eternity that he was becoming acquainted with.

A puttering cry jerked Jacob's gaze to Levi's side, where a blanketed bundle was protected by pillows and Levi's arm. A tiny fist pushed out of the covering. Levi jostled the baby, wincing as he moved too much. "Gabriel's hungry."

"He'll have to wait another minute."

That voice he knew. Yet it took a long, drawn-out moment for Jacob to shift his gaze away from his brother, as if he would never again have the chance to behold Levi. Then he saw Hannah.

A crack began to open in his heart. She sat in a rocking chair, a contented smile on her face. She wore a white night-dress that was unbuttoned, the fabric folded back, and she stared down at another baby suckling her breast. "Gideon is hungry too."

*Who can find a virtuous woman, for her price is far above rubies?*

The love he'd harbored for Hannah was still there, like a safe haven. It had survived the transition from his old world to this new one. Yet the anger and resentment had burned away like chaff. For what else mattered? She was happy. She was well taken care of. She was blessed. That's all he could have ever asked for. He held no animosity for his brother either. Could Levi help that Hannah loved him? Could Hannah do anything but love his brother? Levi was a good man, always had been. He was the older brother Jacob had looked up to, resented at times, and strove to emulate. Yet, it had all been wasted effort, an impossibility. Forgiveness that he never could have found while alive pulsed through him.

Surprisingly, Remiel had been right. It was good to see Levi and Hannah and know they were living the kind of life they had always wanted. Glancing around the perimeter of the room, he was also relieved to know they were well guarded, whether they knew it or not, for there were other angels milling about, soaring toward the ceiling, slipping out through walls and windows as if no barrier existed.

"Not as horrible as you imagined, is it?" Remiel spoke to him.

"How did you know?"

He blinked slowly. "I've seen it before."

Jacob thought of those feelings, once so real and palpable, now only a wisp of a memory. "But how is it possible?"

Remiel turned his attention back to Levi and, of course, did not answer.

"Are they"—Jacob indicated the other angels—"here to protect Hannah and Levi?"

Remiel nodded. "No harm will come here—not of the supernatural kind—unless they themselves open the door to evil."

Jacob's thoughts veered sharply toward his younger brother, Samuel, and he stiffened. Caught in a tide and swept from the room, Jacob hollered, "Wait!" He tried to hold on to

Hannah, then Levi, but it was too late. He was whisked into a hallway and through another wall.

Green shades were drawn in this smaller room. Twin beds took up most of the space. Samuel lay sprawled across one, his feet hanging off the end, one arm flung wide. His duffel bag lay on the floor unzipped, his boots tossed near his clothes as if he'd shed everything in one fell swoop and collapsed on the bed.

A chill entered the room, and yet Jacob suspected it was something more than the weather. It felt as if the air had thinned and something malevolent hovered nearby. Remiel gripped his sword, his expression never changing, but he looked battle ready. A dark form circled above Samuel, similar to one of the creatures that had grabbed Jacob's ankle. Was it a demon, some supernatural creature, some evil force?

Frantic to protect his sleeping brother, Jacob swung around and almost ran into Remiel. "Fight that thing off. Tell him to leave. Get him out of here!"

"This is not my—"

"You've said that before. What good are you?" Jacob whirled back toward his brother. "So, where is Samuel's angel?"

"He has none." Remiel stared out the window, as if seeing what lay beyond the shade. Was that a shadow passing in the dark? "Samuel has made no decision."

The dark creature circled the bed, dropping lower and lower, swooping over Samuel's sleeping form.

Panic rose inside Jacob. "What can I do?"

Remiel did not answer.

Jacob rushed toward the bed. "Bah!" he shouted and flung his arms out wide. "Get out of here!"

The creature jolted backward, tumbling through the air.

Rather than arms or legs, the creature looked shapeless, like a black jellyfish, shifting shapes and sizes, its body fluid. Before Jacob could exult, the creature reared up. A cruel, distorted face rushed toward him, snarling and snapping sharp, gray teeth. Jacob fell back. But the creature did not fall upon him. It swerved sharply and shot toward the ceiling, then began circling above the bed, over the sleeping Samuel.

A book lay open beside the bed. Jacob moved closer and recognized some of the books. Many were of the occult and dark forces, mysterious and secretive in nature.

"Close the book," Remiel said.

Jacob startled at the sound of the angel's voice. "What?"

"Close the book," he repeated.

Jacob attempted to do just that, although he wasn't sure why, but his hand slid right through the pages, hardcover, and table as if he didn't exist, as if he had no form or substance or purpose. "How?"

But the angel gave no answer.

With a heavy sigh, Jacob searched the room, desperate for a way. Then he remembered he could whisper thoughts. Not that Samuel had listened before, but his girlfriend had. Still, he leaned close to Samuel. This time he didn't fool around trying to inject his thoughts. "Samuel!"

The young man flopped over, his long limbs wrestling the covers, and one arm swiped the books right off the table. They fell to the floor in a heap, pages crumpling, spines cracking, and out of them poured a fresh hoard of creatures.

Black disfigured beasts plunged into the room with a rush and flutter. They swirled about but steered clear of Remiel, who never blinked at their appearance nor seemed afraid. He stood completely still, his hands resting on the hilt of his sword, blade pointed toward the floor.

"Great!" Jacob exclaimed with a heavy dose of sarcasm. "Now what?"

"Close the books," the angel repeated, without really offering any help at all.

*But how?* Jacob couldn't close the books himself. He'd have to force Samuel to do the task. Jacob hollered, "Samuel, wake up!"

Eyes fluttered, then his brother grunted and shifted.

Before Samuel could settle back into sleep, Jacob whispered, in what he hoped was an imitation of his father's voice, "Samuel, you are late."

Those eyes sprang open. The youngest Fisher brother sat bolt upright, rubbed his chest, and blinked against the darkness of the room. Jacob grinned at his success. But before he could congratulate himself, Samuel flopped back onto the pillow and rolled onto his side. He lay very still, staring at the side table for a moment.

Once more, Samuel pushed himself upright. Swinging his long legs out of the bed, he scooped up the books, closing those lying open. Some of the creatures were sucked back into the pages from which they'd come, but a couple escaped through the walls of the house in a whoosh.

"That will not fool them for long," Remiel said. "They will be back."

"Then what can send them running for good?"

The first glint of a smile tugged at Remiel's firm lips. "Someone like me."

"How can I get one of you for Samuel?"

Remiel stared down the sharp slant of his nose. "You think you have this power?"

"You do. You could do it!"

"It is not for me to decide."

Jacob sighed and moved toward the bed. He peered down at his brother, blissfully asleep again. Leaning down, he whispered, "Samuel, *you shall know the truth, and the truth shall set you free.*"

# CHAPTER THIRTEEN

HEFTING THE WHEELBARROW, SAMUEL steered it toward the stalls, the wheel wobbling and making the cart go catawampus. With a pitchfork, he tossed in fresh straw, and tiny bits and pieces fluttered in the air. His head felt muzzy from lack of sleep.

Swiping a sleeve over his face, Samuel filled a bucket with feed, then reached up to put the scoop on the shelf. A square object snagged his attention. What was a book doing out here? Samuel dusted off the cover and felt his skin tighten. His hand splayed the cover and then he thumbed the pages.

> When some Beloveds, 'neath whose eyelids lay
> The sweet lights of my childhood, one by one

He recognized the poem Levi had sent. Was this Jacob's book, the one he'd given to Hannah? He flipped more pages.

> There is no one beside thee, and no one above thee;
> Thou standest alone, as the nightingale sings!

A wisp of a smile felt like a soft spring breeze drifting over his face. The poem made him remember a girl from his childhood. She sat in the wispy, dry grass along Hallelujah Creek, her face shaded by her bonnet. She was hunched so far inside her winter coat next to a hickory stump, Samuel had missed her until she spoke.

"I heard them making fun of you."

He stood at water's edge, his boots muddy, and Mamm would not be pleased. He shrugged and kicked a dirt clod. "Who cares? Book learnin' is stupid."

When she didn't respond, he looked back at her. She scribbled in a notebook. Ignoring her, he picked up a rock and chucked it in the water. It made a glump of a splash. Stupid as it was, it made him feel better, so he picked up another rock.

"Here," the girl said.

Samuel tossed the rock in the air and caught it. "What?"

"I wrote something for you. Wanna read it?"

He huffed out a breath. What did this Wagler girl want from him? To torture him more because he couldn't read as well as the rest of the kids his age? "Why would I wanna do that?"

She gave him a slow, steady look, and he threw the rock as hard and as far as he could. But it broke apart midair and made tiny plops in the creek.

"I'll read it to you if you want."

"I don't want."

"But I wrote it for you."

He scooped up another rock and tossed it impatiently. "I reckon then, go ahead. If you have to."

She studied the paper, her lips moving over the words as she read silently, then she gave a tiny nod. "Okay, here it goes. *Words are like seeds. They help you to read. Plant them deep in your head, and you'll be well read.*" She raised those soft brown eyes toward him. "Was it dumb?"

"Nah, it wasn't too bad. You really wrote that?"

She nodded. Then she tore out the page and held it out to him. "You can keep it."

With a scowl, he snatched it from her, folded it, and stuck it in his hip pocket.

"You can learn to read."

He hurled the rock, and it crossed the creek and landed on the other side. "What if I can't?"

"Then we'll just have to try harder."

Samuel leaned on the feed barrel, fond memories of sitting beside Hallelujah Creek on warm afternoons swimming around in his thoughts. That Wagler girl had helped him stumble through the fourth and fifth grade readers. She never laughed at him, never grew frustrated. And finally, he'd made progress.

It had been a long while since he'd thought of those relaxing days, and remembering soothed a ruffled part of his soul. He set the book back on the shelf for when he had more time, finished feeding the livestock, and gathered eggs in the henhouse. He hoped breakfast was ready because he was starving.

With the sun's rays turning the horizon pink, Samuel carried the plastic bucket of eggs toward the house. No frost this morning, so maybe winter was finally behind them. But the influx of warmer air had brought wisps of fog that swirled and hovered over the fields. Pale light shone around the green shades in the windows along the side of the house where the kitchen was located. His stomach was already rumbling.

He barreled through the side door, leading into the kitchen, and nearly mowed over someone standing in his way. His arms came around the slight form. The bucket swayed precariously, and he joggled around, holding on to what he now realized was a girl, as if they were dancing, but he simply tried to keep them from falling splat onto the floor and scrambling the eggs.

"My goodness, Samuel," Hannah said, laughing as she stirred something on the stove. "You must be awful hungry to be in such a hurry."

Samuel grinned, then looked down apologetically at the girl...woman, whose brown eyes instantly transported him back to another time, another season. Those upturned, solemn eyes had once upon a time captured his attention.

Naomi's face brightened with embarrassment. Once he was sure she wasn't going to go sprawling across the floor, he released her and backed away, rubbing his damp palms on the back of his trousers. With her face scrubbed as clean as summer-dried linens, she looked far younger than someone like Andi. Back at Miller's schoolhouse, she had captured his interest, and he had quietly (without anyone knowing) gone to see her in the middle of the night once they were of running around age. She was like a still water, quiet and reserved, but thoughts and truths ran through her like a deep undercurrent.

"Samuel," Hannah interrupted his thoughts, as she clinked a spoon against a pan, "do you remember Naomi?"

He cleared his throat to dispel the emotional congestion. "Sure. Sure do. Yes." But she was no longer the girl fixated in his mind from memory. She was a woman full grown. "It's good...I mean, fine to...uh, see you again."

She gave a somber nod, her eyes wide and watchful. She offered no smile, but her expression held no malice either. So much had changed since those innocent days.

"Welcome back to Promise, Samuel."

A steep barrier separated them now, whether she knew it or not, and that barrier was a knowledge that no one in this

Amish district suspected. But a wider world existed, even if he didn't value much in it. For a second, he wondered what would have happened if he'd never left Promise, if Jacob had never died, if his own innocence had remained intact. Would Naomi and he have taken the next steps in life together?

He could never go back to being that boy again. Still, the fact remained that he'd left and never said good-bye to Naomi. He could have written her. But she was the writer, not him. What would he have said? Putting words on the page was sometimes as difficult as making sense of words stuck in books. How could he have explained all that had happened? Speaking of it, writing about it, probing it was like ripping a bandage off a wound and picking a scab until it oozed. It was better to forget the time they'd shared and stuff the experiences he'd had over the last few years. It was different now.

"Did any eggs break?" she asked.

"I hope not," he said with a rush of uncertainty, feeling edgy and uncomfortable. "Here."

She acted calmer than he felt. Setting the bucket on the counter, she began to count the eggs. Was she angry at his silence over the years? Maybe she hadn't cared as much as he had. Maybe she had moved on and was seeing someone else now—which somehow eased the pressure of guilt in his chest. Yet it also stirred something else. Or maybe she was here because he was, because she'd heard he was back.

"I'll need two extra eggs," Hannah told Naomi, then she explained, "Naomi is here to help me with the babies and around the house."

"Of course." He was a fool to think she was there for him. He felt as if he should say something. "And we're very thankful for your help." He breathed in the warm scents of eggs, bacon, and what he hoped to be biscuits in the oven. "And very grateful for your good cooking last night."

Her cheeks stained the color of summer strawberries. "I'm glad you liked it."

Their gazes locked and for a moment they were young teenagers sitting on the creek bank. Samuel cleared his throat. He needed out of the kitchen, something to do. "Where are my nephews?"

"I'll get them," Naomi offered. She handed the extra eggs to Hannah and left.

Samuel drew a deeper, more relaxed breath and peered over at the fluffy biscuits Hannah pulled out of the oven. She smiled. "Go ahead and take one."

As he bit into the fluffy, buttery richness, he groaned with pure pleasure.

"I'm glad you're so easy to please."

He grinned.

Footsteps sounded in the hallway, and Naomi appeared again, cradling a bundle in each arm. She looked flushed and pleased. He moved closer and peered down into the little faces. Their eyes were closed, pink mouths relaxed, cheeks round and full. They looked healthy and strong, not that he knew much about babies. Still, they were fresh and pink-skinned and beautiful.

"Would you like to hold them?" Naomi asked.

He looked to the mother for confirmation. "If it's all right with Hannah."

"Of course." She laughed as she scraped scrambled eggs into a bowl. "But you best sit down. They can be a lot to handle."

He settled into a chair at the table, and not knowing what else to do, he held his arms out awkwardly.

"Here." Naomi leaned close. "Bend your arm." She

touched the soft place inside his elbow and slipped one swaddled baby into the crook of his arm. She tucked his arm under and around the baby.

His gaze rose to meet Naomi's and he said, "Do you still write?"

A blush flash-burned her cheeks. She backed away, glancing quickly at Hannah, then fussing over the baby she still held.

*Why had he asked that?* Shifting in his seat, he focused on the baby in his arms. "Which one is this?"

"That's Gideon." She joggled the other baby until he held out his other arm.

"Don't fret. I won't drop him."

She leaned down again, and Samuel breathed in a scent of sunny meadows and wildflowers, flour and cinnamon. He drew in Naomi's scent like a memory to be savored. Then she deposited the other baby in the crook of his arm. "Gabriel, meet your Uncle Samuel."

He grinned. "I like the sound of that."

Her gaze met his, and she backed quickly away. But she kept watch over him like a mother bird fluttering about her nest.

"How do you tell them apart?" he asked.

Naomi smiled as if she held a secret and leaned forward, jostling free the end of one blanket. A loose blue thread looped one baby's ankle. "Gideon is blue. Gabriel is yellow."

Grinning, Samuel leaned back, gazing down at his two nephews. Something in his chest opened, and he imagined what it would be like one day to bounce them on his knee or teach them to climb a tree or ride on the back of a horse... and maybe get into a little mischief. After all, that's what uncles were for. His own Uncle Matthew had taught him how to swipe cookie dough from his mother, who had scolded her big brother with an easy chuckle. Then there was Uncle Dan and Uncle Joseph. They hadn't been filled with as much mischief, but when he was a boy, they'd kept him on the straight and narrow path and offered a listening ear if ever he needed one.

Samuel longed to protect these babies from knowing what he knew, from experiencing the pain and guilt he'd suffered over the past few months and years. Was it possible to keep something so beautiful from being tarnished by this fallen world?

"Hannah," he said, his throat thick, "you've been blessed for sure."

She turned, wiping her hands on her apron. "We have, *ja*." She carried bowls of biscuits and eggs to the table. "Breakfast is ready."

"Is Levi coming?" He offered one of the babies back to Naomi.

Hannah reached for her other son. "I'll go put the boys down and see if Levi feels up to coming to the table this morning."

After helping Hannah hold both of her babies, Naomi began cleaning dishes at the sink.

Samuel sat at the table. Alone. The air in the room seemed to shrink. "Aren't you going to eat too?"

"Of course. But if I can get a bit of this chore finished first, then Hannah can relax later."

He smiled, knowing her kind disposition. She was always thinking of others rather than herself. Even back in school, she'd looked out for the younger children. He spotted a few pots and pans on the stove and decided to help her out. But when he touched the pan, which had held the biscuits, he jerked back, and the pan clattered against a skillet.

Naomi turned. "Are you okay, Samuel?"

"*Ja*." He shook his hand. "Burned myself though."

She went to the freezer and pulled out a plastic bag of frozen peas. "Here." She laid it against his palm. "I've done that a few times myself."

"I wasn't thinking." Which seemed to be a sudden problem.

Her eyes were solemn and assessing, her touch light as she held his injured hand between her palms. "You were trying to help."

His attempts at helping often backfired. Maybe he'd made a mistake coming back here. Maybe he should have left the past behind him.

"You never answered my question." He tossed the bag of peas and caught it. "Are you still writing?"

"Sometimes."

# CHAPTER FOURTEEN

ANDI HITCHED HER GYM bag over her shoulder and headed to her Toyota Yaris. She didn't bother zipping her jacket as the night air cooled her heated skin. The parking lot still had a number of cars lined up, but she had no more clients for the evening. And she had less than twenty minutes to make her appointment.

Tossing her stuff in the backseat, she backed out of the parking space. She peered over her shoulder to check for any approaching cars.

A face appeared in the side window. Her heart shot into her throat. She slammed on the brake, jolting her forward and back. The features settled into place, and she recognized the new trainer at the club. He had curly blond hair and a casual I-know-I'm-hot smile. The dashboard clock warned she had little time. Rolling down her window, she offered a tight smile. "Hey, Seth. What's up?"

"Wanna get a beer?"

She'd been anticipating this since the first day Seth had walked into the club with that cocky swagger and roaming eye. "Can't tonight. Sorry." But she wasn't.

Disappointment blinked, but his smile remained in tact. "Gotta hot date?"

"Don't you know it?" She kept her personal life personal. Samuel had been gone less than a week, and already she felt the itch of needing to be out and about on the town. She'd thought about meeting friends last night but had ended up staying home, watching a rerun of *24*. How sad was that? And she'd just turned down a hot guy, who turned her off more than on. What was wrong with her? "Tell you what. Get a group together and we'll all go out Friday, okay?"

Two blinks later, he took it in stride. "Sure. Sounds good."

Backing out of her parking space, she imagined Samuel in his hometown of Promise. Oh sure, he'd made it sound like he would be working hard. But didn't he always? That didn't slow him down when it came to partying. Probably every hormone-addled girl in his old district was baking him apple strudel in an effort to gain his attention. No matter what the Amish said, they knew what was what and played for keeps— especially where men were concerned. Some plain teenage girl was probably already trying to get her short, blunt, claws into him. Probably thought she could latch on to his heart through his stomach. But Andi knew how men worked. And their heart had a direct link to a lower organ. Those Amish girls didn't have a thing on her.

She parked with three minutes to spare. The rearview mirror revealed makeup intact, lips moist. She jerked out her ponytail and swung her hair over her shoulders.

When she'd met Brydon, he'd introduced her to a book by some crazy British dude. At first, she'd thought Brydon was simply coming on to her with the Brit's recounting of his sexual exploits, but he'd actually looked embarrassed by the topic when she brought it up. And boy, she'd thought folks from the eighteen hundreds had been stuffed shirts, but she'd been wrong. They were adventurous.

Over the past week, she'd read about crazy secret groups that believed wacky stuff about angels or gods visiting them and dispensing freaky religious orders. The British dude probably just wanted to get laid. And boy had he. The women back then must have been gullible or stupid or maybe they wanted it just as bad. But with him? From the pictures she'd seen, he wasn't much of a catch.

And neither was Brydon, but she figured he wanted something for himself. Didn't they all? And maybe it would be fun to try out some of the bizarre Brit's exploits.

"Andi?" The voice came from a shadowed hedge to her left.

She whipped around and smiled with relief at the dark figure. "Brydon! What are you doing out here?"

"Watching for you."

"Am I late?"

"I got off early." He stepped out of the shadows. "So I waited out here for you." He tilted his head back to survey the stars. "Nice night, huh?"

"Yeah." His awkwardness, she decided, made him cute.

"Found some books you might find useful. Checked them out with my card." He held out a small stack. "Found a couple of interesting articles that might benefit you too, so I copied them. Would you like to…uh…" He paused and tilted his head awkwardly.

She smiled. Nerdish maybe, but definitely cute. And innocent in the ways of women. Oh how she could educate him. "How about we grab some coffee?" she offered. "There's a diner nearby. And we can look over what you found."

His Adam's apple plunged and surged when he smiled. "I'd like that."

Something in his dark gaze made her feel off kilter.

# CHAPTER FIFTEEN

S AMUEL WALKED INTO THE bedroom carrying a tray of food. Levi sat upright in bed, propped up by a bank of pillows, his middle still bisected by stark white bandages. Across the room, a crib held both sleeping babies. Samuel settled the tray across Levi's straightened legs, picked up a plate for himself, and plopped into the rocker. After offering a silent prayer, he forked some noodles.

Levi tore apart a piece of bread. "Everything okay at the barn?"

"Good." Samuel chewed the beef and noodles.

A strange noise hummed in the room. Searching for the source, he heard it again and his gaze locked on to the blanket covering Levi. A patch of the blanket twitched and shook. Then Samuel recognized the sound as one he'd heard at Andi's apartment. "You have a cell phone, Levi?"

A few Old Order Amish were allowed to have mobile phones, depending on the district and its elders. Sometimes the accommodation was made for businesses, as long as the phones were stored out in the woodworking shops or barns. Some Amish even had special sheds built between farms to house telephones shared by neighbors. The purpose of avoiding telephones wasn't a fear of technology, so much as an attempt to separate the Amish from the fracturing influence of the secular American culture and the ability of phones to lure one away from family and community. Samuel had seen enough *English* teens answering cell phones and texting while sitting at restaurant tables with their friends and family to know firsthand that cell phones did not bring unity to a community.

Still, Levi didn't have the kind of business needing a phone. Maybe it was for medical emergencies? After all, Hannah had recently delivered twins and he'd been injured. An Amish neighbor in Harmony Hollow carried a cell phone so he could hitch rides to the hospital for cancer treatments. Still, that was the exception, not the rule.

Levi didn't answer Samuel's question directly or quickly. Instead, his lips flattened, and he set the bread back on the plate, slid one hand beneath the blanket, and retrieved a small black cell phone. He lifted it to his ear, cleared his throat. "Yes?" Levi listened to the voice on the other end before saying, "Better."

Levi sounded awkward. *Was it because he wasn't used to talking on a phone? Or was it because Samuel was watching him?*

Samuel focused on his plate of noodles.

"All right," Levi said. "I will do that then. Good. And thank you." Levi clicked a button on the phone and laid it back on the bed, this time above the covers, as if saying, "Well, now that the secret is out, what's the point of hiding it?"

This new development was his brother's business. Samuel wouldn't sit in judgment of Levi, just as he hoped Levi would return the favor.

After an awkward minute, Levi cleared his throat again, scooped up peas, and then gulped iced tea. "That was Roc Girouard. On the phone there."

Samuel's gaze snapped toward Levi. "You keep in touch with Roc?"

"I do. He is a good man."

Samuel chewed on that for a moment. He thought back to that time six months ago when Roc and Rachel lived in his parents' home. "Didn't Roc go back to New Orleans?"

"He lives here now. He married Rachel."

Surprised, Samuel nudged a noodle with his fork. Roc and Rachel had claimed to be married while staying in Samuel's parents' home, but then Samuel had learned that was false, a lie created so Roc could better protect Rachel. They must have fallen in love then and gotten married. Samuel sighed in frustration. Of course no one had told him—simply more lies from his father.

Since they were now married, it made sense why Levi would keep track of Roc. Rachel was his sister-in-law through Hannah. "How is Rachel? Her baby?"

"Good. One day my boys will play with their cousin. But I see Roc more often," Levi said. "Easier since Rachel is being shunned."

Samuel looked up, ignoring his dinner. "Marrying an *Englisher* is not taken lightly."

"They married not long after they returned." Levi smiled. "Hannah and I attended their wedding. It was very small. But I believe they are good for each other."

"Then you don't think she should be shunned?"

"It is not for me to say, is it? Hannah grieves for her sister, though. So we see them occasionally, but…not for reasons you might think. And we do not discuss these visits with others." Levi gave a warning glance.

Samuel raised an eyebrow, but he gave a nod of understanding. He would not say anything either.

"I do not lie," Levi added, a tone of defiance in his voice. "I want you to understand that, Samuel."

"You're not Pop."

"No, I'm not. Our actions—Hannah's and mine—could lead to our own shunning at some point. But I must protect my family, and I will."

This man who lay in the bed seemed so different from the brother he had known growing up. Levi acted more like Jacob, skirting the rules and playing with fire. Maybe that was simply part of adulthood. Samuel had done his share of that in the past few months, so he wouldn't judge. Besides, it had been three years since he'd seen Levi. Yet in a world where nothing with the Amish changed in hundreds of years, much had changed.

"When I was injured," Levi said, "Roc canceled a trip he'd planned to find a missing friend so he could help out. He is a good man. And he loves Rachel as she loves him. They are devoted to each other and to Josef's son."

"The child won't be raised Amish then?" Samuel asked.

Levi shook his head. "Both Rachel and Roc understand we are all in a battle. And this battle strips away the dividers between religious institutions."

Samuel's eyebrows rose. *A battle?*

"But I get ahead of myself." Levi scratched his beard. "Samuel, our father sent me a letter a while back. He expressed concerned about you...about an *English* girl you have been seeing." Samuel opened his mouth to deny it, but Levi rushed on. "Hear me out. You are a man now, Samuel, and can make your own decisions. I will not lecture you as Pop most probably already has." He shrugged. "Besides, as you can tell from what I've said about Roc and Rachel, I do not think marrying an *Englisher* is the worst you can do—if it's the right *Englisher*. Rachel's situation is different, of course, because she was baptized. If you were to marry an *Englisher*, you would not be shunned because you have not been baptized."

"Are you telling me not to get baptized?"

"I'm not telling you anything you don't know, Samuel. You must make your own decisions. However, marrying outside our community can be a rocky path. You were raised Amish. When you become a parent, you might be—"

"Whoa, I'm not about to become a parent."

"It is a consideration before you make a big decision. Like marriage."

"I'm not about to get married either."

Levi nodded slowly. "Now that you know about…Jacob and how—"

"I don't know anything about Jacob." Samuel stiffened in response to Levi's jabbing words. His gaze shifted to the cell phone beside Levi. "Or about you."

"A lot has changed in three years."

"Yes," Samuel agreed, "it has." He dropped the fork onto his plate, having lost his appetite.

The gravity of the discussion weighed on Levi's expression, making his face look long and shadowed. Blue smudges deepened his eyes. "I regret that you were lied to, Samuel, about our brother. I never wanted to be a part of that. And I regret the last few years we were separated. A family should be together. But I believe you are here now for a reason."

*Reason? What reason? Had it been the plan all along? Was Levi's injury just an excuse? Was this Pop's way of getting him away from what he considered a bad influence?* But Andi hadn't put him on the path to truth. His father's lies had—

"Wait a minute." Samuel stood, grabbing the plate he'd forgotten about which almost toppled. The fork, however, clattered against the rocker and hit the floor. Samuel shoved the plate onto the tray. "Are you saying Pop sent me here? Was this some kind of a trick you were both playing?"

"Samuel," Levi said, his tone too parental, "I only know that you volunteered to come here and help on the farm while I am laid up. For that, I am grateful."

"Was Pop ever going to come here himself?"

"Not that I was aware of."

So he had been manipulated. Anger curled his hands into fists. Pop had played him for a fool. Maybe Levi was speaking the truth. Then again, maybe not. *Who could he trust? Only himself.* And he'd surprise them all by not playing their game. He'd do what he wanted. And coming here was only the first step on his own road.

"Samuel," Levi continued, "I had a private hope that the trip might be useful for me to explain some things to you, things I was never able to discuss with you before."

Samuel crossed his arms over his chest, feeling betrayed once again. "You mean about Jacob? About his death? Did Pop tell you? Or maybe Roc did." He hesitated before speaking the words, which sliced at his throat like serrated knives, but he wasn't going to hide from the truth either. He threw the words at his older brother with careless aim. "I killed Jacob. I was the one."

Levi blanched.

"And I have to live with that." Samuel slapped his chest. "So yeah, now I wanna know what my brother was doing in Ohio when I thought he'd been long buried in Pennsylvania. And yeah, I've been trying to figure things out. And maybe I've even hung out with an *English* girl. Because I like her. Because she doesn't *lie* to me."

"Samuel"—Levi gestured toward the rocker—"I want to help you understand."

"Where's Roc? He'll tell me the truth."

# CHAPTER SIXTEEN

**B**RYDON WALKED BESIDE THE woman to the diner, keeping a respectful distance. The night was pleasant and the streets deserted. His natural instincts were to pounce and enjoy the taste of her. But he liked the game, the anticipation, and the pursuit more. He also liked them to eat sugar and caffeine. It made a powerful kick, and he got a nice buzz afterward.

Her thoughts told him what a fun evening she was planning, and he'd let her tease and toy with him, then he'd jolt her with a surprise of his own. He hadn't yet decided if he would drain her or change her. She might be open to this lifestyle. She had certainly latched on to the information about Aleister Crowley. If the articles he'd copied for her intrigued her, then he would find an appetizer for them to share.

His sharpened senses detected a presence behind him, and he felt the tiny tentacles probing into his thoughts, which told him another vamp was nearby. But in his experience, vamps only came around other vamps when they encroached on their territory or wanted something. Never good. Always required caution. He kept walking, very aware that Andi was even more vulnerable. Another vamp might fight him for her and ruin his plans.

Finally, Brydon asked, "What is it you want?"

Andi gave him an odd look. "What?"

A deep, rumbling chuckle came from ahead rather than behind.

Brydon came to a sudden halt. A body materialized out of the darkness and stood in front of them, blocking the sidewalk. More than one vamp meant danger. He pushed Andi toward the building. A low guttural growl came from his throat. Three vamps looking like the dark-of-night mafia stood in a wide half circle, barring any escape route.

The lead vampire spoke first. "We are here for you."

Brydon lifted one eyebrow. "What for?"

"You have much to answer for."

Brydon crossed his arms over his chest. He suspected this to be a ploy to get him out of the way so they could feed on Andi. They would think nothing of dispatching him quickly to the hereafter. "About?"

One vamp stepped forward and grabbed Brydon's right arm. "You can tell Jezebel."

"Who the hell is that?" Brydon struggled against the vamp's grip.

"Didn't Giovanni tell you?" The vamp gave a vicious smile. "Did he ever mention the one you should fear? Your day of reckoning has arrived."

The other vamp edged forward, sniffing the air and staring at Andi, hidden partially behind Brydon. "We might be delayed."

"She won't take long." The one that seemed to be the leader licked his lips. "A *ménage à trois*, eh?"

"Andi," Brydon warned.

"I'm not afraid of them." Her voice sounded like steel.

The leader laughed, and the other two joined him. "You should be, my dear. But if you aren't now, then you will be. Oh, you will be."

She stepped out from behind Brydon and walked toward the leader. "And why's that?"

"Because—" But he never finished his sentence.

Andi yanked her hand out of her bag and aimed something right at the vamp's head. She sprayed something in his eyes. The vamp hollered, swiped at his eyes, and doubled over.

Several things happened at once. Brydon blocked one of the other vamps from advancing, shoved Andi toward the street, and yelled, "Run!"

And she did.

Brydon grabbed each of the other vamps—a sleeve, the back of a jacket—and hurled them against the building. They fell in a heap, rolling across the sidewalk and snarling and snapping at each other and him.

# CHAPTER SEVENTEEN

THE SUN BLED RED across the evening sky, smearing a trail along the horizon. Following Levi's directions, he took Highway 30 West on his motorcycle. Samuel noted the distance wasn't far the way a crow flies, but the drive took longer, as he had to take the accessible highways and byways, turning onto Tower Road and then Furnace. He passed through Buzzards Roost and Schulls Rock, the terrain much rougher than typical Amish farmland throughout Pennsylvania. Eventually the roads lost their names and were simply dead-ends or forks that led in new directions. Remote didn't come close to describing this out-of-the-way place. He'd thought Harmony Hollow, where his parents lived now in Ohio, had been in the backwoods.

Thick growth surrounded him on either side of the narrow road, sometimes making it difficult for his motorcycle to pass fallen limbs or broken branches, dips in the neglected road, or even hairpin curves. Obviously not too many traveled this way. Tree limbs overhead dappled the remaining sunlight, and he drove through shade and flashes of light and then into darkness.

Rocks and remains of dried, wintry brush obscured the splintered turnoff. He had to stop his motorcycle, turn it around, in order to take the even narrower road up a steep embankment. Off to his left, the Susquehanna River stretched below him. He veered away from the river, through more woods where leaves had collected and shadowy areas still held snow. Spring had not yet arrived here, and he felt a chill in his bones.

Samuel approached one last decline only to come to an abrupt halt where the road jutted straight down the embankment. It looked more like one of those climbing walls at Andi's gym. For a moment or two, he pondered his options before deciding to leave his motorcycle hidden in a copse of trees. He half slid down the embankment and continued until he came to a flat section. Searching, he located what appeared to be the remains of a trail and followed it until he came to a bend.

A field opened before him, and farther back a small home nestled into the base of a rolling hill. The wind blustered through this tiny valley, which seemed to be cut off from the rest of the world, and slapped the laundry hanging on the line. Samuel followed the footpath to the gate, noticing an unpaved road leading from the barn into a forest, the tall, thick trees, hiding the trail.

*Did Roc and Rachel now reside here? Was it even a farm?* Roc had never seemed the farmer type, and he chuckled to himself as he remembered Roc trying to muck out the stalls in his father's barn. But this tiny farmhouse didn't seem to have any farmland accompanying it. A corral, however, kept a horse and a lone cow. The horse's ears pricked upward at his approach, and the mare eyed him warily. An oversized barn dwarfed the house.

He angled across the yard, toward the porch steps. Something felt wrong—very wrong. Whoever lived here didn't value company. He stood at the base of the steps for a moment, hesitating, wondering what he should do. It felt too still, too quiet. Again, he waited and watched, noting the wave in the tree branches, the sway of the sun-bleached sheets, the deceptive tranquility. He couldn't name what it was, but he felt…like he was being watched again.

Glancing right, toward the barn, then left, toward the woods and even behind him, he saw nothing out of the ordinary, nothing that should alarm him, nothing to make him think someone was spying on him. And yet that uncanny, eerie feeling crept along the base of his neck, like a cold finger trailing his spine.

Shrugging off the sensation as simply memories or paranoia, he jogged up the steps, his heavy boots hollow on the planked steps. When he set foot on the porch, the boards beneath him sagged and gave way, dropping out from under him. He crashed through the opening, knocking a shoulder against a wooden plank, and landed with a hard thump on a dirt floor. Pain hit him in several places at once—shoulder, side, hip.

Coughing, he struggled to sit upright and pulled air into his lungs. He blinked against darkness, thought he saw a shape loom over him. Then something kicked him hard in the chest.

The next thing he knew, a bright light hit him in the eyes, and a deadly voice said, "What the hell do you want?"

# CHAPTER EIGHTEEN

NAOMI CRIMPED THE FOIL around the metal pan to keep the lemony chicken casserole nice and warm for the evening meal. With each pinch, words popped into her head. Spring. Blue. Daffodils. Silly words that began to pair up into phrases.

> Blue skies smiled.
> Daffodils danced.
> Hearts collided.

She shook her head at her wayward thoughts. Her skin prickled even now at the memory of Samuel dancing her around the kitchen. Not really dancing, yet he had held her in his arms. Only to keep her from falling.

A creak of a floorboard brought her back to reality. Hannah came into the kitchen, holding one of her babies against her shoulder.

"Can I get you anything?" Naomi asked.

"*Danke*, Naomi," Hannah gave a tired smile, "you are such a godsend. Did you know that?"

"I'm happy to go where God asks." Naomi pulled the cherry crunch from the oven. "Would you like some lemonade?"

"I should be helping you."

"Not to worry." Carefully, Naomi set the pan on the

stove, the cherry filling bubbling up around the crumbly topping, and she sprinkled on bits of walnuts. "I forgot to add these."

"That's easy to do anytime. It smells delicious. You have spoiled me rotten."

"Every new mother needs rest and some pampering, so Mother says. I'm just glad to be able to help you, Hannah."

"Someday, I hope I can help you when you've got a little one." Hannah smiled.

But Naomi felt the needle of reality piercing her dream. She hid the deep ache, which she seemed to be doing more and more.

Hannah gently shifted her baby, peeking down at the sweet, slumbering features. "Levi was saying what a mighty fine lunch you fixed. Beef and noodles is his favorite. You'll make a fine wife and mother one day."

"If it's God's plan." The words tasted sour in her mouth. Bitterness, like milk left out on the counter, turned quickly and benefitted nothing. Naomi forced a smile. "I'm delighted Levi liked it."

"We should let Samuel know dinner is almost ready." The baby stirred and Hannah joggled him, patting his back until a soft burp came from the parted lips. "Is he at the barn?"

"I don't believe he's here at all."

Hannah's eyebrow went up in question.

Naomi shoved the pan back into the oven. "Samuel took off on that motorbike. I would have thought you heard it too. It's awful loud."

Hannah's expression closed like a door. "Maybe Levi sent him on an errand. Well, we'll save him some dessert for when he returns."

Nodding, Naomi kept her questions to herself. What was

there to say? It wasn't her business where Samuel had gone. And yet, she wondered.

Her feelings for him at one time had been infatuation. He'd liked her. And she'd liked him. Or so she had believed. But they had been young, awkward, inexperienced, passing glances back and forth at singings and other social events in the district. She'd helped him with schoolwork in the meadow beside Hallelujah Creek. He'd even surprised her with a late-night visit when they were beginning their running around years. She had believed they would court, get baptized, and then marry. Then things had changed.

Now, although she was still just as inexperienced, she understood more about relationships. She'd watched her sister Grace and other friends being courted over the years. No one in their district talked openly of such things. It was done quietly, often in secret, but one who paid attention could learn much.

After Jacob Fisher died, Samuel and his parents had left town almost immediately, which had not afforded her even the chance to offer condolences, especially because there had been no funeral to speak of. In fact, many had spoken in hushed tones about the oddity of the situation. Most had agreed that the sudden and senseless death had been too much for Jonas Fisher. The loss of a son at such a young age might have made any of them behave in peculiar ways.

At first, her teenage sensibilities had been wounded, because Samuel never even said good-bye. But she'd let go of any hurt years ago. How did she know what it was like to lose a sibling? To up and move so far away from what you'd always known as home? To have your family split? Over the years, she'd come to understand grief and suspected Samuel's interest had been eclipsed. She'd prayed for him and his family to find peace.

Of course, there had been no promises between them,

and she held nothing against Samuel for his actions or lack thereof. The whole experience, however, had made her wary of stoking an infatuation again, and she'd kept her eyes off boys. Her older sister had chided her gently that she should be more encouraging, but that only pretzeled her nerves. So she'd kept to herself and ended up feeling lonely as many of her friends paired off, and most had already married.

Seeing Samuel again brought all those sheltered feelings from deep inside her heart to the surface. She hadn't realized those feelings still existed—feelings that made her hope his return was an answered prayer.

"Can you hold Gabe for a moment?" Hannah asked.

"Hmm?" Stirred out of her thoughts, Naomi wiped her hands on her apron. "Of course." She reached for the baby, taking the bundle into her arms and cradling him close to her body. The newborn fussed for a moment, then quieted. Naomi smiled down at the infant and cooed nonsensical words to him. He was such a beautiful baby to behold that watching him sleep made her chest ache with longing. Babies were a special blessing from the Lord.

After a minute or so, Hannah emerged from the pantry. "I thought I had—" She stopped when her gaze landed on Naomi. "Is everything all right?"

It felt as if she wore her emotions plastered on her sleeves, and Naomi attempted to erase her hopes and wishes but her embarrassment only deepened. Her skin tingled and grew hot beneath Hannah's studious gaze. She pretended to fuss over the baby.

Rushing forward, Hannah asked, "Something's wrong. What is it, Naomi?"

Flustered by the question and attention, she angled around toward the stove. "It's warm in here is all."

"It is indeed," Hannah finally said. "I thought it was just me." She set a five-pound bag of sugar on the counter and unlatched the window above the sink, pushing it open. Then she turned on the faucet and filled the sink with sudsy water.

"Oh, I'll take care of that, Hannah."

"I don't mind." Hannah pushed up her sleeves and plunged her hands in the water. "Feels good to get my hands good and clean. Might as well scrub the pots at the same time. Gabe looks like he's finally content. He's been fussy this afternoon. He had a gas bubble, I reckon."

Naomi readjusted the blanket around the rosy-cheeked baby. "Do you think Samuel will be back?" She could have bit her tongue for asking such a question, but the words had tumbled out before she'd thought. "I mean—"

"Of course he'll be back." Hannah offered an understanding smile. "Samuel is trustworthy. He simply went on an errand for Levi. He'll be back. Don't you worry."

Despite the cooling breeze drifting in through the open window, Naomi felt her pulse pounding in her temples. She turned away and walked the perimeter of the kitchen, giving a light bounce to her step for the baby's sake. "I wasn't really worried, I just wondered…" She shouldn't be wondering about Samuel Fisher at all. "I mean…"

A warm, damp hand touched her arm, and Naomi looked into Hannah's kind brown eyes. "He's a nice man, Naomi. I'm glad he's come home to Promise."

This time, she kept her thoughts to herself, but in her heart she heard the whispered words—*me too.*

# CHAPTER NINETEEN

S TUNNED BY THE BLOW to his chest, Samuel lay flat out, unable to move or breathe. His chest pinched as if his lungs had collapsed, then slowly, by tiny, painful degrees, his chest expanded and dank air seeped back into his lungs. He stared at a wickedly sharp object aimed right at his throat, but the bright light above blinded him from seeing who held it.

Scuffling noises surrounded him.

"What happened?" A new voice came from above him, from the hole he'd fallen through. "Who is that?"

"How do I know? A shoe nudged his leg. "Who are ya? Speak up before I ram you through."

"Samuel," he managed, coughing again, his side aching with the effort. "Samuel Fisher."

"What are you boys doing?" a commanding voice, distinct from the others, boomed from above. "Let him up. Bring him on up here."

Strong, rough hands grabbed him and hauled him to his feet. Stern faces spun around him. The room where he'd fallen was small, like a dugout beneath the porch, and was made even smaller by the other men crowding around him. A rope ladder hurled downward, and someone shoved Samuel toward it.

His limbs protesting, he struggled but finally grasped hold of the rope. His foot slipped once, and the rope's rough edges scraped his shin. Slowly, he started to climb toward the rosy light. When he emerged back onto the front porch, feeling shaky and tense, Samuel looked into a familiar face.

The man clapped him on his bruised shoulder. "Good to see you, Samuel."

"Father Hellman?" He faltered and blinked. "Is it really you?"

"It's been a while." Roberto Hellman gave a toothy grin, the white collar at his throat brighter than his teeth. "But once you go through life and death with someone, it's not like either will ever forget, eh?"

Samuel nodded, swallowing hard, and tried to get his bearings. He leaned against the railing, felt the deep ache in his side and the skin on his shoulder scraped raw.

"You hurt?" The priest's gaze settled on the arm Samuel cradled.

"Nah. I'm okay. I think." Samuel released his arm, wincing, as it relaxed and hung loosely at his side. He flexed and fisted his hand a couple of times, testing and stretching the muscles. Nothing seemed broken, but he suspected he'd have a few bruises by tomorrow. "I'm fine. But what are you doing here?"

Three men emerged, one by one, from the hole and joined two others on the porch. They had serious faces, wary gazes. A couple had dark skin, the others varying degrees of light; some stood tall, others shorter; all had thick muscles, shaved heads, and wore plain blue jeans and black T-shirts. He had no doubt these men might have killed him if not for the priest's intervention. They circled around Samuel, keeping a distance and yet stayed close enough—too close for Samuel's comfort.

"Shawn"—the priest nodded toward someone behind Samuel—"go get Roc."

The sound of his friend's name brought relief. The young blond who looked even younger than Samuel jogged off. Roberto waved at the hole in the porch, and two of the men looped a thin rope behind the trapdoor and raised it up until it clicked into place.

"Nice trick," Samuel said.

"Isn't it?" Roberto beamed. "Guess you're wondering what's going on here, who we all are. Think of these as my own personal monks."

"Monks?" one very burly man protested.

"I'll let Roc explain," the priest said. "But in answer to your previous question, Samuel, I'm here helping Roc."

"Helping him?"

One of the men cleared his throat.

"Yes, of course," Roberto responded to the prompt. "We're all here helping Roc. You all get back to work now. I'll hook up with you soon. Don't worry about this fellow." He settled a hand on Samuel's shoulder. "He's the one that shot Akiva."

Those words stabbed Samuel with guilt, but the gazes staring at him shifted from suspicion to guarded respect. Instantly, Samuel hated each one of them.

Following the priest's orders, the group backed away. A couple leaped over the porch railing, and the others jogged down the front steps. They fell into step with one another, walking side by side, two by two, like soldiers, and hooked a right at the corner of the house. One glanced back and received a reassuring nod from Roberto.

"They look more militaristic than religious."

The priest laughed. "They do indeed. I call them a hit squad."

The comment surprised Samuel. *What was going on here?* But before he could ask any more questions, the front door to the house opened and Samuel turned, unsure what might pop out at him next.

Rachel stepped out on the porch. With a relaxed smile, she greeted Samuel, carefully stepping around the trapdoor. She wore her hair pulled back, but she no longer wore Amish clothes. Instead, she wore a long skirt and loose sweater. "How are you, Samuel?"

He brushed the dirt off his trousers and jacket. "Okay. I guess."

She looked toward the yard. "Did you walk here?"

He shook his head, which felt like it was spinning from all the surprises. "No, I…um…rode. My motorcycle."

"Roc will want to take it for a spin if you don't mind."

"Sure. Yes. Of course."

She moved toward the railing beside Father Roberto. "Where did you park?"

"I came a different route."

She quirked a brow. "Levi's path?"

"I guess you could call it that."

"He believes in precautions," Father Roberto said.

"I'll have Roc give you better directions for next time." Her easy smile and calm demeanor helped him start to relax.

She watched him, her brow crinkling. "Are you sure you're okay?"

He nodded too enthusiastically, burning off nervous energy. "Fine."

"You weren't hurt by…" She eyed the place in the porch where the planks could give way.

"He's tough," Father Roberto testified.

"Be careful where you step," she warned. "There are other traps around."

"Now don't go telling all our secrets." The priest grinned.

Samuel struggled to find something to say. The aftermath of Jacob's death had been so intense that it made the mundane awkward. The weight of so much loss—Jacob and Rachel's first husband, Josef—settled on Samuel's chest. Too many had died. And for what? What was the purpose? Was there some connection in all this hurt?

He rubbed a hand over his face to erase the dark thoughts and tried to focus on things more suitable for conversation. "How is…uh, David?"

Rachel smiled, her eyes twinkling at the mention of her six-month-old son. "He's growing like a weed. You'll see him later when he wakes from his nap. Would you like to come in? I have a cinnamon crumb cake fresh out of the—"

A dark blur dropped from the roof and landed with a thud on the porch, jarring the planks. Every muscle in Samuel's body clenched tight. Rachel gave a shriek. Father Roberto dropped into a defensive posture and aimed a wooden stake he yanked from his jacket at the blur, which solidified into a black-clad Roc.

"What's going on here?" Samuel asked, bewildered by all the crazy antics—floors dropping away and roof jumpers descending. *What was next?*

Rachel batted Roc's shoulder. "You scared the daylights out of me. Samuel too."

"Sorry, darlin'." Roc Girouard hooked an arm around his wife's waist and kissed her on the cheek, making her flush with either pleasure or exasperation. Turning solid brown eyes on Samuel, Roc grinned, the planes of his cheeks creasing with ease. "Thanks for dropping in, Samuel. Good to see you."

"What's with all the…" Speechless, Samuel stared up at the roof, searching for the right word. Two more shaved heads peered down at him.

Roc clasped Samuel's shoulder and moved him into the house. "Just a few things we're testing."

"Roc likes to keep us on our toes." Rachel trailed behind her husband, Samuel, and Father Roberto.

"How's Levi feeling?" Roc asked, the door closing behind them.

"Good. Well, not so good. It will take some time. Falling off the roof..." Glances shifted between the others and made Samuel's voice trail off. "What's the matter? Did I say something?"

"Not at all." Roc indicated a chair at the table and seated himself at the head. "How are your folks?"

"The same." It was a careful answer, one he figured Roc would understand.

"And your girl? Andi?" Roc had met her when he was staying at Samuel's parents' home in Ohio. He'd interrupted them in the barn late one night.

At the memory, Samuel felt heat burn its way up his neck. He shrugged in answer to Roc's question, not knowing what to say or frankly where she was at the moment. He hadn't spoken to her since he'd left Ohio.

"Who would like some coffee and cinnamon crumb cake?" Rachel asked.

The men agreed. While Rachel served the dessert along with cups of hot, black coffee, Roc went to check on the baby and came back carrying David, who had deep blue eyes like his mother. Samuel was introduced to the little tyke, and then Roc placed the baby in a high chair between Roc and Rachel. They alternately fed bits of cut-up grapes and buttered bread to their little boy, who babbled and cooed.

After what all four of them had experienced back in Ohio, it felt odd to be sitting here, enjoying a normal, carefree moment. Rachel kept the conversation going with questions about Hannah's babies, and Samuel tried to answer as best he could.

"I'll send some fresh baked bread home with you. With so many more mouths to feed, it'll come in handy."

Samuel nodded, not bothering to explain how he'd have to climb that ravine to get to his motorcycle and then there wouldn't be much of a place to put the bread. But he'd make do. He finished the crumb cake and pushed the plate away. "So what's going on here, Roc?"

"I think the best way to explain would be to show you."

"Do you think that's wise?" the priest asked.

Roc leaned toward Samuel. "Did you bring your motorcycle?"

"You wanna ride?"

Roc grinned. "Absolutely."

# CHAPTER TWENTY

S MOKE ROSE FROM THE candles like prayers, the flames wavering like his faith had over the years, until his had been completely snuffed out, the last red glowing ember cooling and turning black. But the tiny wicks and flickering flames around the church mocked him.

Years ago, Brydon lit a candle for his father, his mother holding his hand and guiding the flame to touch match to wick. The glow held his gaze until his eyes burned with unshed tears. His mother's eyes filled and spilled over, her mouth quivering from a fresh round of grief.

It had been years since he was five years old. His mother had been gone since the year he graduated high school, but he had never lit a candle in her honor—never stepped over the threshold of a church until today.

Memories of his previous life in New Orleans wisped about him, thin as smoke, but they could not hold or bind him. He felt isolated, with no place to run, no one to turn to, no one to lean on. He hadn't dared return to his hometown. They, whoever those vamps were, would know where he lived. They hadn't been after Andi. They'd wanted him. And the reason couldn't be good.

So he'd been forced into hiding. New York City seemed as good a place as any, where one could get sufficiently lost. The spires of St. Patrick's drew him to the sanctuary as if the church could protect him, as if it had the answers he sought, and he'd run through the door, like a child throwing himself into his mother's open arms.

His thoughts ran to the past, searching for answers and comfort. Yet it became more difficult to dredge up memories. Ryan Wynne had the late shift at the docks. He came in each morning, just as his wife left to drive Brody to school. He'd always carried a sack lunch in those days—ham and cheese sandwich, Little Debbie dessert. Then she went to her job at the hospital, helping sick folks. But that fateful winter morning, Brody heard the knock on the door. His mother was still applying her makeup and hollered, "Let your daddy in. He must have forgotten his keys again."

But they never left for school that morning. His lunch box sat on the counter for days afterward. A policeman stood at the door. He'd had a stern face, but his throat had jerked upward at the sight of Brody, and he'd rearranged his features. The officer had knelt, his black leather belt and holster creaking. "Hey, buddy. Your momma home?"

There'd been a wreck. Years later, when Brody became a police officer, mostly because of that tall cop who'd shown some heart that day, he'd looked up the official paperwork on his father's wreck. Ryan Wynne fell asleep at the wheel, rammed his Buick LeSabre straight into the grill of an eighteen-wheeler. DOA. Even the toxicology and autopsy reports couldn't fully explain how a little boy lost his daddy.

Somehow, that incident had snuffed out Brody's emotions. His heart atrophied over the years and felt dead. Maybe it was. Maybe that's what allowed him to do the acts he now committed on a regular basis, acts he once would have considered hideous, vile, and obscene, but which now gave him life.

Unsure why or what for, he stood from the seat in the pew, which he'd occupied half the day, and walked as if in a trance to the table of candles. With a steady hand, he lit one candle when he should have lit a thousand. He breathed in the smoke and let it sear his lungs.

Covered in the breath of prayers, he once more took a seat, weary of the chase and the burden of loneliness. He had no prayers to offer. Who would he pray to anyway? He sat alone, not bothering to look at the tourists taking a tour of the cathedral, not even searching for the faces of those chasing him. Let them come. Let them take him right here. In this holy place. In an unholy act.

The day waned as he remained in one spot, waiting... waiting for what he didn't even know. To be found? To receive an answer? An answer to his questions or his unspoken prayers? He wasn't even sure.

A clearing of a throat garnered his attention. Brydon blinked. A darkly clad young man bent toward him. He wore a white collar and an apologetic expression. "The cathedral will be closing, sir, in a few minutes."

Brydon rose, feeling stiff and hollow. He walked the long aisle toward the door and then disappeared into the evening crowds.

# CHAPTER TWENTY-ONE

*T*HUNK.

Levi plunked the book onto the wooden bench. Samuel set down the broken tool he'd been trying to fix for the last half hour. The book cover looked familiar, one he'd checked out from the Cincinnati library. A book on occultist rituals. Last night, Samuel had read about the sanctity of blood and its many uses in spells and potions.

"What do you need, Levi?"

His oldest brother's face held no tolerance. "Hannah found this in your bedroom."

"What was she doing—?"

"It's my house, Samuel. She was cleaning, not snooping. But it has her very upset."

Samuel leaned back and crossed his arms over his chest. He felt defensive, and he wasn't sure why. "You too obviously."

"Yes, me too. You don't understand what you're fooling with here."

"It's a book. Nothing more or less. I'm trying to understand what has happened in our lives to our brother."

Levi took a calming breath and leaned heavily on a cane. "I understand, Samuel, more than you think I do. But what you don't understand is that reading stuff like this is what took Jacob on the wrong path. *Finally, brethren,*" Levi took on a solemn tone as he quoted from the scriptures, "*whatsoever things are true, whatsoever things are honest, whatsoever things are just, whatsoever things are pure, whatsoever things are lovely, whatsoever things are of good report; if there be any virtue, and if there be any praise, think on these things."*

"Is that why you keep Jacob's book in the barn?"

"I keep it there because it reminds my wife of difficult days."

Samuel sniffed dismissively. "So you're saying I should just think of roses and lilies and sunshine, *ja*? I shouldn't try to understand how my brother went from being like you and me to dying at my own hand? How'd that happen, Levi?" Pressure built in his chest. "How did we get from there to here?"

Tears welled in Levi's eyes. He looked older. Maybe it was the beard. Maybe it was simply the travails of life. He settled a hand on Samuel's shoulder. "I wish I understood it all but I don't. I never will. There are some things we're not meant to understand. For some reason, Jacob was lured by all this evil. Hannah too was drawn to this darkness. Maybe we all are. Maybe it's our pride, like in the Garden of Eden. Maybe we all want to be like God. But we aren't God. And we can't handle the temptation...or this evil. It will destroy us. Even looking at this"—he indicated the book—"turns my stomach. Why would Jacob continue on that path? Why didn't he turn back?"

"Maybe he did," Samuel said. "He came home. Remember?"

"But maybe it was too late. There are doors that should never be opened. There are consequences for our actions."

"And what have we opened here?" Samuel asked, his voice cracking. *What was going on here and at Roc's? Why were there still secrets?* "What are you doing, Levi?"

"I'm trying to stay on the side of God. I'm battling evil."

"But what exactly is evil, Levi? Some say religion and faith in God has led to more destruction than any other source. Religion started many wars and atrocities."

"You know that's not our beliefs, Samuel. Our God is true. Our God is a god of love, not destruction. But our God is also holy and demands holiness. And there is the devil. The Father of lies. He is God's enemy. *Be sober, be vigilant; because your adversary the devil, as a roaring lion, walketh about, seeking whom he may devour.*"

Samuel shrugged, uncomfortable sitting on the proverbial fence where he found himself. "I know the differences between faiths, between what we believe and what other faiths claim, but aren't you doing the same as those who have done harm in the name of God? Don't you feel led by God to make this so-called stand?"

"What's right and wrong?" Levi spluttered out the words. His face darkened. "Samuel, I don't decide. You don't decide. *God* decides what's right and wrong. I simply live by His laws. When you put yourself in God's shoes and try to determine right and wrong for yourself, then you are in serious trouble and are further down that path than you want to be."

Samuel stood and met Levi squarely, eye to eye. "Who are you to say what's right and what's wrong when you are the one lying to your family and neighbors? You weren't raised this way, Levi. Does Pop know how you broke a rib? I sure don't, but I don't think it was feeding the chickens. Who else are you lying to? Hannah?"

"She knows," Levi said, his voice soft but firm.

But Samuel wasn't finished. "Is this the life you want to live, Levi? Are you so right that you can't see the wrong in what you are doing?"

Levi took a breath and released it slowly. "Many...no,

most wouldn't understand. But, yes, I know the risk I am taking. I know the wrongs I've committed. You and I know the risk of not doing so. Would you have had me not do anything? Not help the woman I love from being devoured by that roaring lion? Or what about Roc? Should he have not gone after Rachel, not saved her? What would have happened to our family then?"

Samuel had no answer.

Levi took one step toward Samuel, leaning heavily on his cane. "There is a time, Samuel, when we all have to grow up. *When I was a child, I spake as a child, I understood as a child, I thought as a child: but when I became a man, I put away childish things. For now we see through a glass, darkly; but then face to face: now I know in part; but then shall I know even as also I am known.*

"You have choices, Samuel, as a man, that you must make now. Are you going to run, like our father did? Try to hide from the truth? Try to evade evil and ignore its existence? Are you going to keep reading this filth"—he nudged the book—"and follow in Jacob's footsteps? Because if you are, I can guarantee the outcome."

Samuel jerked his chin upward. "Are you going to kill me then?"

"It won't matter if it's me or Roc or someone else. But the end will be the same. And you don't want that." Levi placed a hand against his chest. "I don't want that. You are playing with fire."

Frustration boiled inside Samuel. "I am simply trying to understand."

Levi picked up the book and placed it in Samuel's hands. "Get rid of this. Only bad comes from it. I don't want it in my house."

"Are you telling me I can't read it?"

For a long moment, Levi remained silent, as if gauging his answer. "It's your decision. You're a man, Samuel. But you cannot read this book or anything like it here in my house. Opening a door like this threatens my family."

The fierceness in Levi's eyes ended Samuel's arguments. "Are you asking me to leave too?"

"No. No, I'm not." *Was Levi convincing himself?* "But maybe you need to spend more time at Roc's. Maybe he can explain to you the dark side of evil. Maybe you can understand the battle we are in. *Be strong in the Lord, and in the power of his might. Put on the whole armour of God, that ye may be able to stand against the wiles of the devil.*"

"I'm not sure that's what they're doing at Roc's, Levi."

"Go see more for yourself."

---

The barn structure had been built recently and smelled of raw lumber. But the usual earthy odors of a conventional barn did not accompany Samuel as he followed Roc inside.

His last trip to Roc's, Samuel had taken him up the cliff where he'd left his motorcycle, then, sharing a ride, Roc showed him another road to the training center. It was still far off the beaten path. It would be hard to find, even if someone was searching for it. The easy laughter and shared interest in motor vehicles had reestablished their friendship.

"Where's that fancy car of yours you told me about, Roc?" Samuel had asked, hoping he could drive it.

Roc shook his head. "I sold it. I'm a family man now. Had to buy a kid-friendly car."

Samuel had climbed aboard his motorcycle and revved his engine. "That's a shame, Roc."

"Go on, get out of here." They'd shaken hands and agreed

Samuel should return in a couple of days and learn more about the center.

Now, they walked through a room crowded with wooden cots stacked three high.

"Our dormitory," Roc explained.

Samuel noted the beds were all made, the blankets tucked neatly around mattress corners. A row of lockers stood like soldiers. Then they passed a bathroom with showers and sinks, folded white towels, and an industrial-sized washer and dryer.

At the end of the room, they came to a door, which Roc opened. "This is our training facility."

Samuel stared at the knotted ropes hanging from the rafters like long jungle vines. Storage shelves held not only boxes but also ropes, knives of all shapes and sizes, and stakes, the likes of which he'd seen Roc carry and use. An oversized gun case sported a sturdy wheel lock. Along another side of the building, weights and workout equipment took up considerable space. In another area, chairs gathered around a chalkboard.

"We start here each morning." Roc indicated the few plastic chairs stacked and pushed against the wall. "Father Roberto takes care of us."

"Just a few prayers," the priest added, joining them on the tour, "along with confession and communion. We discussed it, Roc and I, before we began. Surprisingly, Roc agreed."

"Not surprisingly," Roc shot back. "Remember I've seen our enemy." Roc's gaze remained steady, not looking away with embarrassment. "The spiritual is as important as the physical, if not more so."

"If you're going to fight evil," the priest added, "then your own soul should be purged and purified first."

Samuel looked up at the rafters above as if they might hold the answers to his many questions. Thick boards bisected the ceiling. Pulleys were attached, and they held the dangling ropes, which were hanging as loose and wide apart as the statements Roc and Roberto were making. "I don't understand. Who are you training and for what?"

"Those you met earlier." Roc grabbed a clipboard and flipped through a few pages. "We've made a lot of progress, but we have much yet to do."

Samuel huffed out an exasperated breath.

Roc looked up from the papers and burned Samuel with a heated gaze. "We're fighting vampires."

*Vampires.* Even the word sent a chill through Samuel. *But could such a thing exist?*

"Exactly like we did in Ohio," Roberto added almost nonchalantly, swiveling a chair around on one leg and then sitting on it like a cowboy riding a horse. He hooked his arms on the back of the chair. "But we're taking better precautions this time. And our training has been more thought-out and organized."

For months, Samuel had tried to push away the memories of the fight in Ohio, which ended with the death of his brother. Roc and Roberto had insisted the man Samuel killed was not Jacob because he was "changed." He went by the name Akiva. But Samuel hadn't wanted to listen. He hadn't wanted to believe. He hadn't wanted to think about any of this. And yet, at some base level of consciousness, he knew.

That horrific day, Samuel had brought the priest named Roberto from the bus station in Kentucky to his parent's Ohio homestead. The moment they arrived, the priest warned Samuel to leave. "There's imminent danger."

"But—"

"Leave, Samuel! Go now. Quickly, before it's too late."
The priest had rushed to a hiding place and worked his way
toward the side of the house.

Samuel stood transfixed for a moment. His father would
have demanded he leave. But he couldn't. He thought of
the pregnant Rachel in that house. And Roc. *Who were they
fighting? Who were they running from?* Samuel wondered. *What
would happen if he left? Could he live with himself if Rachel and
Roc died? If her unborn baby never had a chance?* No. He had to
stay and help if he could. *But how?*

He'd raced to the barn where Pop kept the rifles they
used for hunting. His hands fumbled with the latch. Then
someone grabbed him from behind and slammed him against
a wall.

He must have blacked out because when he came to,
his head pounding, he lay on the hay-strewn floor, his face
pressed into the dirt. It had taken him a minute or two
to reorient himself, each breath chasing the next, then he
pushed himself into a sitting position. Light poured through
the doorway, silhouetting a man he'd never seen before. He
paced back and forth, in and out of sunlight, through shade
and shadow, his footsteps agitated and brisk.

Samuel stood, but the barn tilted. He lurched toward the
wall. A pail clattered.

The stranger whipped around, black eyes fixed on Samuel.

The world tipped sideways again, and he braced a hand
against the wood-planked wall. It felt as if he was falling but
never hitting bottom. "Who are you?"

Those black eyes bore into him, and Samuel felt as if flames
licked his body. He heard himself cry out. Pain engulfed him
with such intensity he thought he might black out again.

As quickly as the attack began, the man released him. Samuel's legs gave out beneath him, and he plummeted to the floor. Then the man shrank into nothing and disappeared.

Since then, Samuel had read enough to truly know that evil existed and mystical things were possible. He'd read of depravity and wickedness. Maybe he'd even experienced a small token when he'd looked into that stranger's black eyes and felt as if he was falling...falling into a deep pit.

"Levi knows about all of this?" he asked, looking around at the expansive building.

Roc nodded. "He helped build it."

"Was that how he was hurt?"

"He fell during one of our exercises," Roberto explained.

So his brother was making up stories too. Nothing was as it seemed, which disturbed Samuel the most. Had everyone lied to him or misled him? He rubbed his forehead, trying to put the pieces all together. Where would it all end?

Roc tossed the clipboard back on the table. "We're working not only on the physical aspects with strenuous workouts and fighting techniques, but also with the mental, emotional, and spiritual preparation. For this plague we are dealing with, we must be as fully prepared as we can be."

"So why the surprise attack when I arrived?" he asked.

Roc crossed his arms over his chest and leaned back against the table. "We take security very seriously."

"I got that." Samuel rubbed his still sore shoulder.

"Unfortunately, because we are new, we only have a few rudimentary security measures set up to surprise and detain. What we are doing here is top secret and there are many who would like to destroy us. Hopefully, once we have more funds, we'll add security cameras and other high-tech measures. But that all takes funding."

"Funding from where?"

"We rely on donations," Roberto said without elaborating.

Samuel glanced back at the room with the cots and re-membered all the men who had pounced on him when he'd first arrived at Roc's. "Where do these folks in training come from?"

"All over." Roberto scratched his jaw with his thumb-nail. "We get referrals from priests, those who believe in evil, those who've experienced these supernatural events, or some of our members we've acquired by word of mouth."

"Most of the men here," Roc added, "have experienced the supernatural and have personal reasons for wanting to see this evil eradicated. Most have lost loved ones."

Roberto nodded his head. "But so far, many men of the cloth have closed their minds to this pandemic. It's a sad state when the church has quit believing in evil and quit training in exorcisms and combat. Because make no mistake, we are in a war."

Samuel nudged one of the ropes, which swung sideways and back. "What do you do with these?"

"Training." Roberto smiled.

Roc straightened. "You're welcome to find out, if you want to join our fight."

# CHAPTER TWENTY-TWO

FOG CREPT IN OVER the valley like a serpent surveying the land and readying itself to strike. Brydon watched from his perch in a crypt of a room that wasn't much larger than a coffin. There was nowhere for him to run. No one whom he could run to. The only vamp capable of helping him was Giovanni. And he was dead. Besides, vamps only acted if it benefitted them, and Brydon had nothing to offer. He was completely and utterly alone.

From New York, he'd headed north to one of the most remote locations he could find. All in an effort to stay alive. If that's what this changed life could be called. Or maybe it was simply a different kind of hell. But he feared what worse torment awaited him if he was eventually destroyed. When he'd almost died at the hand of Roc Girouard, he'd glimpsed darkness, true darkness, and the endless torture awaiting him in the hereafter.

For the first time, Brydon was the hunted, not the hunter. During his days as a police officer in New Orleans, he'd hunted criminals. Not always easy, but sometimes easier than he admitted. It mostly took patience and determination. Then he'd been changed, changed into a predator of a different kind. His hunting skills had come in handy as he fed off the indigent, lost, and helpless. At first, he'd kept to those who wouldn't be missed or who had such a crappy life that death seemed a step up. It hadn't required much patience or skill to find prey. But now, life had once again flip-flopped on him. And he was the prey.

Those he'd chased in a previous life—murderers, robbers, rapists—deserved hell. He knew that unequivocally. Yet now, he too had killed. Was he to blame as well? He hadn't killed out of rage or passion or anger or plain ol' meanness, only as a matter of survival, no more or less than when a wolf killed a rabbit. *Was he now to suffer the same fate as the scum he'd tracked down, arrested, and put in prison for so many years? Could the good he'd done as a cop outweigh his sins?*

*And who was this Jezebel? A leader like Giovanni? What did she want?* He'd probably violated some secret vampire code, the way Akiva had. Forgiveness wasn't common in the vampire community. The only forgiveness was death.

Brydon had never feared death, at least not when he was alive. He'd faced the wrong side of a gun and the pointed end of a knife when he'd been a cop, often enough to know death wasn't an *if* but a *when*. He'd accepted his own inevitable death when Roc had sliced his throat. He'd allowed it. He'd wanted to die—until the darkness began to swallow him.

Then Akiva saved him, provided a sacrificial lamb, whose blood had healed his fatal wounds. Of course, he'd owed Akiva and had helped him find Rachel. But that was where his allegiance ended. When Giovanni arrived on that tiny homestead in Ohio, he had fled, knowing Giovanni was there to kill Akiva. Brydon hadn't been willing to die for anyone. Now, he wasn't about to be some patsy or die at the hand of another vamp.

Maybe all wasn't yet lost. Maybe he could still get away, make a life, and live alone. This wouldn't be such a bad place.

Holed up in a cold, stone monastery high in the mountains

of Nova Scotia, he stared out the open window, watching the slow progression of fog. The crimson morning sunlight gave it an eerie iridescence and enflamed the valley. The chill rippling through him had nothing to do with the weather.

A knock on the door turned him away from the window. A monk usually brought coffee, boiled egg, and scone for breakfast. All of which he discarded. Otherwise, they left him alone. "Come in."

The heavy key turned the lock and the wrought iron handle creaked. Head lowered, a monk entered the room, carrying a tray. He wore a brown tunic. Brydon faced the window again. The monks were accustomed to visitors not being verbose, as many sought spiritual renewal and tranquility here among the mountains and valleys. They respected one's privacy.

At the click of the door closing again, he moved to the desk, finding the tray on the desk as he had expected. But he stiffened at the sight of the monk still in his room. Not just one monk, but two others had joined him. Together, they moved forward. Instantly, Brydon recognized the black gazes.

He took one backward step toward the open window. "Hello, boys."

The three did not speak. They separated, the two on the outside arcing around the edges of the room to outflank him.

"How do you like the cold—"

In the middle of his question, Brydon lunged for the window, morphing into a winged creature. But before he could completely transform, talons sunk into his neck. The valley stretched out before him, and like a squadron of fighter jets, the group soared over the tree line with Brydon helpless to escape.

# CHAPTER TWENTY-THREE

SWEAT ROLLED DOWN HIS sides, and still Samuel raised the ax, swung it over his shoulder in a high arc, and brought it down with a hard slant. The blade bit through the pulpy wood, splitting it down the middle, until the ax hit the chop block and jarred his arms, shoulders, and back. He tossed the spliced wood into a pile, grabbed another thick piece, and chopped it in two.

The heavy scent of smoke hung in the air, and he paused long enough to throw more feed bags onto the burning trash pile. With the wind almost nonexistent on this sunny spring day, it was a good time to get this chore accomplished. It, coupled with the wood chopping, helped him burn off his confusing emotions.

Anger and fear wrestled within him. Periodically, one got the upper hand. He often felt the prickly sensation of being watched. Noises startled him. Nightmares haunted him. Then his thoughts lingered on the lies Pop had told, how he'd packed up his family and wrenched them away from home, family, and community. Part of Samuel had always wanted to return to Pennsylvania. But now, where did he belong?

He wasn't sure he believed in what Roc was doing. Should he discuss it with Levi? Or not? Levi had also lied. Confused and unsure, Samuel didn't know what he believed or who he trusted.

He'd hoped a change of location—the land of his child-hood, the growing fields and yielding crops, the pastures dotted with docile cattle—would settle whatever had been stirred up inside him months ago and he'd feel at peace once more. But now tension knotted his muscles and uncertainty rocked his stomach.

*What was he to do? What should he believe? Should he shun whatever knowledge he'd garnered or did it require him to act? Levi lived in both worlds. But could Samuel?* He felt caught between the two.

Footsteps sounded behind him. His heart jolted. Without another thought, he whipped around, raising the ax in a de-fensive motion, surprising himself and Naomi.

Her prayer *kapp* in place, her apron clean and ironed, she greeted him with a calming smile, not seeming to notice his wild look and agitated stance. She carried a tray with apple slices, muffins, and a tall glass of lemonade and set it on the chopping block. "I thought you might be thirsty."

He swallowed his heart, which had lurched into his throat. "*Danke.*"

Laying down the ax, he wiped his sweaty palms on the back of his trousers, then swiped a sleeve over his brow. He gulped down the tart liquid, which left a surprising sweetness on his tongue.

"You were thirsty," Naomi noted with satisfaction. "I'll come back later to collect the tray and bring you more lemonade."

"Why don't you take a break yourself?" He spoke before he thought, but he realized he didn't want to be alone with his questions and insecurities anymore. Company would at least distract him. And maybe this was the moment he'd been searching for. "Surely, you could use a snack too. I know you've been working hard in the house."

She eyed the whitewashed home. "The babies are napping, as are Hannah and Levi. Maybe it would be good to stay out of the house so I don't wake them."

Samuel flipped over an empty plastic bucket for Naomi to use as a seat, and he plopped himself down on the ground next to the chopping block, feeling bits of wood chips beneath his trousers.

"Hannah's been wearing herself out fussing over Levi," Naomi said. "But he seems to be healing in good time."

"It's good to see them again. To see them both happy."

"They are sweet together," Naomi agreed.

Samuel reached for a blueberry muffin. He peeled the muffin paper off the bottom, and crumbs flaked around him. The little cake was fluffy and light, and the sweet berries burst inside his mouth. "Mmm," he mumbled. "This is good."

Naomi smiled and crunched into an apple slice. "I'm glad you like them."

He nodded as he finished off the muffin. "It's good you're here to help out. It's lots of work though."

"Taking care of the babies doesn't feel like work at all. It's a pleasure."

For a moment silence settled between them. But it was a comfortable silence, like sitting by a fire in the cool evening. Despite the tension Samuel felt with Levi, he was glad to be home in Promise again. He'd missed his old district and his friends and extended family more than he'd allowed himself to realize.

Had he missed Naomi too? When he'd been younger and visited Naomi in the middle of the night, as many Amish did when they courted, he'd felt awkward and unsure. He'd been naïve to the ways of men and women, hadn't known what to do or how to act. Andi had taught him what *English* women liked and the fine art of seduction. He was not the same boy who had attempted to court Naomi so long ago. He was a man now. Naomi was a woman, not the young girl he'd known, but she was plain. Not just in dress but in matters of the heart.

"You said you still write some?" he asked, trying to find any of the common ground they'd once shared.

"Not much, no. But sometimes words come to me in a prayer or poem." She shrugged and chose a muffin.

"I liked your poetry. You should write more."

"I have no one to read it to now." Her eyes widened and locked with Samuel's until she looked away. The telltale signs of embarrassment stole up her neck and flamed her cheeks. Was she remembering the quiet, tender moments they'd shared at the creek? Or was she embarrassed that she had no one to listen to the words of her heart?

"You could have written me in Ohio," he said. "I would have liked that."

She kept her head bent as she picked at the paper stuck to the muffin.

"I'm sorry."

She looked at him, curiosity brightening her eyes. "For what?"

He shrugged. "For not writing you. I was never good that way."

"You were better than you thought, Samuel."

"It's been three years since I've been back in Promise. A long time. I didn't contact anyone. Not even my friends."

She accepted his confession with a nod. "Paul will be happy to see you. As well as David and Eliam. You four were always together, like peas in a pod."

He finished off the rest of the muffin. "And usually in trouble."

She chuckled. "Not overmuch, I'm thinking."

His head tilted as he studied the soft line of her jaw. "You were always quiet and good."

A tinge of pink brightened her cheeks and she stared at her lap, twisting a tie of her *kapp* between her fingers.

At her silence, he regretted saying such. Maybe he'd said too much. Or maybe he hadn't said enough. Doubting his motives and unsure of his intention, he changed the subject. "What's Paul been up to? Has he found himself a girl yet?"

The color in her cheeks brightened even more. Was she seeing Paul? That jarred him until finally settling into irritation, even though he had no right to feel such. Amish teens tended to keep their affections to themselves. "Sorry," he said, "I didn't mean—"

"Oh no. It's all right."

"I shouldn't have said—" He didn't know what to say. "Sometimes I don't know when to quit talking." *Like now.*

"I'm the opposite. I never know what to say."

He reached for another muffin. As he unwrapped the base, he said, "Someone has to be quiet, I expect, so those of us who blather on will have someone listening. But I have a feeling you're busy thinking of things to write."

Her eyes twinkled. "I always think of things to say in my head, but by the time I get them to my mouth, they jumble into a tangled mess, much like my knitting."

He laughed and filled his mouth with part of another blueberry muffin.

She rubbed her thumb against the palm of her other hand in a back and forth motion as if trying to erase a thought that wouldn't go away. "Samuel," she spoke again, this time her tone somber. "I never had the chance to speak to you about..."

Her gaze met his, and her words trailed away. He braced himself for some confession that she was seeing Paul or one of his other friends.

She swallowed hard, licking her lips, before continuing. "About your brother...Jacob. I am awful sorry for your loss. And it's probably too late to say anything. There's nothing I could say to take away the pain, but I didn't know how or when or...I should have written you maybe. Or maybe I shouldn't have. And now maybe I should have just stayed silent and not said anything at all."

Her words were rushed and breathless, and yet they wrapped about him, a soothing bandage on the wound in his heart. His throat tightened. Finally, he nodded his understanding.

"I'm sorry," she said again. "I shouldn't have said anything. I didn't mean to upset you by speaking of it and yet..." Her voice trailed off. He wished she would go on talking because now he couldn't seem to find the necessary words. Finally, she added, "I have prayed for you." An awkward pause hummed between them. "For your family."

Emotions of the past three years rose up inside him. He'd hoped to forget or at least banish his questions, and all this had done was twist his tangled emotions into a tight knot in his belly.

Suddenly, she stood and dusted off her apron. "I better get back to work," she said in a rush. She left the tray and hurried toward the house.

# CHAPTER TWENTY-FOUR

A NOISE STARTLED HER.

It wasn't the first time she couldn't sleep at two in the morning. Andi sat in her darkened apartment. Watching the doors and windows. Listening to creaks and noises from the street. Waiting. No one was ever going to surprise her again.

First, she muted the television, strained her ears to hear the noise. *What had it been? Someone crying out? A bird? The screech of a tire?* As a precaution, she folded her hand around the hilt of her semi-automatic weapon. Years ago, she'd bought the Beretta at a gun show. No guy was ever going to get the upper hand on her again. A single girl couldn't be careless, which is why she carried pepper spray.

Good thing too. The spray worked on that loser who'd ganged up on poor Brydon. She hoped the librarian was okay. She'd run for her Yaris and called 911, but she'd driven straight home. *Good luck, buddy. You're on your own.*

To be certain the sound that woke her was of no significance, she crept toward the window and peered out at the parking lot. Nothing stirred. Cars were lined up neatly, with one Camry parked crookedly. Windows remained dark. Headlights off.

Slowly, she eased the blinds together and went back to the sofa. She hit the volume button on the remote, and voices floated over her. Images flickered past. She paid little attention to the television. It was just a distraction from the nightmares. And they'd been coming more often since that night a week ago.

As she'd run, leaving Brydon to fend for himself, she'd lost two of the books he'd given her, but she still had one. It sat ignored on the coffee table. She'd called the library a couple of days after they'd been attacked to check up on him, but when she'd asked for Brydon, the answering librarian had said, "Who?"

"Brydon." She felt foolish because she didn't know his last name. "He works there."

"No one by that name works here."

"He works at night." Irritated at the stupid girl, Andi hung up and called later. But she'd received the same reaction.

*Had she been duped? Who was Brydon?* Not that she really cared. It didn't matter anyway. *Good riddance!* She'd plopped the book on the coffee table and hadn't given it or him another thought. *Or had she?*

Maybe she should at least take the book back to the library. *No*, she'd fumed. Served the guy right. He could pay an exorbitant library fee.

But now, her curiosity nudged her to reach for the book. Why had he wanted her to have this one? What had been the purpose? Was it a sex game book? What exactly had the pervert had in mind?

She snatched the book off the table and flipped open the cover only to have a folded piece of paper slide into her lap. She discovered it was a mimeographed newspaper article, one on each side of the page. Skimming the first, she read about a bunch of animals missing or killed in Lancaster County. Ho-hum. Was he trying to spook her? It would take more than that.

Flipping the paper, she felt her heart pounding as she read the second one.

Missing high school student Arianna Davenport has been found. After two weeks, she was discovered walking along Highway 27 in West Babylon near Walmart in a state of undress. After being checked at Good Samaritan Hospital, she was released to the care of her family. The emergency room doctor said that although slightly dehydrated, she was in good shape. He made no other comments as to her state of mind or what might have happened to the seventeen-year-old.

One of her classmates worried that Davenport had been abducted by a Satanic cult. Other sources, wishing to speak under the protection of anonymity, believed she had been involved with a vampire coven. When the teen went missing, her family had been featured on ABC, CNN, and FOXNews, where they showed pictures of their active high school senior who was a straight-A student, cheerleader, and volleyball player. Her family adamantly denied the teen ran away. They feared foul play. The police did too, yet they had the family and friends under close observation.

This morning the chief of police, Ryan Huldoon, conducted a press conference and said they would be speaking to Miss Davenport once she had rested and eaten.

Andi folded the article. *What was that all about?* Had Brydon wanted her to read that article? To have her nerves electrified? What was the point?

But her attention was drawn to the picture of the girl. She had wide eyes and an eerie expression, haughty and distant.

Was the girl disturbed? Or had the girl truly been abducted? Did such things as vampire covens exist? It seemed preposterous, and yet she'd seen enough in her life that made her think anything was possible. Or was it?

And more than that—forget Brydon—why would Samuel be interested in things like this? Something had happened with his brother, something terrible enough to shake Samuel and his faith.

She remembered sleeping beside him several months ago, not long after his brother died, when he sat bolt upright in bed, muscles clenched, releasing a hoarse cry. Had he called his brother's name?

"What's wrong?" she'd asked sleepily, trying to snuggle against him.

A cold sweat coated his skin. He'd grunted and swung his feet to the floor.

"Samuel?"

"Go back to sleep." His tone had been harsh. *Or had he been distressed?*

Scooping his crumpled shirt off the floor, she'd pulled it on and followed after him into the den. With the lights in her apartment out, and only the glimmer of a light from the parking lot shining through the open blinds, she couldn't see much but his outline. He stood in front of the window, oblivious to the fact that he was naked, staring out and yet looking more inward.

She laid a hand against his bare back. "Samuel, can't you tell—"

He'd shrugged off her touch. "Don't. I'm—" But he'd stopped himself.

"What?"

He'd shuddered. Slowly, his gaze shifted toward her, dark

and frightening. Not scaring her, but as if he were the one scared. "Do you believe in evil?"

"What do you mean? Like in the garden of good and—"

"Evil," he injected. "Pure evil."

Did he think he'd been tainted by something sinful? She knew the Amish viewed life in black and white. Maybe his religion was confusing him, making him think something she couldn't fathom. *Was he having guilt over their sexual relationship?*

"Do you mean like sin?"

"More than that. Not just one man or woman, but humanity and beyond."

"Like that man is inherently evil and all that bull—eh." She'd stopped herself because Samuel hated cursing. "All that garbage?"

He didn't answer. He simply looked at her, his gaze begging for an answer, relief, something she wasn't sure she had to give.

She smoothed a hand over his shoulder trying to distract him. "I don't know about humanity, but let's go back to bed and we can talk about that man/woman thing. I have a question about—"

"Do you believe?"

"Okay. Okay." No joking. *Evil. What did he want to know exactly?* "I think," she ventured into this unknown realm, "people are basically screwed up. Heck, we all are. Blame your mother, your father, whoever. We've all been screwed one way or another. We're all probably one push away from committing murder."

"I'm not talking about why we do things. I'm talking about evil. As in Satan. Supernatural. Ghosts and demons and va—"

She'd laughed. It had burst out of her. Had he been about

to say vampires? Or something else? She regretted her response now, but she'd wanted to get him off the weird topic
and back to bed. It was late. She was tired. And who cared
about that stuff anyway? "Look," she'd said, "that stuff is
just figments of our fertile imagination. Or some writer's.
Stories handed down. You know, like myths. Stephen King
and Cujo. Come on, really?" She'd taken his hand. "Trust
me, Samuel, I've seen every horror flick Hollywood ever
made, and it's all made-up stuff. It's funny. You just had a
bad dream, is all."

He'd blinked and turned back to the window. That was
the last time they'd ever spoken of the nightmares haunting
him. And it wasn't long after he'd told her he had things he
had to work out. Alone.

*So had he seen something supernatural? Had he experienced
some of those missing animals back in Promise? Had he seen his
brother's ghost?* Something had spooked him.

Leaning back into the sofa cushions, Andi tried once again
to focus on Tom Cruise trying to save the world through
some impossible mission. But her mind drifted off until it
landed on her work friend, Skylar. The yoga instructor kept
telling her about a psychic she claimed was really in tune with
the supernatural and hereafter. Maybe she'd give this psychic
a chance to explain things, and maybe even she could reach
out to Samuel's dead brother and give her some answers she
could pass along to Samuel.

# CHAPTER TWENTY-FIVE

The day began at four.

Samuel worked Levi's farm, feeding livestock, preparing fields. He ate meals with Levi (who made it to the table more often), Hannah (who often didn't make it to the table because she had to feed one or both of the babies), and Naomi (who occasionally ended up the only one at the table with Samuel).

Today was that kind of day. Both babies were fussy, and Hannah stayed in the bedroom feeding one while Levi held the other, using a pillow to prop the child and relieve the pressure on his healing rib.

Naomi sat opposite Samuel at the kitchen table. It seemed too quiet between them, and he could hear himself chewing. But what did he have to say?

Thankfully, she passed him cheesy potatoes and asked, "Will you be working in the fields again this afternoon?"

He shook his head and swallowed a bite of roll. "I have an errand to run."

"Will you be hitching up the buggy or the wagon?"

"I'll take my bike." He sliced into the ham that the Miller family had brought over. Many of the Fishers' neighbors had brought meals to help out.

"Then you'll be getting…" She paused as if waiting for a location, but when he didn't supply it, she added, "There faster."

"I suppose." He dug his fork into the cheddar-topped potatoes.

"Sunday services are this week," she added. "Will you be going?"

He tasted the potatoes, which were thick and creamy. He doubted he'd find a convenient excuse not to attend Sunday services. "I suppose so."

"That will be nice." Her cheeks splotched pink, and she sipped her iced tea. "For Levi to have his brother there with him…and Hannah…and the babies."

"If Levi can manage himself," Samuel said.

"He's stronger every day. Won't be long before he'll be going full steam."

She was an optimist. Samuel seemed to have lost that trait, if he'd ever had it. He nodded, keeping his elbows braced on the edge of the table.

"After Levi is mended, will you be staying on, do you think?" Her gaze skittered away from Samuel's.

A warning bell clanged in his head. *What was she wanting?* Maybe nothing. And yet, he'd learned enough about women through Andi to know that every question, gesture, smile had purpose. *Didn't it?*

"I don't know what I'll do," he hedged.

"The Lord will show you in His own good time, *ja*?"

Her words jabbed at him. He hadn't prayed lately…at all, not since he'd shot his brother. How could he? How could he ask God for forgiveness? He felt like Cain. Was there now a mark upon him? Was his punishment eventual separation from those he cared about, his home, even his faith? Or only eternal?

"Samuel?" Naomi spoke softly. "Are you all right?"

"Sure." He cleared his throat. "I just wish I knew all the answers."

"Father says, 'If we know all the answers then we haven't asked all the questions.'"

That tugged a smile from him. "Wish I didn't have so many questions."

———————

Late that afternoon, Samuel rode his motorcycle into Roc's compound. The sun's rays slanted down through tree limbs and budding leaves, speckling the ground with shadowy spots. On the pebbled driveway, a blue Jeep Cherokee jerked to a stop, backed up a few feet, and again wrenched to a stop. Eyeing the car warily, Samuel set the brake on his motorcycle and disengaged.

The passenger door of the Jeep opened first and Roc climbed out. He rubbed a hand over his face then waved at Samuel.

"Everything okay?" Samuel asked as Roc approached.

"Sure. Or it will be once my stomach catches up."

Behind Roc, the driver's door opened and Rachel emerged. She sent a smile and wave toward them but walked back toward the house.

"Teaching Rachel to drive, are you?"

"Yeah, she…uh…yeah." Roc cocked his head sideways and popped his neck. "Good to see you, Samuel. How's Levi?"

"Good."

"But you didn't come here because of Levi, did you?"

Samuel jammed his hands in his back pockets but looked straight at Roc. "I want to know more. Not just a tour. I need to know…to do—" His voice cracked on the hard emotions.

"Of course. Come on." He clapped Samuel on the back. "We'll get you started."

Roc led Samuel into the barn structure. The men he'd

seen earlier in the week worked at different stations. One lifted weights, another climbed one of the many ropes leading up to the ceiling where a bank of swivel pulleys waited, while another threw knives at a board, the point stabbing with precision into the black outline of a man.

"Joe?" Roc waved over one of the men. The man's muscles bulged out from beneath a black T-shirt. "Get Samuel started, all right?"

"Sure thing." Joe had a few inches and more than a few pounds on Samuel. His head was shaved, and the intensity in his gaze was unsettling. "Let's go, kid."

Samuel's gaze dragged behind, lingering on Roc, who took off in the opposite direction. With no other recourse, Samuel followed Joe toward the ropes. "You, uh, been here long?"

Joe grabbed one rope by a knot and swung it toward Samuel. "Start climbing."

Samuel caught the rope. "Why?"

Joe's deep-set eyes, the color of whiskey, carried potency. "No questions."

"Why not? What's the point then?"

Joe took two steps toward Samuel and through tight lips said, "The point is you do what I tell you. Got it?"

Samuel shrugged out of his coat and tossed it on the floor. Grasping the rope with both hands, he gave a sharp tug to make sure it was securely fastened to the pulleys above, then heaved himself upward. His muscles strained, his shoulders knotted, and his feet dangled above the ground, kicking and struggling as knees and ankles trapped the rope. Samuel released a breath, drew another, then released it before he lurched upward. No problem. He'd show these guys he could match them in strength.

"Who's the kid?" someone from below asked.

A crowd of shaved heads and black T-shirts formed, but Samuel kept his eye on the prize at the top.

"Samuel," Joe answered, his thick voice rough and deep. "Roc put me in charge of him."

"Poor kid." A deep laugh offered no sympathy.

"How long you think it'll take him to quit?" came another voice.

"What time is it now?" Joe asked.

"Ah, give him some credit…and maybe ten minutes. Tops."

The rope burned and chafed Samuel's palms. He blocked out the voices and focused on inching upward, but his progress slowed as his muscles felt a deep burn. He was twenty feet above the floor. His arms were trembling, his knees and hands raw. Ten more feet. He could make it. Right hand. Left. Yank upward. Then right again.

"Pete," Joe bellowed, "whenever you're ready."

"Geronimo!" The yell came from Samuel's left. A growing blur raced toward him. He had no time to do anything but blink and hang on tight as a pair of boots slammed into his gut.

Air whooshed out of Samuel. One hand lost its grasp on the rope. He dangled for a moment, the faces below blurring as he twirled and swayed. Pete swung past Samuel again and hollered a victory whoop, which was applauded by the others. Samuel's hand slipped, and he slid a couple of feet down the rope, his legs flailing.

"Better make that two minutes." Someone laughed.

"Or less."

From behind, a full body blow smashed into Samuel. This time, Pete successfully dislodged Samuel completely. He fell backward but made a grab for the rope. He caught it with first one hand, then embraced it with his limbs, scraping and burning every piece of flesh the rope touched.

All the while, Pete hollered and yelled, twirling and swinging past like he belonged in a circus.

Wincing at the pain searing his raw flesh and straining muscles, Samuel shifted upward, trying to hang on to the rope. He wasn't going down. *No way.* He clung to the rope as if it was the only thing keeping him out of the jaws of hell.

The rope shook and trembled. Someone below had grabbed it and was shaking it…and Samuel. The vibrations rocked him to the core. Still he held on. He would not let go. Would not. He gritted his teeth, breathing hard.

One look down was all it took. The faces below made it clear falling was not a recommended option.

"Get to the top, Samuel," Joe yelled. "Go on now. Chris! Dwight! Harry, you too. Show this rookie the ropes." He laughed, the sound sharp and biting. "Come on now. Move! All of you!" He clapped his hands in quick succession.

Praying like he hadn't prayed in a long time, Samuel strained to look up at the pulley as if it were heaven itself. He'd lost five feet at least. How would he ever make it?

"Randy," Joe ordered, "stay here in case he falls. Show him what it means to fail. You hear me?"

"Yes, sir!" the black man responded without hesitation. And even from this distance, he looked as if he could do some serious damage.

Then Joe grabbed his own rope and started to climb.

The muscles in Samuel's arms quaked with fatigue. His hands were raw, his fingers numb. With each yank upward, he grunted, forcing himself to climb, no longer to prove himself—this felt more like self-preservation. If he didn't make it to the top, then he wasn't sure what would happen. But these men did not pamper weaklings.

Pete swung past again, too high now to give another

body blow or kick, but as he passed Samuel's rope, he gave it a shove, and Samuel's world spun. Dizzy, he felt his stomach clench. He sensed more than saw others climbing fast around him.

"Ten bucks for whoever brings him down," Joe called.

"Only ten?"

"Doesn't look like it's gonna be that hard," Joe replied.

Another yell made Samuel glance left...right...no, behind, and Samuel yanked himself higher to avoid being knocked loose. A blurry shadow swung past and Samuel felt the kick in his back thigh. He clenched his knees around the rope, jerked upward again. *Keep climbing*, he coached himself.

"He's mine, boys!" Joe hollered, he'd reached some sort of platform and leaped off it, holding his rope, and flew right toward Samuel.

*Not this time.* Samuel twisted, swiveling his rope, and faced Joe's oncoming assault. The leader aimed his boots right at Samuel, but Samuel was ready. Clinging to the rope with one hand and arm, he snagged the other man's calf and twisted hard. With a sharp cry, Joe flipped upside down and barely hung on to his rope.

Samuel didn't look back to see if Joe fell or recovered. He yanked his body upward again...and again...and again even as his muscles screamed. Finally, he touched the padded planks at the top. He hooked an arm over it and sucked in the warm air, breathing heavily, his body coated in sweat.

"Well, lookie there," Joe laughed, "the farm boy might be tougher than he looks."

The black-shirted men all swung down to the floor without acknowledging Samuel's small victory, which seemed to shrink by the minute. Blistered and stripped palms were his reward.

"When you're ready," Joe hollered up at him, "come on down and you can take a shower. We won't push you too hard today." Then Joe, followed by the others, left the building, turning out the lights as they went.

Samuel was left alone. In the dark. The only sound his ragged breathing. It took a long while before he stripped his shirt off, wrapped it around his bloody palms, and fisted the rope again. He hissed and slid his way back to the blessed floor. His legs wobbled and buckled beneath him, and he collapsed in a heap.

"Not bad for your first day," a voice came out of the shadows.

Samuel scrambled to a sitting position. "Who's there?"

A light in the dorm room came on and illuminated the ropes and mats. Footsteps came toward him, and Samuel recognized Roberto. "They don't mean any harm. It's just their way."

Samuel had no response. He felt depleted, like a summer corn stalk relieved of its last husk and bending to the pressures of winter's approach. His eyes burned. What was he doing here? He wanted answers, not this.

"These men," Roberto said, "aren't playing a game, Samuel. They're not checking things out. They're in this. All or nothing. This is life or death to them. They have to know whether or not they can trust you. They would rather you quit now. For if you continue, you will surely face death, and they have to know you will keep your wits and watch their backs."

"I'm not a quitter."

"I didn't think so." Roberto pulled something from his pocket and tossed it to Samuel.

He caught it, wincing at the pain, bumbling. His fingers stiff, he examined the plastic rectangular object. A cell phone. "What's this for?"

"To keep you safe." Roberto crouched down, arm propped on a knee. "It's preprogrammed with all our numbers. You get in trouble; you realize you're being followed; you see, hear, sense something out of the ordinary, you call one of the numbers on that phone. And we'll come, like the cavalry."

Samuel frowned. "But why would anyone be after me?"

"I'm not saying anyone is. But if someone is watching us, if they see you coming and going, then you could be an easy target." Roberto tilted his head sideways. "Not easy per se. But easier. Isolated."

Samuel nodded gravely. It explained why Levi had a cell phone. So now he was in. In some secret society. Committed. Whether he liked the idea or not. Whether he wanted to be or not. *Did he really have a choice?*

"But it works two ways," Roberto said, his voice weighty. "You get a text or a voice message, then you have five minutes to respond. Five minutes. Which means, you keep this phone with you day and night. You understand?"

"I just want…" His voice trailed off. Too exhausted, he simply shook his head.

"What do you want, Samuel?"

He flopped back onto the ground, his arms and legs splayed outward. "To understand all of this."

"You understand plenty." Roberto's tone turned hard. "You've been denying what happened, haven't you? Well, now it's time you gave it a hard look. Your brother died. Yes. But you didn't kill him. He died a long time before that. He gave what was left of his life to save Rachel. A most noble act for a vampire."

"See!" Anger shot through Samuel. "I don't understand—"

Roberto leaned down, his hand pressing hard on Samuel's chest. "You understand what you choose to understand.

Open your eyes. Look around you, Samuel. This world is full of mysteries and darkness. You've lived a simple life, plain, and yet that's what it all comes down to—the difference between black and white, good and evil. Pretty simple, don't you think?"

# CHAPTER TWENTY-SIX

NOTHING SEEMED SIMPLE AT all. Samuel felt beaten, defeated, broken.

All the way back to Levi's, his motorcycle wobbled beneath him as he could barely clutch the handlebars, which caused excruciating pain in his hands. He arrived long after dark, way past Levi and Hannah's bedtime, and he sat outside while he gathered the energy to head inside.

With the tips of his fingers, he turned the knob and entered the house. A single lamp remained on, surprising him. Naomi, head bowed over an open Bible on her lap, sat in a chair. Everyone at the farm, including the horses and chickens, were tucked in for the night. And she should have already returned to her folks'. She looked up as the door swung open, and a smile spread easily across her features.

"What are you still doing here?" he asked, not moving forward.

She closed the Bible and stood, straightening her apron. "Gabriel was fussy, so I told Hannah I'd sit up with him for a while. I just got him down a few minutes ago." Her brow furrowed. "Are you okay?" She stepped toward him. "What happened to you...your face...hands?"

"Nothing. I...uh—" *How could he explain tonight?* He touched his cheekbone with the back of his hand. The rope had scraped a raw patch. His shirt was wrinkled and bloody with only a couple of the buttons fastened, as that was the best he could manage. He'd forgotten his coat.

Reaching toward him, she cupped one of his hands, then the other, drawing it toward the light, and studied his bloody, raw palms. "Sit down. Here."

Before he could protest, she tugged him over to the kitchen table. She hurried to the sink and pulled several rags from the cabinet, dampened them, and returned to him. She knelt and dabbed at his wounds with the clean cloth. Her silence made Samuel feel as if he should explain. *But how?*

"It's nothing really." When she pressed the cloth to the bloody blisters, he hissed out a breath. "And not what you think."

"And how would you know what I'm thinking, Samuel Fisher?" Her face was calm but her words stung.

"I'm sorry, I—"

"Was it that motorcycle you ride?"

"My—? No."

She watched his face, concern in her eyes. "Were you in a fight?"

"No." But he read the doubt in her troubled eyes. "My knuckles would be raw if I'd been in a fight. Not my palms."

She drew her lower lip between her teeth as she contemplated his injuries. "Are you in much pain?"

"I'll be fine."

She finished cleaning his hands, applied ointment, and wrapped them in clean bandages she found in the pantry. Finally, she sat back and surveyed her handiwork. "I'll check them in the morning. The aloe vera should help."

He had to admit his palms no longer stung and throbbed. She surveyed his cheek and neck, then cleaned those wounds and dabbed on more of the green goop, but as her finger slid just inside his collar, she stopped, her face just inches from his, her breath warm on his skin. Her gaze darted toward him, then she backed away. She stuck out the aloe vera leaf and said, "Here. In case you need any more."

He cupped it between his wrists and plopped it on the table. "Thanks."

"I should be getting home. It's late."

"I'll walk you." He stood, but it took more effort than he anticipated, and he grunted.

"I know the way." She readjusted her apron and seemed out of sorts and restless, her hands fidgeting.

"You shouldn't walk alone at night. It isn't safe."

"Hannah made me promise to ask you to see me home but"—she touched her *kapp*—"really I'll be fine. You're injured, and I'm not worried. The good Lord will protect me." The speed of her words revealed her sudden nervousness.

*Was she nervous to be alone with him?* He couldn't imagine that. He was as harmless as a ladybug with his hands wrapped, his arms and shoulders stiff and sore, and his body aching.

"Hannah's right. It isn't safe. I'll take you home." Samuel hobbled toward the door, feeling every joint, every muscle protest. "I don't mind."

"Really, Samuel, it's all right. This is silly. What ever happens in Promise?"

Apparently, plenty happened here. Even though he didn't feel capable of protecting a fly, he wasn't about to send Naomi out into the dark alone.

"What happened to you tonight?" she asked, her voice barely audible, her gaze scanning his slightly bent posture.

He couldn't straighten his arms fully. With his hands cupped and wrapped, his shirt wrinkled and bloody, he must look a sight. "I was"—his mind whirled for an answer—"helping a friend."

Her silence revealed her doubts, but she kept them to herself.

"Come on." He reached for the door but hesitated before placing his hand on the doorknob.

"Here"—she rushed forward—"let me." She opened the door and shut it behind them.

"Do you want me to hitch the horse to the buggy?" Samuel asked, his hands throbbing at the thought of grabbing the leather reins. Riding his motorcycle had been nearly impossible by himself. No way could he manage with Naomi behind him.

"I like to walk. And it's not far. But I don't mind going alone—"

Samuel raised a bandaged hand to stop her protest. "We'll walk. Together." He kept even with her pace as they descended the steps. "What's wrong with Gabriel?" he asked to change the subject. "Is he sick?"

"I don't think so. Probably a gas bubble."

They walked to the end of the drive and turned onto Slow Gait Road, which would take them to Naomi's parents' farm. "Hard to tell with babies," he surmised, "since they don't talk."

"Exactly. Maybe he just wasn't sleepy. The twins are awake more now. And they're so sweet." She gazed up at the stars and released a contented sigh. "*When I consider thy heavens, the work of thy fingers, the moon and the stars, which thou hast ordained; What is man, that thou art mindful of him?*"

He remembered the verse from Psalms and felt very small indeed beneath the vast sky. Was the God of the universe mindful of him? Sometimes he didn't understand those around him who prayed constantly and managed to rely on God for every morsel and breath when he sometimes forgot to pray, forgot to even think about God. *How did others have a relationship with the Almighty?* For God must see man like a flea.

Naomi seemed wrapped in her own thoughts as she crossed her arms over her stomach, rubbing her arms with her palms. The night was calm, the air cool but not chilly. At least for him. "Are you cold?"

"I'm fine. I've been indoors all day and it feels good to be outside."

Right now, it would feel good to be in bed. Every step pained Samuel. When he took a deep breath, his side pinched. He figured he'd have a good-sized bruise by to-morrow. His thoughts drifted back toward his conversation with Roberto. Was he right? Did he only understand what he chose to understand? Many Amish were closed-minded, especially to the *English*. Others were more practical, utiliz-ing things from the *English* world when it made sense, and yet simply choosing the Amish way. His father camped in the first group; Levi remained in the second. And Rachel had ventured way beyond the careful and plain Amish way of life. But what would he choose?

Even though he didn't want to be a remake of his father, he realized he'd reacted the same way—running from the memory, the guilt, the horror of the unknown. Yet the super-natural world was not unknown to the Amish. They believed in the afterlife, the presence of angels, the reality of evil. Was it all manifested in a way he had simply not wanted to see?

"Samuel?" Naomi's voice called to him.

He stopped and looked around, startled that she wasn't beside him. She stood a few feet back, at the turn into her family's drive, and he retraced his steps.

The moon illuminated the slight smile tugging at her lips. "Are you all right?"

He rubbed his jaw with the back of his hand. "Sure. Just thinking about…"

"Can I help?" she asked when he didn't complete his sentence. "Is it some girl?" A teasing tone lilted her voice.

He arced an eyebrow at her forward question.

She dipped her chin and peered up at him beneath her lashes. "You have the same baffled look my brothers get when they are seeing someone."

He shook his head. "No, it's nothing like that."

"Well, that's good." Her words startled him. And apparently her. Her eyes widened. "I, uh, mean…well…it's good that you aren't missing some girl from Ohio. That would be hard. For you. For her. For…you know."

The air around them crackled with tension. It made Samuel shift uncomfortably. He had the urge to change the topic again—for Naomi's sake, as well as his own. "Can I ask you a question?"

Her eyebrows rose this time. "Sure."

"You believe in evil, *ja*?"

Her chin jutted backward. "Yes."

"And man is inherently evil."

She nodded.

"But do you think it's possible for a man to do good?"

She weighed his questions carefully before speaking. "Yes, I do. Not of our own abilities, Samuel, but through God's grace. Through the good Lord's help, it is possible to do good. Yes, I believe that."

"And is living this way, in our own district, minding our business, keeping out of *English* ways, is that the best way?"

She tilted her head and studied him. Moonlight slanted across her cheek, illuminating her pale skin. "Not always, no. Does it surprise you I'd admit that?"

He felt his heart kicking his rib cage. "It does."

"Are you feeling a calling beyond home, Samuel?"

He released the breath he'd been holding. "I don't know."

"Evil isn't locked out of our district." She spoke each word carefully. "It lives in the heart of man, no matter if that is in the *English* world or Amish, *ja*? It is Christ who changes our hearts for good."

"But how do you think that change takes place? Do you think it's instantaneous?"

"I think it takes a lifetime of perfecting through our own trials and carrying the cross, like Christ. Take up your cross daily and follow me. *Ja*?"

He nodded.

"And what do you think your cross is, Samuel?"

She asked hard questions. He crossed his arms over his belly, but it hurt his arms. He felt a cramp in his bicep. "It's a cross I'm not sure I can carry."

She laid a hand on his arm and squeezed. "You are stronger than you think."

He wished he could believe that.

# CHAPTER TWENTY-SEVEN

I F ONE WANTED TO buy cheap land, this was the place. Brydon and his guards, riding in a U-Haul truck, hadn't passed a town or even a lonesome house in miles and miles. Grassy fields undulated outward from the two-lane road, which led nowhere. Or so it appeared. Kansas didn't seem to have much of a population. He spotted not even one cow or tornado.

The miles rolled along, the clicking of the tires, the hum of the engine, all while Brydon considered his two options: find out who wanted him and for what, or these three vamps—Kachada, Walden, and Lamandre—he'd have to kill.

The driver, Kachada, gave orders. He had coppery skin and long, black hair with a feather tied in it, a throwback to Cochise. Was he the new *Dances with Vampires*? Brydon had discovered that many vamps, in losing their normal lives, embraced their families' or make-believe ancestry. Lamandre, who looked like he'd embraced the rapping world of Snoop Dogg, sat beside him in the passenger seat. The third vamp, Walden, was in the enclosed part of the U-Haul truck, torturing their prisoner. Occasionally the back end lurched, and Brydon heard a wretched scream. Over the course of several hours, the cries had grown weaker.

Hunger gnawed at him. They had deprived Brydon of any blood, and he felt weak, which he assumed they wanted.

Ahead, as if sprouting out of nowhere, a large, flat building emerged, surrounded by several others. This one, lone road led toward the conglomeration, and they followed the long stretch of it. Brydon sensed their journey was coming to a quick end.

The compound sat all alone in the heart of a vast prairie, surrounded by a sixteen-foot chain-link fence with loops of wire along the top. Nothing seemed unusual about these buildings other than their very existence and the lack of windows.

"What is all of this?" Brydon asked, but as with every question he'd posed during their journey, he was once again ignored. He'd attempted to probe their minds but gave up after learning their names. The work was exhausting, and they were experts at hiding their thoughts.

They came to a halt at an impressive gate. A guard stepped up to the U-Haul truck. He wore a beige uniform but carried no weapon. He didn't need to. His black eyes told of his abilities. He looked straight at Kachada, then Brydon, and finally Lamandre. No words were needed. The guard gave a nod and the gate behind him slid sideways.

The U-Haul eased down the deserted pathways, moving at a slower pace. Did no one work here other than the guard? Or did they stay inside the buildings? Kachada needed no directions as he turned into a bare-bones parking lot, where a small assortment of vehicles of all makes and models were assembled.

Flinging his hair back off one shoulder, Kachada gave Brydon a hard, fierce look. "Don't attempt anything. There's no escape. You understand?"

"You mean from Shangri-La? Wouldn't think of it. Looks like a real happenin' place." Brydon added a heavy dose of sarcasm.

Without comment, the two vamps disembarked from the

truck. Lamandre waited for Brydon to follow. He stood so close that they bumped into each other.

"Really, dude," Brydon said, "give me some breathing room. Okay? I'm not going anywhere."

The black vamp stood his ground and scowled. Brydon ignored him and walked toward the back of the truck, where Kachada unlocked the latch.

Walden stuck his blond head out the opening. "Here already?" He sounded disappointed. Hopping out of the back, he yanked on a leather cord. "End of the road, *schatz*."

Attached to the end of the five-foot strip was a disheveled young woman. Her eyes were glazed, and she moved in a jerking fashion, as if she were barely conscious. When they'd found her, she'd reeked of living outdoors, and her stiff, filthy jeans and bulky sweater hid most of her waiflike body. She wore mismatched gloves, scarves, and a ragged coat. The leather strap chafed her neck raw.

She blinked slowly and raised a hand as if to shield her eyes from the sun's intensity, but she didn't have enough energy to lift her hand. She stumbled out of the opening.

The three amigos had snatched her and a friend in Topeka. The friend hadn't made it far. She'd been dinner, her remains left on a deserted roadway.

The woman whimpered. "Can we rest here?"

Kachada grasped the woman's chin and jerked her head sideways. He stared at the wound on her neck and snarled at Walden. Shoving her away, he slammed a hand against the tall blond's chest. "What were you thinking?"

"She was too feisty. I had to calm her down."

"She's a present," Kachada spoke in a chilling tone, his lips thinning.

Walden grinned. "I can attest to the fact that she's tasty."

Kachada pushed past Walden with a growling sound. "This way."

His stride stiff with confidence and irritation, Kachada led the way. His long black hair swayed behind him. They bypassed the outer buildings and a concrete slab where a multitude of eighteen-wheelers were parked. The compound was laid out in a methodical manner with several outbuildings surrounding an inner square, which protected one main building at its center. When they reached the most protected structure, cameras popped up in unexpected areas, aiming lenses at each door and walkway; most had motion sensors and followed their progress. The monitoring system appeared quite sophisticated.

"What kind of a place is this?" Brydon asked again.

"Store supplies." Walden treated the woman like a mangy mutt, jerking on her leash when she strayed off the path.

"Store?" Brydon asked. "What kind of store?"

The sound of a metal door behind them had Brydon looking around when someone hollered, "Hold up there!"

The one who called was slight of build and wore the same uniform as the gate guard. He carried no weapon either, but once he drew close, Brydon saw he had all the weapons he needed in his own fingertips and incisors.

"What's the problem?" Kachada puffed out his chest, exerting his own authority.

"Did you check in?" the thin vamp demanded.

"We've been under orders."

"*Everyone* must check in. You know the rules."

Kachada glowered at the intruding vamp but gave a jerking nod to his cohorts. Lamandre clasped Brydon's arm and turned him in the direction of another building. Brydon jerked his arm away and straightened the sleeve of his leather jacket.

No number or sign indicated which building was which or what the purpose was for any of them. All of the buildings were nondescript, appearing to be exact duplicates. Walden swiped a trickle of blood off the woman's neck and licked his finger. Feeling the gnawing hunger in his gut, Brydon breathed in the sweet scent of her blood, his nostrils flaring. He quickened his steps, inching closer to her. Her hair swung sideways, revealing a fist-sized bruise on the side of her face.

Before he could satisfy his own thirst, they entered the side of a warehouse. A pungent odor nearly knocked Brydon over. Death saturated the very air around them. His eyes adjusted quickly to the shadowy darkness. A dozen or more bodies dangled from the rafters, strung upside down on scaffolds, the heads removed. Beneath the bodies were drains set in the concrete where the blood could be washed away. But the stench of this place would never leave him.

The woman beside him bucked and began screaming. Walden backhanded her and she slammed into the floor, out cold. The ensuing silence filled the cavernous warehouse.

"Now you done it," Lamandre said, stepping over the unconscious woman. No one else paid any attention to her. Screams here were commonplace. With an irritated sigh, Walden lifted her over his shoulder and carried her toward a long table.

"Breakers," Walden explained with a sniff of disdain aimed at the bodies. "Vamps who broke the law."

"What law is that?" Brydon asked, more curious than scared, although he figured he might be dangling and headless soon enough.

"*Her* law," Kachada said. "There is no other."

If he had learned anything in the past nine months as a vampire, he'd learned vampires had their own rules and hierarchy. This was no democracy. The bloods respected strength, not weakness. Being dragged in here, he knew, looked pathetic. But he didn't have much of a choice. *Or did he?*

A cold stone settled in his gut. He wasn't sure why he had been summoned. If Jezebel wanted him destroyed, then her minions could have done so already. Or maybe she wanted to do it herself. What he'd done to tick her off, he had no idea.

At the end of the aisle, they reached a table where a child-sized vamp sat. She had straight black hair cut into sharp angles, but her cheeks were rosy, as if she'd just eaten, and her eyes glittered brightly. She opened a book and neatly printed each of their names along with the date. From a box, she pulled a plastic tag and each of the guards looped the attached cord around their necks and waited while Brydon did the same. Only a bar code went across the middle. Slowly, he slipped it over his head, and the tag slapped against his stomach. They did not give one to the unconscious woman.

The child slid a disdainful gaze over the unconscious woman. "You can't take her in looking like that." The younger vamp jerked her chin and two teenage boys, tall and wiry, hurried toward them. "Take her and get her readied."

The teenage boys carried the unconscious woman away.

Walden nudged Brydon's back. Through a side door, they were escorted into another building. A maze of shelves held thousands upon thousands of crates and boxes. Was this merchandise? Brydon read a few labels: fake blood, plastic mace, cobwebs, clown wigs, candy vampire teeth. Then Lamandre gave him a push, and they hurried through walkways wide enough for forklifts to navigate.

Flanked on either side by two of the black-clad thugs, Brydon walked through the well-organized horror warehouse,

passing other vamps going about their business without paying much attention to them. They reached the end of the
hall in front of a pair of doors that were heavy oak. Carved
into the corners of the doorframe were skulls. The wood
was streaked gray, giving it a sinister look. Along one panel,
someone had scratched "Save yourself!"

He suspected Jezebel was on the other side of the door,
waiting with his fate. But he had other plans.

# CHAPTER TWENTY-EIGHT

L ET'S GO OUTSIDE." NAOMI spoke calmly, although she felt exasperated. Taking Matt's hand, she led her five-year-old brother out of the kitchen. He'd come with her to Hannah and Levi's house for the day and had managed to up-turn a bowl of flour onto himself. She dusted off his shirt and pants while he wiggled and squirmed. Straightening, she planted her hands on her hips. "There now. You're a sight better."

He wrinkled up his nose and plopped down on the top step. "How long do I have to wait?"

"Until…" Her voice trailed off as her gaze latched on to Samuel. He walked out of the barn carrying a bucket. When he saw her, he waved and headed in their direction.

"Who's that?" Matt asked.

"Samuel Fisher, Levi's brother."

"Don't he live somewheres else?"

"Not now." She straightened her apron. "Good morning, Samuel."

He gave a nod of greeting.

"Have you met, Matthew?"

Samuel held out a hand, and the five-year-old stuck out his to shake the larger one. "Nice to know you, Matthew."

He shot an aggravated look at his big sister. "Everybody calls me Matt."

She pursed his lips. "He came to help me today."

"I see." Samuel grinned. "Were you helping grind flour?"

Naomi brushed her fingers over her young brother's hair. "He wanted to see what I was making and turned the bowl over."

"Why don't you let Matt help me?" Samuel asked. "Do you like chickens?"

Matt jumped to his feet. "Sure do."

"He likes to chase them," Naomi warned.

Samuel crossed his arms over his chest. "Do you like eggs, Matt?"

"Not so much."

"You like cake, don't you?"

"Yeah!"

"Me too. Peanut butter is my favorite. What's yours?"

"Lemon." Matt grinned. "With lots and lots of frosting."

"That does sound good." Samuel bent down to Matt, bracing his bandaged hands on his knees. "Did you know eggs are in cake?"

Matt's eyes widened.

"If you scare the chickens by chasing them, they won't lay eggs. Then no more lemon cake."

Nodding his understanding, Matt raised a finger and declared, "No more chasing chickens." His focus shifted to Samuel's bandages. "Did you fall off your scooter?"

Samuel laughed. "Not exactly."

"Did you need stitches?" Matt scratched his head. "My big brother got stitches. Busted his chin wide open. Blood everywheres. Papa took him to the clinic. They stitched him right up." He leaned closer to Samuel. "Do they have special needles for that?"

"Probably." Samuel held out the pail toward Matt. "Here, you can carry this."

Matt looped an arm through the handle. The pail clattered against his short legs.

"You sure you can carry that?" Naomi asked.

"I can do it." Matt waddled as he carried the pail toward the chicken coop.

Samuel stayed behind with Naomi. He grinned, and she felt her stomach flop over. "Don't worry," he said. "I'll take care of him."

"I'm not worried so much about Matt but you." She watched her little brother and laughed. "He can be a handful." Cupping her hand to her mouth, she called after Matt, "Mind Samuel now."

"We'll be fine." Samuel jogged toward Matthew. Turning, he offered her a wave and a shared smile. "He'll keep me in line, I'm sure." He ruffled the boy's blond hair. Man and boy walked side by side. Naomi overheard Samuel say, "If we give your sister some time, then we'll sneak in the kitchen and swipe some batter from that bowl."

Naomi returned to the house with a smile and a spring in her step.

# Chapter Twenty-Nine

B RYDON WAITED AT THE door, staring at the skull knob and waiting for it to turn. The young woman they'd brought to this freakish compound had been returned. She swayed unsteadily. The grime had been washed away, her hair brushed into long, dark strands, and new clothes provided. She looked paler, her skin pearlescent. Her eyes appeared vague and disconnected, as if she'd been placed in a trance or given a tranquilizer. Even though she wore a skimpy dress, revealing bony arms and legs, she no longer shivered. No longer screamed either.

For a brief moment, he wondered what her name was, why she'd been living on the street, what her hopes and dreams had once been. It was an odd thing for him to consider. It didn't matter. In a few minutes, whoever she was would no longer exist.

Her gaze sought out Brydon's. What was he supposed to do? He had his own problems. He was at their mercy. Even if he could do something, he wouldn't. Whatever heroic traits he'd once possessed had now vanished.

Brydon figured they were both on their way to their own executions, although he wasn't at all sure his would be quick or painless. He remembered the warehouse with the gutted, beheaded bodies dripping blood.

Now, the door opened, and through the opening Brydon

glimpsed what looked to be a cobweb-infested dungeon, except these decorations didn't come from a cardboard box. Spiders peered at him and skittered away from the intrusion of light. Torn and tattered purple velvet curtains hung from the vaulted ceiling. A rat's beady eyes glinted from a shadowy corner.

The homeless woman, who had been docile and unsteady, bolted. Kachada grabbed her. The scuffling and subduing gave Brydon his one chance. And he seized it.

With a bold kick against Kachada's groin and a hand chop to Walden's throat, Brydon lunged for Lamandre, seized his head, and yanked. Dark, tainted blood spewed. The body remained standing for a moment before collapsing. Walden bent double, gasping for air. But Kachada subdued the woman. Brydon tossed Lamandre's head toward Kachada. He hesitated but at the last second released the woman and caught the head.

The woman looked to Brydon as if he were her savior.

Wrong.

He grabbed her by the hair and dragged her behind him into the dark dungeon.

# CHAPTER THIRTY

AFTER A DAY OF hoeing a field at Levi's farm, then climbing ropes and throwing knives at Roc's school for crazy vampire hunters, Samuel hooked up with his old friends: David, Eliam, and Paul. They all had the same bowl-cut hairstyles. Both David and Paul wore traditional Amish trousers and plain, black work boots. David had shed his coat and rolled up the sleeves of his white store-bought shirt. Paul had untucked his shirt but still wore his suspenders. Eliam, however, was more the rebel, wearing faded jeans that looked torn and ragged but which had cost him a hefty sum. He'd doffed his Flo Rida T-shirt and showed them a cross tattooed on his bicep.

David leaned forward to get a better look, his eyes widening in the moonlight. "Your folks know about that?"

"Not yet."

Samuel had expected at least a nipple piercing from all the lead-up to the revelation. "You done anything really wild and crazy lately?"

Eliam laughed. "That not enough for you? What about you? What have you been doing in Ohio and since you got back?"

David grabbed the last biscuit from the bucket. "You waited long enough to say you were back."

If only his friends knew half of it. "Nah, nothing much. My life is boring."

"Eliam's gonna get a nose ring next," Paul said.

"Can't hide that from your mamm," David cautioned.

"My girlfriend has one through her belly button," Samuel admitted.

Paul shook his head. "Don't get it. Met a gal who had her tongue"—he stuck out his tongue—"pierced."

"You know what they say about that—"

Eliam punched Samuel in the arm, right on a ripe bruise, and interrupted him. "Your girlfriend, huh? Must not be Amish."

"Probably not my girlfriend anymore either. Can't say she was happy I was coming back to Promise."

"Maybe she should come"—Paul leaned an elbow on his knee, grinning and giving a knowing nod—"here."

"So she's *English,* huh?" David asked, missing the sexual reference. "She hot?"

"What do you think?" Eliam took a pull on his beer.

The field where a goodly amount of Amish teens hung out most nights was dark with only a smattering of stars overhead. Cars and buggies congregated around the truck, and teens meandered, some hooking up, others single. Somebody's radio blasted rap music. Booze, cigarettes, and weed were passed around.

Samuel leaned back against the tailgate of Eliam's truck. His head felt woozy from too much beer, his belly full of greasy fried chicken. The empty bucket lay on its side in the truck's bed.

Paul drew deeply on a brown cigarette and passed it on. His eyelids looked weighted. "Thinking"—his voice sounded tight—"I'll go see Sara Stutsman tonight."

"She wouldn't give you the time of day or night with you all stoked."

"You keep saying that about Sara." Eliam shook his head. "But you haven't done nothing about it."

"No use bothering now." David crushed a beer can beneath his shoe. "She's seeing Reuben Sommer."

Paul's eyes narrowed. "Since when?"

"Last Sunday's singing."

"Maybe you should think about Naomi Wagler." Eliam leaned back against a bag of feed. "She's awful pretty."

Samuel's muscles tensed.

Paul coughed. "You've got to be kidding."

"What's wrong with Naomi?" Samuel asked. She was pretty, sweet, attentive. If he weren't busy with all the chores at Levi's and training at Roc's and if he didn't have a relationship already with Andi, then it would be natural to be interested in her. But, of course, he wasn't.

"Oh, well, nothing." Paul grabbed another beer out of the cooler. "Nothing at all, if you're aiming to settle down and get married. She don't put out though."

"Is she seeing someone?" Samuel asked before he could stop himself.

"Doubt it." Paul eyed Samuel carefully. "She keeps to herself."

"Maybe she has standards," Samuel snapped.

"You high and mighty now too?" Eliam challenged.

"He's got that *English* girlfriend," Paul said, "remember?"

"Go back to your wet dream." Eliam reached for the weed.

"Why do you care about Naomi Leave-Me-Alone Wagler?" Paul asked, still staring at Samuel. "How many girlfriends can you handle at one time?"

"Oooh!" David laughed.

Samuel leaned sideways on a small stack of feed sacks. "She's a nice girl, is all."

Paul crossed his arms over his chest. "Uh-huh."

"What's wrong with—" Samuel's defensive question was interrupted by Eliam poking David with his boot.

Eliam laughed. "Think David's hiding something."

Paul pushed up with his elbow, which slipped, and he clunked his head on the side of the truck, which led to a round of rumbling laughter. When they'd all settled down again, Paul narrowed his gaze on David. "What? What are you hiding?"

"You seeing somebody?" Samuel asked, eager to turn their attention away from Naomi.

David flushed red.

"You are! Who is it?" Eliam heckled. "Does she give—"

David shoved Eliam.

He fell over laughing. "Oh, he'll never kiss and tell. He'll be married before he loses his virginity anyways."

"Not me." Paul hooked his thumbs in his waistband. "I'm doing exactly what you were with that *English* girl. What's her name anyway?"

"Doesn't matter." Samuel chugged the rest of his beer, trying to drown his past and the helpless feeling he got when he thought of Naomi.

# CHAPTER THIRTY-ONE

THE FLOOR WAS STREWN with body parts and dried blood. Brydon strode down the center of the vast room, dragging the nameless woman behind him.

The smell of fresh blood sent Brydon's pulse racing. His head felt woozy from hunger. Flies buzzed around a nearby corpse. Candles flickered ahead of him. Tarnished silver candelabras and dead roses surrounded a solitary casket. It sat on a dais. The wooden exterior was ornately carved and polished. The lid creaked open. The inside shimmered with inlaid mother-of-pearl and white satin. The candles' flames quivered with anticipation and dread.

Brydon strode straight for the casket even though he heard the fluttering of wings, stamp of feet, and gnashing of teeth, as bloods swarmed out of crevices and shadowy nooks and flooded through the doorway behind him.

A body emerged from the casket—a woman—sitting upright. She leveled a pair of heavily lashed black eyes on him. Arching her neck back, she rose out of the casket, arms outstretched as she descended slowly to the dais in front of the casket. She had long white-blond hair and, despite her small stature, had a commanding presence. With one finger raised, she silenced those crowding the hall.

Her beauty was exquisite, especially when she smiled. Which she did now—closed lips tugging to one side, as if intrigued and amused. Brydon summed up this blood. She was old, older than most here, certainly far older than he, and possibly many centuries. After all, she'd established this fortress and had a conclave of bloods to serve her. Her territory far outreached Giovanni's. Yet she had not aged since her awakening. But life for her, Brydon determined from keen observational skills, had become dull and uninteresting. Yet he'd managed to surprise her.

Steadily, he walked toward her. Her lips were the color of blood, which made her skin appear even paler and flawless. He flung the woman forward, and she slid across the floor until she lay sprawled and unmoving at the base of the platform.

"A present for me?" Jezebel asked, her tone amused. Her voice held the tiniest trace of an English accent, subtle and yet carrying an air of sophistication and superiority.

Brydon returned her reserved smile. "It can't be easy to find live bait way out here. Unless you dine on vermin."

"As much as I like it when dinner puts up a fight, I prefer fur not to fly." She folded her hands together. She had long, graceful fingers, giving her a delicate look, but he was not fooled. "So"—she assessed him with a long gaze—"you are Brydon."

He gave a slight bow out of respect. "And you are Jezebel."

"Have you heard of me?"

This one had an ego. "Hasn't everyone?"

"If they're wise." She drew a hand along the length of her hair. "And what have you heard about me?"

"It isn't for the faint of heart."

She laughed, apparently delighted. "Now that we have that straight, who's who, and such…." She tapped her long, slim index fingers against her lips. Her gaze slid over him, like a long caress. "And I have heard of you too."

He cocked an eyebrow at that.

"Not exactly how I imagined you, but still…" She elongated the last word as if tasting it like a fine wine.

It felt like she was dining on him, swallowing him with those luminous eyes. He cleared his throat, not wanting to consider if vampires were cannibalistic. "These fellows said you wanted to see me. All you had to do was ask."

"And what would your reply have been?"

"Curiosity. And"—he paused, stoking her curiosity—"an offer for dinner."

"A dinner date?" She laughed, a gleeful sound full of sinister undertones.

"A vamp like you should go out on the town. Or are you a homebody? In your"—he glanced at the cobwebs and shabby dwelling that appeared a remake of *The Addams Family*—"dungeon."

She tapped her index fingers against each other, and her mouth curled in that amused manner. "Do you like it? My little joke. I like to greet all new arrivals here. It's what many expect." Whatever hint of a smile there had been disappeared, replaced by a stony expression. "You killed one of my staff."

"Lamandre?" Brydon shrugged. "You will not miss him."

"And why is that?"

"He spoke of you in a dishonorable way. What was I to do? Allow such insolence?"

Her eyes narrowed to slits. *What could she say? Who would ever know the difference? Would someone defend Lamandre?* Doubtful. Brydon's defense of her honor provided a way of reaffirming her position. But he waited, unsure how she would react, unsure what Lamandre had really meant to her. Maybe he had been a lover, or maybe just a simple lackey sent to carry out her demands.

The moment stretched like the fragile thread of a spider's web. Finally, she said, "That is the price one pays for shame." The slightest head tilt signaled a blood hovering nearby. "Have Lamandre's body strung up, drained, and burned."

The servant bowed before disappearing behind a black velvet curtain.

"Now"—she focused on Brydon—"what shall I do with you? A renegade."

"I wasn't running from you."

"You ran, didn't you?"

"I was attacked. What did you want me to do? Submit?" He tsked. "Not my style. And I suspect it isn't yours either."

"I can see that's true." Again, her gaze trailed over him in an appreciative manner. "So what am I to do with you, Brydon Renegade?"

He gave her a cocky smile. "Anything you'd like."

# CHAPTER THIRTY-TWO

"WHY ARE WE HERE?" Jacob trailed behind in the shade of a live oak. The sidewalk had wide cracks and rifts. The houses crowded together in the little neighborhood as if unsure of themselves. A bold red flag flapped beside one front door, declaring the Buckeyes #1. "Samuel isn't here," Jacob complained. "How can I help him if—"

Remiel stopped abruptly.

Jacob swerved to keep from plowing into the arc of the angel's wing. He tracked Remiel's laser-like gaze to a young woman who climbed out of a miniature car. She dressed seductively in tight jeans and tighter T-shirt, which emphasized every asset.

"*At twilight,*" he whispered, the words coming back to him with a rush, "*as the day was fading, as the dark of night set in.*"

Remiel nodded with the cadence of the words from Proverbs. "*Then out came a woman to meet him…*"

Jacob knew her, knew women like her. She'd lured his brother away from his family and beliefs. Through tight lips, he continued, "*Dressed like a prostitute and with crafty intent. She is unruly and defiant; her feet never stay at home.*"

"*Now in the street—*"

"*Now in the squares, at every corner she lurks.*"

Samuel had sniffed after this woman, unable to control

himself. Sure, she'd helped him avoid the vampire, Brydon, but now she was simply trouble. A terrible trouble.

Jacob felt it, like a cloud blocking the sun, as a sense of darkness swept over the neighborhood. The air felt heavy and oppressive. He stuck close to Remiel as the powerful angel resumed his walk toward the unassuming house, where that girlfriend of Samuel's headed. All over the roof, dark creatures perched, their yellow eyes glowing, as if ready to leap on some unsuspecting human.

"I don't think this is a good idea." Jacob sidestepped one of the dark creatures, who leered at him and snarled.

"You have nothing to fear," Remiel stated, his tone firm.

Then why did it feel like he walked through the valley of the shadow of death?

The door opened, and more creatures spewed out of the house. A woman stood in the threshold with a bright smile and auburn hair the shade of Lucille Ball's once-famous locks. She looked to be in her late fifties, yet she dressed like she was sixteen. Her too-tight jeans pinched her middle and a roll of flesh lopped over the waistband. A cross and dove tattooed the crest of one plump breast. She wore a clump of crystals around her neck and silver rings on her fingers.

"Andi Mitchell? Come in, come in." The woman introduced herself as Philly. Philly Raven. A made-up name if Jacob ever heard one.

"Who is she?" he whispered to Remiel as if the two women could hear him.

"A medium."

Jacob sized her up. She looked petite. "Medium what?"

Remiel placed himself in the corner of the room and surveyed the area. "She sees into the spirit world."

That stopped Jacob. "Can she see us?"

Remiel remained silent.

The small room had a plaid sofa and two brown chairs on either side of a fireplace. Candles had been placed on every table, and the different scents of lavender, sage, and jasmine were heady and cloying. Tiny sticks stuck out of bottles and emitted exotic fragrances. A dusty bookshelf behind one of the chairs held books on chakra, yoga, eastern mysticism, palmistry, tarot, and the spirit realm.

Philly led Andi to a small table, holding on to her hand longer than necessary. "Oh my. You are so warm. And I can tell you are open to—" The woman stopped abruptly, her blue gaze shifting sideways away from Andi. *Was she seeing Remiel?* Her smile faltered, then regained strength. She stumbled into her seat on the other side of the table.

"You okay?" Andi asked.

"Of course." Philly found her smile again. "I won't waste your valuable time. *Tempest fugit.* Right-ee-o? We'll just get right down to it." She laid her palm open on the table. Andi placed her hand on top, but the medium cleared her throat.

"Oh, sorry." Andi pulled a stack of twenty-dollar bills out of her bag. Philly didn't bother counting the money but folded her hand closed and stuck the bills in her hip pocket. "Now, I prefer that you not tell me anything about yourself or what you're seeking." She spoke in a manner as if she'd said this same spiel a hundred times. "Just answer yes or no when I—" She stopped, looked over Andi's shoulder again, and sighed. "Apparently you brought someone with you. Well, he's right there behind you about to beat the band for my attention."

Jacob saw him, a dark creature across the room, mirroring Remiel's stance.

"Andi," Philly cleared her throat, "have you lost someone close to you recently?"

"No."

"A while ago?"

An indentation between Andi's brows deepened. "Well, could be—"

"No-no!" The medium held up a stout finger. "Don't tell me. Only yes or no."

"Uh, yeah." She shrugged one shoulder. "I guess."

Philly looked beyond Andi's right shoulder at the dark creature, who broke his stance and moved toward the women. "So who are you, huh?" The medium gave Andi a quick wink. "He's tall and not bad looking." She waggled her brows then frowned. "And he's clutching his throat."

The creature's distorted hands wrapped around his own throat. If Philly really saw the true nature of the beast, she would have run from the house and never stopped.

Instead, she calmly tapped the table. "Was this person who passed on…did he die from strangulation?"

Shock hit Andi's features from the tiniest detail of her eyes dilating to her skin blanching. She began to tremble all over.

"Are you all right?" Philly asked, her concern more smug than anything. "Did I say something—"

"M-my father," Andi stammered. "My father died."

"Really?" the medium seemed surprised and yet pleased with herself. "Your father was strangled?"

"He choked on some food and died when I was eight."

Remiel made a slight noise at the back of his throat. "She's not quite telling the whole story. Or maybe she doesn't know all of it."

His curiosity growing, Jacob asked, "What happened?"

"Her father, Bob Mitchell, was a drunk. Choked on his own vomit." Remiel's expression shifted into compassion.

Empathy filled Jacob. He'd had his own trials as a child

with a very strict father, and yet how much worse for this young girl? He wondered what he would tell Andi if he had the ability to speak to her. Would he tell her to run? Or would he simply encourage her to seek God? After all, hadn't he learned running never solved anything?

The creature, who had been choking itself, rushed forward and, with a burst of foul draft, disappeared. Jacob looked to Remiel, but the angel was stoic and reserved.

Philly leaned forward, confidence exuding from her. "Your father wants you to know he loves you. He's always loved you." Her forehead collapsed in rows of concern as she watched something from the great beyond. Her mouth gaped.

"What?" Philly asked of no one then shrugged. "I don't know if this will mean anything to you, Andi, but your father says"—she slowed her words to make them very clear—"do *not* go to Pennsylvania."

A glacial chill swept the room. Andi leaned back as if she'd been struck.

"Were you planning on going to Pennsylvania?" Philly asked.

"I have to go."

"Well, you heard him, or I did. Don't go. Not to Philadelphia…er, Pennsylvania…wherever."

Andi stumbled out of the house, her face pale, her steps unsteady. Remiel nodded for Jacob to follow.

"Now what? What was the point of that?" he asked the angel, not understanding why they were here or what they were doing. "Can we get back to Samuel *now*?"

But Remiel focused on the young woman sitting in her car, her hands clenching the steering wheel. Her lips thinned as she rolled them inward. "Not go to Pennsylvania?" she asked herself. "Is she crazy?" Andi shook her head, read-justed her hands on the wheel, tightening her grip. "I'm a fool for coming here. What did my old man ever do to help me? Why would I listen to him? Now or ever." She snorted and shoved the gearshift into place. "And I'm not about to start now."

# CHAPTER THIRTY-THREE

W HAT'S THE NIGHTMARE WE'RE walking into tonight?" Samuel flexed his hands, which no longer
required bandages, then shook loose his nerves. For over a
week, he'd participated in bizarre games, which had no actual rules, but where a combat of wit and strength mattered.
The last man standing seemed to win. But win what?

*And what was all this for? Training to fight some creatures
Samuel didn't even know if he believed existed? Some mystical force
of evil?* Maybe they were all mad and he was too for going
along with them.

"Hey, Samuel," Shawn greeted him, followed by a chorus
of other team members, who gathered in the meeting area. A
caffeinated aroma permeated the air.

Roc took his place in front of the white board. "I don't
want to spoil the surprise. We'll get started in five."

Everyone continued their private conversations, and Roberto
hooked an arm around Samuel's shoulders. "You okay?"

He would never voice his doubts to the others, who had
slowly begun to accept him, but in a low voice, he confided
to the priest, "What if I don't buy into all of this?"

Roberto's features turned solemn and thoughtful. "Why'd
you come then?"

"I don't know."

"Well, that's a start. It's those who think they know

everything that we can't work with." Roberto clapped Samuel on the shoulder. "Come on, we're going to go easy this evening."

They started with a few calisthenics followed by a light run. They finished with climbing the ropes to the rafters. Samuel, his hands still tender, was the first to descend.

Roc clapped him on the back. "Good going, Samuel."

"I don't get this." Shaking his stiff fingers and arms, he asked, "Do you usually have to climb a rope to reach a vampire?"

Joe's feet hit the floor next. "Vampires can change."

"Change?"

"Into birds or bats," Joe explained, his brown eyes glittered with golden specks, "and critters of all kinds."

"Interesting." Samuel rubbed his sore biceps. "So what's the point of this?"

"A vampire's strength is unmatched." Joe swung his arms, making his shoulder joints pop. "To even have a shot in battle, we must be in top physical shape."

"But that's only the beginning," Roc added. "You should stay late one night for one of our nightly runs."

Samuel swallowed. "Not sure I want to."

"If you want to be one of us, then it's a requirement."

Samuel laughed. "What do I get at the end? A certificate?"

Roc shook his head but he didn't laugh. "Help."

"What do you mean?"

"If you want to leave here and do battle, then you'll need help. And if you want help, then you have to pass our requirements." He looked at his watch. "Come on, time for Father Roberto's class on the proper way to gut a vampire."

"Couldn't we eat dinner first?" Samuel asked with a dying laugh.

# Chapter Thirty-Four

B RYDON WAS LED TO Jezebel's private quarters, which dispensed with the gothic horror décor and this time expressed a soft, turn-of-the-century romantic flair. A sitting area and library contained shelves filled with hardback books, all from previous centuries. A French door opened to a courtyard. Where the land surrounding this conglomeration of warehouses seemed lifeless and drab, this little respite had been transformed into a lush garden of pink and white roses and shade trees, which were just beginning to bud and leaf. Trellises bordering the bricked walls allowed English ivy and yellow jasmine to climb uninhibited. Cobblestones made a footpath toward a white-painted gazebo. Beneath its canopy sat a white wrought-iron table and chairs. There, Jezebel sipped from a dainty teacup. With a wistful smile, she greeted him and gestured to the empty chair across from her.

As he joined her, giving a slight, respective bow before sitting, his escort disappeared back inside the warehouse. No other door led to the courtyard. No window looked out upon it. But above, on the flat warehouse roofs, guards paced the lengths of the buildings. He was being watched and monitored. But then, so was Jezebel.

Brydon waited for her to speak first, but she seemed content to enjoy the slight breeze against her face. With her eyes closed and chin slightly tilted upward, she looked young and carefree. But the silence made him anxious. "Quite a place you have here."

"Does that mean you like it?" She opened her eyes and the blackness engulfed him. "Or are you just being polite?"

"Let's say this place is full of surprises." His gaze flickered upward toward the guards. "You've taken great care at security."

"One can never take too many precautions."

"And from whom are you hiding? Other vamps? Or vampire hunters?"

"Hunters? Please." She gave a slight sneer as if she never even gave humans a thought. "But there are those like you and me, who would overthrow me in a heartbeat." She poured blood from a teapot. "I've heard you know something of defensive measures. Is this correct?"

"A little." He took the cup she offered. Since his first encounter with her in the dungeon, he'd been fed regularly while he waited for her to see him again. "I was a police officer—in my former life. Is that why you wanted to see me?"

She nudged a delicate bowl in his direction. "Sugar?"

He leaned back, holding the warm cup between his hands. The temperature was a perfect ninety-eight degrees.

She appraised him thoughtfully. "And do you miss your former life?"

"I use the knowledge I acquired daily."

She smiled, a tolerant expression that never reached those penetrating eyes. He felt her attempts to probe his thoughts, and he resisted. "That doesn't answer my question."

He set the cup on the table, revealing his self-control. If he was going to get anywhere, then he'd have to play her game. Or at least pretend. "Do you miss your old life?"

She looked skyward. "I barely remember. It was so"—she twirled her wrist—"long ago."

"What did you do?"

"Do?" She laughed. "Women had nothing to do. No way to make a living. No way to survive on their own. So what I do remember, I'd rather forget. It was not an easy life. This one is much better." She sipped her drink, enjoying it. "I have choices now. I've established a place for myself. I've accomplished more than I ever could have."

The lush trees and blooming plants made him think of the Deep South, the place of his birth, during a gentler time. "You have indeed."

"Many covet my place here. My power. They would overthrow me if they could." She was testing him.

"And do what?"

She lifted one eyebrow as if there was only one answer. "And rule."

"Seems to me vampires make their own rules. Do you worry about those who serve you here?"

"No." Her reaction was quick, almost too quick.

"Why? What is your hold on them?"

"Now, why would I tell you that? I like to keep my secrets secret. Isn't that the point?" She gave a sly smile. "But all these bloods, I created. For life, they vowed their loyalty. And they know the consequences of infidelity. There are, of course, renegades." She tilted her head, shaded the blackness of her eyes with long lashes. *Was she wondering if he was a rebel to be squashed?* "But insurgents often die."

He remembered the hanging bodies in the first warehouse. A bleak reminder to any vamp. "So I've seen."

"Yes, you have." She steepled her fingers beneath her chin. "You were with Giovanni when he was destroyed. Is this true?"

"Not exactly."

Both of her eyebrows shot upward. "But I thought—"

"I wasn't there. But I do not doubt that he was destroyed. Or the other vamp with him, Akiva."

"Why do you say that?"

"Because I know who they were up against."

The skin at the corners of her eyes looked pinched with strain. "Who?"

"Someone…not another vamp…but someone *you* should be worried about."

She waited.

But he wasn't quite ready to reveal all he knew. First, he wanted something from her. He stood and walked the perimeter of the gazebo, surveying the intricately carved woodwork. "Do you ever feel trapped here? In this little fortress you have created? Unable to venture out into the world?"

She lifted her chin in defiance. "I choose to be here."

Fear clearly ruled her heart. And he could use that against her. She thought she could control things and therefore manage her fear, but she was wrong. He faced her again. "You would be safe with me."

She simply watched him with those heavy-lidded eyes.

"If you chose," he emphasized the word she had utilized, "to venture beyond these ivy-coated walls"—he leaned casually against a wooden post—"I could show you a good time. Elsewhere."

"Where?"

"Wherever you wanted to go."

She leaned one elbow on the armrest of her chair and propped her chin on her hand. Her eyelids drooped seductively. "And where did you have in mind?"

"We can discuss that later." His gaze traveled up to where

four guards protected the sanctity of her courtyard. "In a more private setting. When we are truly alone."

She stood and moved toward him, not fully approaching. She leaned against the opposite post. "You speak quite scandalously."

"Do I?" He knew this was the moment. "I'd like to propose an alliance."

She stiffened slightly.

He was taking a huge risk. "There is a vampire hunter. One you should fear."

She rolled her eyes and looked away, disinterested. "There always have been those who believe they can destroy us. But they are mistaken. Fools."

"Are you so sure?" He injected doubt into her overblown confidence.

"Why should this particular one concern me?"

"Because he's building a force. A force of vampire hunters."

Her reaction to the news was nonexistent, as not one muscle moved, yet she gave him her full attention. "Go on."

"They're not sniveling individuals who would be inconsequential. They are organizing and planning a full-out assault."

"And you know this how?"

"Because I know the vampire hunter. From my previous life. He too was a police officer. And I know his abilities. I know his determination. I know what drives him."

"And why should I be afraid of such a man?" Her condescending tone had a frosty irreverence. "What do we have to fear from a mere man?"

"Because Roc Girouard killed Giovanni and another vampire, Akiva. He would have killed me if I hadn't escaped. And who knows how many others he has killed in his quest to avenge his wife's death? He will not stop until he is dead."

"That can be easily rectified." She blinked slowly. "Well, now"—Jezebel rested her chin on the tops of her fingertips—"I am intrigued. Your passion is compelling." Her dark eyes gleamed. "Most compelling." Her tongue curled to touch her upper lip, then she pressed her lips together. "Most vampires bore me. But you"—her gaze bit into Brydon as if she'd sunk her teeth into his neck and savored the taste of him—"you're interesting. And mortals"—she examined one of her nails—"mean nothing to me. But this Roc sounds like an amusing challenge."

Brydon would have bet a vat of blood that Jezebel hadn't been challenged in a long while.

The corner of her mouth tipped into a half smile. "It might be entertaining to toy with him, to see if we can make a rock bleed."

She gave two quick claps of her hands, and a vampire rushed out of the French door toward the gazebo. This vamp was Jezebel's opposite, tall and majestic with thick brown hair and a voluptuous build. She gave a slight bow toward Jezebel. "Madam?"

"See that Brydon receives all he needs in reinforcements and help." She leveled her gaze back on him. "Bring me this vampire hunter."

He straightened. "Of course."

"Alive. He must be alive. They're much more pleasurable that way."

He bowed again, ready to leave the premises, escaping with his life—at least temporarily.

"And Brydon?" she asked.

He stopped at the bottom of the steps and faced her.

"That outing with just you and me that you had in mind?"

"Yes?"

"When you return."

He gave another slight bow, and a full smile emerged. "I look forward to it."

Turning on his heel, Brydon walked out of the courtyard, realizing he was lucky to still draw a breath.

# CHAPTER THIRTY-FIVE

S NEAKING OUT WAS NOT as difficult as sneaking in, which was why Samuel took extra caution as he approached Levi and Hannah's house.

The dark sky was clear, bright with stars and a smiling moon. Samuel parked his motorcycle near the barn. Gentle stirrings of sleepy animals gave the impression all was well. No lights shone in the house or around the green shades covering the windows.

Entering through the kitchen's side door, he removed his jacket and placed it on a wall hook. He sniffed, detecting if there was any of those fried pies still around. The scent of grease, butter, and warm peaches lingered. As his eyes adjusted to the dark kitchen, he searched the counters and found a plate covered by a cloth. Beneath, a handful of peach pies hid.

"Hungry?" the voice came out of the dark behind him.

Samuel dropped the pie, grabbed the stake from his belt, and swung around. The speed of his move would have impressed Roberto. He blinked at the shape.

"I won't stand between you and a fried pie." A bubble of laughter infused Naomi's voice. "I promise."

"Oh. Uh." He straightened, dropping his hand and the stake to his side and maneuvering it behind his back. "Sorry. You, uh, startled me."

"I should be the one to apologize." Her voice remained light as a feathery touch.

"You're here late again."

"Gabriel. He was fussy."

"I can take you home." He moved toward the door, but realized she wasn't following. "What's wrong?"

"I'm not in a hurry."

*What did she mean? Did she want to talk?* If she had been *English*, then he might have thought she was implying something untoward. But Naomi wasn't like that.

"Go ahead," she said, "and have a pie or two. Would you like some milk to go with them?"

He laughed, but abruptly stopped, glancing in the direction of Levi and Hannah's room. The laughter acted like a pressure valve, releasing the sudden tightness in his abdomen. "Let's sit outside. I'll grab the pies."

"And I'll get the milk."

A few minutes later, they settled on the back steps, a plate of pies between them, along with two glasses of cold milk. The night air felt warm, and a delicate breeze ruffled the wisps of hair dancing free around Naomi's face. She was a pretty girl, sweet and guileless, and he felt somewhat protective of her, especially in light of the earlier conversation with his friends.

Naomi would have been mortified if she'd known how his friends had spoken about her the other night. Yet, he'd been inexplicably relieved to find out she wasn't seeing anyone. There were girls one ran around with, and then there were girls only meant for marriage. In Ohio, Samuel had experienced much with Andi. But returning to Pennsylvania, he found he was already starting to take life more seriously. Roc had asked him once if he intended to marry Andi, but he hadn't been thinking of marriage when he was with her.

He'd been thinking of fun. Now he realized how different their lives were. He'd been foolish or hardheaded to believe there was any future for them.

But he couldn't imagine what his own future would be anymore. Would he get baptized, marry an Amish girl, raise a family, and farm or woodwork, like Levi? Or would he derail his parents' plans for his life and strike out on his own? Or even help Roc? After all, he understood things his family and friends couldn't. If he embraced the Amish life, would he be turning his back on Jacob's memory? But how could he forget what Roberto and Roc had been teaching him about the threats of this world? Could he bury his head the way his father had? Or could he live, one foot squarely planted in two separate worlds, the way Levi did?

"Don't you want a pie?" Naomi asked, her voice as soft as the breeze.

"Oh, yeah. Thanks." He bit into a flaky outer shell and gooey, sugary inside. "Did you make them?"

She nodded.

"Delicious," he mumbled around another bite.

She nibbled at a pie, laughing lightly when some of the insides oozed out onto her chin and she had to wipe it away with her thumb. But he wasn't smiling. He felt a tension inside him, as if he was being pulled in too many ways.

"Have you seen Paul, Eliam, and David since your return?" she asked.

He picked a chunk of crust off the pie and popped it in his mouth. "We got together the other night."

"Good." She refrained from asking any more questions. Maybe she suspected them of the drinking and smoking they did and didn't want to know about it. Worse, maybe she didn't care. "You seem troubled, Samuel."

He tried to focus on the pie but his thoughts spiraled downward again. *How could he explain what he was thinking and feeling when he didn't fully understand it all himself?*

"Is there something I can do to help?"

He shook his head and chewed. *What would he tell her? How could she help?*

"I understand," she said, "if you don't want to discuss personal issues. But I will be praying for you."

*Praying for him? Praying what?* It was the Amish way not to pry and he appreciated her concern, her respectful boundaries, and even her prayers. Maybe he needed those more than anything. He remembered Andi's solution when he'd been "in one of his moods" as she'd called it. She'd snuggled close to him, twisting a finger into his chest hair. "Come on," she'd cajoled. "Tell me what's bothering you." And her playful toying had eventually become a distraction. It had always left him feeling misunderstood, as if she didn't really want to know what he was thinking but only wanted his undivided attention. In contrast, Naomi remained respectfully silent, never intruding into his thoughts or trying to pull him out of his mood. He couldn't decide which approach or woman he preferred.

He finished the pie and brushed his hands off on his trousers, pressing his palms along the tops of his thighs. "I'm trying to figure out—" He stopped himself, but he wasn't sure why. Something about Naomi made him confide, "I don't know…where I'm going…what I'm doing here."

She sipped her milk before replying. "It's not easy to know God's plan sometimes."

Guilt punched him in the stomach. He hadn't consulted God at all. Shame washed over him and made his throat tight. He gulped half the glass of milk and released a pent-up breath. "You know Rachel, Hannah's sister, right?"

"Of course."

"She's being shunned," he supplied in case she didn't know. She nodded but didn't speak.

"Do you think it was wrong of her to marry an *Englisher?*" he asked.

She finished swallowing and set the rest of the peach pie on the plate. "I don't know. It isn't for me to say anyway. It's between Rachel and God, I expect."

"That's not what the elders say."

"I'm not an elder." She reached for her pie again just as he reached for another one, and their hands brushed. She pulled back first. "I'm sorry."

"No, go ahead."

She cradled the pie in her hands. "It's hard to understand someone without walking in their shoes. Have you heard that saying?"

He'd heard a lot of handy platitudes from his mother through the years.

Naomi brushed a crumb off her lap. "Rachel is a young widow with a baby. It would not be an easy situation for anyone. Of course, family and neighbors would help her, but she had a second chance at love. Why wouldn't she take it?"

In that moment, Samuel glimpsed a part of Naomi's soul. She was a dreamer, a romantic. It wasn't a trait that was encouraged in the Amish community. Yet, maybe that characteristic gave her empathy for Rachel. For some reason, understanding that quality about Naomi made him nervous.

A vibration hit his pocket. His cell phone. *Not now. Come on!*

"I know what others are saying," Naomi distracted him, "but I don't hold with gossip. There were plenty of young men in the district who would have married Rachel. Even with all the stories going around."

"Stories?" Samuel asked.

She shook her head. "I tried not to listen to such things. But Rachel loved Roc Girouard, and…"

She hesitated, and he suspected her reason, which wasn't a particularly Amish view. Amish men and women married for love, but it was a love based on faith, understanding, friendship, and vows that were irrevocable and indivisible. But she hinted at a kind of love that swept you up and away, carrying you on a current that drowned reason and sometimes even faith.

"Go ahead," he encouraged her.

"Well," she picked at the flaking crust on her pie. "She loved Josef. *Ja?* I don't think anyone doubts that." This time when Naomi spoke, her words were measured, not rushed with nervousness, but as if she'd given this particular topic careful consideration. "Obviously, Rachel knows more about marriage than I do, and maybe she knew she could never marry someone she didn't love. I don't know." She shrugged her shoulders. "It's probably silly, me rationalizing her thoughts and feelings, pretending to know when I don't. I haven't even spoken to her, so I'm not divulging any secrets. But she's been through a lot. Why should we make that worse now by judging her?"

Her gaze bumped into Samuel's, and he saw tears making the blue in her eyes as deep as the ocean.

"You have a good heart, Naomi."

"I don't know about that." She averted her gaze. "We are all easily deceived, are we not?"

"*Ja.*"

"So"—she looked up at the thin smiling curve of the moon—"you said you were thinking about your life, of where to go, what to do. Are you thinking of leaving your family and district? Or is it more than that?" Her gaze shifted to him. "Are you considering entering the *English* world altogether?"

He released a breath, as if a rush of indecision and uncertainty poured out of his heart. "I don't know. Really, I don't. Before…in Ohio, I was just living day to day. Not thinking about the future other than—" He broke off, not wanting to describe the anger and resentment which had pushed him. He picked at the fried pie until gooey filling leaked out of a tiny hole in the side and he sucked at the sweetness. "But now, I see how happy Levi and Hannah are. How blessed they are with their boys. And yet, Roc and Rachel, they are happy too. And also blessed." His gaze sought hers. "Would you ever consider leaving your family…friends…all you've ever known?"

She breathed several slow breaths. Most Amish would deny quickly any possibility of leaving the district. But he appreciated Naomi thinking it through, taking his question seriously. Finally, she raised her chin and spoke out into the night, as if a prayer. "If God wanted me to do so, then yes…yes, I would."

"What about"—again, he pick at the fried pie and kept his gaze off her as if he wouldn't reveal too much of himself—"marrying a guy like…I don't know, someone on the wild side like"—*Me.* But he didn't say that aloud—"like that Roc Girouard?"

"Since you're not asking me…" she teased but grew serious. She did not full out laugh at his question either. She placed a hand on his forearm, her touch light yet steady. "If it was God's will."

He felt a jolt through his whole body. He wondered if she felt it too, because she pulled her hand away.

"Do you remember the story from the Old Testament," she asked, "the prophet, Hosea, who married Gomer?"

"*Ja*. She was a prostitute."

"His people believed he had acted foolishly I imagine, and yet he knew it was God's will." She flushed. "Did I surprise you?"

"Only with your understanding biblical matters."

"Oh well. I'm quite the scholar." She laughed.

But he didn't. Naomi was wise, and he was impressed.

She raised a finger and announced, "Do not mistake temptation for opportunity."

Samuel cocked an eyebrow. "That some saying or Bible verse?"

Her lips tugged sideways into a secretive smile. "A saying I read from a fortune cookie."

He burst out laughing, and she joined in with him. When she threw a glance over her shoulder at the house, he quieted. Their gazes met and locked. Again, he felt a shimmy of desire rocket through him.

She looked away first. "Sometimes, Samuel"—her tone was solemn again—"it's difficult and painful in obeying God while not listening to those around us. I do believe God places people in our lives to exhort us and also correct us. But at times, God's will makes no sense to any of us here on earth. But we are not to make sense of it. We are simply to follow."

"What if you don't know where He's leading?"

"He doesn't ask you to plan the route or mark the destination on a map. He only asks you to take one step at a time." She leaned forward, resting her elbows on her knees. "What step is He asking you to take?"

"A difficult one." Uncomfortable revealing too much, he dropped the rest of his uneaten pie back on the plate and dusted his hands on his trousers. There were a lot of things he didn't understand, but one thing he was certain of: he liked Naomi Wagler. More than he should. And that was not good—not for her.

He leaned toward her, peered deeply into her eyes. She looked troubled. In the pale moonlight, he detected a warming of her cheeks and felt heat burrow in his gut. "Are you all right?"

Her gaze dropped to his mouth, then sprung back. "Yes. Of course."

"Naomi"—he touched her shoulder lightly, felt the hum of anticipation between them, and turned her to face him— "are you seeing anyone?"

She squared her body toward his. "No, Samuel."

He swallowed any reservations he had and leaned even closer. He focused on her full lower lip, which she dabbed at with her tongue nervously. "I would like to see you more."

"More?" she whispered, her mouth angling toward his.

A snap of a twig made them both freeze. Samuel braced a hand against her shoulder and met her surprised gaze. "Don't move."

She gave the tiniest nod, and Samuel wheeled about, rising to his feet in a low crouch. He'd left his stake, his only weapon, inside. *What a fool he was.* Every muscle tensed, ready for action. He would fight to keep Naomi safe. No matter the cost—even if it was his life.

"Aren't you going to kiss the girl?" a voice came out of the dark.

Samuel recognized the voice as Joe's. He straightened. "What are you doing here?"

"We'll wait," came another voice, this time Chris spoke from behind a tree, his blond hair showing in the moonlight.

"It was Harry who gave us away," complained Pete.

"Samuel?" Naomi asked from behind him, her voice tremulous. "What's going on?"

"A little shenanigan, I'm afraid." Samuel straightened and descended the two steps. Turning in a circle, he said, "What are you all doing here?"

"The five-minute rule," Joe replied. "Answer our text next time."

"Okay, well, you've had your little fun. Go on now." He held out a hand to Naomi. "I should be getting you home."

"Ah, come on and kiss the girl first." Pete chuckled.

Naomi picked up the plate of fried pies. "I'll take these inside."

Samuel sent a scowl to those hidden around him. "You can go away now."

"I think he needs help," Joe said, humor lacing his deep voice. "Want me to show you how to kiss a girl?"

"I can manage fine."

"So that was your intention, eh?" Harry had the last laugh.

Samuel glared at the team.

---

The early spring night had turned chilly, but Naomi had no doubt she'd stay warm. Her heart still beat lickety-split as it had when Samuel almost kissed her.

She stepped out onto the porch, eyeing the shadows and darkness. "Did your friends leave?"

Samuel waited for her at the bottom of the steps. "Yes."

She smiled to herself and felt a glowing warmth deep inside. She headed toward the road, but he angled away from her and stopped.

"We don't have to walk," he offered, gesturing toward his motorbike near the shagbark tree. It made her stomach tangle into knots. Or was riding with him, her body nestled against his, what made her nervous?

"I prefer to keep my two feet on solid ground if you don't mind."

He laughed but not in a condescending way. He didn't argue with her or even hesitate before he redirected his footsteps. Together, they walked toward the road at the end of Levi and Hannah's drive. It was about a mile to her parents' farm.

"What was all of that about?" she asked. "Who were those men?" She hadn't recognized their voices. They certainly hadn't sounded Amish or spoken Pennsylvania Dutch. Samuel's reactions had not exactly been friendly. "You looked like you were ready to fight them."

"Not them."

"Then who?"

"It doesn't matter." He turned and walked backward, making full eye contact with her. "But I would have defended you. Do you know that?"

"From what?" She blinked, not understanding. She wished she could recapture the moment they'd shared together, but it seemed to have evaporated. She wrapped her arms across her middle against the cool night air.

"Are you cold?" Samuel asked.

The deepness of his tone rattled something inside her. She picked up the pace. "I'm fine. A brisk walk will set me right."

He shrugged out of his coat and laid it over her shoulders. "Here. This will help."

His warmth embraced her and yet made her insides quiver uncertainly. Her feelings toward Samuel baffled her. He seemed both Amish and *English*, which both intrigued and frightened her.

When she was younger, she had been drawn to him. She'd sympathized with the trouble he'd experienced in his family and wept for him and his family when his older brother Jacob died. Her oldest sister had been rebellious at one time, and her family had prayed for her over several tumultuous years until Lizzie had returned to the fold. It had been a day of rejoicing for her family, and yet Naomi had understood how close they had come to losing her, especially as the Fishers experienced such a terrible loss. Now, the Fishers were scattered between Ohio and Pennsylvania with Samuel not knowing where he belonged, even planting a foot in both Amish and *English* worlds. "You are different, Samuel."

"How so?"

"You don't always act Amish."

He released a breath. "I don't want to *act* any certain way. At one time, my life seemed laid out…almost easy. But things happened and changed me. I can't explain…"

"You don't have to."

His hand brushed hers, and he linked his little finger with hers. "One thing you should know, Naomi, I've learned some things are worth fighting for. Not very Amish of me, I reckon. Maybe if we'd fought for Jacob he'd still be here."

He wasn't speaking from pride or bitterness but from deep conviction. Even though she should have been, in many ways, shocked by his statement, she wasn't. In fact, his revelation moved her deeply. Awareness of the delicate link between them made her nervous. She'd never kissed a man, never felt this way about one either. It made her want to both run away and stay at the same time. She hoped she had the courage to stay.

Silence stretched between them and unnerved her. *What was Samuel thinking…or wanting?* She attempted to draw him into conversation with, "It's a nice evening."

Samuel studied the night sky. "A storm is coming."

A gauzy swath of clouds hovered in the endless sky, but they appeared harmless. Still, she felt a similar turbulence inside her. "Maybe we should have taken your motorbike. I was being selfish. Do you want to go back?"

"I've walked in the rain before. I don't usually melt."

She smiled shyly. "Me either."

A soft spring breeze accompanied them, along with the sound of a bullfrog. She felt a surprising sense of peace and was grateful she didn't feel as if she had to say something just to fill up the emptiness. Young men often made her nervous and also seemed ill at ease. But Samuel seemed different. Even though he had confessed he wasn't sure about his future—and who really could be?—he had a self-assuredness and confidence that belied his years.

"Sunday services are this week," he said.

"Yes. Are you going?"

"It's been a long time since I was here in the district."

"I'm sure you would be welcome." She offered him a reassuring smile. There had been much talk after Jacob's death, especially after the Fisher family up and moved so quickly. Samuel returning to Promise had stirred up some of that idle talk, which she hoped he hadn't heard. "Many in the district will be happy to see you again."

He walked several steps before asking, "What about Sunday singing? Will there be any?"

"There always is." Her insides jumped with enthusiasm.

"What if I asked you to go with me?"

Her cheeks grew warm, and she was grateful for the darkness. "Are you?"

"Yes." He took hold of her whole hand. "Do you mind?"

Even as her skin burned, her gaze remained steady, not

looking away, not searching for an excuse. "I'd like that, Samuel." She savored the taste of his name. "*Danke*."

He gave a succinct nod of agreement. A smile bloomed inside her. It was the Amish way, not to court with fanfare but quietly, and yet she wished everyone in Promise knew that Samuel Fisher was courting her. *Her!* Plain ol' Naomi Wagler. Naomi and Samuel. Words spun around her head along with all the possibilities this could bring. She felt like she might burst with happiness.

They reached the drive leading to her parents when a light drizzle began. The rain felt cool and refreshing. Neither of them hurried their steps. It felt as if they both wanted to draw out this moment together. But they eventually reached her parents' two-story home, the windows dark, the side door unlocked, as usual.

"Naomi"—Samuel came to a stop and captured her elbow in his light grasp—"about earlier…when we were interrupted—"

"It's all right."

"I hope you weren't frightened."

"Not with you there." Her heart pounded at his touch and concern.

He took a step toward her. The drizzle continued, and his shirt looked damp and clung to his skin. Inside his coat, she felt protected. Still, he didn't rush and neither of them moved. A fluttering erupted in her stomach. A surge of blood rushed to her head. She felt off kilter. But Samuel's hand steadied her. He cupped her jaw, tilted her chin toward him, and his mouth closed slowly, sweetly, delicately on hers.

The kiss was unhurried. They stood inches apart yet deeply connected. She felt drawn to him in ways she could not understand. She never wanted the moment to end, but it did.

When he pulled away, his breath still warm on her mouth, her heart throbbing, he touched her bottom lip and a half smile curled his.

"I'll see you tomorrow." He backed away, releasing her. She shrugged out of his coat and handed it to him. As she turned for the house, she felt a lightness to her step, and she had to restrain herself from skipping, running, exulting.

When she crawled into bed several minutes later, she took her notebook, pen in hand, and began to write, the words flowing from her like water along a brook.

# CHAPTER THIRTY-SIX

Silent, Jacob stood, arms crossed over his chest, and watched Samuel. "I don't like it."

"You don't like anything." Remiel sharpened his giant sword.

Jacob shook his head at his younger brother, who was pining over some young woman. Even though she was Amish, and probably better for him than that loose woman, the situation concerned him. "He needs to focus. He needs to—"

"And what were you doing at his age?"

A frown formed on Jacob's brow along with a knot in his stomach. "Much as he is…searching…chasing after women."

"It's what young men do." Remiel slid a stone along the sleek blade, and it made a grating sound. "Since the beginning."

"As in…*In the beginning*?"

"What else?"

Jacob watched Samuel, who stared up at a light-shrouded window. "Hasn't gotten us very far, has it? Look where it took me."

"Not every young man ends up the way you did, Jacob."

"But he's playing with fire. If he's going to fight Brydon, then he has to focus. Or get burned. This isn't some little game. Brydon isn't coming here just for Roc. He's coming here to take out his revenge on me. Against my family."

"Why don't you tell your brother?"

"If I could!" Jacob's voice rang out and yet couldn't cross

the invisible barricade between this side of life and where his brother lived.

Remiel focused on his blade. "Don't complain to me."

"Am I supposed to pray now?"

"You can. But not to me."

"And will prayers help? Will God call down ten thousand angels on my behalf?"

"I don't know."

Exasperated, Jacob asked, "What do you know?"

Remiel stroked the sword, honing the blade, polishing the steel. "*Though I speak with tongues of men and of angels, and have not charity, I am become as sounding brass, or a tinkling cymbal.*"

*What but love had brought him here?* Jacob shoved his fingers through his hair. *How was he to get through to Samuel? How?* Stalking toward his younger brother, he inched close to him and whispered, "Samuel."

His brother's chin jerked up and he looked over his shoulder. After a moment, he shook his head and turned away from the darkened house, walking back toward the narrow-lane road.

"Did he hear me?" Jacob asked. "Do you think—"

"Are you talking to me?" Remiel asked.

Shooting the angel a disgruntled look, Jacob caught up with Samuel, walked alongside him. "Samuel," he whispered, "what are you doing? Roc needs you. Focus on your training."

His brother rubbed at his shoulder, rolling it forward as if testing it for soreness. He was damp from the light drizzle. Tilting his head to one side, then the other, he began to jog in a steady rhythm.

"That's it." Jacob kept pace and urged him on. "You need

to train. You must train. You have to be strong. It's the only way."

*But was his brother really listening?*

# CHAPTER THIRTY-SEVEN

Y OU MUST BE FEELING better," Samuel said at the sight of Levi coming into the barn.

"Stronger, *ja*." Levi started to lift a pail of feed but pressed his arm against his rib cage in obvious pain.

Samuel took the pail. "But not well yet."

"*The way of the slothful man is as an hedge of thorns: but the way of the righteous is made plain.*"

Samuel grinned. "I've heard Mamm say that a thousand times in my lifetime, but I don't think she would call you lazy for resting when you're injured."

"I'm better."

Samuel carried the pail into the second stall and set it down. The gelding clopped over to his feed and stuck his nose in the bucket and began chomping on the grains. "So are you telling me its time for me to go?"

"Go?" Levi's brow knotted.

"Hannah told me the bishop came to see you last night. I don't want to cause you trouble, Levi."

"I'm glad to have you here, Samuel. I'm grateful for your help. You can stay as long as you like." Levi placed a hand on Samuel's shoulder. "You and I were separated for several years. Sometimes I wonder if it was a mistake that I didn't go with all of you to Ohio."

"And yet, what would have happened here if you had?" Samuel asked.

Levi studied the ground at his feet. "You've been learning much over at Roc's."

"Is that bad?"

"Regrettable—and also necessary. I'm glad there are no longer secrets between us."

"Me too."

Levi drew a deep breath, wincing only slightly as his chest expanded. "With that knowledge comes responsibility. You will have to make a decision. If you want to live like our father...or like me...or even—"

"Like Roc," Samuel supplied, knowing his brother spoke the truth.

The words hung between them like an anchoring weight.

"What about the bishop?" Samuel asked. "What did he want?"

"It's not your concern. It is in the good Lord's hands."

# Chapter Thirty-Eight

Samuel stepped out of the communal shower at the training center, toweled off, and hurriedly dressed. He wanted to get back to Levi's before Naomi headed home for the night. Half hopping and half walking, he yanked on his boots, moving through the bath facilities toward the door. He was midway through the sleeping quarters when he realized something was amiss.

It was quiet—too quiet.

His eyes strained to peer through the darkness into the bunks. But his eyes hadn't adjusted yet. Cautiously moving forward, he bumped something hard with his shin.

Usually some of the men lounged on their bunks, milled about, or snacked after their evening session. But tonight, he was alone. *Where was everybody?*

A sound—*a snicker?*—came from his left. He jerked around and something small and light smacked him in the forehead. Laughter rumbled around him.

The lights came on, and Samuel squinted against the sudden glare. "What's this?"

"We thought you needed a little help." Harry pressed forward with all the team members. His brown features split with a generous grin.

Samuel met the other smiling gazes and tried to gauge

what was coming next. With these guys, one never knew. "Have you all gone loony?"

Joe bent down and scooped up something off the floor. *Was that what hit Samuel in the head?*

Dwight moved in close, bumping his shoulder. His grizzled face split with a grin. "We thought you needed some help."

"How's that?" Immediately, he regretted asking the question.

"We bought you a gift." Lance nudged him from behind. Shorter than Samuel, Lance was wiry with a whiplike strength.

The team gathered around Samuel, pressing in close. Samuel braced himself for whatever would come next.

Before he could bolt, someone grabbed his arms and pinned them behind his back. This was gonna hurt.

Joe moved forward and jabbed something under his nose. Samuel jerked his head but too many hands held him. Joe's look was serious, threatening, but in a blink, his expression shifted to creases in the corners and a spark of humor. Gripping the sides of Samuel's face, the leader smeared something across his mouth. Samuel bucked but was held secure.

Harry made kissing sounds. "Some lip gloss for when you see your lady friend."

Laughter rose around him. Samuel yanked free. Or maybe they let him go. Someone jabbed him playfully in the ribs and clapped him on the back. Stumbling away, Samuel swiped his sleeve across his mouth, tasted strawberry.

"Ain't lip gloss," Shawn corrected Harry. "It's lip balm. Makes your lips supple and smooth."

"Oh, you're making me horny now!" Pete grabbed Shawn from behind and lifted him in the air. Pete's eagle tattoo bulged on his bicep.

"Hey!" Shawn broke free and pumped a fist at Pete.

"Remember what Roberto said about impure thoughts and unholy, unsanctified acts."

"Don't worry. You're not my type. I prefer the ladies." Pete hooked his thumbs in his belt loops and rocked back on his heels. "Besides, I didn't sign up to be no priest."

Randy placed a thickly muscled arm around Samuel's shoulders. "You need some advice about women? You come to me. I can tell you all you need to know."

"Yeah." Shawn waggled his white-blond eyebrows. "Randy's good at diagrams."

Feeling his face burn, Samuel ducked his head. "No, thanks. I'm doing all right on my own."

"I'll say!" Joe's laugh resonated through the room. "Maybe the Amish boy can give you some tips, Shawn! How long has it been since you got any? Like never?"

More laughter followed, and they shoved and clapped Samuel on the back as they rubbed the top of Shawn's head playfully. But Joe lifted his hand and halted the shenanigans. The others quieted quickly, their gazes following Joe's toward the door.

Roberto gave a polite nod. "It's late, boys."

"It is." Joe dusted off Samuel's shoulders. "Now, go straight home. No detours tonight. You need your beauty sleep."

Roberto trained his gaze on Samuel and tilted his head for him to follow. Samuel lightly punched Joe in the thick bicep and wove his way through the rest of the team members. He snatched the tube of lip balm out of Shawn's hand. "You boys won't be needing this tonight. But I might."

With a grin, he followed Roberto into the workout center.

"Don't mind them," Roberto said. "It's just their way of accepting you as a part of the team."

"So I measure up?"

"You always have. See you tomorrow, Samuel." Roberto turned away.

But Samuel stopped him with one question. "How?"

Roberto tilted his head and gave him a hard, assessing look. "They've watched you during the training sessions."

"They know I can take a beating."

A hint of a smile appeared, then disappeared. "They trust you. And they know what happened in Ohio."

Jacob. They knew he'd killed his own brother. It felt like a knife stabbing his chest. The good feeling the team had roused was drowned out by the guilt pouring out of him like blood.

For a long moment, he stood in the dark, fighting back the memories, the self-reproach. He had a sudden urge to run as far as he could...or drive. Yes, drive. He'd hop on his motorcycle and take off. For where he didn't know.

Only dim lights illuminated his path, and he wove his way through equipment and dangling ropes, around the wrestling mat, to the side door. A clicking sound stopped him. He peered into the lecture area, where Roberto taught about the spiritual aspects of the battle and Roc taught tactics. In the tiny, blocked-off area, surrounded by chalkboards and chairs, Roc knelt in front of a table with three lit candles and clicked beads together.

Samuel watched his friend, who seemed to have many burdens weighing on his shoulders these days. But Roc carried the stress and responsibility well. Just when he thought he knew all there was to know about this man, Samuel learned something new. He looked up to Roc, respected him, wanted to be like him. But was he ready to take such a bold step? Was he ready to walk away from all he'd ever known?

Roc glanced up, saw Samuel, and stood. "Everything okay?"

"*Ja.*"

"You're doing good work, Samuel." Roc walked toward him, pushed open the door, and they stepped outside into the cool evening together. Crickets chirped and it sounded like a bullfrog looking for a lady friend.

"Roc, I…" He hesitated and decided against voicing his doubts and concerns. "Good night."

Roc's hand snagged Samuel's arm. "No secrets here. If you have something to say, say it. Makes going into battle together easier."

"You think it's coming to that?"

Roc breathed in the night air and looked up at the stars filling the sky. "I do."

"How can you…how can *we* win?"

"Because we have to. We have more to lose. Which translates: we have more to fight for. More important than that, we're on God's side. And whether we lose a battle here or there isn't as important as the end result. We know how it will all turn out."

"I didn't know you were so religious."

Roc shook his head. "Religious? No, I'm not that."

"But you pray."

"I'd be a fool not to."

"But what do you pray about?"

Roc stared up at the stars and rocked back on his heels. "For answers. Guidance. Protection over my family." He nodded toward Samuel. "My team. And"—he breathed in then out—"forgiveness."

That word twisted inside Samuel. "And do you believe God forgives you?"

"I do." His tone was confident. He raised three fingers. "I light three candles. One for my first wife, who I failed. She died because of those sons of bitches. The second is for my mother. I couldn't protect her from my father. And the third is for my father, who I couldn't help—and who is probably dead."

"Is that your fault?"

Roc shrugged one shoulder. "Maybe. Maybe not. I pray for their souls, for my loss, and for the mistakes I make."

"You?" A measure of humor entered his tone but Samuel wasn't joking.

Neither was Roc when he said, "I do. Everyone does."

"You think God would"—Samuel swallowed hard—"forgive me?

"I'm not a priest. But yes, I believe he would."

"You've killed before, Roc. You don't feel guilty and light candles for those you've killed?"

"Because I was defending someone, sometimes myself. Self-preservation kills guilt, I suppose. But also, I know what I'm called to do here, Samuel. I have no doubts about that. Every time I kill one of those vampires, I'm protecting an innocent from being killed or becoming one of them. And maybe that's how you need to look at Jacob. He wasn't innocent. He wasn't the brother you knew. He was a killer. He killed innocent people. He would have killed Rachel that day. And her baby. Without one ounce of guilt. So the next time you feel guilty, think about that. Think of the ones you saved. Maybe someone like Naomi."

At the mention of Naomi, Samuel's hands became fists. He would protect her, without hesitation or regret. "And pray, right?"

Roc nodded, his mouth compressed in a thin line. "All you have to do is ask."

The Fisher family sat at the kitchen table, along with Samuel and Naomi, passing bowls of scrambled eggs, a platter of bacon, and a basket of biscuits. He stole a look at Naomi and remembered her soft kiss from last night. He'd met her at Levi's and walked her home. But a dose of uncertainty pinched him in the gut. Was he wrong for wanting to be with her? His discussion with Roc had made him look solidly at the life that awaited him if he took that path.

What would it mean for Naomi? He understood the risks on his own life. But was he also putting Naomi's life in danger? What would be her response if he told her what he was doing every evening over at Roc's? Would he risk her derision, astonishment, or disappointment? Even her rejection?

She caught him looking in her direction and smiled. The pleasure in her eyes erased all his doubts and concerns.

The crunch of tires on the gravel alerted everyone at the table. Samuel's worried gaze collided with Levi's. He rose first and strained to peer out the window.

"Who is it?" Hannah asked.

"I don't know." Levi stood now. "Don't recognize the car."

"Could be a lost tourist," Naomi suggested, who seemed to be the only one at the table who wasn't concerned.

Shrugging off his initial concern, Samuel sat back at the table and piled his plate high with a mound of scrambled eggs, biscuits, and diced potatoes. It wasn't unusual for strangers to stop in, tourists trying to get a glimpse of the Amish world, travelers who got turned around, even occasionally a reporter wanting an interview or a novelist doing research. "Probably someone who got a whiff of this food. You outdid yourself this morning, Naomi."

A blush crept into her cheeks. She kept her eyes averted and passed him the butter.

Levi headed toward the door. "I'll see who it is and if they need help."

Hannah pushed back from her place at the table. "I'll cover your plate until you get back."

One of the babies began to cry, and Hannah waved off Naomi, who started to rise. "They're both probably hungry."

Naomi nodded and took the foil from Hannah and covered Levi's plate, pinching the edges to seal in the heat. She avoided Samuel's gaze as he did hers.

"Never a dull moment around here, is there?" he asked.

She smiled. "Oh, I forgot the marmalade."

He tried not to watch as she went to the refrigerator but his gaze was drawn to her. Only one thing stopped him from full-out pursuit. No matter where he lived, whichever lifestyle he embraced, he'd be forced to lie. There was no real choice, which didn't sit well with Samuel. His own father had lied to him. He didn't want to be that kind of a man. He didn't want to lie to Naomi. *But how could he tell her the truth?*

"Is everything all right, Samuel?" She returned to the table, head tilted as she studied him.

"I was"—he poked his fork into his scrambled eggs, suddenly not hungry—"just thinking."

She didn't pressure him to say any more. The sweep of her eyelashes shadowed her cheeks. Her innocence staggered him. His heart was lost to her. But how could they ever have a future together?

The back door opened, and Levi peered inside. "Samuel, there's a woman out here, says she knows you. Her name is Andi."

# CHAPTER THIRTY-NINE

ROC SAT ON THE edge of the small desk in the corner of his training facility. The whiteboard held Roberto's writing—

> *Then the earth laid accusation against the lawless ones.*
> *There is no darkness, nor shadow of death, where the*
> *workers of iniquity may hide themselves.*
> *The light of the body is the eye: if therefore thine*
> *eyes be healthy, thy whole body shall be full of light.*
> *But if thine eye be evil, thy whole body shall be full*
> *of darkness.*

Some of the scriptures were from the canonized Bible, others not. Roc recalled his old friend Anthony, who had shared these with him before he'd bought into all this vampire lore.

*Anthony.* Roc pressed his forehead with his hand. Where was he now? Was he even alive? Roc should have gone searching for him sooner.

Roberto swiped his hand over the whiteboard. "Kind of a depressing lecture, wasn't it?"

Roc reread the line at the top—*The devil is one of God's creations*—as it disappeared beneath the eraser's arcing sweep. Roc sighed. "Better hear it now rather than find out the truth the hard way."

"We all have the capacity to embrace evil."

Roc had seen it with his ex-partner on the New Orleans' police force. Brody, who now went by the name Brydon, had done precisely that. Maybe not of his own free will, not at first anyway, but Brydon now enjoyed the perks of being a vampire. He would not be easy to kill. At least, not a second time. "Do you remember what you first told me when we met?"

Roberto paused. "What's that?"

"Not to trust anyone. Not even you."

"Exactly." Roberto went back to cleaning the board, but markers had discolored it and it would never be pure white again. "You can't trust yourself either."

Roc nodded, knowing all too well he too carried a thirst for iniquity. The virtues in his life—Rachel and baby David—continuously pulled him toward the light.

Roberto tossed the eraser onto the desk. "So what do you think?"

"About?"

"Samuel. Is he ready?"

"Not yet, no." Yet he was hopeful. With Samuel here in Pennsylvania, maybe Roc could finally pursue what had happened to Anthony while Samuel kept an eye on Rachel and David for him. "But maybe he's ready for a test."

Roberto sat in a chair and surveyed Roc with those keen blue eyes. "You're finally going after Father Anthony, are you?"

Roc leaned forward, his elbow braced against his thigh. When he'd tracked Rachel to New Orleans and rescued her from Akiva, he'd been wounded by a vampire. The first person he'd gone to for help was Anthony Daly. But another priest had moved into his parish house. Roc had promised himself he'd find Anthony one day. "I owe him that much."

"Roc," Roberto said in that fatherly tone he often invoked, "one of your best traits is loyalty. But don't let the enemy use it against you. Anthony would never want you to risk your life for him. You know the two possibilities as well as I do. If he is dead, then Anthony knew the risks he took. If he is not one of us anymore, then it would be wise to avoid him."

"Because you think I couldn't do my job?" Roc's hand fisted. He hadn't hesitated to kill his ex-partner, Brody. He should have stuck around and made sure he'd been dead. It was a mistake he wouldn't make again. "You think I wouldn't kill him?"

Roberto laid a hand on Roc's shoulder. "You would do what must be done, just as I would do. What else is there? And ultimately you would be helping Anthony, yes?"

"Then why shouldn't I go?"

"Besides that you are committed here? Besides the fact that your wife and son need you too?" Roberto gave a squeeze to Roc's shoulder before releasing him. "There is something—I don't know how to explain it but—much more dangerous in encountering a vampire you once knew as human. First, it is easy to underestimate them. You believe they will react as they once did, as if they were human. You expect the same weaknesses, the same emotions. But they are no longer human. They no longer have the same love, fear, kindness we have. And for some reason, they are more vicious toward those they have known. It is as if the love they once had is distorted and twisted into a powerful hatred."

Roberto's gaze shifted as if he was remembering something from his own past. "I have thought this hate stems from a jealousy over their loss of the life they once loved. Or maybe it is that those they knew remind them of what they lost, what they can never have again. I don't know." He leveled a steady gaze on Roc. "But I do know that if Anthony has been changed, then his hatred of you and all you represent will be mighty in its intensity."

Roc understood what Roberto was saying, and yet he couldn't abandon his childhood friend any more than he could have abandoned Rachel or his son, David. He shoved his fingers through his hair. "He never quit on me, and I won't quit on him."

# CHAPTER FORTY

SAMUEL HAD CHANGED.

Instinctively, Andi recognized the signs. It wasn't just that he wore traditional Amish attire, when she'd become accustomed to seeing him in jeans and T-shirts. His resigned facial expression turned the corners of his mouth downward rather than his usual affable smile. His reluctant footsteps brought him closer to her but not close enough. Maybe this wouldn't be as easy as she had anticipated.

And those weren't all of the changes she saw in Samuel. He didn't reach for her, didn't offer a hug, not even a greeting. His eyes were cold and flat.

"This place wasn't easy to find," she said but immediately regretted it. Maybe she should have started with a simple hi. But it was too late. Maybe the psychic had been right. Maybe she shouldn't have come. But she had. So she lifted her chin a notch, defying Samuel to pretend he didn't know her.

Behind Samuel, the Amish man who had greeted her looked on from the porch. She moved toward Samuel but realized she was only making this worse.

"What are you doing here?" he asked, his tone flat.

Anger fired inside her in response to his coldness. "Actually, I thought I was doing you a favor. But I was wrong. I can find my way home just fine." She turned back to her Yaris.

"Andi...wait."

But she ignored him and jerked open the driver's door.

"I'm sorry. You surprised me is all. I wasn't expecting you."

She hesitated but didn't close the door. "I sort of surprised myself coming here."

"What's going on?" he asked, his words and tone even.

"That research you were doing, remember? Well, I did some of my own. And I found some information I thought you might want."

He rubbed a hand over his clean-shaven jaw. "Maybe we should start again." A slow smile emerged. "Hi."

She rewarded him with a hesitant smile of her own. "Hi." She'd make Samuel want her, come to her, so she resisted reaching for him. Not yet. Patience. "How have you been?"

"Good." He nodded. "Busy."

"And your brother? He's getting better?"

"Levi is stronger every day. You met him, *ja*?"

She brushed his sleeve with the tip of her finger. "Since he's getting around now on his own, will you be coming home soon?"

"It's complicated." Samuel rubbed the back of his neck. "You said you had information for me, something about my brother, Jacob?"

"Can you get away for a couple of days?"

*Don't push.* She heard the voice in her head and rebuffed it. She knew what she was doing.

Samuel ducked his head. "I don't know that it's a good time."

Irritated with herself and even more so with Brydon, she waved her hand toward the fields. "You've probably got chores. I could come back this evening and we can discuss it."

"Maybe I could meet you."

She smiled. *Perfect.* Some secluded spot would be better. She'd have more weapons in her arsenal to use in convincing him. "Works for me."

# CHAPTER FORTY-ONE

NAOMI'S HEART PUMPED IN an unsteady rhythm, jerking ahead before slowing. *What was wrong with her?* While Hannah held one baby and Levi the other, Naomi tried to focus on cleaning the dishes. Through breakfast, she had smiled and fussed over the babies and forced down as much food as she could, all the while her mind lingered on what Samuel was doing outside. With that woman.

Who was she? An *English* woman, at that. One who drove a car. According to Levi, she'd come all the way from Ohio. What kind of a woman struck out on her own like that?

*The same kind of woman*, Naomi realized, *who let her heart lead her.* The way she had about Samuel. There was no understanding between Samuel and her. He'd walked her home a few times, kissed her even, and yet he'd made no promises. But even so, she'd carelessly allowed her heart to gallop ahead, unrestrained.

Her older sister had her heart broken over a man who chose another as his wife. It had taken Lizzie months of heartache to move on and turn her attention toward someone else. Naomi had vowed not to let that happen to her. But something odd had happened since Samuel had arrived here. He'd rushed in to help his brother, risen early each day, worked hard in the barn and fields, and been kind enough to see her home at night. Other young men she knew seemed

so sure of themselves, so confident in their purpose and beliefs, sometimes overly confident, that it had been refreshing
to hear Samuel's doubts expressed honestly.

Eager to banish those thoughts, she removed the dishes
from the table and scraped the plates into the sink. Standing
in front of the window, she caught a glimpse of the *English*
woman. A snug top outlined her feminine assets and even
tighter blue denims rode low on her hips, revealing a wide
expanse of flesh. Morning sunlight poured over those long
auburn waves, worn loose around the woman's shoulders,
her glory revealed for all to see. Dark glasses hid her eyes and
gave her a mysterious and alluring look. Worse, the woman
edged closer to Samuel, placing a hand against his chest in a
familiar way that made Naomi's stomach clench.

Heat burned her cheeks, and she turned away from the
sink and refused to spy on them. It wasn't her business. She
would not judge either Samuel or this woman. But she
caught an intimate moment between Levi and Hannah as he
leaned toward his wife, brushed a finger along her neck, and
kissed her on the mouth. Tears surged inside Naomi, and she
fled the room.

She found herself in Samuel's bedroom. Flustered, she
turned to leave but heard Hannah ask Levi, "You reckon
Naomi's all right?"

Determined to prove she was fine, she straightened the
sheets on the single bed and pulled the quilt toward the pillow. Smoothing her hand over the soft fabric, she imagined
touching Samuel's blond hair. The dangerous thought prickled her skin.

Rushing on to avoid thoughts that took her down a rocky
path, she detoured into Hannah and Levi's room. She fussed
with the crib sheets until her breathing calmed and her heart

settled into its normal rhythm. *What was wrong with her? Why was she so desperate for love? Was she that lonely?* Covering her heart with her hands and twining her fingers with the ties of her prayer *kapp*, she whispered a prayer to the good Lord, laying her wishes and needs in His hands.

# CHAPTER FORTY-TWO

H IS BACK PRESSED AGAINST the tree trunk. Shaded by the overarching branches and thick foliage, Brydon watched the lonely two-lane road. A slight breeze ruffled the leaves overhead.

Snatching a blade of tall grass, he creased it between his fingers, digging his thumbnail along the central vein. It hadn't taken long to put his plan into action. Of course, it would be all too easy to race into Promise and simply kill Akiva's brothers, Levi and Samuel. Then Roc Girouard would give chase. But what would be the fun in that?

Death wasn't the revenge he sought. It would have to do for the older brother. There wasn't any alternative for him, since he'd chosen a path that could not be diverted. But the younger brother, Samuel? Ah, he had plans for him. Plans that would twist Akiva's black soul.

At the rumbling sound of a car motor, he tossed away the blade of grass. The Toyota Yaris puttered toward him, and he wished she'd at least had the perk of a better car. It slowly passed him before pulling off the road into patches of grass. It idled for a few moments until the driver's door opened.

There was a spring to her step as Andi alighted. She left the door open, the engine running.

Brydon pushed away from the tree's trunk and walked out of the shadows toward her. "You pushed too hard."

She raised her sunglasses and met his dark gaze with her own. "I know Samuel, how he responds. We're meeting tonight."

It had only been a couple of days since her awakening, but she had adapted very well. Still, she could not be trusted. "If that's the best you could do."

She crossed her arms over her stomach. "Why can't I change him here? Why do I have to take him all the way to New York?"

Brydon's gaze narrowed. He didn't like to be questioned. He didn't like to have to explain his reason, motives, or plans. But he needed her cooperation. "When Samuel goes with you, Roc will follow."

"Will you meet us in New York?"

"No."

Her jaw jutted back. "Why not? I thought—"

"I have something else I must do."

"But—"

He cupped her jaw firmly. "We will rendezvous later."

"What about Samuel?"

"You said you know him." He tossed her own words back at her. "You can handle him, can't you?"

"But you said the change can be dangerous, that if I didn't have patience...that my hunger could get out of control..."

He pressed a finger to her lips and caressed the soft, pliable skin. "You will be careful."

She touched him boldly, her fingers skimming over his shoulders as she wrapped her arms around him, her fingers seeking out the faint scars along his neck. "Who changed you?"

He shrugged. "We all have the same birthmark. Doesn't matter anymore." He placed his hands on her bare midriff. "But neither of us had the baggage Samuel carries. All that religiosity. Still, he's questioning. And that's good enough for now."

"But what if he chooses"—she drew her bottom lip between her white teeth—"another life."

"It's up to you to make sure he doesn't." Brydon pulled her against him, his hands cupping her backside. "But from what I've seen, you're very persuasive."

She brushed her lips along his jaw. "Is it time?"

He chuckled. "You're insatiable."

"Please." Her breath felt hot and moist on his skin.

"All right. You pick where you want to dine."

"Ooh, a date."

# CHAPTER FORTY-THREE

In late afternoon, promising himself he'd return from meeting Andi in time to walk Naomi home, Samuel parked his motorcycle far away from the road and walked around the house toward the barn. Rachel struggled with a hefty load of laundry. He hurried toward her, taking the basket in his arms.

"*Danke*, Samuel." She shook her head as if admonishing herself. "Thank you," she repeated, this time in clear, unrepentant *English*. "Old habits are hard to break." Her cheeks flushed. "Don't get me wrong. There's not a law that I can't speak the way we were raised but..."

Samuel lifted his eyebrows, waiting for her to finish.

She gave a slight, awkward shrug. "I don't know how to explain it."

"I reckon Roc prefers you speak only *English*."

"He's never said. I don't think he cares much one way or the other. He's understanding, and he's fine with David learning both. I still have family speaking the old way."

"But you don't see them much. Or do you?"

Her gaze dropped for a long, awkward moment. "Not as much as I would like. My folks not at all. But Hannah I've seen some."

He thought of Mamm and Pop back in Ohio. He missed his mother, her eagerness to please and help, her soft heart and kindness. But the shadow of anger toward his father overrode the softer emotions. "You miss your family?"

"Awful much."

Samuel understood. He'd felt the same being separated from Levi and worse when Jacob had died. Still, he struggled over the loss of Jacob and whether he would ever see his brother again, in another life. He stared at the ground before he got up the courage to ask, "What did they say when you left to marry Roc?" He nudged a rock with the toe of his boot. "I'm sorry for asking, Rachel. It's none of my business but—" His throat tightened and closed off any excuses.

She placed a hand on his forearm. "I understand, Samuel. Of course, Mamm and Dat were upset. I'd been baptized, and so it's all the more complicated. I'm being shunned. I can't go to their house. They're not to speak to me. And"—her voice became pinched—"well, I miss them. I wish they could see David. But I understand that they don't want to get into trouble. I worry for Levi and Hannah, that our seeing them occasionally will get them shunned as well." She lifted one of Roc's shirts out of the basket and hung it on the line, attaching it with wooden clothespins. "Are you thinking of leaving?"

He looked across at the training center. "It's crossed my mind. I won't deny that. My being here, training with Roc's team, is testament."

"It's not an easy decision."

"I don't want to think about what my folks will say if I do. Pop will rail that I'm headed straight for eternal hell." He could have swallowed his tongue. "I'm sorry, Rachel, I didn't mean to say...that you...well, that—"

"It's all right, Samuel. I'm not offended. I struggled with that myself before and after I left. We both know some-one who has left. Some left the faith altogether. Others just wanted to live in the *English* world, go to school, get a job. Many are still believers, but they don't adhere to the old ways. Still, some of their folks have told them they're heading for eternal hell. Mamm and Dat haven't said that to me. I hope they don't believe it because I don't."

She lifted a pair of jeans and attached them to the line, her fingers moving deftly, but her gaze drifted sideways. "I don't believe I'm going to eternal hell. I believe the same as I always have…in Jesus…in God the Father. Do I think God wouldn't let me in heaven because I don't dress a certain way or that I drive a car on occasion?" She shook her head. "No, I don't believe that. Still, I've been asking a lot of questions, talking to Father Roberto. He's very educated, you know. He's tried to explain things to me from both the Catholic and Protestant views."

"What have you learned?"

"I'm no expert, and I'm not sure I reckon all that he's tried to teach me. But I read and I pray. Since marrying Roc and moving here and starting the center, I've read more of the Bible than I ever have in my life. Read it for myself."

Samuel handed her another shirt and kept handing her clothes, moving down the line with her.

"I've been thinking about this a lot, Samuel, and realizing that many of the Amish believe in salvation but act like works get them to heaven. Remember, even the demons believe in Jesus. The difference is, I fall at his mercy, ask forgiveness for my sins. There is nothing good I can do to make up for the bad I've done. Only Jesus's blood can cleanse me of my sins. And since he has, then whatever happens in this life, I'm heaven bound." She smiled back at him, as if it were a relief to grasp that, then her smile faded. "I know you're struggling with all of this, Samuel, and there is much to consider."

"There is."

"God will reveal His plan when it's time."

"Do you miss our ways? The simple, plain ways."

"Oh, *ja.* Yes." She laughed at herself. "Of course. And yet, I have to say I like the washing machine Roc bought for me. I still prefer sun-dried clothes though." A sly smile spread across her face. "And"—she looked sheepishly at him—"I like driving a car too."

Samuel laughed.

For a few moments they silently hung the clothes on the line. When the basket was empty, Rachel picked it up. Together, they began to walk toward the house. "Are you comfortable here, Samuel?"

"*Ja.* Well, as comfortable as I can be straddling this fence— one foot at Levi's and one foot here."

She nodded. "I reckon you're missing your folks and friends back in Ohio."

"I'm glad to be with Levi again after so long though."

"Oh, yes. I'm glad for the both of you."

He stopped halfway to the house. "I should be going." He hooked his thumb toward the barn. "I have an errand to run."

"Of course. It was good talking to you. And thank you again for the help."

"Same here, Rachel." He took one step but stopped again. "Do you know what it feels like?"

"What's that?"

"When I was young, I felt so free, running outdoors in my bare feet. But as I grew up and learned all the dos and don'ts, I felt penned in, like a horse or pig or chicken."

"Those fences are there to keep them safe, Samuel," she admonished.

"I know. And God's laws are like that. But maybe you

and Roc have the right approach. You're living the way you want, without a bunch of rules other than what God set forth, and so maybe you understand true freedom."

Her smile was answer enough.

---

With the sun dropping, shadows lengthening and deepening, the sky bled over the horizon. He drove his motorcycle out toward Lincoln Highway, taking a turnoff, and veering another onto a narrow road usually traversed by horse and buggy. Andi had said she was staying at a bed and breakfast nearby.

When he reached the tiny Amish school, which he remembered so well, he turned at the corner and came to a dead stop. He moved not a muscle, yet his heart raced. The motorcycle hummed and vibrated beneath him. Darkness crept over him. *Why here? Was it a cruel joke? Did Andi not know the significance of this location?*

Swathed in the souls that seemed to linger, waiting, watching, wondering when would be their chance to rise, the cemetery stood in the heart of the district. Weathered stones held silent testimony of those who had hoped and dreamed, walked this earth, worked this soil, lived, and died. Some markers stood straight, rock solid, as many of these Amish had withstood oppression and prejudice, and others tilted at odd angles, the ground beneath them shifting and uncertain. Samuel wondered if any of those buried here, some his own relatives, had ever wavered in their beliefs.

He maneuvered his motorcycle off the road and onto the slanted edge of dirt, rock, and sprigs of green grass. Memories pushed into his consciousness. His grandparents, Amos and Martha Fisher, had been stoic, never complaining about arthritic hands or infirmities brought on by old age. When Jacob had spouted out his shocking questions and doubts, their lips had thinned, but they had refrained from saying anything. But should they have?

He remembered the cloudy morning Pop gathered Levi, Mamm, and Samuel in the cemetery around a freshly dug grave. The wooden casket lay at the base. Pop could barely speak. Mamm cried into her apron. No friends attended. No one else knew Jacob was gone—not yet anyway.

Even now, he felt the same stark emotions tighten his throat. Even though it had been a lie then, it was truth now. Although Jacob's body had never been buried here, his ashes had blackened a field back in Ohio.

The charcoal sky darkened, the last rays of sunlight snuffed out as if a giant artist rubbed a fist over a pencil drawing, smudging lines, smearing distinctions. A soft breeze stirred the grass around him. He felt alone. Lost. Not that he didn't know where on a map he was, but lost in the sense of where he was in life.

He imagined all the arguments Roberto and Roc would have against him being here in an isolated field. Their warnings shot through his mind. *This was not a good idea.*

Yet, here he was. He took one step back toward the motorcycle when he heard his name like a whisper. *Samuel.*

He searched the road but saw nothing, no one. He called out, "Andi?"

"Samuel." The voice came from the graves.

He whirled around. Andi stood only a couple of feet from him, silhouetted in a shroud of darkness, her shadowed eyes looked like deep black pools.

"Where did you come from?" he asked, startled.

"Ohio. Remember? I've been waiting here for you." She

closed the gap between them and placed her hands gently against his chest. Her breathing sounded uneven. Her heady scent enveloped him. Something about her was different. If he hadn't known her so well, he wasn't sure he would have recognized her. Which seemed crazy because she looked the same. She felt the same. But her scent had a deeper quality. Earthier. Her voice sounded more exotic.

Or maybe he had changed. He knew his heart had.

"I've missed you, Samuel." She breathed the words against his lips.

Her kiss was light but provocative. His hands automatically lifted to her waist. But he didn't want to pull her close. Instead, he wanted to push her away. "Andi, I, uh—"

Her open mouth grazed his jaw and brushed along his neck. "Have you missed me?"

*What could he say? Had he missed her? Really?* He hadn't. And yet, something about her was so familiar. It felt like falling into water, at first shocking, then floundering and finally relaxing and moving in a timeless manner that seemed as ancient as the stars above. Their bodies knew instinctively how to come together. The problem was not his body but his mind…even his heart.

"Andi"—his hands tightened on her waist and his arms straightened to put distance between them—"what did you come all this way to tell me?"

Brushing back her hair, she released a sigh. "Don't you want me anymore?"

"I just want to know what you came here for. Can't we talk? Or do we only know how to—"

"What if I came here for you?" She tilted her chin downward and set a weighty gaze upon him.

For a moment he felt as if he was falling. And he would

not. Frustrated with her, with himself, he forced himself to look away from her. She held no answers for him. He stared up at the stars searching for an answer. "But that's not what you said. You said—"

"I came here to help you."

"How?"

"You were looking into your brother's death"—irritation hardened her tone—"into the path he chose."

"I still am."

"Have you found anything?" she asked.

"I've found—" He hesitated, not eager to share about Roc and his training center. Yet it was more than that. Something restrained him. *Could he trust her?* He decided on another track. "I haven't had much time for reading or research." Which was true. He hadn't even had time to search through Jacob's book. Yet he wondered if he'd begun to lose the desire to know more. Maybe he'd begun to accept the loss. Or maybe he'd simply been distracted.

"Well, I've had lots of time," she said, "and you won't believe what I've discovered."

Having diverted her attention off sex for the moment, he breathed easier. "What's that?"

"I know this is going to sound kind of crazy, and I'm not even sure I could tell you how I got to this conclusion, but do you know anything about…vampires?" Her voice dipped seductively on the last word and it resonated through him.

It felt like the first time he'd visited Roc's home and had fallen through the floorboards of the front porch, his breath knocked out of him.

"You have, haven't you?" She placed a hand on his arm, an urgency pressing her fingers tight against his skin. "It's okay. I've been learning all about it myself."

Samuel felt as if he was being shaken from the inside out.

"What if your brother was into some cult like that? Do you think it's possible?"

He cleared his throat, tried to find his voice. "Maybe."

She tugged on his arm. "Then you have to come with me."

He held firm. "What? Why?"

"New York." Her grip possessed more strength. "It's not as far as you think. There's a coven"—she touched the dip at the base of her throat where he knew her pulse throbbed—"and from what I can gather, they're just a normal group of teens. Nothing bad or evil. No hocus-pocus kind of stuff. Still, it might help you—"

Her words rushed over him as her gaze probed his, and he felt disoriented, breathless. "When do you want to go?"

She looked as surprised as he was by his question. She stepped closer to him, her eagerness radiating off her. "How about now? Tonight."

"But—"

"It's only a couple of hours' drive."

This was sudden. Too sudden. Yet, if they went tonight, then he could be back by tomorrow. Tomorrow night. Maybe afterward Andi would return to Ohio. He would tell her there was no future for them. And he could take Naomi to the Sunday singing and walk her home. Maybe then he could put all of this behind him.

"All right. Let's do it."

He considered calling Roc or one of the team. But what had Andi said? This was a group of high schoolers. What danger could there be?

# CHAPTER FORTY-FOUR

THE EARLY MORNING HAZE was disorienting. Levi left the barn, keeping his right arm tight against his side. His rib had healed well, but it still caused him some pain. After lifting feed bags, he was sore. He stood on the gravel drive and squinted against the mist swirling around him. A spring storm was on its way, but something else worried him. *Where was Samuel's motorcycle? More to the point, where was Samuel?*

Since he'd arrived, Samuel had fed the livestock each morning. Although Levi had begun making his way to the barn, most of the chores still belonged to Samuel. But this morning, Samuel hadn't shown up. Was he still in bed?

A quick check revealed an empty, undisturbed bed.

*Could Samuel still be at Roc's?* Sometimes maneuvers and drills kept him late. Maybe Samuel had bunked there. Levi ducked back inside the barn and pulled his cell phone out of his pocket. The phone rang several times before Rachel answered.

"Good morning," Levi said.

Her greeting was warm and friendly. "How are you feeling, Levi?"

"Better. Managing to do some chores today." He nudged a clump of straw with his boot. He breathed in the earthy aromas before plunging into the reason for his call. "I was wondering if Samuel might be handy."

"Sure, he's—" She paused. "Did you say Samuel?"

"*Ja.* I thought he might have stayed overnight at—"

"Hold on a minute, Levi." The phone clunked onto a counter or table.

Dread plunged into Levi's gut like a baited hook in water. He was responsible for his brother. He'd promised Pop he'd watch out for Samuel, keep him safe, help him through this difficult time. Samuel was going through many of the questions and doubts he himself had faced when he was the same age, when Jacob had died and his family had moved to Ohio. And yet, Samuel had so many other issues Levi had never faced. Had he failed Samuel?

After all, he'd introduced Samuel to a shadowy world, where black and white faded into gray, then splashed with bold intensity once again. It was a world of lies. Yet it also put one's faith into practice and one's life in jeopardy.

"Levi?" Roc's voice came over the line sharp and piercing. "Rachel says Samuel is missing."

Levi had faced this kind of crisis before when Rachel had disappeared last summer, but all had turned out well. Believing it was simply a miscommunication, he released the tension in his chest. "I wouldn't say that, Roc. He wasn't here this morning, and I thought he might have stayed over at your place, after drills last night."

"No," Roc's voice held a southern lilt, but his tone was decisive and firm.

Panic shot through Levi.

"Samuel left earlier than usual last night," Roc explained. "Said he had to get home. I thought it was to see Naomi."

"Naomi?" Mind racing with possibilities and fears, Levi faced the doorway and witnessed the sun demolishing the haze. "I'm sure all is well." He hoped. He prayed. But he was anything but sure. "Maybe he—" Levi hesitated. "Roc, a woman was here yesterday. An *English* woman. Samuel knew her, said she was from Ohio. He didn't say she was a girlfriend or anything but…it wouldn't surprise me. So maybe he"—Levi cleared his suddenly congested throat—"spent some time with her."

"What's her name?"

"I just barely met her." Levi rubbed his forehead. "Andi. I remember because it didn't sound like a girl's name. Andi Min—Mix—no, Mitchell. That's it. Andi Mitchell."

"Okay. I better get on this. Call if he shows up."

The phone line clicked, then went dead. Levi held it for a moment, frozen, his pulse racing. He stared up at the rafters in the barn and prayed.

# CHAPTER FORTY-FIVE

SAMUEL DRIFTED UP FROM sleep, his head cloudy as if he'd drunk himself into a stupor last night. He rolled onto his side, and the room tilted precariously. He lurched, bracing himself with a hand against the bed. His head felt woozy. But this was not his bed. Not the single bed he used at Levi's. Not a bunk at Roc's. *Where was he?*

He pressed thumb and middle finger against his temples to settle the world back into its respectable place. Squinting his bleary, aching eyes, he didn't recognize anything in the room, not the dresser, drapes, or television.

He was alone.

A memory sprang up, blurry and fleeting. Andi. He'd driven with her to New York. She'd clung to the back of him on his motorcycle. They'd arrived about one in the morning and found a motel with an available room.

She'd curled up against him, one leg thrown over his, her hand flat against his chest. She kissed his neck, lavishing attention in one place, and sending rippling chills through his body. Her voice was husky but not with sleep. "Have you thought of changing your name?"

"Why would I do that?"

"Just to be different." Her foot caressed his calf and she kissed his mouth. She tasted salty and earthy. Slowly, she'd worked her way back to his neck.

He couldn't remember anything after that. He forced his gaze around the room, but his eyes felt heavy, oh so heavy. Where was she now?

A car horn blared outside followed by a siren's wail. Samuel staggered out of bed and over to the window. He parted the heavy curtains and stared downward at the street. Traffic didn't seem particularly heavy but moved at a lethargic pace. He guessed it was still early, as the sun, which he couldn't see for the buildings, seemed as weak as his eyes.

Turning away from the window, he realized he was nude, his clothes tossed haphazardly onto the floor. He rubbed his chest, trying to remember. *Had he made love to Andi?* His muscles felt stiff and sore and weak. He flopped back onto the bed.

Closing his eyes, he tried to remember the night but it was a hodgepodge of sights and sounds and smells he couldn't place, couldn't articulate. He drifted back to sleep and awoke when he heard the lock on the door click. His eyes opened just as the door did.

With a bright smile, Andi waltzed inside. She carried a brown paper bag. "Just the way I like my man. In bed." She nudged his bare foot. "Come on, lazybones."

"This the one you've been bragging about?" a strange man walked into the room and closed the door behind him.

Samuel jerked upright, scrambling to cover himself with a sheet. "Who are—"

But he stopped mid-question as two black eyes greeted him. The teenager had Howdy Doody hair and freckles. But it was the eyes that captured Samuel's attention. Those eyes made him feel as if he was falling.

"This is Maddox," Andi said in an offhanded way, as if she didn't notice Samuel was naked or care. "He's going to take us to meet some of his friends. They're having a get together this morning. Believe me, you're going to like it." Her hand slid up the length of Samuel's calf. "But you might want to take a quick shower before we go."

The teenager plunked down in a chair and propped his feet on a desk. "Don't take too long though. We don't want to be late."

The room swayed as Samuel pushed himself to a standing position. His hands clumsily wrapped the sheet around his hips. "What's going—"

"That's some love bite, my friend." Maddox's gaze narrowed on Samuel's neck.

His hand automatically went there, jerking away at its tenderness. The mirror over the desk revealed a bite mark. A light brown smear of blood trailed down his neck.

Andi shrugged. "Couldn't help myself." She stepped behind him, smoothing her hands over his shoulders. "You're so delicious. Now go get dressed before I can't restrain myself any longer." She pushed the paper bag into his hands. "And here's a bagel. When in New York, eat like a New Yorker. Right, Maddox?"

He winked. "At least for now."

Backing his way to the bathroom, Samuel's knees wobbled with each step. Something was wrong. Very wrong. *Where was his phone?* He needed to call someone…Roc…somebody.

# CHAPTER FORTY-SIX

WHERE ARE YOU GOING?" Rachel stood in the doorway, baby David perched on her hip. The baby wore a gleeful smile as his arms and legs flailed happily, but his mother's look was stark with concern.

Roc tossed a box of hollow-point bullets into his duffel bag next to his toothbrush. "Going after Samuel."

"You think he's in trouble?"

"I know it."

"But how?"

He met her concerned gaze. "The same way I knew you were. Even when I didn't want to admit it."

"But how do you know where to go?"

"The team has been out scavenging information for the last hour. It wasn't difficult to find out Samuel was seen riding his motorcycle with a woman behind him. So I did a little checking on the name Levi gave me. Andi Mitchell." He swallowed past the thickness in his throat. "A body of a runaway teen was found in her apartment."

Rachel gasped. "A body? But if it was her—"

"It wasn't her. It was a runaway. Andi Mitchell is missing. Her place of employment reported her not showing up for work. Another death was reported at the downtown Cincinnati library. Had the same MO."

"Roc, please—"

He faced her and braced himself against the tears in her eyes. "Look, Rachel, we talked about this. You knew this would be our life. For better or worse."

"It's one thing to talk about it."

He nodded. "It's another thing to live it." He moved toward her and the baby. She came into his arms, pressed her face against his shoulder. "But you know I have to go."

"Who's going with you?"

"No one."

She straightened, jarring the baby, who squealed. "Why are you training these men if you're not going to use them?"

"They're not ready. Besides, this shouldn't be that difficult." But he suspected who was behind this disappearance, and if it was Brydon, then it was his own fault, and he'd have to rectify the situation. He rubbed his hands along Rachel's arms, wishing he could hold on to her. But he had a job to do. "I'll be back soon. With Samuel."

His phone rang, and he stepped away to answer it with a clipped, "Roc here." He listened intently to the police officer describe Andi Mitchell's white Toyota Yaris, which they found abandoned. Roc added, "All right. Thanks."

Returning to his packing, he zipped his bag and hooked it over his shoulder. "I'd tell you not to worry, but—"

"You know I will."

She pressed her cheek to David's downy head as if to hide the tears welling in her eyes. "Something doesn't feel right about this."

"It feels all too familiar." Roc wrapped his arms around them both one last time, felt their soft warmth against him.

"I just wish we were making progress against these evil creatures."

He kissed the top of her head. "We are. Or else they wouldn't be coming back."

"You think that's what this is?"

"I don't know. But I'll find out."

A shudder went through her, and he felt it deep in his soul. She looked up at him, her blue eyes like twin oceans. "Take care of yourself, Roc. We need you too."

"I know what I'm doing, Rachel. And I know why." He kissed her hard, taking in her sweet taste and scent, and she clung to him with one arm until the baby squirmed. With his eyes he made her a solemn promise. "I'll be back." Then he took the first step away from what he loved most. "Until then, Roberto is here, as is the team."

She nodded, even as her lower lip quivered. He memorized the way her hair curled over one shoulder, the baby's soft fist against her breast, her determined and brave stance. Just in case he didn't return.

# CHAPTER FORTY-SEVEN

THEY SAT IN THE back of a yellow taxi, Samuel sandwiched between Andi and Maddox. They drove out from the city on I-495. None of them spoke, not even the driver. A speaker box on the dash crackled. Air rushed into the car through the partially opened windows. Andi's hair whipped about, slapping Samuel, until she fisted a section.

Maddox jiggled the lock button on the door, up and down, up and down with the tips of his fingers. "These are high school kids." His voice was deeper than his freckled face implied. "Most are here for kicks, especially the devil's dandruff and angel dust, but there are a few true believers."

"Believing what?" Andi asked, staring out the side window.

"That they are like us. They pretend to drink"—his gaze shifted toward the driver—"but they are not true believers."

Andi laughed. "This I gotta see."

The words flew past Samuel, dancing around him, in a whirl of sounds and syllables that he understood and yet did not. Nor did he care. He hadn't found his cell phone. He'd searched his pockets in the hotel room, under the bed—

"What are you looking for?" Andi asked.

"I-I thought I lost something."

"Come. The taxi is waiting, and we don't want to be late."

After a half hour or so, with little traffic, they pulled through a gate to a sprawling estate. It looked like an all-American

home, although upscale…way, way upscale from the places
Samuel had lived. Still, the looming house sat on a wide,
immaculate, green lawn surrounded by groomed trees and
bushes, which gave the place a secluded feeling. Samuel
swallowed hard, wishing he hadn't come on this journey or
met Andi. It had been his choice. Hadn't it?

Maddox climbed deftly from the taxi and slammed the
door, forcing Samuel to follow Andi. She paid the driver and
waited for Samuel. He inched toward the opening, hesitating, peering at the house, which looked more like a mansion.
It wasn't the structure itself that made him doubt the wisdom
of this venture. It felt as if someone were whispering in his
soul: *Turn around, Samuel!* This place felt as if a dark presence
hovered over it. He voiced his doubts to Andi. "I'm not sure
about this."

Through the black lenses of her sunglasses, she stared at
him. "What are you afraid of?"

"I'm not afraid, just not sure this is where I should be."

"Oh, yeah? You're the one who wanted to understand
what your brother was into. Well, here we are!" She turned
in a circle. "Does this place look scary?" She waggled her
fingers. "Oooh. Are you scared?

"Samuel." Andi bent forward, her glasses sliding downward. Hard black eyes bore into him. "What have you got
to lose?"

The world felt topsy-turvy. He couldn't think straight. He
couldn't think of an argument, so he pushed himself out of
the back of the taxi. His limbs felt stiff. His stomach clenched
with doubts and regrets. "Who lives here?"

Andi waved to the taxi driver, who began backing out of
the driveway. "Some rich slob apparently."

"You don't know?"

"A kid who's in this group lives here. His folks own it, but they're gone for the weekend." She touched his hand, slid her fingers between his. "So lots of fun." Pulling him toward the house, she added, "Come on."

"But"—Samuel pulled back—"how do we know this had anything to do with Jacob?"

"How do we know it didn't?"

She jogged up the stone steps, dragging him with her, and entered through the front door as if she owned the place. *Had she been here before? Or was she simply following Maddox? Where had he gone?*

At first the house seemed deserted, in an encompassing quiet that swelled and throbbed around them. Samuel could have sworn the house breathed, its chilly breath puffing out of the slatted vents. Ornate paintings hung on the walls. Some were brash with color, bold with their lines and suggestions. Cherubs danced and floated above them in the entryway, where the arced ceiling had been painted with clouds and baby angels.

A noise off to the left turned them in that direction, and they wandered into a kitchen with more gadgets than Samuel had ever imagined. A teenage girl, wearing a bikini that looked like it was made of string, stood at the extra-wide refrigerator. Her eyes were glassy. "Hey there."

"Hi," Andi said. "Maddox brought us."

"Cool." Her gaze traveled lazily over Samuel. "We're downstairs. Grab something to drink or eat if you want."

Andi tugged him toward the stairs that led downward. "Party this way!"

They went through a doorway and down a shadowy passageway of carpeted stairs, which opened into a wide space. None of the electric lights were being used. Heavy curtains covered expansive windows. A few black candles had been set up on a table and the flames wavered invitingly. A lamp was turned on, its light bulb purple, which gave off an eerie glow.

A dozen or more men and women gathered, some older, some younger than Samuel. A few lounged on chairs, others quietly talked in small groups. A sickly sweet odor saturated the room.

"How can you see in those?" He pointed toward her sunglasses.

"I can see very well in the dark." She smiled and raised the glasses to the top of her head, which pulled her hair back around her ears.

When her eyes locked with his, he felt the room dip and sway. The only time he'd ever felt that way was the day he'd killed Jacob.

Sudden understanding came over him. *Andi.* She was different. She was like Jacob and that stranger who had attacked him in the barn of his parents' home.

He had to get out of there.

# CHAPTER FORTY-EIGHT

H E WATCHED HER FROM the window.

Rachel moved about the kitchen, stirring this, pouring that, handing her baby a cracker. David had blond fuzz on his head and wide blue eyes. Waving a spoon, knocking it against the high chair's tray, he gummed the cracker.

Roberto stood outside the door for a long time, peering in at the domestic scene and regretting his reason for intruding, and delayed his knock. The late morning sun hurled rays in his direction like Zeus throwing lightning rods from Mount Olympus. But the sweat pouring out of his pores was from stress rather than heat.

Many times during his days as a full-time priest, he'd delivered heartbreaking news to parishioners. Some were stoic, others hysterical, and some begged questions he could not answer. *Why? Why did this happen? Why did God allow such a thing?* Roberto never pretended to understand the ways of the Lord. He doubted Rachel would ask that of him. *For my thoughts are not your thoughts, neither are your ways my ways, saith the Lord.* Rachel knew the scripture from Isaiah as well as he did. But it might not be enough to hold her together when he told her the news.

Over the past few months, he'd not only presided over Roc and Rachel's unorthodox wedding, attended only by a police officer from Philadelphia and an Amish couple, the bride's sister and brother-in-law, but he'd watched the young couple. The wedding had been a somber occasion and yet joyful because the happy couple had a glow of contentment and eyes only for each other. When Rachel was shunned, their relationship deepened, and the couple relied on each other as they planned and built this place together. When Rachel walked into a room, Roc's eyes lit up. If they were within a foot of each other, one's hand sought the other's.

*But now…who would help put her back together if she fell apart?*

The door opened before he knocked. Rachel smiled at him. She was breathless and energetic. "Hi. Have you been standing there long? Sorry I didn't hear you knock." She eased back, opening the door wider. "Come on in."

He stepped inside, ducking his head slightly and doffing his hat. "I'm sorry to bother you, Rachel."

"Oh, no bother at all." She fanned her face. "It's warm out today."

"That it is."

Waving toward the kitchen table, she offered him a seat. "Would you like some iced tea or lemonade?"

He shook his head. "Not now. Thank you, though."

She clasped the back of a chair, her cheeks rosy with exertion, her eyes bright with happiness. Her baby cooed from his highchair. But Rachel's gaze grew wary. Her brow knit together. "Is everything all right, Father?"

He smiled at her use of "Father." She'd never felt comfortable calling him by his given name, so they'd settled on something that made sense to her, because he'd taken on a fatherly role with Roc. He indicated the chair. "Can you join me for a minute?"

He sat, but she remained behind the chair, staring at him as if stunned. He stood.

"I'm sorry." She skirted the chair and perched on the edge. Concern darkened her eyes. "Has something happened?"

Again, he settled in the chair and searched for the right words. "I don't know."

Her eyes widened and her lips parted before she managed, "I'm confused."

"Yes, well, it's about Roc. We don't know the problem, but we've sent scouts."

"Did he call?" Without waiting for a reply, she hurried to the counter where a cell phone was plugged into a socket. She punched the buttons quickly. "He hasn't left a message." Then she punched another set of numbers— or started to. She had to stop and restart. Her hands were trembling. She placed the receiver against her ear, her gaze flitting around the room, as she waited for Roc to answer his cell phone.

"Rachel," Roberto said, keeping his voice as calm as he could manage, "you haven't spoken to him since he left?"

"That's right."

Roberto released a breath and drew another. "It could be nothing, nothing at all. It could simply be that he's lost a signal or out of range. It does happen occasionally."

She clicked off the phone and her gaze slammed into Roberto's. "But you don't know where he is?"

"Exactly."

She looked away, staring off as if her mind were racing and she was attempting to track it. She braced a hand against the table. "Are you doing something?"

"Of course. I sent out a team."

"When?" Her tone was clipped, demanding. "How long have they been gone?"

"Just now." He stood. "Rachel, sit down, please. Let me

get you some coffee or something. I'll stay here while we wait to hear. The team will check in regularly."

"No. You go. Do something…whatever you can to bring him back. And I'll—" She stopped abruptly.

"You'll what?"

She looked at her son. "Do what I have to do."

# CHAPTER FORTY-NINE

R OC COULDN'T OPEN HIS eyes.
Not that it would do any good. Someone had bound a tight bandage about his head, and the material pinched his scalp. His hands were tied behind his back, the rope connected to his bound feet. When he jerked his hands in one direction, the rope tightened on his ankles. So he lay on the warm metal, feeling it sway beneath him. No point in struggling anyway. Each time he lifted his chin or twisted his neck, he felt the gash at the back of his head ooze and warm blood trickled down his neck. His head throbbed, and moving set off fireworks inside his eyelids, splashing red and blue sparks, which ignited a chain reaction of pain throughout his body.

It didn't take a genius to figure out he was in a truck of some kind and rumbling down some forgotten or hidden highway. But who was driving? And where were they going?

He'd been a fool to go off by himself.

One thing he'd learned from Rachel in the few months they'd been married: when hopeless and defenseless, pray. It had become a habit with him, influenced by both his wife and Roberto. But his feeble attempts were constrained by his own inadequacies and failures. Still, he prayed his team would not find him. If he were to die, and the possibility seemed relatively high, he'd rather be a martyr than the first in a massacre—or worse, the last.

So he laid as still as he could, drifting in and out of crazy sleep, his dreams a parade of faces from the many he'd killed. They peered down at him, elongated and hollow eyes, eager to watch his demise, lips spread in wide, impatient, hideous grins. He jerked back away from them and woke himself. Then he prayed, his fingers moving behind his back as if he held his mother's rosary beads, his thoughts reeling and swaying with the rhythm of the truck.

When the truck came to a stop, he jerked awake. The engine rumbled for several minutes. The air grew stuffy and warm. When he thought the invisible weight on his chest would suffocate him, he heard a clank and scraping sound of metal against metal. He faked unconsciousness and forced his muscles to relax.

"Is he dead?" a heavy voice asked. Male. Deep. Old.

"Doesn't matter," came another voice, this one familiar. But his memories felt fractured. "Just haul him out of there and take him to get cleaned up." The commanding voice uttered something indistinguishable. "Stinks in there."

Roc heard footsteps walking away and felt the truck bed dip and the metal floor quiver. Something jabbed him in the neck and he lost consciousness.

# CHAPTER FIFTY

ENOUGH OF THIS. HE had to get out. Fast.

A panicked fist twisted his gut. This was not right. Not right at all. With frantic gaze bouncing from section to section, Samuel searched the basement in the enormous house. The covered windows. The stairs. Only one option.

While no one paid attention to him as Andi spoke quietly with Maddox, who now wore a long black robe, Samuel bolted for the stairs, stumbled, then righted himself. Two steps. Three. A shadow fell across him. The bikini-clad teen leaned an arm against the doorjamb at the top of the stairs. She wore a black robe too. A grin spread slowly across her face. It was the kind of smile that gave Samuel an eerie feeling.

But he had no other choice. He scrambled up the stairs, his legs weak, as he clawed at the railing.

"Samuel?" Andi called from below. "Where are you going?"

He reached the top.

But the teen blocked the doorway. She flicked a lock of blond hair off her shoulder. "Going somewheres?"

"Yeah, I forgot…" Samuel smiled. Or hoped it was a smile. "Don't worry. I'll be right back."

But the young woman never moved. That's when Samuel saw her eyes were solid black—the color of Andi's. Was this a dream? A bad dream? Those eyes felt like holes Samuel fell into and he wavered unsteadily on the top step. His heart felt feeble. *Where could he go?* He looked back.

Andi stood midway along the passageway, her hand on the rail. Slowly one foot mounted the next step. She spoke carefully in what seemed to be an effort not to startle him. "Samuel..."

Fear plunged into the depth of his stomach.

"Samuel," she repeated, reaching a hand toward him, "they're wanting to get started, so we don't have time to go—"

Samuel bolted for the door, putting a solid shoulder to the young woman's breadbasket. She grunted but didn't budge. Samuel's shoulder throbbed as if he'd slammed into a boulder. They grappled in the doorway for a moment, shoving each other one way, then the other, but Samuel was no match for her supernatural strength. He felt himself tipping backward. Twisting his torso, he ended up falling. Andi moved out of his way and let him crash, tumble, and roll to the floor below.

He laid there, his breath knocked out of him, his limbs flailing, chest burning.

She stood over him. Andi's eyes chilled him. "Put him on the table."

# CHAPTER FIFTY-ONE

STRIPPED, SOAKED IN SCALDING water, then rubbed dry, Roc stood, no longer blindfolded, in the center of a white-tiled room as cold as a tomb. Even though the tile appeared white, the grout, which ran between the squares like regimented veins, was stained with his blood.

No longer bound by hands or feet, Roc felt no urge to fight or run or kill. He had no energy at all, as if it had swirled down the drain hole with the water, dirt, and sweat. Two young vamps tended him. They acted disinterested and devoid of emotion, perfunctory in their motions, never speaking as they tended the wound on his neck, slapping a bandage over it, and dressed him in jeans and a button-down shirt, stiff with starch.

When they finished, they led him out of the room and down a hallway. They never touched him. Roc simply followed, hearing occasional thoughts in his own mind. *Left. Now right.* The same had happened when they'd scrubbed away the grime. *Lift arm. Right arm. Turn around.* Roc had no real self-awareness, no thoughts of "what is happening?" or "where are we going?" or even feelings of fear or panic. It felt as if he was watching himself like a casual observer.

The hallway stretched a long way, and Roc's limbs felt weighted as the three of them aimed for a door, a metal one which had no bolts or locks but remained closed. When they reached it, Roc heard a fluttering on either side of him, and the two vamps disappeared. Befuddled rather than relieved or worried, Roc searched one direction, then the other, and turned to look behind him. He was alone.

He should do something. But what? He couldn't formulate a thought. Couldn't imagine what he should do or how he should respond to this situation. He simply stood and waited. Until the door opened.

Brydon, his ex-partner, once known as Brody, stepped through the doorway. His gaze was like black magic. "Roc," he said, as if not surprised at finding him, "it's good to see you again."

Those eyes locked on to Roc, and he felt himself sway, the walls tilting. He should say something. He should do something. A fleeting thought came to him to ask, "How's it?" the way he once did in their days back in New Orleans. But he couldn't speak the words. They fled before he fully grasped them.

Brydon rubbed a hand over his neck. "Remember the last time we met? I do. But don't worry, Roc. I won't hold it against you." He grinned, but his eyes remained dark, unconvincing pools. "Come on, I want to introduce you to someone." He pushed open the door again. "You're quite the prize, you know."

---

It couldn't have happened to a nicer guy.

Brydon relished the look of glee on Jezebel's features when he presented Roc to her. In the shade of her gazebo, she rose immediately and came forward.

Roc stood stone stiff, his coloring deathly pale.

"Oh my." Jezebel circled Roc, her hands fluttering in

an eager dance, her gaze devouring him. "He's delightful. Truly." When she faced Brydon, her eyes blazed. "Anything you want. Name it."

"I'm glad you like him." Brydon walked up the steps of the gazebo. Sitting in her chair, he gripped the armrests, his fingers curling over the edge possessively. He matched her smile but kept his request to himself. "There is plenty of time to discuss that later."

"Until then..." She sucked in a breath as if tasting Roc's deliciousness. "What do you recommend we do with our guest?"

"We wait. They will come for him."

"How do you know?"

"I know how they work. I know Roc's devious little plan to mount an army. But it is miniscule. And I left a trail even a blind bird could follow."

Jezebel laughed. "I haven't felt so much anticipation since"—she laughed like a young girl—"since ever."

# CHAPTER FIFTY-TWO

NAOMI WATCHED THROUGH THE window, her hands submerged in the soapy water as she washed dishes, but her gaze was trained on the two sisters outside.

Standing on the drive beside a boxy blue automobile, Hannah and Rachel spoke. Hannah held one of her boys and Rachel held her baby, who was a few months older. He was waving an arm excitedly. But the two women had worried looks, they sent furtive glances toward the house, and it gave Naomi a sinking feeling in her stomach. Something was wrong.

She shouldn't be so nosy. It was none of her business. Hannah shouldn't be speaking to Rachel since she was being shunned, but what was a sister to do? Rachel had driven over here, but Hannah had not yet invited her inside. But would that be so awful bad? Even though the elders didn't allow socializing with those being shunned, wasn't it one's Christian duty to help those in need? What if Rachel was in trouble? What if she needed help? Who else could she turn to?

Gabriel began to cry and Naomi dried her hands and went to him. She scooped him out of the crib and cuddled him close, cooing and joggling to quiet him. She didn't know the answers or problems the young women were discussing, but God did. And so she began to pray that the good Lord would give them answers and the grace to deal with whatever problem they faced.

When Gabriel fell back to sleep, Naomi gently laid him in the crib. She went back to the kitchen and slid her hands into the water, which had cooled. The cinnamon sugar mixture had stuck to the pan and she scraped at the hardened mess. Not meaning to but unable to stop herself, she stole a glance out the window. Rachel was gone, as was her car. But where had Hannah gone?

By the time Naomi had finished cleaning the kitchen and begun working on a load of laundry, Hannah entered the back door. Gideon had fallen asleep on her shoulder and she went straight to the bedroom to put the baby into his crib next to his sleeping brother. Naomi swept the floor until Hannah returned.

"I'm sorry I deserted you in here, Naomi." Hannah sat at the table with a bucket of green beans and began snapping them. "I meant to help you clean up."

"It's all right, Hannah." She kept sweeping even though questions begged to be asked. They were not her concern.

The snapping of the beans stopped suddenly. Tears dappled Hannah's cheeks, and Naomi rushed to her side. "What is it? What's wrong?" She knelt beside her friend. "Are you in pain? Should I get Levi?"

Shaking her head, she sniffed and tried to shake off the tears and Naomi's concern. "He knows."

Naomi waited, searching Hannah's face for some clue on how she could erase the pain. But maybe she couldn't. Maybe there was nothing she could do. So she clasped her friend's hands, bowed her head, and fervently prayed. The Lord would know how to help her. Sometimes prayer wasn't the least someone could do but the most.

"Oh, Naomi," Hannah whispered.

Still, Naomi prayed. When she had poured out her heart and concerns, she lifted her head.

Hannah's tears had dried and peace had settled over her features. "Thank you."

When Naomi started to rise and pull away, Hannah squeezed her hand and tugged her back. "Wait, please…"

"What can I do?"

"There's so much you don't understand." A mixture of emotions flitted across her friend's face like fireflies lighting and disappearing. Hannah drew a shuddering breath. "It's all starting again. I know it is."

"What is starting?"

"Have you ever done anything and it was like adding too much yeast to a batch of dough and suddenly you have way too much dough? And it was all because of your mistake? Oh, of course you haven't. But I have. And all of this is my fault." Her eyes filled with more tears.

Naomi wanted to say the right words but she didn't know what those might be. She patted Hannah's hand. "Is this about Rachel?"

Hannah's eyes widened.

"I saw her outside earlier," Naomi explained.

"It is in a way. Or partly. But it also has to do with Samuel."

It felt like she'd swallowed a rock.

Hannah squeezed Naomi's hand. "You like him, don't you?"

She considered sounding carefree with "of course" or "who wouldn't?" but those words stuck in her throat like a fish bone. All she could manage was the truth. "Yes."

Hannah patted her hand. "I'm so sorry, Naomi. So sorry to tell you this."

The pulse of her heartbeat throbbed behind her eyes and

pounded loud in her ears. *Had he left? Had he gone off with that English woman? Was the young woman pregnant?* Too many possibilities arose. "What?" she breathed.

"Samuel is missing."

She blinked, at first not comprehending. "Missing?"

"Yes. And Roc…Rachel's husband…went to go find him to protect him but now he's missing too."

"I don't understand. Protect him from what?"

Hannah swallowed hard. "I can't say anything else. I wish I could."

Naomi stayed on her knees, clasping Hannah's hands tightly. "I don't need to know anything else. We must pray."

"Yes." Hannah found her voice. "We'll pray."

"And we must ask others to pray," Naomi said. "The more prayers, the better."

# CHAPTER FIFTY-THREE

JACOB DUCKED BEHIND REIMEL. The clash of swords echoed in his head. He leapt over the sweeping arc of Reimel's wing and caught sight of the dark beast. He had tarnished and rusted wings but a vicious glare and brutal thrust.

Something grabbed Jacob from behind, and he whipped around. A smaller fluttering creature wrapped what seemed to be a long tentacle around Jacob's shoulder. He slapped at it, pushed the creature back, but it came at him again. Jacob shouted, "Git!"

It skittered away into the vestiges of shadows. He'd learned the tiny creatures were powerless unless he gave them power through his fears. And he was finally no longer afraid.

Swords clattered again, and Jacob dodged back and around to the other side of Remiel. He waved at the beast Remiel fought, trying to distract him, stuck out his tongue, and whooped triumphantly when Remiel landed a hefty blow. The beast listed sideways but thrust and parried. Remiel was quick, able to dodge and weave like a boxer.

Remiel did a quick, evasive move, his blade lifting the creature's weapon right out of his hand, metal clattering and sword cartwheeling over itself into oblivion. The dark creature narrowed red eyes at Jacob's audacity, Remiel's agility, then vanished.

Remiel smiled. Jacob offered his knuckles.

"Are you wounded?" Remiel asked.

"Give me your hand."

Remiel offered his hand, and Jacob closed it into a fist and knuckle-bumped it with his own. "And what is that for?"

"Just means 'way to go.'"

"Go where?"

Jacob laughed. "No. It means 'nice job.'"

"I see." Remiel studied his knuckles, then shrugged. He looked over his sword, the broad flat side, then the length, before he sheathed it.

"You do that often?" Jacob asked.

"I've had years of practice." Remiel's smile disappeared. His gaze drifted, and Jacob knew he was receiving some kind of word. No matter how badly Jacob wished they followed his own interests, the angel never ignored commands. "We must go."

"Where?"

"You will see."

# CHAPTER FIFTY-FOUR

S PLAYED OUT ON A table, hands and feet bound, Samuel stared up at the ceiling. He remembered Roberto's words: *Don't ever discount prayer. It is your most powerful weapon.*

At the moment, it was Samuel's *only* weapon.

The group of robed individuals lined up at a table, where one of the leaders poured out little white lines of powder, and as each member passed, they ingested it. All but Andi partook. She stayed near Samuel, guarding him, not in a protective sense but to keep him from escaping.

"Is that cocaine?" he asked, having heard about it from a few of his friends.

She smiled. "It is more powerful. Called bath salts. Have you heard of it?"

"No."

"Sometimes it causes cannibalistic behavior."

He strained his neck, lifting his head off the table. "Are you telling me they're going to eat me?"

She looked down at him with those black eyes that were no longer her own. She drew an invisible line from his jaw to his collarbone, sliding her short, blunt nail along his neck and sending a dreadful shiver through him.

Worry was too mild a word for what he felt. Sheer panic was a better fit. He fought the restraints—tugged, yanked, pulled—but nothing worked. He jerked his knee upward but whatever was wrapped around his ankle held tight. In one violent, terror-filled fit, he shook and struggled and wrestled. But none of the restraints gave way.

The robed men and women circled his table and chanted, their bodies swaying to the rhythm. The words were low, ominous, and unintelligible.

Andi's hand settled on his chest, her fingers smoothing out the wrinkles in his shirt before they began to slowly unbutton it and spread the material, exposing his flesh. In spite of the warmth in the room, he felt chilled, his skin puckering and recoiling against the chants spinning around him and over him. He stared up into Andi's sinister gaze. She stood behind him, her belly bumping the top of his head, as she leaned slightly forward. Her lips were as red as ripe strawberries. She smiled down at him, her hands splaying across his chest.

"Get me out of here," he said.

"Don't worry," she whispered. "You are mine. And I am yours." Her eyes closed and she rocked to the rhythmic chanting. "And we will be together—"

"Andi," he sounded harsh, desperate. His heart battered his chest cavity.

"No matter what happens," she said, her eyes closing, as she began swaying to the heady rhythm, "I will save you. Even when you don't think it will happen. Even when all seems lost. Trust me." She pushed against his chest, placing more and more pressure on him as her gaze bore into him. "Do you?"

He did not trust her. He knew he was going to die.

Maddox, a hood shading most of his face, stepped forward. In his hand was a knife. The thick blade gleamed in the candlelight. He moved toward Samuel, the knife rising above him. Samuel stared at the blade. Firelight flickered over the metal, making it seem alive and even deadlier.

Samuel squeezed his eyes closed, bracing himself for what was to come. And he prayed. Because it was his last resort.

A scuffling sounded on the stairs. A flood of footsteps descended. Samuel opened his eyes. The knife hovered above him. Maddox froze, his head turned toward the stairs. Samuel strained to see. *What was happening?*

Anger darkened Andi's face. She gripped his head and forced it sideways. Her lips parted in a hissing snarl. Her teeth flashed. Then she bit into his neck, her teeth sinking deep in the same place she'd wounded earlier. Pain rocked through him. Samuel's back arched off the table. The chanting rose in an insistent rhythm.

"*Vade retro, Satana!*" a voice boomed.

A shriek ripped through the room.

Andi fell back, her mouth wet with his blood. The room spun on some invisible axis for Samuel. Those wearing robes scattered. They threw open the curtains. Light shot into the room. Some raised windows. Others broke glass. Pandemonium charged the air.

Deserted on the table, Samuel saw a solitary man descending the stairs. He wore all black, except for a white collar, and held a silver cross. "*Vade retro, Satana!*" he repeated, his voice powerful and commanding, his footsteps determined and quickening. "*Nunquam suade mihi vana. Sunt mala quae libas, ipse vinena bibas.*"

The slight man moved forward into the room, holding the cross out like it was a sword. The robed men and women scrambled up and out through the windows. Some raced up the stairs behind him, like cockroaches escaping the light. Soon, only this odd man and Samuel remained in the room. The grave face peered down as he muttered more words Samuel did not understand. The older man touched a cloth to Samuel's neck wound and laid his palm on Samuel's forehead. Closing his eyes, the man's lips moved in silence.

The keen eyes opened and locked on Samuel. "We arrived in time, did we not?"

Samuel swallowed. What could he say? "What's happening?"

"Look at me."

Samuel looked into a pair of calm gray eyes and felt a peace descend on him.

"Do you believe in Jesus, the Christ, the son of God?"

Samuel licked his dry lips. "Yes."

"Good. Very good indeed. Now I know I can release you." He pulled a knife from his hip pocket and slashed the binds. Helping Samuel to sit upright, he gave him the cloth and said, "Keep this pressed to your wound. It does not look too serious but it is bleeding. Did you drink blood?"

Samuel shook his head and scrambled off the table, his knees wobbly as feeling rushed back into his feet.

"What just happened?"

"It's a long story." His gaze shifted around the room. "First we should get out of here. Before they gather their forces and get brave again." He hooked a hand under Samuel's arm to steady him. "Stick close to me."

"And who are you?"

"Father Anthony."

# CHAPTER FIFTY-FIVE

LEVI HITCHED HIS HORSE to the buggy. Before he climbed aboard, he touched his wife on the cheek, a brief but emotional connection that Naomi observed from the porch. It made her throat constrict and her thoughts drift toward Samuel.

*Where was he? Why hadn't he called or returned?*

The horse's hooves clomped on the gravel as Levi drove away. Hannah stood strong, shoulders straight, her gaze following her husband. Slowly, she turned back toward the house and came up the steps. "*Danke*, Naomi."

"No thanks necessary." She opened the door for Hannah. "I'm happy to help."

"Will your folks be worried?"

"They're aware the babies have been fussy. They will simply think I'm helping you with them. They will not worry."

Hannah looked back toward the drive, her gaze searching for one last glimpse of the buggy and her husband. "I suggested Levi might send Rachel and little David here to stay the night too." Her questioning gaze sought out Naomi. "Would that be all right?"

"If she needs our help, I cannot see the harm in that."

Hannah's gaze narrowed on Naomi. "If it causes trouble, I will make it clear you did not know and hopefully that will keep you—"

"I am not worried," Naomi reassured her friend. She wasn't worried about the bishop or gossip, but she was worried about Samuel.

The two women went about the rest of the chores, tending the babies, preparing a light supper. While Naomi kept working and moving, her mind whirred and her heart murmured one long continuous prayer.

After the babies had gone to sleep for the night, Hannah hugged her. "I'll see you in the morning."

"Call if you need help with the babies...or anything." Naomi went to the spare bedroom and knelt beside the bed, the one Samuel had slept in. She breathed in the lingering scent of him on the pillow. Time moved at a snail's pace as she whispered her prayers. Her knees ached, and her back hurt. Still, she prayed.

Some time past midnight, she heard the clop of horse's hooves and wheels on the drive. She pushed up straight, her back and knees stiff. She straightened her prayer *kapp* and apron.

Hannah met her at the back door. Still dressed in her white nightdress, she looked wide-eyed with fear.

"Who could it be?" Naomi whispered.

Hannah peered out the window, and her hand touched her heart. "Levi." Relief washed away the fear in her features, and she rushed out the door.

Naomi waited, trying to hear what was happening, but she remained inside in case the babies awoke. Her fingers pinched together. She leaned against the door, praying all was well, praying for good news.

Soon, Hannah was back and squeezing Naomi's arm. "Samuel is safe and on his way home."

A pent-up breath rushed out of Naomi, and she breathed

easier. "Thank the good Lord." But then she thought of Rachel. "But what about Roc? Is there—"

"No word yet."

Naomi's heart felt heavy. "Rachel must be sick with worry."

"Levi is going back to stay with her and help if he can. He said he's going to get me a cell phone. He's been worried about us here by ourselves. I don't want one, but I'll do as he thinks best. Still, I'm so relieved he came to tell us the news. He wanted us to know about Samuel. He didn't think we'd sleep all night for worrying."

"Why doesn't he bring Rachel here?" Naomi suggested.

Hannah shook her head. "She wouldn't hear of leaving. She wants to be there in case Roc calls or comes back."

"Of course." Naomi nodded. "But Levi should stay with you. I'll go to Rachel."

"Naomi, you could get in trouble."

"I will go," she said firmly. "I want to pray with her."

# CHAPTER FIFTY-SIX

S AMUEL MET UP WITH half the team in New York. He'd
called them with Father Anthony's cell phone. Now,
they sat in a church that had been deserted by its parishioners, but it was the only place they could speak openly. A
thunderstorm raged outside. Inside the sanctuary, they could
hear the rumble of thunder and crack of lightning.

Father Anthony placed a guard at each door. He was not
taking any chances. "We reached our hand into a hornet's
nest, a small one, but we should expect some of the hornets
to exact their revenge. So we should be ready."

"Where's Roc?" Joe demanded, his deep-set gaze fierce as
a wolf's as he glared at Samuel.

The question jarred Samuel. "How should I know?" He
didn't want to admit his disappointment that Roc, their leader, hadn't come to help him. But he had more questions than
just that one. "I want to know—"

"Roc Girouard?" Father Anthony asked from his seat
on the front row. He had hawkish features and a slim build
that looked as if the stiff wind outside could blow him to
New Jersey.

"You know Roc?" Harry asked, leaning back in one of
the pews. The whites of his eyes glowed brightly against his
dark complexion. "He runs our training center."

An awkward grin crossed the priest's face, his gray eyes

lighting with pleasure. "I'm glad to hear that. Very glad indeed. Glad to know he finally became a believer."

"He's a believer all right," Joe spoke with solid conviction. "But we can't waste time here." He stalked up the aisle. "We need to get back to Promise."

"Might not be a good idea." Father Anthony's warning stopped Joe.

"No offense, Father, but why the hell not?"

"You could be leading those hornets right back to your own home. If you have anyone back there you care about, then you want to keep them safe."

Joe crossed his arms over his thick chest, and his gaze narrowed on the priest. "How do you know Roc?"

"We grew up together. He chose the police department to fight truth and justice. I chose the priesthood. Neither of us knew we'd be doing this though."

Joe assessed the priest for a long moment. "Well, you should know—Roc's missing."

"What?" the question burst out of Samuel, and he lurched to his feet, still feeling weak and unsteady.

"When?" Father Anthony tensed, his face darkening with serious intent. "What happened?"

"Once we realized Samuel was in trouble, Roc headed out to track him." Joe nodded toward Samuel. "I'm thinking it was a trap of some kind. I think that girl vamp lured Samuel away. So when Roc took out after him, all alone, I think she nabbed him."

"How could she take Roc if she was with me?" Samuel questioned. "I never saw Roc." His mind raced back to the night Andi convinced him to go to New York. *Was it only yesterday?* His disjointed memories made it feel as if weeks had passed.

"When Roc no longer answered our text messages," Joe said, "or phone calls, we knew he was in trouble. But I thought"—he shook his head at his assumption—"hoped he'd be with Samuel."

"Did you check the house where you found Samuel?" Joe asked the priest.

"As best I could. But I was alone." Father Anthony propped a hand on his narrow hip. "And I had to get Samuel out of there. But I'm fairly certain no one else was there."

"Maybe Brydon took him," Samuel suggested.

"Brydon?" Joe snapped his attention in Samuel's direction. "Roc's old partner?"

Samuel nodded. "Andi mentioned Brydon…or I think she did. My memories are blurry."

"It's the best we have to go on now," Anthony said. "But where would Brydon have taken Roc? And why?"

The why seemed obvious to all in the room, and for a moment silence descended on them with dread. But these were men of action, not regret. The discussion picked up and went round and round with Joe arguing against Anthony. Samuel's head ached, and his gaze drifted to the front of the church. Jesus hung on the cross, his hands and feet and brow stained with blood. He understood why this church was empty, devoid of hope or believers. They'd left Christ on the cross instead of focusing on the power of His resurrection.

"Roc could be dead already." Father Anthony spoke calmly. Overhead, a boom of thunder resounded in the church. "Then again, because he's in the thick of this battle, whoever took him might have a purpose." The religious man had an amazing ability, in spite of his slight size, to go toe-to-toe against these burly men. Slowly, he rose out of the pew, straightening to his full height, like a warrior ready to enter another battle. "We'll return to Promise."

Samuel's stomach trembled. "But you said we shouldn't go back, that it was too dangerous."

"I changed my mind. Now we have to get ready."

"Ready for what?" Joe asked. The stained-glass windows looked dull without sunlight, but lightning flashed, making the colors spark and flare.

In a hushed, reverent voice, Father Anthony said, "A war."

---

They rode in the van the team brought from Pennsylvania, keeping to farm roads and staying as much as possible out of congested cities, which Father Anthony explained were "feeding grounds." The night was dark with heavy clouds. The roads shimmered from the earlier rain.

Joe drove, one hand on the wheel, not worrying about the speed limit. From the seat behind him, Samuel could see the speedometer's needle pushing ninety. Most of the time, he closed his eyes to ease the invisible talons digging into his skull.

"Roc told me," Joe said to Father Anthony, who was sitting in the front passenger seat, "that you'd been missing yourself. You don't have the signs, so I know you're not a vamp. So what happened to you?"

Father Anthony held a bottle of water in his hand. "It's a long story, my friend."

"We're not exactly friends," Joe answered in his gruff way. "But we have time."

"Joe," Samuel argued, "you don't have to—"

"It's all right," Father Anthony reassured him.

"Yes, I do." Joe clenched his teeth. "I'm not taking him

all the way to our base camp without knowing more about him. Some vamp could be following him...*us* right now."

"Multiply that," Father Anthony chuckled, "and you'd be closer to the truth. I understand Joe's precautions, Samuel. He's a smart warrior. One thing you should all know right from the start—never trust anyone. Not anyone."

Joe switched lanes, swerving around a slow-moving truck. "So why should I take you to our one safe place? Where innocents could be killed?"

"You're a fool if you think any place is safe. But Roc has trained you well."

"So what gives? Where have you been?"

"Where haven't I been?" Father Anthony spoke more to himself than Joe. "I wasn't aware that I was missing actually. But I have been out of touch with Roc for a while. The last I knew he had been sent to Pennsylvania on a murder case. I suspected vampires were involved, but he wasn't ready to hear the truth. Not then. I'm glad to know he has seen the light, so to speak."

He gave a grim smile, untwisted the cap on a water bottle, and took a sip. "I have been studying these creatures for many years, reaching outside the confines of the church for answers. It was somewhat ironic that I would find answers then within the church. I came into contact with another priest in Italy and went there to learn from him and just recently returned. In fact, I was just landing in New York when the Lord prompted me to travel outside the city."

"Is that how you found me?" Samuel asked.

"Yes. And no. Actually, a parishioner in a friend of mine's church had deep concerns about her teenager. This parent contacted my friend, who then called me. Many within the church community have ostracized me for my radical beliefs.

Then again, when supernatural things begin happening, I'm the first one they call in desperation." He shrugged a narrow shoulder. "We all come to knowledge and wisdom in our own ways. Still, I did not know Samuel or that he was in trouble when I went to that house on Long Island. I went to break up an occultist ritual, where I suspected a sacrifice would be made."

"Would they have really killed me?" Samuel said, remembering Andi's dark gaze devouring him. *But she had promised to save him.*

Father Anthony glanced back at Samuel. "You do not know what they are capable of. Even those who are not vampires, they take all sorts of drugs. They *believe* they are vampires, whether they are or not. They drink blood. And they have been known to kill. They do all sorts of abominations. None of it should be taken lightly. They are dealing with evil."

"No, you don't understand." Samuel leaned forward. "My girlfriend...really ex-girlfriend," he corrected himself, "said she would protect me."

"Is that the one who took you to that place?" Joe asked.

"She wanted to show me—"

"She wanted to *change* you," Joe said. To Father Anthony, he added, "Samuel has not finished his training."

Defensive, Samuel challenged Joe. "You don't know what she wanted."

"And you do?"

"This girlfriend," Father Anthony interrupted. "She's a vampire?"

"I-I..." Samuel shrugged. "I think maybe so."

"Is she the one who bit your neck?"

Reflexively, Samuel touched the tender flesh. "Yes."

"She would have changed you," Father Anthony confirmed. "That or killed you straight out. Better that I rescued you. Or now you would be hunting us."

"I wouldn't—"

Father Anthony shifted to hold Samuel's gaze. His blue eyes pierced. "Yes, you would."

Samuel felt his face swell as blood pumped furiously through him, but he drew a steadying breath. He owed this man much for saving his life. "Thank you, Father Anthony. I do appreciate your good timing."

"The Lord's timing," Father Anthony corrected gently. He shifted back around in his seat. "Anyway, in Italy I learned these creatures are not the walking dead, as I had once believed them to be. No, these creatures are simply inhabited bodies."

Joe glanced from the road to Father Anthony. "What do you mean?"

"I went to Italy to study the art of exorcism."

"The art?" Joe asked.

"Exactly. Almost a lost art now. Very few priests practice it. Even fewer are allowed to openly. It is a travesty the church has allowed. A travesty."

"Allowed?" Joe repeated. "You have to get permission to perform an exorcism?"

"Of course."

"Why?" Samuel asked. "Is it so difficult?"

Father Anthony took another sip of water and dabbed his mouth with the back of his sleeve. "Modern man doesn't like to look to the spiritual, for spiritual matters are deep and quite often unseen. Over the years, modern science and psychology has taught us we must see in order to believe. So we have put names and labels on conditions in our effort to understand…and control.

"Demonic possession has been rationalized and explained away by psychosis and other psychological maladies, remedied by prescription drugs. At least sometimes. But many, many cases never see positive results. Many mental disorders cannot be solved by simply popping a pill. The church, I am sorry to say, has bought into all of this modernity. It has forgotten we are in an ancient battle. *Not against flesh and blood.*" His tone deepened. "*But against rulers, against the authorities, against the powers of this dark world, and against the spiritual forces of evil in the heavenly realms.*"

# CHAPTER FIFTY-SEVEN

NAOMI FELT A CATCH in her chest, her heart hiccupping. She stood inside Rachel's house, staring out the window as the van pulled into the drive. Rachel rushed outside. Smiles were passed around, hugs exchanged as Samuel climbed out of the van.

The early morning sun cast red-tinted light across the yard, but Naomi's gaze was transfixed on Samuel. His hair appeared golden, his shoulders broader than she remembered. He wore a small patch of a bandage on his neck. *Was he hurt? Had he been wounded somehow?* She remembered cupping his large hand in hers and bandaging the blisters and stripped flesh. He shook hands with a couple of the men. One wrapped his thick arms around Samuel and lifted him off his feet. Naomi smiled with them, even if from a distance, and whispered a prayer of thanksgiving.

The baby fussed, and Naomi went to check on him. David was standing in his crib, his little legs wobbly, making him bob and weave. He wore a proud smile on his face.

"And what have you done there, David?" She smiled.

Cooing, he bounced until his legs buckled, and he sat down hard. His blue eyes widened.

"Wanna try again?" She held out her hands for him to grasp. The baby wrapped his little hands around her fingers and she pulled him up until he stood, jouncing and swaying. "There you go!" She smiled at his eagerness. "Happy now?"

He made a squealing noise as he tilted sideways. She caught him and lifted him out of the crib.

"You're a strong one." She hitched him on her hip. "I bet you'd like a little snack, huh? Your mama and I made some bread. It's still warm." She carried the baby into the kitchen and set him in his high chair. He pummeled the plastic tray while she cut a slice of bread and spread some butter on it. Pinching off little bites, she scattered them over the tray. "Here you go."

The back door opened and Samuel walked in. Her breath caught in her throat. She wanted to rush to him but held back, unsure. *Did they have that kind of relationship?* Her heart jerked crazily at the sight of him. Maybe the memory of the woman who'd come to see him…had taken him away… stopped Naomi from throwing her arms around him and kissing him. There were too many questions and not enough answers for her to reveal her heart.

Samuel locked gazes with her and swallowed hard.

She gave him a warm smile but remained where she stood. "Samuel, it's good that you are back. We were awful worried."

"Feels good to be home." He closed the door behind him, and Naomi realized Rachel wasn't coming inside.

"Is everything all right?" she asked.

He cleared his throat. "Can we talk?"

"Of course." Her gaze drifted toward the window, but she could no longer see Rachel or any of the men outside. David was gumming the bread and his cheeks and mouth glistened with the greasy sheen of butter. She wiped her hands on a dish towel.

"Rachel will be back soon," Samuel said. "She went to make a new member of the team comfortable in the bunkhouse."

"I see."

He approached the table slowly. "It was nice of you to come and help her. I hope it will not cause you trouble with the bishop."

"I'm not worried."

He leaned onto the back of a chair. "I wanted to explain what happened."

"You don't owe me an explanation, Samuel. We are all glad you are home safe. That is enough."

"I need you to understand." He crossed his arms, then let them fall to his sides. "That woman...the one who came here. Andi. That's her name. She was my...we used to see each other...sort of...but not anymore. Not anymore," he emphasized. "Not since I left Ohio. She had information about Jacob. That's why I went off with her. Not for any other reason."

The tension along her neck and chest eased. There was something incredibly sweet about his awkwardness. He was making it very plain there was nothing between him and that *English* woman—at least not anymore. He looked like a lost little boy when he spoke of Jacob. The raw need to know more about the brother he'd lost forever touched Naomi's heart. "And did she?" she asked, her voice soft. "Did you learn more about Jacob?"

Samuel gave a slight shrug. "I don't really know. It was..." His voice trailed off and he finally said, "Not good."

Her gaze shifted toward the bandage on his neck. "You were hurt."

He touched the edge of the bandage. "I'm okay."

"You're sure?"

He nodded. "I learned a couple of things while I was gone."

She waited, her hand folding over the top of a chair that stood between them.

"I learned I couldn't trust her…Andi." A hardness glinted in his eyes.

*Had the woman betrayed him? Hurt his heart?* "I'm sorry."

Samuel gave her an odd questioning look.

"I know how it feels to be betrayed. And well…I am sorry."

"It wasn't the kind of betrayal you might imagine. But, Naomi"—he moved forward and took hold of her hands— "I also learned there are some things worth caring about… worth dying for." His words pierced her heart, and she felt a charge in the air humming between them.

David gave a sharp cry, and Naomi startled, focusing on the baby. "What is it? Oh, are you thirsty?" She hurried to the cabinet and pulled out a sippy cup and filled it with apple juice. The baby guzzled the juice, and she turned her attention back to Samuel.

"Things?" she asked.

His mouth quirked with a half smile. "A leading question, Naomi."

Her cheeks warmed and she looked away, but he moved toward her and took her hands in his again. His touch was warm and insistent. "I'm sorry I involved you in all of this."

"It was my choice."

"Was it?" The smile had left, replaced by a seriousness that unnerved her.

Nervously, she licked her lips. *Would he kiss her now?* A longing to hold him, hold on to him, welled up inside her.

"Naomi." He spoke quietly. "You should go home. It's not safe here."

His words punched her. *What was he saying?* She felt a

fracture crack open her heart. "Not safe?" She scrambled for a reason to stay. She didn't want to leave. She wanted to be a part of his life. *But how? When he apparently didn't want her...* "But Rachel," she managed. "She needs help. And you..." She was squeezing his hand, not wanting to let go. "I will help you."

"There's nothing you can do."

"Yes, there is. I began a prayer chain. We will continue to pray for your protection and of the others. The good Lord has brought you back." She felt tears rising and struggled to hold them back.

For a long moment, he stared at their joined hands. "That may be what saved me. That and Father Anthony arriving in time."

"Saved you?"

"Naomi"—his voice cracked—"as much as I may want you to stay here with me, I want you to stay safe. That's my utmost concern." He released her hand and stepped away. "We're leaving soon, the team and I, and so should you. Levi will take you home."

Her heart jolted. She felt herself reeling. She placed a hand against the counter. "Where are you going?"

"After Roc. We've had a couple of leads. Randy, Pete, Lance, and Shawn, one half of our team, are tracking leads on Roc." He balled his hand into a fist. "This is all my fault. And now, the team is split. Roc is gone." His voice cracked. "We have to get him back."

She threw caution out the window and clutched his arm. "You will, Samuel. I believe. But it will be dangerous, *ja*?"

"Like dropping into hell." He covered her hand on his arm with his other hand. "But don't worry. God willing, I'll be back. In the meantime, you must go home. Do you understand?"

She didn't understand why someone would want to hurt Roc Girouard, but it didn't matter if she understood or not. She simply knew these men had to help their friend, just as she felt driven to help Samuel. "Do not worry about me. I will be praying for you...for Roc." She squeezed his arm even as she felt her heart contract. "The Lord will give you the strength you need."

"I hope so."

She peered deeply into Samuel's eyes. "I know he will. Believe, Samuel. And bring Roc back to his family."

His mouth thinned to a straight line. He started to pull away but stopped and leaned toward her. He tilted his head, and she felt her stomach plummet as her soul soared. The line of his mouth softened as he touched his lips to hers.

It was the briefest of kisses—soft, gentle, chaste—and yet it flipped her world upside down, turned it inside out. Her heart jerked crazily in response. She longed to grab on to Samuel, to hold him close, and yet she held herself in check.

When he backed away, he held her gaze. "I'll return. I promise."

# CHAPTER FIFTY-EIGHT

THEY SPENT THE NIGHT at the training center, readying equipment, preparing the van and themselves. The day was muggy, as if the weather was awaiting some sign or cue. By evening, clouds rolled in but no word came.

"We must wait," advised Father Anthony, who had been conversing with Father Roberto.

"Randy will contact us when they've discovered something," Roberto agreed. "Until then, we should rest. There will be plenty to do in time."

"Yes." Anthony looked each team member in the eye. "You will be no good to anyone if you are exhausted. Get some sleep."

Joe stepped forward. "The van is packed. We are ready to move, so everyone hit the sack. Now, while we have time."

Solemnly, everyone found a bunk and fell into it. Shifts were established and patrols guarded the grounds. Silence descended, except for the occasional tossing and turning, rustling of sheets, squeaking of springs, and a cough or grunt.

Samuel stared up at the darkened ceiling, not seeing anything, yet seeing everything he had been missing. His mind churned over the events of the last couple of days. *What if Father Anthony hadn't arrived? What if Andi had changed him? Was she out there, even now, planning another attack?*

For what seemed like hours, he tossed and turned, his

mind chasing thoughts like his old dog, Buster, after a rabbit. He worried about Naomi. She had stayed with Rachel,
refusing to go home. He worried what Roc was enduring.
Or was he already dead? But Roc was prepared for death. He
had a strong relationship with the Almighty.

Words from a story he'd read, one of Jacob's favorites,
came to him. *Deep into that darkness peering, long I stood there,
wondering, fearing, doubting...*

How long had he been staring into that darkness, trying
to make sense of it? Had it crept into his soul? Or was the
darkness there because of an innate bent toward evil? Was he
ready to die? He'd already faced certain death once in the last
day. And he'd understood his errors. For too long, he'd put
it off, but now was the time for a decision.

Flinging his covers off, he climbed out of the bunk,
pulled on his clothes, and quietly left the room where one
or two were snoring. He made his way through the darkened training center to the place where Roc used to pray.
Several candles, their wicks blackened, sat on the table.
Samuel lit one and the light wavered over a leather-bound
Bible. Father Roberto's. Samuel picked it up and flipped
through the crinkly pages, landing on a passage in 1 Kings
where Elijah, the prophet, competed against the prophets of
Baal. Elijah said to the people, "*How long halt ye between two
opinions? If the LORD be God, then follow him: but if Baal, then
follow him.*"

How long had Samuel been sitting on that fence, unde-
cided, reluctant to make a choice? Now was the time. He
closed the Bible and blew out the candle; the pale gray smoke
rose and drifted off. He no longer needed a candle to light
his way.

*Behold, I stand at the door, and knock: if any man hear my voice, and open the door, I will come in to him, and will sup with him, and he with me.*

He knelt in that place, where he'd seen Roc praying. How long he stayed there he couldn't be sure. He went through the long list of sins as they came to mind and asked the God of the universe for forgiveness. A quiet peace filled him, and when his mind had stilled, he rose.

"Am I interrupting?" a voice startled him. Father Anthony stood nearby.

"I was...uh..."

"No need for explanations, Samuel." Anthony placed a hand on Samuel's shoulder. "We all should be readying our souls."

"Has there been word yet?"

"Not that I'm aware. I've been on patrol, but Joe has taken my place. Father Roberto will rouse the troops when it's time." He sighed and rubbed his face wearily. "I'm not sure I'll be able to sleep. Seems to be my own thorn. Need some reflective time of my own, I fear. Are you back to bed then?"

"There's one more thing I need to do." Samuel searched the wisdom in the older man's face. "Could you help me?"

# Chapter Fifty-Nine

"Who is that?" Jacob asked Remiel. Another angel, large and gleaming with bulging muscles and stern expression, had appeared in the training center, giving a solicitous nod to Remiel. He took the same stance Jacob had become accustomed to seeing—sword drawn, planted, with hands on hilt.

"It's our signal." Remiel turned away and walked through the wall of the center and into the night.

Jacob gave chase. "What do you mean?"

"It's time to go, Jacob."

"Go? How can we go?" He glanced back at the center. "Samuel is still in trouble. It's just getting worse." Jacob felt a sudden tug on his body, and he was being lifted into the air, along with Remiel. "No! I'm not ready. I can't leave my brother."

"Samuel's fate is already sealed." Remiel leveled his blue gaze on Jacob. "And so is yours."

"I don't care about my fate—"

"That's admirable, but we still must go."

A wall of emotions crashed over Jacob. "But I failed."

Remiel stopped, his gaze softening into sympathy. "There was nothing you could do. Don't you understand that yet?"

Frustrated, Jacob fisted his hands. "So what was all this? An exercise in futility?"

"You requested more time, and it was granted. But it wasn't allowed for Samuel's sake." Remiel hooked his hand around Jacob's arm. "It was for you."

"What do you mean?"

"Samuel had to make his own decisions." Remiel spoke slowly as if speaking to a child. "He had to choose—just as you made your choice."

Fear gripped Jacob, its fingers tightening their hold on him. He searched the shadows for the dark creatures. "Are they going to take me away now?" Frantically, he looked for the shadowy creatures. "Don't I get a choice?"

"You made your choice."

"But I wasted my life."

"Yahweh never allows waste. Come, Jacob."

Once more, he drew back, but the force pulling him was too strong. "But I don't deserve anything."

Remiel smiled, and his face shone like a star. "Exactly."

# Chapter Sixty

A CLICKING SOUND WOKE HER. Naomi lay in the spare bed, her heart galloping, and waited for it to calm. After a moment, the sound came again. A flutter against the windowpane. *Was it the weather? A storm brewing? A branch or leaves?*

More awake now, she pushed up on her elbows. A tap-tap on the window brought her to an upright position. Tap-tap. Tap-tap. The rhythm had no equivalent in nature. Someone was at the window.

She scrambled out of bed, and the corner of the quilt tripped her. She righted herself, headed toward the window, and stopped. *Who could it be? Was it safe to open the shade? Or should she get Rachel? No, she didn't want to disturb her.* Rachel needed her rest. Naomi stood in the middle of the room and forced herself to breathe. She was being a silly goose. *Get a hold of yourself, Naomi.*

*What if it were Samuel?* Maybe they'd heard from Randy's team. Maybe Samuel was leaving and wanted to say good-bye.

She wrapped a sweater about her shoulders and pulled the green shade away from the edge of the window. The night remained dark and gray, with a heavy covering of clouds overhead. Her eyes strained to make out shadow from form. A twig scratched the glass, and she startled, her heart leaping into her throat.

Samuel's face appeared below. He smiled and motioned for her to come outside. Automatically, she nodded and closed the shade.

She dressed quickly, scuffing into her sneakers as she crossed the room, and pinned her *kapp* in place, pricking her finger with a pin. She hurried to the back door, unlocked it, and stepped out into the cool night.

Samuel stepped out of the shadows and took her hand in his, closing his fingers over hers. "Come on."

"Where are we going?" she whispered.

He pulled her toward dense foliage that bordered the property. "Not far, but we have to hurry. There's not much time."

She followed close behind him, her shoes snagging on roots and fallen branches. Leaves and bracken crunched beneath their footsteps. It sounded like they were loud enough to wake the dead, but no lights came on in the house behind them. Farther away was the barn, which Rachel called the training center, and it appeared even darker and quieter. Branches stretched out their prickly fingers to scratch at them, but Samuel pushed them back and made a path for her. With both hands, she clung to one of his, forming a lifeline between them.

She heard the soft, rippling sound of the Susquehanna River. They broke into the open at the same time, side by side, and a few feet more brought them to the edge of the water. She felt the soft, damp ground beneath her shoes.

"Now we can begin," came a voice out of the dark.

Her hand tightened on Samuel's. He squeezed back in reassurance. "It's okay. It's Father Anthony. He's the one that saved me yesterday. And he's an old friend of Rachel's husband."

"Did you explain to her?" the older man asked.

"Not yet. I didn't want to wake anyone else." Samuel faced Naomi. "I made a decision tonight. Not an easy one, one I've been wrestling with. You were the one that said the Lord would guide me, *ja*?"

She nodded.

"I'm a believer, Naomi. I can never go back to who I was, what I was, not now. Not after all I've seen and experienced. I'm not asking you to follow or be a part of this. But I want you to understand. I wanted you to be a witness. My faith in the Almighty is no less than any Amish person who is baptized. But my baptism is not for membership into a district but simply to declare that I am a believer and forgiven."

She touched his arm and smiled. "You're to be baptized?"

"Tonight. Here and now." With one final squeeze of her hand, he turned toward Father Anthony, stripped out of his shirt, and waded into the water, which came to his waist.

The pale moon's glow filtered through clouds and bathed his bare skin. He bowed his head. Father Anthony made his way out into the river and stood beside him, placing a hand on Samuel's shoulder and raising the other to the heavens. Uttering words that sounded like another language, the priest scooped up a handful of water and poured it over the top of Samuel's head. Rivulets of water ran unhindered down his neck, chest, and arms.

When he opened his eyes, he beamed. Feeling privileged he would want her here in this sacred moment, she dabbed at the tears in her eyes and met his smile with one of her own.

# CHAPTER SIXTY-ONE

THE CALL CAME JUST before dawn arrived, and the team set out immediately. The van bisected Ohio. They did not bother keeping to back roads but drove a relentless pace, rarely making stops and then only for gasoline.

Samuel watched the blur of landscape out the passenger window. In an odd way, it looked both familiar and foreign. He kept to himself that his folks lived southeast of Cincinnati, never mentioned he'd lived in the state for three years, never even thought of his folks or friends here. His life was back in Promise, Pennsylvania, and his heart was with Naomi. But if he allowed her into his thoughts or an image of her to settle in his mind, then he might hesitate or falter in battle. He had to break any ties to what he held dear. His focus fixated on rescuing Roc.

Joe stayed in contact with the second team, which had followed Roc's trail this far. They were camped somewhere in the middle of Nowhere, Kansas, outside a suspicious compound, waiting for the van holding Samuel and the rest of the team. Together, they would attack the compound and rescue Roc. At least, that was the plan. They would not leave without their fearless leader.

One if not more on their team could die. And he wasn't sure he would make it out alive either.

All of those in the van were good men, bold in their

determination, honorable in their decision to fight this pestilence. Chris drove and chewed gum, his jaw popping as each mile disintegrated behind them. He never entered the conversation but bounced from radio station to station, searching for country music. Occasionally, he'd say, "Joe, you heard from the boys? They still waiting for us?"

"They will," Joe said without opening his eyes. He rested on the far backseat.

"They don't have a choice," Father Anthony stated. "Not if they want to survive this ordeal."

The priest sat in the front passenger seat, his head bent over his cell phone, his finger scrolling through messages or websites or maybe even scripture. With a calm and serene demeanor, he acted as if he already knew the outcome of this venture.

Earlier, when the call came, Anthony had confided in Samuel, "Roc's my dearest friend. I hope I don't have to kill him."

"You think it'll come to that?"

With a nonchalant shrug, Anthony said, "If it were me, if I were changed, I know he would do me the courtesy. Still, Roc is strong willed. It would not be easy for them to change him. It's more likely we'll find him dead. If we find him at all."

Over the past few weeks, Samuel had watched Roc and Rachel, the tender looks between them, the gentle teasing, and their deep affection. They shared the kind of love that should be the foundation of a marriage. They were good together, and he couldn't understand why anyone, Amish included, could believe it was wrong for them to be married.

Samuel determined they would find Roc. They would rescue him. But if Father Anthony was right, and Roc had been changed, Samuel would not tell Rachel. He would simply declare her husband's bravery to her.

He remembered Naomi standing beside Rachel on the porch as the van pulled away. She would be a comfort to Rachel if something went wrong—and vice versa.

# CHAPTER SIXTY-TWO

THUNDER RUMBLED OUTSIDE. THE clicking of knitting needles echoed in the sitting area of Rachel's home as Naomi kept at her knitting, determined to make progress on the scarf for her little brother, Matt. Yet her mind continuously drifted toward Samuel and Roc and all those men in danger. Not one had voiced fear or concern. Brave determination had squared their shoulders and made their gazes steady. But she felt the cold dread of fear, even if she didn't completely understand what danger they faced. It felt as if her heart counted each second, each minute and hour since they'd left.

Naomi missed a stitch. With an irritated sigh, she plunked the whole scarf into her lap. "Rachel," she asked, "how did you know?"

Rachel sat in a well-worn reclining chair but with the back upright, Bible open on her lap. Her finger marked her place. For a moment, she studied Naomi. "About Roc?"

At Naomi's nod, Rachel leaned back with a reminiscent sigh. "The idea had been forming in my mind for a while, I think, or maybe my heart. After David was born, the seed took root. When Roc brought me home to Pennsylvania, I felt like my heart was being ripped out of my chest." A wisp of a smile touched her lips. "I wept most of the train ride. Poor Roc thought I was scared to face my family again. But

I knew—knew I couldn't let go of him, couldn't be away from him. I had to be a part of his life. Somehow. Someway. So I prayed and asked God what I could do, what *we* could do." Her shoulder lifted in a barely noticeable shrug. "And I knew God would find a way. I just had a peace about all of it, even telling my family." She chuckled. "I told them before I said anything to Roc."

Amazed at the story that seemed so different from any of her friends' paths to marriage, Naomi asked, "So he didn't ask you to marry him? Or to leave the district?"

"Oh, he never would have done that. He knew the price I would pay. He'd heard about shunning. Plus, he also knew what his life was like, where he was headed, and he didn't see a way to have a wife or family. But God had another plan."

Concerned for her friend, Naomi prayed God would bring Roc back to his family. She admired Rachel for her courage and strength. "I know you loved him, that's plain to see, but how did you find the courage to leave your home, your faith, everything you'd ever known?"

"I didn't leave my faith. It's right here." Her hand patted the Bible—the thin paper crinkling beneath her palm—then her heart. "What I came to understand and see beyond the white picket fences of our district—there is a hurting world. And there is evil lurking, searching, determined to find it's way into our lives."

"*Be sober*," Naomi quoted scripture, "*be vigilant; because your adversary the devil, as a roaring lion, walketh about, seeking whom he may devour.*"

"Exactly." Rachel closed the Bible and brought it to her chest. "And just because we felt safe and secure in our homes, in our Amish district, behind our green shades, didn't mean we were safe. I found a man who understood that. I couldn't turn my back on what God was showing me or on the man I believed could do something about it."

Truth pounded in the depth of Naomi's heart. "And so you married Roc."

"I did." In spite of the fear and concern in Rachel's blue eyes, she also had complete confidence she was following God's will. And with that came peace.

Or so Naomi believed. But living it out was not so easy. Right now, fear gnawed at her belly and worry twisted her thoughts into doubts. She wanted to hide herself away from the hurt she feared was coming. With trembling hands, she went back to her knitting, picking up the dropped stitch. The long metal needles clicked rhythmically. Her voice sounded small when she asked, "Do you have any regrets?"

"No." Rachel's answer was swift, no hesitation in her voice. She leaned toward Naomi. "You're called now too. Aren't you?"

Her hands shook, but she stared down at the pale green knitting needles, afraid to admit the truth. She kept knitting. The clicking sounded like tiny accusations.

"Naomi?" Rachel pressed.

Drawing a shuddering breath, Naomi gripped the needles hard, feeling the yarn and metal against her palm. The textures were so different yet oddly complementary: soft and strong. Could that work in real life? When she raised her chin, tears spilled down her cheeks. "I don't know. Honestly, I don't, Rachel. I care about Samuel. I do." She stared at the shade and wished she could see out into the night, beyond the light rain, the churning clouds, and to the faraway place where Samuel now was. "But I don't know what I'd do if something happened to him."

Rachel's hand touched hers. "Well, you'll know when the time is right."

"Will I?"

"I have no doubt. You see, Naomi, I was foolish and made many mistakes. I didn't believe God could forgive me enough to use me. But now I understand He can. He's not looking for a perfect person. He's looking for a willing heart."

Her tongue dabbed the corner of her mouth where tears had gathered. "And me?"

"He's already using you, far more than you probably realize. You're far stronger than I am. You already know your source of strength and you wield your prayers and the word like a sword." She closed her Bible and hugged it. The wisp of her smile faded. "Thankfully the devil cannot prevail. I just hope Samuel can learn the worth of being on God's side. Before it's too late."

# CHAPTER SIXTY-THREE

A TWISTING ROUTE AND MULTITUDE of stairs placed Roc in front of a simple, unadorned door. He stood in the dim hallway, stared at the knob, but did not reach for it. He felt disconnected from his body, as if he couldn't have made himself open the door if he'd wanted to, if his life had depended on it.

*What was wrong with him?* The fact that he recognized that he was even considering such things gave him hope he might recover.

"Are you ready for this, Roc?" Brydon twisted the knob. "Brace yourself."

Sunlight flooded the hallway. Closing his eyes, Roc swayed in the warmth. He hadn't realized he was so numbingly cold. But now his body seemed to come alive. Brydon steadied him with a hand on his arm, then gave Roc a slight tug to move forward. Two steps then three, and his eyes fluttered, trying to open against the barrage of sunlight. A sweet, cloying scent enveloped him. Roses. He took in the lush surroundings of floral gardens. He stumbled over a slate stone; the path lead toward a gazebo. If he had to die, this would be as good a place as any. At least it was beautiful. Not that it mattered.

Emma died in a parking lot; Josef, a cemetery; Jacob, a yard. Roc hoped when the time came, he would be brave.

His thoughts turned to Rachel, and his chest tightened.

*Had he put enough precautions in place to protect her and David? What of the sweet baby he had come to love as his own son? What would happen to them? To their family? Their dreams? How unfair for one woman to lose two husbands and one child two fathers. Was it all Roc's fault?* David might never remember him, and that would be for the best. But Rachel…

Anger shot through his veins at the injustice. He had lost Emma. He intimately knew the painful recovery. If there was such. But together, he and Rachel had found comfort in each other's arms, love and purpose. She'd taught him faith. Faith in God. Faith in her. And if he died now, he'd be betraying her trust. He couldn't just give up. He had to fight.

*But how?* He could barely manage the thought much less any action beyond blinking and walking. Yet she was depending on him. David was counting on him to come home. He would not let them down. His hand fisted, like a spasm.

"Well, well, well." A woman—no, a vampire, with eyes as black as death, sat beneath the gazebo's canopy. "I've been very curious about you, Roc Girouard."

No words came to him as a response. He looked in her direction but raised his gaze slightly above her head. He would not directly challenge her. Ever so slowly, he released the tension in his hand.

But he remained aware of every inch of her. Any and every detail mattered because one might reveal a weakness that he could exploit. And, oh, he would.

She was beautiful in an odd sense, and yet those black eyes exposed how death methodically stalked her. It wasn't obvious, just an observation he now recognized, having encountered many of these vampires. She was no different than the others. Maybe more powerful. Maybe not. Maybe she was spoiled and pampered. Maybe that was her weakness.

In a lethally smooth motion, she rose and moved toward him. "I must say you are delicious looking"—she leaned close and breathed in deeply—"and you smell divine. How did you resist, Brydon?"

"I am stronger than you think."

A smile tugged at one corner of her pink, almost red lips. "So you would like me to believe."

"I did what you asked, Jezebel," Brydon said. "Now—"

She held up a rigid index finger. "Enough."

She circled Roc, not touching him with her hands but eyeing him as if memorizing every contour of his shape. When she stepped in front of Roc again, he refused to meet her gaze. That gaze would rob him of attentiveness, knock him off balance, and steal his thoughts. Roberto had taught him well.

"Very nice indeed," she said. "A wonderful specimen."

Roc remained unresponsive.

Brydon stepped toward them. "What about—"

"And they are following?" she cut him off again.

He clasped his hands behind his back. "Of course. I told—"

"Actually"—a full smile bloomed, revealing Jezebel's straight white teeth—"some are already here. We have one." She indicated a pitcher on the table filled with a thick, red liquid. "Or we did. Tasty. But not as tasty as this one, I'd say."

"Suit yourself." Brydon turned away.

"Don't pout." She went to him, slid her fingers along the expanse of his shoulders, tracing the curve of his back, and wrapped an arm around his waist. "I have plans for you too."

"Maybe I have my own plans."

"Of course you do. And I can help you attain them."

# CHAPTER SIXTY-FOUR

No way am I staying here," Lance declared. He grabbed his duffel bag and started toward the motel room door.

The team had arrived only a half hour before and rented a room, so they could gather their thoughts and make ready their plan. The compound was one hour away. Their arsenal of semiautomatics, rifles, and shotguns was collected on the two beds. Each man had knives, stakes, and holsters strapped to their torsos and calves. They looked like a renegade militia prepared to fight every inch to reach their leader.

It had not been a joyful reunion. Samuel, Father Anthony, along with Joe, David, Dwight, and Harry had arrived early, having taken shifts driving through the day and half the night. The faces of three team members—Randy, Pete, and Lance—had been stricken.

"You can't just walk out." Joe stood, tossing the pillow he'd folded beneath his head to the bed.

"The hell I can't." Lance's tone was defiant, filled with anger and resentment, as if he had been betrayed somehow. Meanwhile, the whole team stared at him, their eyes filled with rage because he had become their own personal Judas Iscariot. "I didn't bargain for this."

"What did you think would happen?" Chris leaned against the desk, arms crossed over his chest, papers and notes spread behind him. He chewed gum slowly, making it pop. "Did you think this was some fairy tale? Some mythical journey? Or did you think because we were on the right side that no one would get hurt?"

"I don't know!" Lance's voice exploded in the room. Fear and anguish were etched on his face. "I wanted to help." He lifted a hand but dropped it to his side. "I wanted to do something worthy. But I don't want to die."

"No one does," Joe said. "But walking out sure ain't worthy of nothing."

"But...th-this"—Lance gesticulated in a helpless way—"what happened to Pete—" His mouth twisted. "You're all fools for staying here. You can't win."

His pronouncement resonated through the room and bounced off the determined faces of the team. Samuel's hands clenched in denial. They had to win. There was no other choice. Admitting defeat, playing it safe, was not an option. He'd seen the pictures on Shawn's cell phone—pictures that made this battle very real. Very ugly. And solidified Samuel's purpose.

These men had risked their lives to save him. And now they were doing so for Roc. Samuel wasn't going to run away from fear or death. Regret would chase after him and haunt him forever. No, he would stay. He would fight. Because there wasn't another option. Not now. Not when the image burned in his mind. Even if he was the only one fighting and willing to die.

*Pete.* The one who had always helped others, enjoyed the ladies when he had the chance, and been quick to find humor in a situation.

He was dead. Not just dead but horrifically mutilated when they found him. Then again, at least he was dead. It could have been worse, much worse.

Samuel couldn't let that happen to Roc or anyone else, not if there was something he could do.

He thought of Rachel, her blue eyes anxious, her mouth pinched tight. And her beautiful baby boy. David needed a father. Samuel wouldn't let them down. Another image, another set of calm eyes, sprang into his mind, and he forcefully blocked out Naomi. She was safe. In Pennsylvania. Far away from this danger. That's all that mattered.

"Look," Chris said to Lance in a reasonable tone, "I know you're upset. We all are. Pete was our brother. But running out now…is that how you want to honor Pete's memory? Wouldn't you rather seek a little revenge on those bastards?"

The team nodded in agreement, their bodies as tense as Samuel's, ready for action, ready to draw blood and account for the sins perpetrated on their team member.

Pete had gone on surveillance, scoping out the compound where they believed—and now knew—Roc had been taken. Shawn had gone with him. They'd circled the compound, taking opposite directions, and planned to meet up again. But something went wrong. Very wrong. They'd kept in contact via their phones. Shawn heard, "Hey!" Then a scream. Static came from Pete's phone, which he later found smashed. Shawn took off running, passed the rendezvous point, and kept going, calling for immediate backup from Lance and Randy. But they'd all been too late. They'd only found pieces of Pete. And blood. Lots of blood.

"No," Lance finally mouthed the answer to Chris's question. "I don't wanna die."

"You think we do?" Harry asked. "Come on, man, we have work to do. We have to help Roc."

But Lance shook his head and opened the motel room's door.

"No!" Joe threw himself at Lance, and their bodies collided with the door, shutting it firmly.

"Whoa!" Samuel surged to his feet.

Chris, Shawn, and Randy leapt forward and dragged Joe off Lance.

Joe struggled, his veins bulging in his neck and arms. "We can't just let him walk out! This is a brotherhood."

"What are we going to do?" Shawn asked, holding on to Joe's thick shoulder. "Kill him?"

Chris planted his hands against Joe's chest. "If he wants to go, let him. No use having a coward with us."

"He swore to be a part of this team. What if he goes out there and tells someone what we're doing?"

Randy and Chris shared skeptical glances. "That's a point. Maybe we should...I don't know..." Randy turned toward Lance now as if to tackle him but only grabbed his arm. "We could tie him up at least until this raid is over. Roc will know what to do."

Lance attempted to shake off Randy's grip. "Roc could be dead!"

"No!" Samuel wouldn't believe that. He rushed past Father Anthony, slamming his shin against the bed frame, but he threw himself into the midst of the three arguing men. "Let Lance go. Who is he going to tell? Anyone would think he's crazy."

"But what if *they* catch him?" Randy looked panicked, his eyes wide and bulging.

Dwight glared at Lance, as if he had become the enemy. His grizzled beard made him look formidable. "What if they learn our secrets?"

"You think they got secrets from Pete?" Samuel challenged. From the corner of his eye, he saw Father Anthony nodding in agreement, which encouraged him to continue. "If they catch Lance, he'll face what we all may—death." He drew a breath. "Besides, if they have Roc, then they could already know our plans and strategies."

"I doubt it," Father Anthony said with that calm voice, but his authority ricocheted through the room. "They are too arrogant, too trusting of their own abilities to worry about us. We're like gnats to them. We may be a nuisance but they believe they are stronger and smarter."

"They are stronger!" Lance glared at his once teammates, who now looked as if they might lynch him. Then he bolted out the door, leaving it wide open.

Thick, humid air poured into the room. An uneasy silence settled upon them. Joe moved first.

"Let him go," Father Anthony warned.

But Joe only closed the door.

Slowly, Father Anthony pushed to his feet, looking as if he'd aged twenty years in the last few minutes. His cheeks were sunken, his shoulders slumped wearily, but there was still fire in his eyes. He wove through the men, brushing shoulders with them, and he walked to the door before facing the team.

"Lance made his choice. And each of you must choose, weighing what you believe you have to lose. Some of you have already lost loved ones. I've heard a few of your stories over the last few hours and what brought you to train with Roc and Father Roberto. Each of our stories is unique, as are each of our callings.

"Lance was right. This is not an easy task. They are stronger. Probably smarter too. A few of us may die—maybe even all of us in the coming battle. I cannot tell you what to do. Only God can do that. And then it's up to you whether you are willing to obey the calling on your life or not. It is your choice.

"You will not answer to me but to the Almighty. We need every man here, but we only want those committed to our cause. Today, we free Roc. But we are also striking into the heart of the enemy. Will there be any of us left to continue the fight tomorrow? I do not know. But I do know the Lord raises up His own army. *And the Lord shall utter his voice before his army: for his camp is very great: for he is strong that executeth his word: for the day of the Lord is great and very terrible; and who can abide it?*"

His words resonated in the room, pulsing with the beat of Samuel's heart.

"So"—Father Anthony flung open the motel room door—"if you want to stay and fight, then do so. If you believe you should leave, then now is the time."

Silence had its own beat, its own score. It played differently for each man. Samuel met every gaze—Joe, Chris, Randy, Dwight, Harry, and Shawn. They were soldiers. Every one of them.

"We will not think ill of you if you leave," Father Anthony said. "It is your choice. Just as it is our choice to stay."

Again, Samuel thought of Naomi, and a voice whispered in his head, "Samuel, you can go. This is not required of you."

But his spine straightened. He would not leave. And apparently neither would anyone else. After a long moment, Father Anthony closed the door and sealed their fate.

# Chapter Sixty-Five

THE EXPLOSION WAS FAIRLY small compared to those Samuel had seen in movies, where cars flipped, buildings imploded, planes broke apart. This blast simply garnered attention and created a diversion.

Vampires poured out of the buildings toward the enflamed Dumpster like a horde of angry hornets.

A couple of fire extinguishers, Samuel reasoned, could take care of it without any need for a fire truck. Though, with the windows open in the van, he could already smell acrid smoke. The remaining fire leapt out of the Dumpster's opening and sent up a plume of black smoke.

But it got the vamps moving in the right direction— away from the team—and it didn't jeopardize Roc. Or so they hoped.

The plan, devised by Joe and Father Anthony, was a four-pronged attack. Dwight had lobbed the homemade bomb over the fence and into the Dumpster, setting off the initial explosion, then he'd hooked eastward to meet up with Chris and Harry, who were breaking into the compound from the east. Rotating clockwise along the backside of the compound, Randy and Shawn, having previously clipped the wire mesh, plowed a van through the west fence. Down the only road leading toward the compound, Samuel drove the other van toward the main gates, making a grand entrance with Father Anthony sitting beside him in the passenger seat and Joe in the rear.

Even though the team members carried knives, stakes, and .357 magnums with hollow-point bullets, to create the most damage and heaviest blood loss, Father Anthony only wore a heavy gold cross on his chest and carried a Bible. It was up to Samuel and Joe to protect the priest.

As they drove through the entrance, a young man raced out of a guardhouse and bolted in front of the van. Samuel slowed the vehicle, gripping the wheel hard. Through the windshield, a black angry gaze met him. A vampire. Samuel's heart jolted. Sweat burst onto his forehead.

"Easy," Joe said from the back. "Just keep driving, nice and slow."

Father Anthony began chanting what he had explained earlier was scripture in Latin. "*Vade retro, Satana!*"

The vampire came around the front of the van toward the driver's window, but his footsteps slowed, then faltered as Father Anthony's voice reached him. The vampire pressed his palms to his ears as his face contorted with rage. Hissing and growling, he yanked the side mirror off the van and clawed a hand through the open window. Samuel ducked sideways and stomped on the gas. The van lurched forward. Joe raised his gun. But he never fired a shot. The vampire did not advance but spewed vile words and then fled. Joe exchanged an amazed look with Samuel through the rearview mirror.

"Go! Go! Go!" Joe shouted, moving forward and leaning between the front seats.

Samuel took a sharp turn, and the tires squealed. Up ahead, a pack of vampires spotted them.

"Turn right!" Joe ordered.

Samuel floored it, but before he could reach the next turn, two vampires appeared in front of the van. Stomping the break, Samuel braced himself against the steering wheel as they slammed into them. The hood crumpled, the protective air bag burst out of the steering wheel, and the van came to an abrupt stop. The vampires, standing tall, unharmed, and dangerous, glared through the cracked windshield.

Calmly, Father Anthony raised the cross and continued his chanting of the Holy Scriptures. One of the vampires shrank and disappeared.

"Where'd he go?" Samuel asked.

The other vampire launched himself at the van. But a sound exploded next to Samuel. When the concussion of the semiautomatic weapon died, Samuel could only hear muffled sounds. A hole opened in the vampire's chest, and he fell across the hood.

"Get out!" Joe jerked open the van's side door and helped Father Anthony out. "This side!"

The wounded vampire clambered toward them, and Joe shot him twice more.

"This way!" Joe pulled Father Anthony out of the van and waved for Samuel to follow. "Do not separate."

More vampires approached from behind them. Joe and Samuel bracketed Father Anthony, both aiming their .357s. Father Anthony continued his chanting, and the approaching vampires snarled and snapped but didn't approach any further. The priest looked as if he was in a trance, his eyes blank, his voice hoarse.

Joe backed all three of them toward the fallen vampire, who lay in a pool of dark blood, but he wasn't yet dead. He struggled, but his movements were jerky and ineffective. Joe looped a band around his neck and tied him to the bumper.

The vampire grabbed at them, clawing at their ankles, but they kept out of reach.

"If he bites you," Joe explained, "he'll gain strength." He pulled a blade from its sheath strapped to his back and sliced the vamp's wrists and neck. Blood spurted and poured forth. He glared down at the writhing beast. "Where's Roc Girouard?"

The vampire growled through clenched, bloodied teeth.

"I can make this slow or quick." He flashed the blade in the vamp's face.

But the vampire curled inward and attempted to cover his ears. "Make him stop." He acted like Father's Anthony's intonations were more painful to him than the chest wound. "Please...stop."

"If you'll tell us where Roc Girouard is being held prisoner, he'll stop."

"Who?" The vampire twisted as if trying to escape. "You will die this day, Anthony Daly!"

Father Anthony showed no surprise that the vampire knew his name. "I know where I'm going. Do you? *Nunquam suade mihi vana. Sunt mala quae libas, ipse vinena bibas.*"

They were now surrounded, yet no vamp would come close once the priest began chanting scripture again. An invisible line held them at bay. A pint-sized vampire, who looked to be nine or ten, snapped and struggled against invisible restraints. She caught Samuel's attention. She had long yellow hair and smooth skin. One of her knee socks hugged her ankle. Those black eyes snared Samuel, and everything around him faded and fogged.

*Help me!* the child's voice echoed in Samuel's head. The vampire didn't call out to him, but she reached a hand toward him. *You can help me. Please.*

"Roc Girouard. Where is he?" Joe demanded from the

vampire lying at their feet. He shouted the scriptures with Father Anthony, yelling the words and aiming them at the vampire recoiling and moaning.

Yet it all seemed so far away from Samuel. He couldn't take his gaze off the young child. Samuel felt his own hand reach outward.

"Tell me now!" Joe shouted, his voice sounding hoarse and muffled.

"Okay, okay. Let me go and I'll tell you."

"Not likely. *Vade retro, Satana!*"

"I hate you, Joseph William McBride!" The vampire spewed vile names.

"*Vade retro, Satana. Vade retro, Satana. Vade retro, Satana.*"

"Building four! Now let—"

The priest did not relent; his voice remained deep and powerful as he chanted.

Joe pushed. "Where's building four?"

"Over there."

*Over here!* came the voice in Samuel's head. *Help me, please. I'll show you where your friend is. He's hurt. He needs help. Come! Quickly!*

"Samuel!" Joe snagged Samuel's arm and yanked hard, jerking him around. "Look at me. Me! Right here."

Samuel focused on Joe's hawkish gaze, the brown of his eyes. Somehow the world righted itself.

"You okay?" Joe clapped Samuel on the shoulder.

Samuel shook himself, shucking off the effects of the vampire's gaze. Something brushed his leg. The wounded vampire rolled sideways and strained to reach them. Joe stomped on the arm, and Samuel heard a bone snap.

"Come on!" Joe pushed Samuel toward a plain, ordinary building, which looked like all the others. "Let's go."

This time, Samuel didn't look back, didn't dare even a glance at the rest of the vampires—especially the young one.

# CHAPTER SIXTY-SIX

G ET UP."
Roc rolled his head sideways, unable to lift his chin fully, and his gaze collided with Brydon, who stood in the doorway of the tiny room where Roc was being kept. For how long he didn't know. The concrete floor felt cold to Roc's backside and his limbs were numb. His brain worked even slower, as if it had been put into a deep freeze.

"Come on, let's go. Now!"

Roc blinked but couldn't get himself moving.

Rushing forward, Brydon grabbed him by the arm and hauled him to his feet. He shoved Roc toward the opening. Roc stumbled and crashed into a wall, and Brydon pushed him again, moving him down the narrow passageway.

Then Brydon pulled up short. Roc drew several shallow breaths and slumped against the wall. Down the long hallway, he saw a glowing figure coming closer, and Roc started, his heart picking up its sluggish pace. Had he died and not realized it yet?

As the being drew closer, it separated into three distinct bodies. The faces he knew, but the names stayed out of reach.

"Roc, move!" one yelled.

That voice. He scrambled to find the name to match. But he couldn't follow the command. The men were running toward him now.

Brydon whipped around and shoved Roc in the opposite direction. He stumbled, fell to his knees, and Brydon scooped him up, half dragging, half carrying him.

Something exploded against his eardrums. A gunshot. Then another. It jarred his brain, jolted his heart, and one name fell into place. Joe. Who else was here? Had the whole team come? They shouldn't have. "Go," he managed, but the word came out weakly.

The door at the end of the hall slammed against the inside wall. Jezebel. Despite her slight size, she had a commanding presence. "Bring him."

Brydon shoved Roc toward her, but he fell, splayed out along the floor, his body sliding several feet.

"Roc!" The sound of running feet ricocheted around him, and he watched Samuel running as if in slow motion. He swung a blade at Brydon, but the vampire ducked and grabbed Samuel, hurled him toward Jezebel. Samuel slammed into the wall and fell in a heap, not moving. Jezebel snatched him by the back of the collar, and all three disappeared, the door clanging shut.

Roc struggled to his feet, bracing a hand against the wall, and tried to follow Samuel, but he was stopped.

"Roc!" Joe took hold of his shoulders, his grip unrelenting. "Roc! Come on. We have to get out of here."

He shook his head, struggling to break free. "We have to get Samuel."

A whoosh of a blaze ignited the door where Samuel had been dragged. Heat rolled forward and smoke boiled toward them. Joe hurried them toward the other exit, and Roc stumbled, the other figure grasping his arm in an effort to help. Roc recognized the gaunt features. Anthony. Tony. His friend.

But neither the priest nor Joe would give him rest. Coughing on the smoke, they burst through the exit and out into the sunlight. Roc blinked, his eyes watering from smoke and the brightness of day. *How long had it been since he'd seen sunlight?*

Anthony steadied Roc with a hand. But there wasn't time to speak or make a plan. What met them outside was a war zone.

Buildings were ablaze. Smoke darkened the sky. Bodies littered the drive, their arms askew, legs bent unnaturally. A van had been overturned, the wheels sticking up toward the sky like a swollen carcass's limbs. Together, the three men staggered past, moving as one toward the outer realms of the compound.

"Where are the others?" Roc asked.

"I don't know. We can't stop." Joe directed them between two buildings. "We have to get out. Now. Before it's too late."

"Too late for what?"

"Us."

Something caught Roc's eye, a flutter, a movement, and he jerked his head to the left. Between two buildings, a man bent over a body. But it wasn't a man. It was a vampire, and he was sucking the life out of the helpless victim. A violent reaction exploded inside Roc, and he yanked his arms out of the grip of Joe and Anthony.

"What are you—"

But Roc was already running and stumbling and clawing his way toward the vampire, his fingers scraping the gravel road, his shoulder bouncing off one of the side buildings. He had to stop him. He wouldn't let someone on his team die. Not for him.

Then Roc was shoved sideways, and Joe took aim. He fired three rounds into the back of the vampire, who arched backward and at the same time fell forward.

Joe was the first to reach the downed team member. Roc slid into place beside him. *Samuel.*

Roc's heart almost stopped at the sight of the young Amish man, neck arched, bloody wound gaping, his mouth open as if he was fighting for air.

Placing a hand on the younger man's chest, Roc felt for a pulse.

Anthony reached them, laid his hand on the young man's head, and began praying.

It took a moment for Roc to recognize the words of the priest. Last rites.

Roc shoved Anthony away. "No!" the word burst out of him. "He's not going to die. Not today. Not for me. Not because of them."

"But, Roc—" Anthony said.

"No buts. If you have to pray, make it for a miracle."

# CHAPTER SIXTY-SEVEN

SAMUEL FELT HIMSELF LIFTED, his body weightless, buoyed by an invisible force. Yet when he stared back at the ground, he saw his body splayed out on a table. People scurried about him like ants, retrieving this, grabbing that, poking him with things he couldn't identify. Sharp tones were spoken and triggered a beeping sound, a steady, unrelenting alarm. If he were there, and yet floating somehow above, then he must not be.

He must be dead.

*Dead.*

He felt nothing at the realization. No regrets. No remorse. No fear. Just a simple, flat awareness.

He was dead.

For what seemed like a long while and yet no time at all, he watched the people below working on his body. But he felt nothing. No sensations. No tugging or pulling. No pain. Was that the undertaker working on him already? No, it looked like medical personnel. They wore scrubs. And there was blood.

But…what had happened? They—Joe and Father Anthony—had been searching for Roc. They'd seen him. Down a corridor. But someone had been with him. And Roc had acted dazed and confused. But he'd been alive. Alive! And Samuel ran for him.

And then nothing. Samuel knew nothing.

Now, he remained suspended along the ceiling, a gravity of some kind holding him, tethering him to earth, to his body. He could see through the paper-thin walls where Roc paced along a hallway, his phone to his ear, a worried expression on his exhausted face. At least his friend was safe, alive.

And Samuel's job was completed.

It was in that moment he understood why he'd risked his life to save Roc's. Not that one life was more important than another, but Samuel had killed his own brother. Giving his own life for Roc, to save Roc, somehow evened things out.

Samuel wanted to reach out in greeting to his friend, tell him he was okay, not to worry. For the first time in months, maybe years, Samuel felt at peace. He wished he could ease the burden Roc felt, erase the worry, but he could not bridge the gap to reach Roc and explain. Maybe it didn't matter. In the end, Roc might mourn, but more importantly, he would return home to his family and continue his God-given purposes.

"Samuel."

He glanced around. No one below had spoken his name. Then he saw the sky opening, the clouds peeling back to expose a hidden place, a brightness that defied the sun's brilliance. Standing in that crack of not-quite-here-or-there was his brother Jacob.

*Jacob.*

A sob of anguish combined with relief clutched Samuel's throat. In that instant, he rushed upward toward his brother without thought or knowledge of how he was doing so. He simply was. It felt like the breath of heaven upon him as he moved swiftly forward.

And they came face to face, standing so close, yet neither reached out. Samuel didn't know what to say.

Jacob's eyes were wide, startled with what Samuel interpreted as wonder and love. A million emotions flitted across his features.

Those same emotions reflected in Samuel's soul. A thousand apologies rose up in him. But how could he ask for forgiveness for such an awful, unforgiveable act?

"You're here." Jacob's voice sounded confused, and his forehead furrowed. "You're not supposed to be here." He looked behind him. "Remiel!"

Some invisible cord pulled Samuel backward. He reached for his brother's arm. He had to know. "Jacob." The name came out as broken as Samuel's spirit. "Please."

Jacob shook him off. "You have to go back."

The tugging became more insistent, but Samuel clutched at Jacob, tried to hang on. "But what about you?"

"It's not my time. It's yours."

"But—"

"Go, Samuel. Go live your life!"

With an anguished cry of defeat, Samuel fell backward, tumbling through time and space and nothing, and he cried out, "I'm sorry. Jacob! I'm so sorry."

But his brother was gone. And Samuel once again knew nothing. A thick darkness wrapped him up and bound him in silence.

# CHAPTER SIXTY-EIGHT

SAMUEL DRIFTED IN AND out of sleep. Nurses came and went. His neck felt stiff from a thick bandage, and tubes jabbed into him. It hurt to swallow or move. Roc was there when he woke and drifted off again. He didn't bother him with questions or try to fill the silence with empty words. Mostly Samuel slept or lay with his eyes closed, his thoughts twisting, turning, tumbling over bits and pieces of memories. But he didn't want to discuss what had happened at the compound or with Jacob. He didn't want to think, either. When his thoughts assaulted him, he pressed his thumb against the button that shot medicine into his veins, and he drifted down a river into nothingness.

But slowly, they removed the tubes and lessened his medicine, and the lulling sensation began to subside.

"You need to wake up now, Samuel," a nurse said, her voice perky, as she placed a tray of broth and wiggly Jell-O cubes in front of him.

When she left the room, Roc rolled his eyes. He looked like he hadn't slept in weeks.

Samuel wondered how long he'd been here. He didn't care enough to ask, but there was a question he needed to know. He forced his eyes open when they only wanted to close and located Roc, who sat in the hospital chair. He tested his voice. "The team"—he sounded raspy as a rusted-out motor—"okay?"

Roc hunched his shoulders and stared down at his clasped hands for a long time. Samuel's eyelids struggled against an invisible weight. His head bobbed and weaved before Roc spoke. At the sound of his voice, Samuel jerked awake.

"Dwight." His voice roughened with grief and weariness. "Shawn."

Two. Should have been three. Should have been...but there was. Pete. Hot tears burned Samuel's eyes.

"And"—Roc's voice cracked—"Chris."

They didn't speak any more. What was there to say? Samuel slumped back against the pillow and feigned sleep until it pulled him into flashes of fire and blood. Pressure against his chest woke him.

Roc stood over him. "You're okay. You're safe."

Samuel drew gulps of air.

Slowly, Roc backed toward his chair. "I have dreams too. You'll get used to it."

But sleep had become his enemy. He tried to stay awake the rest of the night but sometime before dawn, he lost the battle.

When he awoke again, an older man in a white coat stood beside him. "You're a lucky man," the doctor said as he scribbled on the chart. "You'll have some scars, I'm afraid. But you'll live to tell the tale." He turned to Roc, who sat in the chair beside the bed, his eyes shaded by dark circles. "Anyone ever find that dog?"

Roc shook his head. "Not yet. But I'll know it when I see it again."

The doctor, an older gentleman, had gray hair and a tired complexion. "We better keep you here for another day. Make sure your blood pressure remains stable. But then you can go home."

The next morning they headed out. Roc drove the van, his friend Anthony at his side, and Samuel rode in the far back, a hospital pillow propped behind him. Anthony had taken care of the bodies, then visited a fellow priest in the area. Joe, Harry, and Randy had already returned to Pennsylvania. Roc had been worried there might be an attack on the training center. But so far all remained quiet.

Now, Samuel was headed home.

*Home.* And he knew it truly was home for him now. Not just because he'd been raised there, but because he'd found his purpose.

# CHAPTER SIXTY-NINE

Y OU'RE STILL RECOVERING." ROC dismissed Samuel's offer as he cleaned a weapon.

"I'm fine." Since returning the night before, Samuel had thrown himself into work. Usually, he answered questions with nods or shakes of his head, avoiding speaking. It was not only difficult physically, as his throat muscles were still sore and the stitches in his neck pinching, but too many emotions welled up inside. He felt frayed and at loose ends, and one conversational thread could undo him.

Roc set his Glock on the table, and his perceptive gaze narrowed on Samuel. "I understand how you feel, how you want to help. But not now." He stood, his motions painfully slow, never complaining about his own ordeal, and clapped Samuel on the shoulder, the gesture firm yet with a measure of gentleness. "Get some rest."

He led Samuel toward the opening of the training center and out into the night air. The air was still warm from the day. The scent of freshly mown grass drifted on the soft breeze. "When you're stronger, you'll get your chance. I promise."

With a heavy sigh, he entered the bunk room, where he'd taken up residence with the remaining team members. His duffel resided under a bunk. He stretched out on the thin mattress, one arm tucked under his head, and stared up at the ceiling.

Joe, Harry, and Father Anthony had taken the first patrol while the others slept. A few feet away from Samuel, Randy snored and shifted on his bunk. It felt like they were all wait-ing…waiting for something to happen. *But what?*

Sleep skirted Samuel too. He'd allowed Rachel to feed him oversized portions of food, and he ate as if he hadn't eaten in days, as if he couldn't fill the emptiness inside him. But it was something else he needed.

Restless, he rose quietly, so as not to wake the others, and left the bunk room. He made his way through the darkened center, maneuvering around equipment and weights, and back out into the night. Along the back of the building, he approached his motorcycle.

"Going for a night ride?" a voice in the dark asked.

Samuel turned toward Father Anthony. He rolled one shoulder and searched for an answer. Finally, unable to locate a reason, he simply said, "I guess."

"Nice night for it."

Samuel nodded and settled one hand on the handlebar. He flung one leg over the seat.

"Samuel?" The priest wore a dark jacket. He lived as plain and simple as the Amish. "If you ever want to talk about it… what happened in Kansas, I'm here."

Samuel pressed his lips together and gave a curt nod.

"Having a close brush with death can change a man." Father Anthony lifted a hand, then settled it back at his side. "If you need to talk…"

Samuel roared off into the night.

He took the roads at a fast clip, pushing himself and the bike faster and faster. He felt reckless and foolish, and only when he was a few hundred yards away did he slow his pace. He turned into Levi's farm and puttered up the drive, the bike sounding loud in his ears as he approached the darkened farmhouse. By the time he'd parked, Levi stood on the front porch and came down the steps to greet him.

His oldest brother's arms came around him, and he hugged Samuel, holding him tightly for a long moment. Samuel's carefully constructed façade began to crumble. A shudder went through him, and he embraced his brother, breathed in the scents of hay and sky and orange marmalade. The aroma of home and hearth brought a smile and yet also heartache. He ended the hug with a clap on Levi's back.

"How are you?" Samuel searched his brother's face in the shadows offered by the moon. "Your ribs healed?"

"Better." Levi eyed the bandage on Samuel's neck. "And you?"

"Better."

Levi gestured toward the chairs on the porch. "Want to sit for a while? Or are you hungry?"

Samuel patted his belly that was amazingly still flat. "Rachel's been stuffing me like a Thanksgiving turkey."

"Good." Smiling, Levi leaned toward him. "I know someone else who's been anxious to cook for you."

Samuel broke eye contact, and his jaw hardened. All he had hoped for ended back in Kansas. Having looked death in the eye, he couldn't drag Naomi into all of this danger. He wouldn't. Not ever.

Together, the two brothers climbed the steps and settled next to each other in the wooden rockers. For long minutes, they simply stared at the stars as the boards creaked with their weight and steady rocking. Everything Samuel had experienced in the last week formed a rock in his gut, and the edges pressed into him. *But how could he share with Levi what had happened? And yet how could he not?*

"You want something to drink?" Levi asked, breaking the silence. "There's root beer and lemona—"

"I saw him," Samuel interrupted.

Levi froze.

"Jacob." Samuel spoke his brother's name. It had been a rare moment in the past few years when Jacob's name had been spoken among his family. It usually prompted Pop to leave the table and Mamm to cry. But Levi...Samuel could talk to Levi. He needed to speak of it.

"When?" Levi asked.

"When I died." He slid his hands along his thighs, flexing his fingers as if he could hold back the memories. "The doctor told me my heart stopped. I lost a lot of blood." He touched the bandage still attached to his neck. "This artery was cut. I don't remember much." He shook his head, wishing he couldn't remember any of it. "I-I saw myself on a table...flat out...being worked on." His chest tightened, and he jerked his chin upward. "I saw Roc pacing in some hospital corridor." Swallowing hard, he took the leap. "Then I heard a voice."

Levi's hands curled over the end of the rocker's arms.

"It was Jacob."

Levi's eyebrows rose. "Our brother?"

Samuel felt his throat closing, and he drew long, slow breaths until the sensation eased. "He stood in...I don't know...some kind of an opening, like...I don't know."

When Samuel didn't go on, Levi asked, "What did he say?"

"H-he acted surprised to see me. And he told me to go back."

Levi began rocking again, slow and steady, as if digesting all Samuel was saying.

"I wanted to tell him I was sorry. I didn't mean to kill him. I wouldn't have...shouldn't have—" Samuel's voice shattered, and he fell forward, bracing his elbows on his knees, his head in his hands, and for the first time since that night so long ago when he had shot his brother, he wept.

And Levi let him. He didn't try to make him feel better. He didn't tell him he shouldn't, as Pop would have. He simply sat beside him, stayed with him in the dark. When he felt spent, exhausted emotionally, Samuel looked up, stared at the heavens, and wondered if that was where his brother was. *Had Jacob forgiven him?* Wiping his face with his sleeve, Samuel shook his head. "Sounds crazy, huh?"

"I wouldn't say that."

Tense, Samuel pushed back in the rocker. "What would you say?"

"I'd say there are things we don't understand. Whether it was the medication making you imagine things or whether you actually saw Jacob..." Levi's voice constricted. "Did he look...okay?" He swallowed hard. "Normal?"

Samuel nodded. "Whole."

Levi placed a hand on Samuel's shoulder, squeezing slightly. "I understand the guilt you feel. The heaviness. But I don't think you need Jacob to forgive you."

"Who then? God?"

"Always, *ja?*"

Samuel nodded.

"But you also need to forgive yourself."

Those words wrapped around Samuel's heart and squeezed until he thought he could no longer breathe.

"It's not easy," Levi continued. "I understand, Samuel, the awfulness. But if you cannot forgive yourself, if you cannot move on, then it will hold you to that moment in your life. And everything you do will be tethered to that."

Samuel leaned back and blew out a breath. "Do you think the Lord forgives such a thing?"

Levi weighed the question carefully.

"God did not forgive Cain, did he?" Samuel challenged.

"He punished Cain, that is true. But I cannot say if Cain was forgiven. Did Cain ask for forgiveness?"

Samuel contemplated the question.

Before he could respond, Levi continued, "Christ died for all our sins. When you hold on to your transgression, you reject the power of his sacrifice."

# CHAPTER SEVENTY

LEFT ALONE WITH HIS traitorous thoughts, Samuel rocked on the front porch in the deep shadows, unable to sleep, unable to let go of his doubts and guilt. He wrestled with what Levi had said and with his trapped feelings. When the moon dipped behind a cloud, darkness shrouding him, his chin dipped, the chair slowed, and he breathed deeply, fully resting for the first time in days.

The crunch of gravel nudged him out of oblivion. His eyes snapped open. The rocker fell forward with his movement.

*What was he doing?* He shouldn't have stayed out here in the open. *Foolish.*

His gaze landed on Naomi. *What was she doing here?* But of course, she was here to help Hannah with her twins. He'd been stupid in more ways than one.

With the morning sun behind her, she walked up the drive, head down, apparently in deep thought and unaware of his presence. But as she came up the porch steps, she paused at the sight of him. "Samuel?" Her voice spiked and a smile blossomed. "You are here. Really here. And safe."

She rushed toward him, a smile breaking free, but she stopped abruptly. Her gaze locked on the bandage covering a good portion of his neck. "You're hurt."

He rose to his feet, feeling a bit disoriented from the late night and abrupt end to his sleep. The sun had risen above the horizon, and he squinted in its direction. He rubbed a hand over his face. "I'm all right."

She came toward him, approaching more cautiously. "Oh, Samuel, what happened?"

Every part of his being ached to pull her to him, hold her, breathe in her scent. But he forced himself to resist.

Her hand lifted as if to touch the bandage or simply reach out to him, but she faltered. Before she could pull away, Samuel's hands closed over hers. He wasn't sure what had made him do such a thing—reassuring her or himself—but at her soft touch, his heartbeat stumbled, his resolve wavered.

"Are you all right, Samuel?" Her gaze sought his for reassurance, her brow furrowing with concern. "I didn't know you had been hurt. Rachel said nothing. Only that you had returned with Roc."

"I'm fine." And his words were true. He hadn't been fully right until this exact moment. *Right here. With her.* He squeezed her hand. "How have you been?"

"Me?" She started to laugh, and his gaze caught on the curve of her lower lip. "All is well here. Just helping out where needed."

"Rachel told me how kind you were, seeing her through those days when Roc was missing."

"It was the least I could do."

"She appreciated the company and support."

"Do you need to sit and rest?" she asked. "I could get you some breakfast." Her gaze shifted toward the bandage again. "It looks as if your injury was awful bad."

He gestured toward the empty rocker Levi had vacated hours ago. When she sat, he resumed his seat beside her. He should explain. He should tell her. *Things are different now.* "Naomi—"

"Samuel—"

They spoke at the same time and he tilted his head and waited for her to continue. But she shook her head.

He drew a slow breath. "I died, Naomi." He needed her to know, to understand. "Roc didn't tell Rachel." He shrugged. "It wasn't something we discussed. I didn't want anyone to worry. But the fact is, I died." He felt the piercing in his soul of those words. It wasn't until then that he understood the consequences. If he had died, if he hadn't returned, he never again would have felt the sun on his face, the closeness with his brother Levi, or shared this moment with Naomi. It was a gift and gratitude welled inside him.

Her eyes widened and her lips parted. "Samuel…"

"The doctors restarted my heart." He touched the tape along the edge of the bandage, then clasped her hand again. "I lost so much blood my heart gave out."

"It's a miracle."

"It is indeed." And it was a miracle seeing the light in her eyes, hearing the emotion in her voice, and feeling the touch of her hand on his.

The corners of her eyes pinched with concern. "No wonder you look tired."

He shook his head. "I wanted you to know."

She tilted her head sideways. "Of course."

"No, I wanted you to know that I understand now."

"Understand what?"

"Why I'm here. My purpose." His hand tightened on hers as he thought back to one of their early conversations. "Do you remember?"

She nodded. "I have been praying for that too. As well as your safety."

His voice closed over the words of thanks that he owed

her, so he simply brushed his thumb over her knuckles again. Her skin felt so soft and he longed for more. But he would be grateful for this moment. "I've made a decision."

He stared at the weathered floorboards of the porch. The once-deep grooves had smoothed out over time and use. "I'm going to work with Roc."

"What about Levi?"

"He's healing and won't need me much longer. As long as I don't cause him problems with the bishop, then I'll help out as needed. But I've moved over to Roc's and—"

A scream split the morning. It sounded inhuman, like an animal dying. And yet, there was a desperate human quality to it. The scream seemed to go on and on, surfing on the breeze, then breaking off sharply.

Samuel leapt to his feet and pulled Naomi behind him. He scanned the drive, trees, barn.

"What's happened?" she asked. "Who…what was that?"

His heart raced. His mind seemed to stop for one brief second, splintering into questions. Fear rose up inside him. Not for himself, but for Naomi. "Get in the house. Stay in the house with Hannah. Lock the doors and windows. Do not come out."

"But, Samuel—"

"Now." He moved her toward the front door, keeping his back to the house and facing whatever danger might be out there. "Hurry. I'll be back."

She stood at the threshold, holding on to his arm. Before he could leave, she embraced him, pulling him close. Tears brimmed her eyes. "Be careful."

He longed to kiss her, to promise his return, to declare his love for her. But he had to go. And if he didn't return, it would be best if those words were never spoken.

He launched himself off the porch but turned back. "Lock the door. And don't open it. For anyone."

"But—"

"Anyone! Even if it sounds like me."

"Samuel—"

"Do as I say. Please, Naomi. Do as I say."

———

"What's going on?" Levi came out onto the porch. He closed the door behind him, and Samuel heard the bolt lock in place.

"I don't know." Samuel shoved his cell phone in his hip pocket. He'd tried calling Roc but got no response. He decided to circle Levi's house first and make sure all was as it should be, then he'd return to the center.

"You heard that, right?" Levi asked.

Samuel nodded, but his gaze moved around the perimeter of the property, as he edged toward his motorcycle. "Stay here, Levi."

"Where are you going?"

"Keep your cell phone handy. Call me if you see or hear anything." He climbed aboard and revved the engine, drowning out any arguments Levi tried to make. Hollering over the roar of the motorcycle, he added, "And get back in the house."

The drive toward the Slow Gait Road seemed longer than when Samuel had arrived last night. As the sun remained low on the horizon, shadows wept from the trees and brush in deep, dark pools. When he reached the main road, he gave one last look at the house. A figure stood at the front window. *Naomi.*

He prayed for God's protection over this house and all inside.

He turned right onto the road. It wasn't long before he saw the van approaching. Joe slowed and rolled down the window.

"What happened?" Samuel asked.

"We caught one."

"Where?"

"Not far from here. In the back now."

"Where are you taking—"

"Back to the center. Follow me."

# CHAPTER SEVENTY-ONE

SAMUEL GOT STUCK BEHIND a horse and buggy. When he reached Roc's, he parked behind the van. Roc appeared at the side door and tossed him a rifle. Samuel caught it with one hand.

"Come with me."

"What happened?" Samuel jogged alongside Roc.

"You were followed."

"By?"

"Your ex-girlfriend, I'm guessing."

Samuel's footsteps slowed but his mind raced ahead. "What are you going to do with her?"

"Anthony is in charge." Roc yanked open the center's door, and they entered.

Tethered in the center of the room, the ropes dangling from the ceiling held her in place—a writhing, screeching vampire, snapping and snarling and clawing to get at any team member who dared approach. In spite of the black eyes and viciously snarling mouth, Samuel recognized the slight form. Andi. Blood covered her mouth and chin and spotted her clothes.

Only a few yards away, Harry leaned against the wall looking shaken, his deeply tanned skin three shades paler as he wrapped white gauze around his bicep.

"*Vade retro, Satana.*" Father Anthony approached the rabid

vampire. Andi reacted to the holy words like acid poured over her. She tried to crawl up the ropes but the strap around her neck, tied to a latch on the concrete floor, prevented her from getting far. Attempting to cover her ears, she curled inward. Father Anthony stood over her and dripped water onto her head, which made her scream, a sound most unholy.

"Not too close, Tony," Roc warned, grasping Father Anthony's elbow and tugging him out of the vampire's reach just as she tried to snare his foot.

But Father Anthony seemed lost to this world.

Randy, Joe, and Father Roberto circled the vampire, staying well out of her reach.

"What's he doing?" Randy asked, his dark skin gleaming with sweat. "Why can't we just kill her?"

"No!" the word burst out of Samuel. He instantly regretted his outburst.

Roc met his ashamed gaze with understanding. "Tony's trying to save her. He's trying to extract the demon from her."

"Why the hell would he do that?" Joe yanked a .357 from the back of his jeans. "Did you see what she did to Harry?" He aimed his gun at her chest. "Maybe she's the one that took a bite out of you, Mr. Save-the-Vampire."

Samuel shielded Andi with his own body, staring not at the Glock but at Joe's eyes. "She deserves a second chance, just like the rest of us."

"She didn't give a second chance to Peter or Chris or—"

A sound from Samuel's left stopped Joe in the middle of his rant. They both turned toward Roc, who aimed a shotgun at Joe. "Put it down."

"Or what? You'll kill me?" Joe's eyes blazed. "I'm not the one who gutted Shawn! Kill her! She deserves it."

"She doesn't know what she's doing." Father Roberto

eased toward Joe, one hand splayed. "It's not her. It's the demon within her. If we kill her, Joe, then the demon will simply find another body to inhabit."

Joe shook his head, glaring at the writhing vampire several feet behind Samuel, and his hands clutched the shaking gun. "But Martha…"

"*Vengeance is mine, saith the Lord.*" Roberto placed a hand over the gun and aimed it at the floor. "Someone else killed your sister. And we'll find that vampire someday." When Roberto had taken the gun from Joe, he settled a hand on the taller, broader shoulder. "Joe, can you take Harry to the house? He needs Rachel to look at his wound."

"You're a fool," screeched Andi. Her face distorted with rage and yet she gave a horrific laugh. "A fool!"

"*Therefore God exalted him to the highest place*"—Father Anthony reverted to *English*—"*and gave him the name that is above every name—*"

"Don't say it!" Foul words spewed forth from Andi. "Don't you dare say it!"

"*—that at the name of Jesus—*"

She fell to the ground and writhed, yanking on the ropes until blood streamed down her arms and legs.

"*—every knee should bow, in heaven and on earth and under the earth, and every tongue confess that Jesus Christ is Lord, to the glory of God the Father.*"

Transfixed by Andi's fierce reaction, Samuel backed away and bumped into Roc. "How is this going to help her?"

"I don't know that it will. It's Tony's theory that it will take an exorcism. Exorcising her of the demon within. But if it doesn't work"—Roc readjusted the shotgun in his arms—"then I'll take care of her so she doesn't hurt anyone else—ever again."

A shot rang out. Samuel looked at Roc, but he hadn't fired a shot. Andi froze. A red hole opened in her chest. She crumpled and lay very still. Only the fingers of one hand twitched. The training center pulsated with silence in the aftermath. No one in the immediate vicinity held a weapon aimed. *Who had shot?*

*Had Samuel thought the question or had someone yelled it?* Roc reacted first, crouching low and aiming his shotgun toward the rafters. Along the padded ledge stood Brydon. He held the weapon he'd used to shoot Andi. *But why?*

"No one tells us what to do. No one!" Brydon's voice boomed and echoed through the facility. "No one, old man! No one!"

Roc fired. But Brydon shrunk and disappeared. Laughter reverberated around them. Wings flapped and a creature took off. Roc tried to hit Brydon but failed.

Samuel raced toward Andi, but Roberto stopped him. "No! She's still dangerous. Get back to the house!" Roberto pushed him toward the exit. "Now, hurry, Samuel. Alert Joe!"

But Samuel wasn't thinking about Joe or Harry. He was thinking where Brydon might have gone. All he could think of was Levi, Hannah, and Naomi, waiting in the house, like lambs. And Samuel was already in a full-out run.

# CHAPTER SEVENTY-TWO

J EZEBEL STOOD ON THE porch, a smile touching her lips. The green shades of the Amish home were pulled down, hiding all that was inside. Yet she could feel the fear like static electricity, making her charged and alive. "I haven't had this much fun in years." She placed a hand on Brydon's arm. "I must remember to thank you later."

"Don't worry. I'll remind you." Then he kicked in the door, splintering the wood as it burst open. He gave a slight bow to Jezebel, indicating she should lead and he would follow.

She stepped over the threshold into the warm confines. The air was still. Not a sound greeted her. But a young woman stood on the other side of the unadorned room. Her shoulders were squared, and her gaze solid, unafraid. She wore a plain dress and silly cap over her head as if it were the 1830s. Hatred rose inside Jezebel. *Women like this still existed?* Nothing had changed.

But this woman had backbone. She didn't run screaming into the back of the house. She spoke with calm conviction. "You must leave."

Jezebel smiled. "And why's that?"

"Nothing here belongs to you."

Jezebel turned in a slow circle, taking in the brown sofa, braided rug, and worn recliner. But she noted Brydon was not behind her, not in the doorway. *Where had he gone? Had he left her?* Fuming, she whipped back around and gave a caustic laugh. "You think I would be interested in anything here?"

"Who are you?" the woman asked. "And what do you want then?"

"Well, Naomi…" Jezebel laughed, feeling more sure of herself and caring less that Brydon had left. "Yes, you are Naomi…an old-fashioned name, isn't it? I am Jezebel, the one you should fear." She ambled forward, unhurried, and flicked a wooden baby toy with the tip of one finger. "Where's the baby? Is it yours?" She tilted her head and studied the woman. "Oh, not one baby, but two."

With slow, deliberate steps, she advanced on the younger woman, who didn't waver or crumple with fear.

"This house," Naomi said, lifting her chin, "belongs to the Lord. It is His. Not yours. And everyone in it belongs to Him."

"The Lord who?" Jezebel mocked.

"The Lord God Almighty," Naomi declared in a clear, strong voice.

Jezebel recoiled, stumbling backward. Her skin felt hot as if flames licked her skin. "Oh, really? What kind of a slut are you to—"

"*I saw heaven standing open and there before me was a white horse, whose rider is called Faithful and True.*"

Jezebel shrieked and hurled a lamp at the woman. It crashed into the wall. Whirling about, she decided a better tactic might be—

But someone blocked the doorway.

# CHAPTER SEVENTY-THREE

THE WORDS NAOMI CLEARLY and fearlessly quoted rang in Samuel's ears. His chest swelled with pride. She'd stood up to the foul creature. He aimed the gun at the vampire's heart.

"You think I am afraid of you or"—Jezebel jerked her chin at the Glock—"anything else?"

"I don't care if you are or not. But I'm betting you're afraid to die." He stepped into the house.

She laughed, then rushed toward one of the closed windows.

"We can help you," Samuel said. "Come peacefully with me, and we'll help you to live…really live."

"You're a fool," she spit out. She grabbed a log from the basket of wood near the fireplace and hurled it through the window, shattering the glass. She stripped away the green shade and came face to face with Roc on the outside. Jezebel spun away.

"There's nowhere to go now," Samuel warned.

The vampire sneered at him. "There is nothing you can do to me."

"Think again."

"You are the one who is scared." Yet, she backed away, her gaze shifting between Samuel and Roc. "I know you. Samuel Fisher and Roc Girouard. I will take care of your wife this day." She tilted her head back as if imagining the obscene act. "And your babe. Yes, how sweet it shall be."

Hatred contorted Roc's features.

"Roc, don't," Samuel warned.

"Don't worry," Jezebel said, "it's unlawful to kill a babe. It would be suicide for me to do so." She continued taking small steps toward a doorway at the far end of the room. "I will awaken your wife though. And she will kill her own. And then—"

Roc's gun fired.

Before Jezebel hit the floor, Roc had leapt through the window and wrapped a leather strap around the vampire's wrist, tethering Jezebel to the china hutch. Her knees crashed into the floor first, then she fell backward, her legs at an odd angle. Roc slashed a knife across her throat and blood spurted forth.

Roc stepped out of her reach. "I'm liking these hollow points more and more."

Samuel rushed forward and stood over Jezebel. "Where is he?"

Jezebel's mouth opened and closed as if she was trying to take in air.

Roc and Samuel turned to Naomi, who stood frozen as if not believing all she'd witnessed.

"Where's Levi?" Roc demanded.

She shook her head, her eyes glazed with shock, and Samuel went to her, wrapped an arm around her shoulders. She trembled even though outwardly she appeared solid and strong. "When we knew they were here—"

"They?" Roc repeated.

She swallowed hard. "Hannah and the babies…" Her voice shook. "They're hiding. And Levi went out." She clutched Samuel's arm.

"It's okay. I'll—"

The back door burst open and Levi rushed in, his work boots heavy on the wooden floor. Sweat poured from his face, and he carried a .22 that he used for hunting deer. "I heard a gunshot—" His gaze swung around the room until it landed on the bleeding vampire sprawled on the floor. "Where's Hannah?"

"I'm okay," came a voice from the hallway. Hannah came around the corner. "I was in the safe room, the one we built under the house."

Relief washed over Levi's face and he rushed to her side.

Naomi sagged against Samuel. "I'll help bring the babies up."

But Samuel stopped her. "There was another vampire here, wasn't there?"

She nodded.

Roc and Samuel looked at each other and spoke at the same time. "Brydon."

"But where is he now?" Levi asked.

Roc spoke first. "Rachel."

# Chapter Seventy-Four

**B**RYDON SAT BRAZENLY ON the front porch of Roc's home. Samuel held Roc back, placing a hand against the solid chest. "Wait."

"Looking for your wife?" Brydon asked.

Samuel felt Roc's muscles quivering with frustration and fear. "Wait."

"You would think," Brydon continued, rocking back and forth as if he had all day…or all eternity, "after you lost your first wife—"

"You know nothing about—"

"Emma? Oh sure I do. I put the puzzle pieces together once I had eyes to see." Brydon stood slowly. "Gotta say you're either braver than I ever imagined or the biggest fool I've ever met."

"What do you want?" Samuel asked.

"The list is long and beyond your pay grade." He laughed at his own little joke.

From the side of the house, Samuel caught sight of Joe, armed and making his way to the porch.

Brydon's smile vanished and disdain settled in its place. "You cannot surround a vampire. I have abilities you can't begin to fathom."

"Enlighten us," Roc challenged.

"You don't have the intellect." Without looking to his

right, Brydon motioned toward Harry creeping up the other side of the house. "Come on, come on, the more the merrier. Don't you agree?"

"If you hurt Rachel…" Roc threatened.

"Then what? What are you going to do?" He stepped sideways, one step then two. "Nothing. That's what. You tried to kill me once before but you failed. And you'll fail today. There's nothing you can do. Don't you get it yet? Oh sure, you can kill one of us…but you haven't even scratched the surface. It's impossible to destroy us all."

"We have a few tricks of our own."

Brydon laughed. "You might be able to shoot me…maybe even kill me. But you'll never find Rachel."

Blood drained out of Roc's face. "What have you done with her?"

"I'm going to enjoy"—he stepped toward the door—"hearing her scream and—"

The planks beneath Brydon's feet dropped away and he fell into the hole, which Samuel had once experienced.

A howling cry tore through the shocked silence. Roc was the first onto the porch, followed quickly by Samuel and the others. They peered into the depths, where Brydon twisted and struggled against two ropes pulling his limbs in opposite directions. Father Anthony held one rope. Father Roberto struggled with his end as Brydon jerked on the ropes and fought for freedom.

"I could use some help down here," Father Roberto hollered up at them. "I'm not as strong as I look."

"Trouble with having a tiger by the tail"—Joe moved first—"is they don't tell you what to do once you have him."

"I know what to do with him." Father Anthony wrestled with his end of the rope.

Gun in hand, Joe jumped into the dark pit. "Just kill him."

"No!" Roc yelled. "He knows where Rachel is. Don't hurt him."

The front door opened. A wide-eyed Rachel peered out from the house. "Rachel is right here. With David. We're fine. We're both fine."

Roc leapt over the corner of the breakaway planks and into the arms of his wife. He held her for a long time. Samuel watched them kiss, then looked away. He rejoiced and at the same time grieved.

# CHAPTER SEVENTY-FIVE

I T TOOK THREE DAYS.

The team kept Brydon restrained. The priests took turns, back and forth, and even together, praying over him, reciting scripture, arguing with the demon, until finally Brydon released Brody. His eyes cleared once again. His features transformed. Exhausted, Brody curled on his side, his face wet with tears, and slept.

Roc stayed by his ex-partner's side, and when Brody awoke, Roc gave him water to sip and food to eat.

They moved him to the training center and gave him a bunk. However, Roc took the cautious route to Brody's recovery. Night and day, two guards stayed with him—always two, never just one.

"How is he now?" Samuel asked.

"He's eating small bits of regular food and appears better."

Together they went into the house and sat at the kitchen table. "Does he remember anything?"

"Doesn't seem to. Said it was like he couldn't stop himself from doing things, and was confined inside himself to a small dark place."

Samuel went to the coffee pot, which seemed perpetually full, and poured two cups. "What now?"

"Father Anthony will help him."

"And so will you." Samuel set the cup in front of Roc.

Straight up and black was how Roc took it, and he sipped the steaming coffee, hissing at the temperature. When he leaned back in his chair, cup in hand, Roc asked, "What about you?"

"Me?"

"You removed your bandage."

"Naomi took the stitches out."

"Naomi, huh?"

Not wanting to discuss her, Samuel pulled his collar away from his neck to show Roc the puckered scar.

Roc's brow furrowed. "I've seen worse."

Samuel laughed. "Where?"

Roc shrugged. "You're staying here?"

Samuel scooped a spoonful of sugar into his coffee. He stirred slowly. "I have no choice."

"Sure you do."

"Then it's my choice to stay."

"Good." Roc seemed pleased. *Or relieved?* "What about your folks back in Ohio? What will you tell them?"

Samuel's gaze drifted toward the open window. Sheets flapped in the spring breeze. The trees and grass were greening up and buds were appearing. Ohio seemed far away. Maybe the distance had given him perspective. Maybe life had too. Still, he wasn't sure how to answer Roc's question. "I don't know."

Roc leaned forward. "I know there's tension between you and your father. But—"

"I forgave him." He stirred his coffee again, watching the granules of sugar rise to the surface. "Back in the hospital. I can't explain it, but I just knew I had to. Maybe it was catching a glimpse of Jacob. He wasn't angry at me. He was, I think, concerned. Worried. Fearful." He shifted in his seat, and the chair creaked. "I think that's one thing death brings you—a broader perspective, an ability to look outside of yourself, where you realize what's important and what isn't.

"Pop experienced things that frightened him, things he didn't understand. And he didn't have the luxury of talking about it or researching what happened to Jacob. If he'd talked to the bishop or ministers, he might have been shunned." Samuel shrugged, feeling sympathy for his father in a way he never had before. "And that's not something easily born."

"You're right." Roc knew all about what Rachel had experienced being shunned. "Not to be taken lightly."

"Exactly," Samuel agreed. "He did what he thought was best for Mamm and me. He wanted to protect us. And I want to protect them from all of this. So I'll tell them as little as possible."

Roc nodded. "You've learned a lot."

"I reckon I've got more to learn."

"Don't we all." Roc smiled empathetically and sipped his coffee. "So what about Naomi?"

The question startled Samuel. "What about her?"

"She was amazing at Levi and Hannah's. You heard her, didn't you?"

Samuel nodded this time. "She's very strong in her faith."

"Yes, she is." Roc eyed Samuel and finally said, "I thought you were interested at one time."

Samuel felt his ears burn. "I was. Am. But I can't ask her to leave her home, all she's ever known, for *this*." He gestured toward the center but realized his words might have insulted Roc. *Wasn't that what Roc had done—bringing Rachel here?* "I'm sorry, Roc. I didn't mean to imply...well, how did you convince Rachel to marry you?"

Roc laughed. "I didn't. She convinced me. Maybe that's how it will be with you and Naomi, eh?"

Samuel shook his head. "I don't think so."

Roc's lips flattened, and he contemplated his coffee cup for a few minutes. Then he gave Samuel the look he'd seen before—serious, uncompromising, hardened by experience. "Samuel, I'm going to tell you the truth. And you may not want to hear it."

"I reckon I can't stop you then."

"You can't protect Naomi any more than I can protect Rachel. Oh I do my damnedest. I take precautions. But I'm only a man and not perfect by any stretch of the imagination. I have to trust God to protect her and David."

"That's a cavalier attitude for this dangerous business."

"No, it's not. I realized eventually, hardheaded as I am, that I owed her the choice. I tried to make it for her. But that wasn't fair." He clunked his coffee mug on the table. "Have you ever considered asking Naomi what it is she wants? Or is it that you still blame yourself for Jacob's death? Maybe you don't think you deserve that kind of love and happiness."

# CHAPTER SEVENTY-SIX

A QUILT HAD BEEN LAID out beneath the old willow, and the three babies—two twin brothers and the other a cousin—scooched around on the squares. The oldest, David, plucked at the grass blades along the edges. The willow branches danced over their heads in the soft, spring breeze. The boys' mothers kept a careful eye on their babies, chatted, and helped Naomi hang the laundry on the line.

Naomi pulled a cotton sheet out of the basket. The cold, wet material slapped her arms as she lifted one corner to the wire and secured it in place. Rachel stretched the material along the line.

"It's such a beautiful day," Hannah said, reaching into the laundry basket as well, "that it's hard to believe only a few days ago there was so much terror."

Rachel nodded. "Are you doing all right, Naomi? Both Hannah and I understood what was happening, but you were in the dark for a while."

"Evil is evil, and I knew the Lord would protect me."

Hannah placed a hand on Naomi's arm. "You are far wiser than I was at your age."

"If so, it's the Lord's doing."

Rachel walked back toward them. "Every day is a blessing. And we must enjoy each as we can."

Hannah's gaze slid toward her twin boys. "And each child

is a blessing too." She gave her sister a nudge. "So when are you and Roc going to give David a little brother?"

Rachel's hand fluttered over her apron. "Soon I hope. 'Tis a lesson you should heed, if at first you don't succeed..."

Hannah laughed. "Try, try again." Her cheeks reddened beneath the morning sun. Her gaze shifted toward Naomi, and she cleared her throat delicately. "We're embarrassing someone."

"Oh no." But Naomi felt her face burning. "I'll check on the boys." She moved to the quilt and sat on one corner, where she could monitor the babies. Gabriel pushed up on his forearms and his little neck strained like a turtle's as he looked around with big blue eyes. Gideon frog kicked his way around the quilt. David pinched a blade of grass and stuck it in his mouth.

"No, no," Naomi said, taking the grass away. She replaced it with a wooden rattle. He banged it against the ground, and Gideon attempted to turn around but flopped over. She situated the baby so he could see but not get whacked in the head. Smoothing a hand over the downy soft hair, she smiled at the happy trio.

Hannah and Rachel joined her, strategically sitting at the edges of the quilt. Hannah patted Gabriel's back. "I wonder if Levi's mother had as much fun with her three boys. Of course, they were of different ages."

"Wait until they start crawling." Rachel caught her son as he lunged forward onto all fours and began scrambling off the quilt. "You might not think it this much fun."

The two sisters shared a smile. Naomi stretched out her legs to prevent Gideon from rolling off the quilt. His little fist grabbed hold of her skirt. "You are both blessed."

"We are," Hannah agreed. "Now what about you?

Now that things have settled down, is Samuel back to courting you?"

Naomi's heart faltered. She ducked her chin and focused on the baby beside her, cupping the chubby bare foot.

"I'm sorry," Hannah said. "I shouldn't have said anything... I was just hoping to have you for a sister someday soon."

"It's not your fault." Naomi shook her head but didn't trust tears not to spill from her eyes, so she kept her gaze on the baby's blond head. The hair blurred.

Hannah reached over and touched Naomi's hand. "I was inconsiderate. Please forgive me?"

Naomi blinked to clear her vision and offered a weak smile. "There's nothing to forgive."

Leaning over, Hannah gave Naomi a hug. For a second, she sagged against her friend and tears sprang forth. But she sniffed and pulled away, brushed her hand across her damp cheeks.

"It's all right. I'm okay, I reckon." Naomi straightened her spine and tucked her feet beneath her. "I made a mistake is all. I allowed my feelings to run rampant, for Samuel to know...and he'd already made his decision." Her bottom lip quivered and she trapped it between her teeth. "He's not going to live Amish anymore. You know that. It's not a secret after all that's happened. And he wants to keep me safe... away from all of that. It's because he cares." She tilted her head and met the concerned gazes of Rachel and Hannah, tried to offer them a reassuring smile but faltered. "I should take comfort in the knowing of that."

Rachel and Hannah looked as unconvinced as Naomi felt. She squeezed her eyes shut, then forced them open. "I understand and respect his decision." She picked up Gideon and snuggled his warm body against her. He gave her a happy, toothless grin, which melted her heart into a puddle of dismay. Sighing, she added, "But why does a man get to make the decision?" Her face suddenly burned with shame at this unexpected outburst. "I'm sorry. I shouldn't have—"

"Oh, Naomi." Hannah moved toward her and placed an arm around her shoulders. "You know what Rachel did, don't you?"

"I asked Roc to marry me." Laughter bubbled out of her. "I did. Plain and simple."

Naomi shook her head. "I could never do that."

"But I know what you could do," Hannah said. "Pray. Let's pray together. *For where two or three are gathered together in my name…*"

Naomi answered with the rest, "*There am I in the midst of them.*"

# CHAPTER SEVENTY-SEVEN

AFTER THE EVENING MEAL and final chores, after the men had gone in different directions—Father Anthony and Harry to sit with Brody; Joe, Randy, and Father Roberto to town; and Roc to his family—Samuel set out on a drive. The motorcycle hugged the curves and hills as he skimmed along the blacktop at responsible speeds. His thoughts spun off in reckless directions, but they always returned to the same place.

The gray of twilight hovered longer and later as the days were lengthening. The moon hung suspended, its pale glow reflective of the hope shining in him. Stars emerged, growing brighter by the minute.

Samuel came to a juncture and stopped at the red sign. Empty fields spread out around him. The motorcycle thrummed in his ears. He looked straight ahead and realized he had inadvertently arrived at Levi's. But he wasn't here to see his brother. He had two options. He could return to Roc's. Or he could stop and see Naomi.

Bidding Hannah and Levi good night, Naomi opened the back door to their home.

"Do you want me to drive you over?" Levi asked, rocking one of his sons.

"*Danke*, Levi. I enjoy the walk this time of night."

Hannah joggled one of the babies. "I'll see you tomorrow, Naomi."

She closed the door carefully. Drawing a calming breath, she stepped across the porch and down the steps. Night sounds chirped around her, and her tennis shoes crunched gravel. The scent of lilacs and freshly mown grass carried on the breeze.

A low hum rumbled, vibrating through her. She slowed, catching sight of a bright orb. The light swung across her and spotted her, keeping her in its beam.

Wondering if she should return to the house or forge onward, she squinted against the light. The thrumming engine stopped, the light blinked out, and silence buzzed her ears. She blinked against the sudden darkness until shapes formed in the waning light. Crunching gravel accompanied footsteps, slow and steady, yet determined. Coming straight toward her.

"Naomi."

Samuel. Her heart leapt. She waited as he approached, his outline forming, the broad shoulders and long legs until he stood before her. Moonlight shone in his eyes.

"You're going home?" he asked.

"It's getting late." She twisted the tie of her *kapp* around her finger. "Are you coming to see Levi?"

"No. I, uh…"

She noticed the white bandage was gone from his neck. "How is your wound?"

"Healing."

"Good."

He slid his hands in his back pockets and scuffed the gravel with the bottom of his shoe. "I wanted to talk to you about something."

She waited.

"I owe you an apology."

His words surprised her.

"I put your life in danger. Can you forgive me?"

"Of course, Samuel." She shook her head, confused by his request. "But you need not apologize. It wasn't your fault."

"I thought I would die when...when you were standing there...so strong and sure...and Jezebel could have killed you." He shrugged, flexing his arms, then giving them a shake. "If anything had happened to you—"

She rested a hand against his thundering heart. "Nothing happened. I'm fine."

"But the battle isn't over yet. It may never be."

"I know who wins in the end. Don't you?"

A shy smile curled his mouth. "Of course. But we may not see that happen in our lifetime."

"Then again we might...or else we'll see it all unfold in the next."

He captured her hand against his chest and held it there. "Naomi, I shouldn't ask you this."

"Shouldn't?"

He stroked her hand, and tingling sensations rippled through her. "But I'm going to because...well, why should it be only me who decides this? So I'm just telling you right now that you should say no."

Confused, she asked, "Do you want me to say no?"

"No, of course not. But it's the right thing to do."

"And I always do the right thing, *ja*?"

"You'll say no then?"

She watched him for a long minute, noticing the longing in his eyes and the urgency in his voice. She felt his heart pounded against her palm. "Ask me, Samuel."

"I can't live in the Amish world anymore. God's called

me to other things…dangerous tasks. But I can't help that I love you. I do. It's probably wrong in sixteen different ways. But it's the truth."

"And you are always truthful, aren't you, Samuel?"

"I try. Yes. I do." He cleared his throat. "You amaze me and surprise me. You're stronger than I ever imagined and more beautiful than a sunrise. So I know you'll be stronger than me and say no, right?"

"How can I? You haven't asked me, Samuel."

"Look, Naomi, you…we have a choice. And if I could have anything in this world that the good Lord would give me, it'd be you."

She inched closer to him, sliding her hand up to his shoulder. She felt his heat through the thin layer of his shirt. "I agree."

"You do?"

"I do."

A smile started to break free, but he caught it and frowned. "But you'll say no. Right?"

"You still haven't asked me, Samuel."

He drew a breath. "Naomi, will you m—"

"Yes." And she kissed him. Or he kissed her. It seemed to be mutual and the kiss went on and on until they rested their foreheads against each other. His hands spanned her waist, and hers splayed across his back. They stared deeply into each other's eyes. His breathing was ragged, and she felt her body trembling.

"You didn't say no."

"You're right."

Then he smiled, his relief and joy mingling, interlacing inextricably with hers. She knew she could live a sheltered life, but without Samuel, without God, she wouldn't really live.

# Acknowledgments

Writing this series was a journey into the unknown. I learned much on my travels across the country, as well as those within the mind and heart. As with any journey, there are many along the way offering help and encouragement. So many have encouraged me as I wrote this last book of the Plain Fear series, from readers (who wrote me emails and letters) and reviewers (who were gracious and encouraging in their reviews) to booksellers and writing buddies. Thank you. I appreciate each and every one of you. I tried to thank you along the way, and I hope I didn't leave anyone out.

A special thanks to Jerri for her prayers and friendship. What a blessing you are!

I'd also like to thank those on my Sourcebooks team: y'all are spectacular! A special thanks to Peter Lynch for believing in this project from the beginning. And a special thanks to Stephanie Bowen for her enthusiasm and work on this final book.

Thanks also to my wonderful agent, Natasha Kern. You're simply the best.

My biggest thanks to my sweet and wonderful family, who are always willing to eat pizza and plot stories. I love you!

# ABOUT THE AUTHOR

L EANNA ELLIS IS THE winner of the National Readers'
Choice Award and Romance Writers of America's
Golden Heart Award. She has written numerous books in
the romance genre as well as the inspirational market. With
her husband, two children, and wide assortment of pets, she
makes her home in Texas.

# Plain Fear: Forsaken

## A Novel

### Leanna Ellis

Although she knows that the Amish way is to move on from grief, on to a new season, Hannah cannot move on from Jacob, who was taken too soon.

Jacob's brother Levi also cannot move on—his love for Hannah burns just as strong as ever. But he knows how much Hannah loved his brother, and the event that took Jacob from them.

And it's a secret he must take to his grave.

So when a mysterious stranger comes to their community, he too carries a secret, one that will force Hannah to choose between light and dark, between the one she wants to love and a new yearning she fears to embrace.

### Praise for the Plain Fear series

"An intense, powerful novel of love and loss, deception and deliverance." —*Nancy Haddock, national bestselling author of* Always the Vampire

"This is a haunting, heartbreaking story told with such beauty and intensity, it took my breath away." —*Lenora Worth, author of the* New York Times *bestseller* Body of Evidence

### For more Leanna Ellis books, visit:

www.sourcebooks.com

# *Plain Fear: Forbidden*

## A Novel

## Leanna Ellis

## How long must we pay for the sins of our past?

She blames herself for her husband's death. But for Rachel Schmidt Nussbaum, redemption may only lie in the ultimate sacrifice.

When a stranger arrives claiming only she can save him, Rachel's impulsive instincts lead her on a perilous journey, one that leads her to a battle that will decide both the fate of her soul and the life of her unborn child.

A far-from-ordinary story of love and desperation, sin and sacrifice, Amish faith and vampire lore, *Plain Fear: Forbidden* is an imaginative thrill ride that's like nothing you've ever read before.

### Praise for the Plain Fear series:

"Ellis creates characters with depth… The story keeps you enthralled from page one." —*Shelf Awareness*

"Truly entertaining… Gripping plot lines and unique characters… There is nothing run-of-the-mill about this paranormal romance story…" —*Long and Short Reviews*

"An emotionally packed journey of love, loss, heartbreak, life and death, good and evil… A stellar read." —*Shelf Awareness*

### For more Leanna Ellis books, visit:

www.sourcebooks.com